THE WICCAN CHRONICLES

BOOK II

THE MIDNIGHT MAN

D. A. BARNEY

FRANKLIN PUBLISHING

THE WICCAN CHRONICLES TRILOGY

D. A. Barney

BOOK II:

THE MIDNIGHT MAN

"You don't have to be afraid - to die."

Published by Franklin Publishers Printed in the United States of America For permissions, inquiries, or additional copies, contact:

Franklin Publishers www.franklinpublishers.com

PROLOGUE

New Orleans, Louisiana
July 15, 1999

"This is bullshit!" Taq, a young vampire in his late teens, said as he moved from the foot of Lucien's bed to the window. He scanned the empty courtyard below, then turned and retraced his steps back to the bed, where the sole heir to the Gerard fortune helplessly lay in an unwakeable sleep. "We should be out there."

"Taq, I swear, if you wake this boy--" threatened his older sister Tik, who sat on the bed next to Lucien, stroking his head with a concerned hand.

Though barely older than Taq, Tik carried herself like a protector forged in fire. Her touch was gentle, her gaze fierce. Like most childless female vampires, Tik carried the Wanting, a gnawing hunger that rooted in her marrow and never let go. Lucien, unconscious and trembling, offered her a kind of peace she could not explain.

"No one can! That's the point!" Taq yelled.

Tik gave her younger brother a look that, even though he was physically bigger than her, made him take pause. He pushed off the bed and trekked back to the window.

"He did this," Taq said, gesturing toward the window, "he's the one that should be punished, not us."

"You think this is punishment?"

"I think I should be out there fighting with the rest of them, not stuck here babysitting with you."

Before Taq could even blink, Tik was off the bed and blurred across the room, slamming him into the wall. Her hand was iron against his chest.

"I was in the courtyard tonight. I saw what he's capable of; felt it. So trust me when I tell you that staying here with me tonight is no punishment," she said.

Just then, Lucien abruptly woke from his sleep and sat straight up. Tik sped over and sat next to him, with Taq taking his place at the foot of the bed.

"What is it, Luc? You okay, baby?" Tik asked.

His body quivered as he stared off into the distance, trying his best to hold back a wave of tears with his rapidly blinking eyelids. He was unsuccessful and one by one, they escaped.

"Baby, what's wrong?" Tik asked as she tried to brush the tears from his face.

He opened his mouth, but the words caught in his throat. His body trembled. Then, barely above a whisper, "My momma's dead."

He knew it. He somehow felt it in every bone, every muscle, every molecule. Tik picked him up and held him tight as he cried on her shoulder. Taq's anger steeped as he watched, knowing there was nothing he could do. Just then, the window burst open with a howl of cold air that smelled faintly of iron and grave soil. It swept across the room like fingers searching for something.

"Taq!" Tik ordered.

Taq sped over to the window and closed it. He paused a moment as he stared at the handle because he knew he had checked and secured it before. As he pondered this window conundrum, he felt some kind of force press up against him and violate his person before it moved straight through him. He shivered and turned, only to see his sister, with Luc's head resting comfortably on her shoulder. He scanned the room, every sense alert, the hairs on his arms rising in response to something unseen. Something had entered with the wind, and whatever it was, it had not left.

CONTENTS

CHAPTER 1

"*I* promise."

"Tik," Taq whispered. She shushed him softly while rocking Lucien, her hand brushing comfort across his back.

"Tik!" he said this time with more urgency.

"Hush!" I'm trying to get him to--" she started, but she was silenced by an unnatural chill that took her breath away. Before she could react, Lucien was ripped from her body and then hovered in the air a few inches away from her. "Luc!" Tik screamed.

She reached for him and was repelled backward and forcefully seated into a chair next to the bed. Taq barely twitched before he was flung against the wall. Both siblings froze in place, unable to move as Lucien hovered, suspended in the air by a force beyond them. His tears stopped as a loving smile overtook his face.

"Momma," he gasped.

"Hi, baby," Camille whispered through a smile equal to that of her child's.

Luc wrapped his arms around his mother as his face melted into her warm, welcoming shoulder. Tik and Taq struggled to move, staring in awe as Lucien floated back over to the bed and sat with his legs crossed, smiling from ear to ear. Camille crawled up and sat across from him. The white was gone from her hair and she glowed as if she were illuminated with a backlight.

"You look so pretty, Momma."

"Thank you, baby. You don't look so bad yourself."

Lucien giggled before the smile was lost on him, and he lowered his head.

"What's wrong, sweetie?" Camille asked.

"I had a dream like Dani does. I thought you was dead."

"Luc, who you talking to, buddy?" Taq asked.

"I'm talking to Momma."

"But your momma's not back yet," said Tik.

"They can't see me, baby, only you can," Camille replied.

"How come?"

"Sweetheart, your dream was real," Camille said as she reached out and grabbed his hands.

Lucien swallowed back his emotions as he looked down and fervently shook his head.

"It's okay, baby--"

"No," he whispered as the tears gushed through his eyes. "I don't want you to be!" he wailed.

Tik and Taq struggled to help him but could not move as Camille swept him up in her arms. She held him tight and let him cry as she comforted him.

"Lucien!" Tik screamed as she violently struggled to free herself from the mysterious hold.

Camille sat Lucien in her lap and wiped the tears from his eyes.

"I'm sorry, baby, but I only have a little time here, and we have so much to talk about," Camille said as she looked over at Tik, who had nearly knocked the chair over in her struggle.

"Tell Tik and Taq that everything is fine and that if they promise to be quiet and not interfere, I will release them."

"Tik, sto-o-op! I'm fine. Momma says if you guys promise to stop struggling and be quiet, she'll let y'all go."

"Okay, okay, we will," Taq said eagerly.

"She says you have to promise."

"I promise!" screamed Tik.

"Me too!" Taq added.

Instantly, the two of them were released. In a blink, Tik charged toward Lucien and was repelled back into the chair. Taq charged for the door. It locked, and he was yanked over to his sister and forcefully seated on the floor next to her.

"She said she ain't gonna ask you again."

This time, the two of them obeyed and helplessly watched what was to come next.

"Now, I need to ask you for a favor, 'kay?" Camille said. Luc nodded. "I need you to take care of Dani for me. I'm not gonna be able to do that anymore, and so many people are going to try and hurt her."

"Why? Where is he?"

"'She', baby. Where is 'she'"

Lucien again furrowed his brow at this.

"Remember that night I got hurt real bad, and you saw that little girl?" Camille asked. Lucien nodded. "That little girl is Dani. She's your sister, your twin. The boy you've grown up with wasn't real, baby. It was just her in disguise."

Luc's eyes began to well up.

"I'm sorry I had to deceive you, but there's a lot of people in this world who are afraid of her, of what they think she'll do when she turns twenty-one, so they're going to try very hard to make sure that she doesn't. That's why I disguised her as a boy, because some people in this house, not all, but some, feel the same way and would have killed her if they knew. That's why you can't ever tell anybody about you helping her."

"Not even--"

Camille placed her finger over his lips, silencing him.

"Nope. Not even him. Your daddy's a good man, but he's the reason why they want her dead. Four years ago, just before you were born, there was a prophecy that--"

"What's a 'prah-pho-cee'?" Lucien interrupted.

"Oh, sorry, baby. It's a prediction, a guess of what's going to happen in the future." Lucien nodded his understanding. "This prophecy said that your sister was going to kill your daddy on her twenty-first birthday."

"I don't want her to do that!"

"She's not, baby. Don't worry, she's not, but there's a bunch of people that believe she is. That's why this has to be a secret for just me and you, okay?"

"...Okay, Momma," he nodded.

"You have to promise me."

Lucien didn't want or deserve to carry this burden and, other than his mom, there was no one else on this planet he would carry it for.

"...I promise."

Camille kissed his forehead and sat him back on the bed in front of her. Lucien resisted, not wishing to be let go, but his struggle was futile as Camille held him at bay.

"It's gonna be your job to look after her and protect her until she's big and strong enough to protect herself."

"No! Momma, don't go! Please!" Lucien wailed, thrashing in her arms as her image began to blur at the edges, like light through fog.

"I love you so much, sweetheart."

"Momma!" Lucien cried as she began to fade.

"You'll always be my big boy," Camille smiled.

"Lucien!" Tik and Taq screamed at the top of their lungs, their cries falling silent with no one around to hear them.

Helpless, all they could do was watch as young Lucien struggled with some unknown force that they could not see.

"No, don't leave me! I don't... even know... how to do... what you want me to!" He sputtered and hiccuped out.

"When the time comes, you'll..."

A wave of fear rolled over Camille's face.

"Someone's trying to kill her and Kaitlin on the train right now."

"No! Momma, don't let them!" Lucien screamed.

"Hold my hands, baby. Quickly!" Camille ordered. Confused, Lucien did as he was told.

"I'm so sorry, baby, but this is going to hurt."

"Momma?--"

Camille's eyes burned red, and her hair rose as if caught in a wind only she could feel. The room hummed with rising power. Lucien followed suit and, for the first time, he went full Mactrouge. Children aren't meant to go full Mactrouge. Their bodies can't hold that kind of power. Camille's heart broke knowing she was forcing her son to carry more than he was ever meant to. He screamed horribly from the pain. He didn't understand what was happening to him. He struggled to break free from his mother but could not. The window doors flew open as the cold night air rushed in and violently jostled the contents of the room.

The energy between them funneled up and swirled around them. Now, for the first time, Tik and Taq could actually see a silhouetted image of Camille on the bed, glowing and growing brighter. They were petrified. Neither had ever seen Camille like this, and they had no idea what she was doing to Lucien as the child continued to struggle and scream. Tik and Taq were forced to shield their eyes from the blinding energy in the room. Then it seemed as if Lucien's eyes opened inside someone else's head. He saw a man—Black, tall, refined—on what looked like a moving train. He saw Kaitlin, and it seemed as if he was crawling toward her. He saw her wrap her arms around him, but Kaitlin wasn't in the bedroom with him; she was with Dani on the train. He realized he was, somehow, seeing what his sister saw. He could hear the black man's strange voice as if he was standing right in front of him.

"Your cognitive skills are equal to that of someone three times your age. You lack power, of course, but that would have come in time. How interesting it would've been to see you in ten years or so..." the black man with the refined British accent said. "Right, then."

Lucien watched as the black man slammed his hands together creating a loud, powerful force that scared him. Air rushed through the open car, jostling him/Dani, and Kaitlin about the floor. Then, the black man formed a giant ball of energy.

"What a shame," the man said, with a calm that made the danger in his hands feel colder.

Just as the black man was about to launch the ball of energy toward Kaitlin and Dani, Camille screamed out an incantation in Latin so that Lucien could not understand.

"GODS AND DEMONS, HEAR MY PLEA! TRANSFER ALL THAT'S LEFT TO HIM, OF ME-E-E-E!!!"

A wave of energy circled around them and shook the room as it exploded. Tik and Taq were released, and when the light subsided, Camille was gone, and Lucien was in a deep, peaceful sleep. Tik and Taq rushed to the boy's side, but neither could wake him from his slumber. Taq raced to the window and closed it, then zoomed around the room, checking every corner, every crevasse, for any sign of intrusion. Tik hovered over Lucien, watching his chest rise and fall. If her kind still had tears, she would have shed them all. She gently nudged the child, but he would not wake.

CHAPTER 2

*W**hen the world gets too big... make it small.*

A quarter of a mile. Four hundred meters. A distance a strong swimmer might cover in under fifteen minutes, on a good day. That was the distance Kaitlin had to travel to remove herself and an unconscious Dani from Canal Pass Manchac at the Lake Maurepas border. A distance that, under normal circumstances, would take a skilled swimmer about fourteen minutes to traverse. Add the weight of a nearly four-year-old unconscious girl and the fact that her only light was coming from a dimly lit crescent moon - fourteen minutes is not a very realistic expectation. More like twenty-five minutes, if she was lucky, and under the present circumstances, she would need to be.

A swimmer losing sight of the shore at night could cost them their life. In this situation, there could be something in this water that could do that job just fine. Alligators like fresh water, their natural habitat. They can tolerate salt water for a few hours, maybe even a day or two, but all in all, they prefer their water fresh.

Lake Maurepas was a brackish estuary, fed by fresh water from rivers and streaked with salt from the Gulf. Alligators didn't usually live here and tonight, that was a fragile kind of comfort. At that moment, that was the only thing Kaitlin had going for her: the fact that alligators *generally* don't live in Lake Maurepas. They do, however, live in the swamp just north of it, the one just south of it, and in that big ol' freshwater swamp on the west side of it. With Lake Maurepas sitting smack dab in the middle of this alligator haven, the crocodilians have been known to dip their claws into the lake and go for a briny swim every now and again, especially between dusk and dawn.

Kaitlin grew up in Gulfport, so she was well-versed in these matters. She also knew that IF she were to reach the shore, things would become exponentially worse. There are a whole hell of a lot of things more dangerous than alligators living in swamps. With all she'd been through tonight, "overwhelmed" would not be a fair choice of words to describe Kaitlin Morrison at that very moment. She had just been blown off a train and fallen a good fifty feet into this lake, perhaps lost a woman who was more her sister than her best friend, and then there was Jean.

Where was he? Kaitlin's heart pounded. Jean would never leave her. He would have given his last breath to save her. So why wasn't he here, and what did it mean that he wasn't here now?

"What am I going to do if I do make it to the shore? Is Julien's crew still out there looking for me? Is Camille really dead? WHERE'S JEAN?! ... Where's Tirin?" She thought.

If he was anywhere within a mile of her, he'd pick up her scent, and there would be no one to stop him from finishing what he tried to do on the train. Those negative thoughts were swimming through her head far better than she was maneuvering through the train debris in this canal, and that was just not acceptable. It would be easy to quit and give in to the negativity of this most precarious of situations, but quitting in this circumstance meant dying, and she was not ready to do that. She stared at Dani's unconscious body floating next to her.

"Somehow, this tiny little girl found the strength to save me from dying on the train. Now, I have to find the strength to save her. But how?" she thought.

She remembered one of the first things Jean ever told her: When the world gets too big, sometimes the only way to get through it is to make it small. Whatever else was to come, so be it, but right then, she needed to make her world small.

"Jus-Just... get to the shore," she shivered as she forcefully pushed herself and Dani through the water. "Just get to the shore," she kept repeating as she picked up speed.

If there *were* gators in this lake, they would have already felt the changing current caused by her strokes, and they would be coming for her.

"Just get to the shore," she again repeated.

If there *were* gators in this lake, they would have already picked up her scent with their incredible sense of smell, and they would be coming for her.

"J-J-Just get to the shore," she said, spitting up some of the lake she had accidentally ingested.

If there *were* gators in this lake, they would have already heard her and would be coming for her; therefore, there was no need to hold back.

"Just get to the shore," she cried, her tears mixing into the briny water as she pushed forward with every ounce of strength. She swam as hard and as fast as she could, toting Dani at her side. Her world had shrunk to a single goal: Get to the shore. Nothing else mattered. One breath. One stroke. One nightmare at a time.

CHAPTER 3

 ustified

The Fat Lady

One hour earlier

The curtain to the most ominous of booths was snatched open. Inside sat an unfazed Barrett, enjoying the last sip of a well-aged single malt whiskey. He had hoped never to return to this place. But one last loose end needed cutting, and it carried the weight of blood. Dani couldn't live, and he didn't want to depend on The Council to get the job done, so one last trip to The Fat Lady was necessary. Even for him, hiring The Talisman to eliminate the granddaughter he had never met scraped against something raw. But if it was her or his son, the choice had already made itself. "Alright, Pops, time's up," said the Maitre' D. "Let's go."

Barrett hid his guilt behind the manufactured smile he had placed on his face. He nodded his approval to D for his excellent choice of alcoholic beverages. D bowed, acknowledging Barrett's compliment, then dramatically swept his arm toward the exit. Barrett crawled out of the booth at D's request and stylishly sauntered across the floor toward the stairs, making sure he locked eyes with the beautiful mocha-colored woman he had shared a drink with before. D was normally indifferent toward the customers who found their way through his door, but for some inexplicable reason, he liked Barrett, and judging from the smile on the mocha-colored woman's face, she liked him, too.

Barrett gave her a wink, then ascended the stairs. He tipped his hat to the Doorman, then stepped into the street without flinching at the metallic groan of the door locking behind him, but the smug smile etched on his face only moments ago had been erased as the pain of his actions became evident. He tried to pretend it didn't matter.

"Camille had hidden the girl for years," he thought. What he'd done was justified. Or at least, that's what he kept telling himself. Others would eventually come around and understand that unleashing The Talisman, a supernatural contract killer, onto an almost four-year-old girl was the prudent thing to do in this situation. He hoped that one day, he would understand it as well.

He closed his eyes and deeply inhaled the ever-present smell of burnt embers in the nighttime air. Nighttime for him, anyway. In reality, there was no passage of time in this place - no day, no night. It was always somewhere just in between. His eyes opened blood red as he released his breath, and the slow-moving mist crept up from the street.

With a puff, a thunderous *'BOOM!'* dispersed the mist, and The Trolly was revealed. Barrett's eyes faded to normal as the door hissed open with a mechanical exhale, and The Trolley patiently waited for its sole passenger to come aboard. The driver eyed Barrett as if he'd never seen him before, but when he dropped the gold coin into the canister, the driver's suspicion melted into a knowing smile, as if the fare had said more than words ever could. He tipped his cap and waited for Barrett to take a seat and get comfortable. Once seated, Barrett nodded his gratitude, and the driver pulled the door closed, rang the bell twice, and the mystical behemoth backed into the rising, slow-moving mist. With another thunderous *'BOOM!'*, The Trolly, along with the mist, was sucked away, leaving the Fat Lady and all her dirty little secrets behind.

CHAPTER 4

$\mathcal{L}$ogs. Don't. Bite

Twenty-seven minutes and sixteen seconds later, Kaitlin could just feel the bottom of the canal with her toes. She strained to complete one final stroke, pulling her that much closer to achieving her goal of reaching the shore. Her legs burned. Her lungs begged for oxygen. Every breath hurt. She desperately tried to suck in as much oxygen as she could to alleviate the pain, but an arduous inhale took in a bit more water than was desirable, and she immediately paid the price by violently vomiting it back into the lake, along with a few more tears.

"Enough," she choked, coughing lakewater and bile into the black water around her.

"Perhaps it would be more prudent to walk the remainder," she thought.

She let both feet touch the lake floor, pulled Dani up, cradled her on her shoulder, and carried her the rest of the way. Her muscles strained as she waded through the chest-high water. Every step was labored but easier than the last as the waterline quickly decreased.

Just a few feet away from reaching the shore, with the water just above her knees, she momentarily took her eyes off her goal as she fearfully trained them on the dark beach and the dangers past the forest line just beyond it. She looked away, just for a second. It was a mistake she'd never stop paying for.

With her next step, her right foot landed on what she thought was a log lodged into the beach floor. As she put her full weight on it, she painfully realized it wasn't. Logs. Don't. Bite. The pain she felt was amplified through the ferocity of the scream she unleashed. Just about anyone would have dropped the small child in their arms, but Kaitlin held on tighter. Pain exploded up her leg like a live wire. She screamed so loud it tore something in her throat. She couldn't move. She didn't want to. All she wanted was for the pain to stop. The only thing she could do in this moment was scream.

"NO-O-O-O-O! PLEASE, A-A-A-W-W-W!" She wailed.

The desired stealthiness that was required for his excursion was gone. Every creature within a quarter of a mile heard that scream and depending on who or what they were, they were either running away from it or moving toward it. Right then, Kaitlin needed to make the world small again. She needed to focus on the problem at hand and somehow get the alligator that had latched onto her lower calf, just above her ankle, to let go.

Contrary to popular belief, gators don't like to get into fights with humans. Not saying they're bullies; they just don't like to take on things that are bigger than they are. A full-grown male is about twelve to fifteen feet long and around eight to nine hundred pounds. Females grow around eight feet long and can get up to two hundred pounds. If one of these two grabs hold of you, you're gonna lose something.

This one here wasn't quite six feet long and was probably around eighty pounds. Not a baby, but nowhere near close to being full grown. If Kaitlin hadn't stepped on him, made him feel like he was being attacked, more than likely, he'd have let her pass. He didn't want to tangle with her either, but now that he'd gotten hold of her and tasted her blood, it was gonna take some effort on Kaitlin's part to get him to let go. Kaitlin was gonna have to fight him, and to do that, she was gonna have to put Dani down.

Alligators drown their victims. They latch onto them and pull them into water deep enough for them to violently roll with the victim without hurting themselves. It's called the "death roll," and once they start it, the likelihood of someone surviving it is greatly diminished. They want you to freeze and be complacent and give up. They don't want you to fight. He yanked Kaitlin's right leg. Her body jerked, and she screamed from the searing pain. He yanked again, this time pulling it out from beneath her. She cried out as she fell toward the wet sand. She turned her body slightly to the left to absorb the fall on her right shoulder while not crushing Dani with her body weight. Her body became a barrier between the gator and Dani, but the position also left her unbalanced, making it easier for him to pull her deeper. He dug in and tugged again.

She was heavy, too heavy for a clean kill—but the gator had tasted blood, and now it was a fight, and she wasn't fighting back. Fortunately, she was much too high on the shore for him to even think about rolling, but he was determined. He yanked her like a dog playing tug-o-war with a bone, pulling her ever closer to where he needed her to be.

Kaitlin was horrified, but she knew what she had to do; everyone who grew up in this part of the country did. Anyone unfortunate enough to be attacked by an alligator has to do exactly what the alligator doesn't want them to do. THEY HAVE TO FIGHT. That is the only chance for survival, and those who know how to do it can definitely win.

A gator's body is like an armored truck, but there are weaknesses, two, to be exact: their eyes and their snout. Although the eyes may be the obvious choice, trying to hit one in the middle of the night while under attack could prove to be as difficult and futile as trying to win a rigged game at a local carnival. The snout, on the other hand, is a much bigger target that's a lot closer to you. The soft tissue around their olfactory nerve endings lies in the nasal cavities that open into their nostrils. Hit it hard enough, and even a hungry gator would back off. One or two solid strikes on their snout, and they're not gonna want to tangle with you anymore.

The gator yanked Kaitlin again, snatching her a little deeper into the shallow water. Any deeper and Dani risked the chance of being submerged. Kaitlin had no choice but to release the still-unconscious child as the gator tugged again, but this time, Kaitlin had something for him. She twisted her body and slammed her left heel down on the gator's snout. She screamed horribly as the action caused the gator to bite down on her leg that much harder. He was letting her know that he didn't like that, but it was a fight now, and whoever the victor was would have to pay a hefty price. He thrashed her like a rag doll, dragging her from Dani. Every second he held on, the water crept closer to the child's face. He shook Kaitlin around enough to make most of her strikes miss, and, yank by yank, he was getting close to a depth where he could roll. Finally, Kaitlin grounded herself and delivered two forceful push-kicks, driving her heel into the front of the gator's snout. He immediately released her but held his ground with his mouth wide open. Kaitlin quickly scooted away, putting a little distance between the two of them as they stared each other down. She could tell he was thinking about giving it another go, so she slammed her left heel down in the water to let him know there was more of that to come if he tried. Acknowledging defeat, he closed his mouth, turned, and swam away. She immediately turned to find Dani. In the heat of the battle, Kaitlin didn't realize how far she had been pulled away from her. Only now did she see how far Dani had drifted. As the waves climbed the shore and receded back into the lake, they were just high enough to graze over Dani's mouth.

" NO!" Kaitlin screamed.

In that moment, she forgot about the searing pain she was experiencing as she lunged to lift Dani's head above the waterline. The lunge, however, was a not-so-subtle reminder that she had, in fact, been bitten by an alligator. She no longer had the leg strength to cover the distance with a single lunge, but she was able to get there in two. She grabbed hold of Dani and painfully dragged both herself and the child to the momentary safety of the sand. In a panic, she placed her ear on the little girl's chest, then a quivering hand just above her nose and mouth. Nothing.

"Ahhww," she cried out as she quickly began CPR, gently compressing Dani's chest in perfect rhythm.

"Don't you die… Don't you die."

After the last compression, she tilted Dani's head back, opened her mouth, leaned down, and tried to fill Dani's lungs with air, then waited for her chest to fall.

"Come on…PLEASE! You gotta wake up!" Kaitlin cried, then went down to deliver another breath.

She had to force herself to stop crying so she could do it properly. Hard as she tried not to, after she administered it, the tears once more began to flow.

"Don't you die on me. Not now. Not after everything. Breathe, damn it! Breathe!"

This time, Dani answered by coughing up a small amount of Canal Pass Manchac and giving it back to the shore. After filling her lungs with air, Dani opened her eyes for a brief moment. She looked up at Kaitlin and moved her lips as if she wanted to say something, but whether it was from all the unwanted water she had consumed or from the stress her tiny body had been forced to endure on the train, her eyes closed again, and consciousness was lost. The third law of magic is that it comes with a cost. It's a price that a young witch should never have to pay. Dani had paid more than her share tonight, and the debt wasn't done collecting.

CHAPTER 5

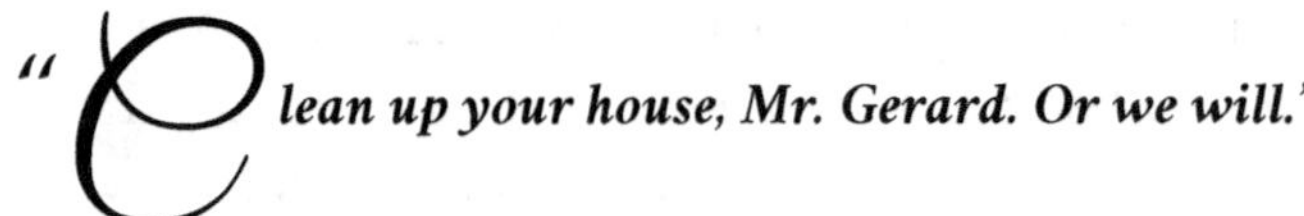

New Orleans, Louisiana

50 minutes earlier

Julien once said that New Orleans was beautiful, but he added a warning: be careful, or it could be the last city you ever see. Although that warning was meant to be a not-so-subtle threat to Jean Laveau, there was a lot of truth to the statement. I suppose one could say that about any place, though. At night, a certain element comes out in pretty much every city around the world. An element that doesn't always exist during the daytime hours. A street-savvy person knows this and takes extra precautions to keep both themselves and others out of harm's way. That being said, those who know New Orleans know the signs. A sudden wind. Mist curling around your ankles. A strange crackle. A boom. That's not weather, it's a warning. MOVE. That wind is a friend. It should not be resisted; it's there to help - to move you. LET IT.

The Trolley burst from the mist, hissing and howling down Conti

Street. Pedestrians scattered. Some stared. Others were not the least bit surprised or concerned. At least not with The Trolley. It screeched to a halt at the corner of Dauphine. Fortunately, there were no casualties – this time. In the past, when Barrett stepped off of this particular streetcar, he was amused by the discord it caused and the attention it brought him. Being the narcissist he was, he looked forward to it, but after seeing the chaos and disarray in the streets was not on his account, the disappointment that followed was epic. Like any city, New Orleans has a smell it's synonymous with. Bourbon Street always smelled like mildew and piss, with a top note of vomit and sweat. Like the cabin of a pirate ship gone sour. Royal Street has its antique shops, upscale boutiques, and fine cafés, while Dauphine has its hotels and fine dining establishments. Those two streets create some of the great olfactory joys for which this great city is known. What it's not known for, however, are carbon monoxide, sulfur dioxide, and hydrogen sulfide. In layman's terms - smoke.

The 'aroma' descended upon the prevailing streets like a plague. It was barely visible to the naked eye but thick enough that you could taste it. Sirens screamed from every direction. Chaos buzzed through the streets, and for once, Barrett wasn't the reason. That unsettled him more than the smoke emanating from several blocks away to the west. The Trolley door hissed closed behind him, and the bell rang twice as the slow-moving mist rose up from the street. Not as impressive an illusion with the air already somewhat saturated with smoke, but it was still a spectacle if anyone cared to pay attention to it. The beast lurched forward, turned on Dauphine, and with a *'BOOM!*', it was gone.

Barrett seemed supremely annoyed by the fear excreted from all the humans around him. He shook his head with disgust as he surveyed his surroundings until his eyes fell flatly upon Mr. Jeffries from The Council. He stood catty-corner across the street from Barrett, wearing a disapproving glare with which Barrett was becoming all too familiar.

"Hmph," Barrett chuckled to himself as he walked across the street to engage with his old acquaintance.

"I wasn't aware Conti Street had trolley service," Jeffries said, his voice sharp enough to cut pavement.

"Oh, it'll come," Barrett smiled. "If you know how to call it."

"Indeed," Jeffries responded. "I was contacted by your buffoonish friend and was told to meet you here."

"Come on, na'," Barrett said with a bit of agitation in his voice. "Cecil's a good boy. The man is loyal to his core."

"I'm sure he is."

"Around these parts, loyalty is EVERYTHING. Sometimes, I think you boys over in London town forget that."

"ORDER is everything, Mr. Gerard." Jeffries responded in a tone to match Barrett's intensity and agitation. "It is the foundation of our society and the only thing that has kept us alive for all these centuries. You, of all people, should know that. But after witnessing firsthand this self-serving, unnecessary, public display of your powers... I wonder."

"I'm just tying up loose ends like I was instructed to do."

"Correct me if I'm wrong, but it was your son's 'ends' that needed to be tied, not yours." Jeffries's eyes looked up to the cloud of smoke in the sky. "And from the looks of things, there may be more 'ends' fluttering about."

"The hell does that mean?"

"Clean up your house, Mr. Gerard. Or we will."

Jeffries handed over a thick manila envelope stamped with The Council's seal. The weight of it felt heavier than the paper inside.

"I'll review this with you and your son later this morning."

"Come on, na'. Let's grab a drink, talk like old friends. Malaffections is just down the block, my treat."

Jeffries looked at his watch and shook his head no.

"I have a meeting with the mayor in an hour to try and curtail this mess before it goes any further. And truth be told, I really don't like what you've done with the place. It was so much more... elegant when Madame P was in charge."

"Well, we can go someplace else, then. We got an hour."

"Do we?" Jeffries asked as his eyes looked to the ominous trail of smoke in the sky. "Seems I may have some more cleaning to do," he said, then looked Barrett straight in the eye, "and so do you."

Jeffries disappeared into the haze, leaving Barrett alone with the rising smoke and a warning still echoing in his ears.

CHAPTER 6

"*Just get to the tracks,*"

Kaitlin held her hand over Dani's mouth. She felt soft breaths against her palm. Dani was breathing, but Kaitlin needed more than that. She needed her to wake up.

"Come on, baby, open your eyes… Please," she begged as she gently brushed the sand off her face. "Wake up."

One by one, Kaitlin's tears bounced off of Dani's face, but still, the child would not wake.

"Please… I need you. I can't do this on my own."

Kaitlin's pleas went unanswered. As the adrenaline faded, the pain in her right leg surged. It was worse than before, sharper, deeper, unavoidable. She rolled into a seated position and extended her leg. It was the first time she had a chance to look at it since the incident. Her jeans at the lower calf were shredded and soaked with blood. She winced as she reached down and ripped the material away, afraid of what she might see. To her surprise, it was nowhere near as bad as she had imagined. The blood was coming from two diagonal lines about four inches apart, each consisting of three to four small puncture wounds from the small, sharp teeth on both sides of the gator's upper jaw. A few bled more than the others because they were ripped from the violent shakes she withstood.

A mirrored pattern marked the other side of her leg, punctures torn wide from the gator's thrashing. All in all, it wasn't bad. If it weren't for the two deep and nasty punctures coming from the extra-large fang-like teeth on the gator's upper jaw, she could have easily considered this a resounding victory. Fortunately, the gator's bottom teeth hadn't developed to their full size yet; however, these two holes were more than enough to cause serious concern.

She quickly tied off the ripped bottom portion of her jeans just below her knee as tight as she could withstand, using it as a makeshift tourniquet to help slow the constant stream of blood. Her eyes followed the crimson trail she had inadvertently made back to the shore. The blood stopped at the waves' furthest point of extension as the water rolled it back into the lake. If there were more gators nearby, the blood would draw them. The water would carry the scent straight to her. With their acute sense of smell, the ones in the swamp behind her were probably on their way now, as well. Of greater concern, however, were the two or three things in that swamp that frightened her even more.

She felt the urge to vomit and wasn't sure if it was because of the blood dripping from her leg or the return of the fear she had momentarily forgotten. Either way, it was time for her to go. She needed to get off this beach and as far away from this lake and the swamp as she could. She needed to make her world small again. One goal. One step. Just get to the tracks. About three hundred meters to the west were the railroad tracks her train had traveled before the accident. Although the swamp would still be within two hundred meters of her, at least the lake would no longer be a threat. Old Highway 51 was just another three hundred feet past the tracks. A seldom-used road, the likelihood of finding help at this time of night was small, but her chances were much better than following the tracks, and it would put her a great deal further away from the swamp. A couple hundred feet more was Interstate 51, the freeway. Surely someone there would stop to help her, but first, baby steps.

"Just get to the tracks," she whispered as she gathered Dani in her arms. "Come on, let's just get to the-- AWWHH!"

She tried to stand with Dani in her arms, and collapsed. Pain exploded through her leg as she hit the sand. She released Dani and pushed herself up using only her arms and her left leg. She swallowed a scream and instead whimpered as she put just the smallest amount of weight on her right leg to test its strength for the pilgrimage they were about to undertake.

"Just get to the tracks," she repeated.

She quietly cried from the pain as she straightened her leg. Tears poured from her eyes as she forced her full weight on the damaged limb. She stood there a moment, taking in the pain, conditioning herself to it. She inhaled deeply, then, without hesitation, bent down and hoisted Dani straight to her shoulder and cradled her.

"AWWWWHHHAAA!!" She screamed as she nearly collapsed to the ground.

She couldn't hold that one in. She needed to recondition herself to take THIS pain. She breathed in focus. Breathed out pain. She wasn't past the agony—just learning how to carry it.

"...J-Ju.. Just… Get to the tracks."

She took one step. Every cell in her body screamed for her to go down, to collapse, but she refused and instead took another, then another. She staggered and teetered, but she would not fall as she steadily made her way across the beach.

"Just get to the tracks… Just get to the tracks."

The phrase became her mantra, with each chant bringing more focus to her mind and more strength to her body. She didn't know how long it took her to cover the distance. What mattered was that she did. She had reached the tracks. As much as she wanted to rest, she was afraid that if she put Dani down, she might not be able to pick her back up. She needed to keep going. The pain had not stopped; it was still there. She had simply learned how to tolerate it. The constant loss of blood from her wound was not a matter of toleration, and with every passing minute, it became more of a concern. There was no time for rest.

"Just get to the road," she whispered.

A new goal. A new mantra. She raised her left leg a little higher than normal to step onto the tracks. It put that much more weight on her right leg, causing a significant increase in pain. Adding to the sensory static flooding her brain was the loud, deep, nasally sound emanating from behind her right shoulder. The sound was deep and rough, like sawing through thick wood. It sent a chill through her that, whether it was because she recognized the sound or couldn't believe she was hearing it, took her breath away... and it was getting closer. Gingerly, she turned and squinted to see something come out of the darkened tree line that no one had seen in over a decade: a jaguar. As far as everyone was concerned, they didn't exist in the continental United States anymore, let alone the bayou in Louisiana. Sure, there were rumors; an old fool would claim they had spotted one here or there, but no one ever believed it. Now, out of the darkness, on this of all nights, two hundred feet away and looking right at her. There it stood. A creature of myth, flesh and blood in the moonlight.

He was beautiful, and from the way he was looking at Kaitlin and Dani, he was hungry. Kaitlin could do nothing. There was no point in trying to run. It was everything she could do to remain standing at this point. By now she knew that Jean, for whatever reason, wasn't coming to save her, yet that's all she had left to believe in. She clutched Dani tightly, closed her eyes, and prayed as the big cat took two quick steps before he transitioned into a gallop.

"Jean," she whispered, clutching Dani tighter. "Please..."

CHAPTER 7

"*Y*es, Daddy."

Kaitlin opened her eyes to the sound of the animal as it awkwardly slid toward her, desperately trying to stop. It stumbled, rolled once, then stopped hard, panting as it locked eyes with Kaitlin. It grunted a few distinctive, wood-sawing sounds, then turned and ran away, disappearing into the darkened tree line from which it came. A jaguar is an assassin. A top-notch killing machine. It has a bite force of two hundred pounds per square inch. Only four animals in the world have one that's greater.

"*What on earth could make it turn tail and run like that?*" she wondered.

"Jean!" Kaitlin exclaimed as her face lit up from the long-awaited return of her smile.

She winced as she painfully pivoted around to face him. The light in her face, along with her smile, diminished just as quickly as it had appeared. Jean was *one* thing that could make the jaguar run away like that. Unfortunately for Kaitlin, there were two other things, as well.

"Who's Jean?" asked the mysterious man with the sprightly smile. "Hmm? Somebody else out here wit' chu,' darlin'?"

Kaitlin had no answer for Mr. Mysterious, who had somehow been able to sneak up behind her without making a sound. Only three beings on this planet had the capability of doing that. Two of them were the things in the swamp she feared more than the gators.

"Hello?..." Mr. Mysterious asked in a mischievous manner. "Can ya' talk?"

Mr. Mysterious wasn't large or loud. If anything, he looked tired, barefoot, clothes stained by swamp mud. But there was something off. Too clean. Too neat, and he was unusually well-groomed for a swamp dweller. Under other circumstances, she might have actually found him attractive. He did, however, lack the very distinctive swamp odor. In fact, he lacked any odor at all. That's what gave him away to her as the tears fell freely from her glazed-over eyes. It seemed Mr. Mysterious was not so mysterious after all.

"Awh, na', don't cry, sugar. You don't have to be afraid, he won't come back," Mr. Not-So-Mysterious said, referring to the jaguar. "What's ya' name, baby doll?" He asked as he gently brushed her hair from her face. She couldn't speak. All she could do was stand there with that blank look on her face, quivering in silence.

"I asked you a question."

Kaitlin noticed the subtle and distinct change in his demeanor as the tension rose up from the ground between them.

"K-Kaitlin," she stuttered. Her quick response was all that was necessary to push that tension back down, temporarily anyway, as the sprightly smile returned to his face.

"K-Kaitlin, huh?… Yeah. I like d'at. Well, K-Kaitlin," Mr. Not-So-Mysterious said, mocking her, "you just sexier than a mu-fucka, ain't chu'?"

Not-So-Mysterious tilted his head and let his eyes wantonly roam over her body in a manner no woman would find complimentary.

"Umph. Yes, ma'am. Yes, you are. You know, back in the day, I turned a few ladies' heads myself."

He tossed up a sincere smile, then darkness came over him as he drifted off to an unwanted and dangerous place.

"I been out here for damn near twelve years, ever since--" The memory, whatever it was, took Mr. Not-So-Mysterious somewhere he didn't care to revisit. Unfortunately for Kaitlin, he was stuck there now.

"A man gets lonely, K-Kaitlin, ya' hear what I'm sayin'? And you just about the most beautiful bitch I dun' ever seen, and I dun' seen a few. What are you, O positive?"

Kaitlin gasped from the question as Not-So-Mysterious stooped down, not even waiting for her to respond, and gently swiped some blood from her wound. His touch was soft and effortless. Kaitlin flinched and whimpered, not from the pain but from the anticipation of what was to come.

"Whoa! Be still, God Damn it!" Mr. Not-So-Mysterious ordered, settling her before he sampled her 'goods.'

He dabbed his finger on his tongue before engulfing it into his mouth. He licked his finger clean with a slow, savoring groan. Kaitlin flinched. It was too intimate, too practiced.

"Ohhh shit, girl! You's O negative!" Not-So-Mysterious said.

He seemed both surprised and excited by this discovery as he looked up to her.

"Sexy as fuck and O negative, too?!" He said as he reached in and scooped another sample from her leg, this time, not so gently.

"Uuuhh!" Kaitlin gasped.

That one hurt. Her knees buckled and she stumbled as she fought to stay on her feet while Mr. Not-So-Mysterious rose to face her.

"Mmmm!" he grunted, "O-mutha-fuckin' negative! You got a little more in you than African, don't you? 'Cuz that's rare as fuck. DAMN! And you dun' brought me this little gift, too? Shi-i-it. You and me gonna get along just fine for a lo-o-ong time."

"Okay, if you--"

"Hold on, na', let me finish,--"

"Please, just let her--"

Not-So-Mysterious backhanded Kaitlin across her face like it was the normal thing to do. Still clutching Dani, Kaitlin twisted her body so that she'd be the one to land on her back in the middle of the tracks instead of Dani.

"If you and me gonna get along, girl, you gonna have to learn proper respect, hear me?" The lack of a quick response definitely stoked his ire. "Bitch, I asked if you heard me?!"

"YES!" Kaitlin screamed. "Now you hear me! You can turn me if you want, okay?! I won't fight you. I'll do whatever you want if you just promise to let her go! You let her go, and I'll be yours!"

Mr. Not-So-Mysterious seemed to find some kind of amusement in her response.

"Bitch, you already mine!" He chuckled. "I don't need yo' mutha fuckin' permission!"

"You do if you want me to stay with you!" Kaitlin yelled. "I'm not stupid, I know how this works! You're not a lycan; I'm not beholden to you, and don't you dare mistake the pain I'm in as fear! You turn me and kill this little girl, I swear I'll leave you the second after I rise if I don't kill you first!"

Not-So-Mysterious stood over her with contempt in his eyes. He wasn't used to his victims speaking to him in such a way.

"Let her live, and I'll stay. Call me whatever you want. I won't run. But hurt her, and I swear, even dead, I'll find a way to make you pay."

He stooped down and snatched her up by her throat to a seated position. Kaitlin released Dani, who fell to her right, onto the tracks.

"Bitch! Are you tryin' to barter with me?!" Not-So-Mysterious laughed at the insanity of her request. Then he got serious. "You know... before all this happened," he explained, indicating his situation, "I was a pimp, and I gotta tell ya', you the sexiest lil' black bitch I dun' ever seen, AND you O negative. For that and only for that, I'm a give you a moment to re-evaluate your situation. Now we can do this the easy way, or I can break yo' fuckin' neck and do it anyway. Either way, it' gon' get done. So, if I was you, I'd stop thinkin' 'bout that lil' baby girl and take a moment to reflect on your own self-preservation."

Kaitlin closed her eyes and took that moment. She knew there was only one answer to give, and she painfully nodded yes.

"Say it," he ordered as he squeezed her neck tighter. "Say it, or I'll kill this little bitch right now and make you sit here and watch. I will poke a hole in her and suck out that young, innocent blood like a fuckin' juice box. Now tell Daddy what he wanna hear."

"Okay," Kaitlin gagged, but he would not release his hold.

"Say, 'Yes,'" Not-So-Mysterious ordered.

"…Y-Yes," she said, struggling to breathe.

"Say, 'Yes, Daddy.'"

"Ye-- Yes, Daddy."

"Now say, 'Please turn me, Daddy, so I can be yours forever.'"

Kaitlin snorted intermittent inhales, trying to take in enough air to speak.

"…Ple-Please, tur-- tur-- turn me, Da-a--" she whispered.

"I can't hear ya'."

"Dad-dy, so I-I-I can… be… yours…"

"Louder, God Damn it!"

"FOR-EVER!"

Not-So-Mysterious instantly released her, and the tears burst through her eyelids as she gasped for air.

"Sho, darlin'," he said with a gratifying smile on his face. "All ya' had to do was ask."

She cried hard as she placed her hand on Dani's head.

"Aww, bitch, come on, na'. Don't do that," Not-So-Mysterious said as he tried to reassure her. "Shit, girl, this ain't even yo' kid. And in a few minutes," he said as his two top incisors began to protrude from his devilish smile, "I promise you won't even care."

Suddenly, Kaitlin's eyelids felt abnormally heavy. Her heart rate began to rise as each breath became weighted and measured. It was the pheromones working their way into her system. Not-So-Mysterious saw the effect and slowly moved in to claim his prize. Kaitlin quickly extended her wounded leg to him and gently guided his head toward it, away from her neck.

"Awww, yeah," Mr. Not-So-Mysterious chuckled. "I knew you was a freak."

He scooched down and ran his fingers the distance of her leg. He grasped her calf with one hand and her ankle with the other, then sensually licked the excess blood from her wound. She inhaled passionately and exhaled an orgasmic groan. Not-So-Mysterious smiled, opened his mouth, and forcefully bit into her leg. Kaitlin's entire body stiffened.

The pain she felt was surreal. She clenched her fist and gnashed her teeth, anything she could do to hold back the scream that was impatiently waiting just inside her lips. Try as she might, she could not contain it all, and a tiny fraction of it burst through, along with the legion of tears she had been holding back.

"Ahww," she gasped ever-so-softly.

Any louder would've alerted Mr. Not-So-Mysterious that his pheromones weren't working the way they should. Kaitlin should be feeling nothing except pure, unadulterated ecstasy at this moment. She should be lost in an orgasmic trance that would seemingly never end, and she would be if not for Jean. Had he not spent months building up her immunity to pheromones, she would be caught in Mr. Not-So-Mysterious's spell. Her fingers found a loose board along the track. She broke it free, gritted her teeth, and drove it into his back with everything she had left.

Staking a vamp through the back to get to his heart is not ideal. It's a further distance to go to reach your target, plus there's just a lot of excess stuff that gets in the way. A good-sized, strong, healthy man under ideal circumstances, maybe hits gold – maybe – but a nearly exhausted, alligator-bitten woman suffering from severe blood loss in the grasp of the strongest of all the malafecs? Not a chance. She did, however, get Mr. Not-So-Mysterious's attention.

"AAWWWHHH!" he screamed as he released Kaitlin and rose to his knees with the makeshift stake lodged into his back.

Despite an intelligence almost commensurate with Rayna's, Kaitlin had neither the tools nor the strength to fight off a vampire in this condition. She had to give in to him and hope she could withstand the pain of her second bite in one night, knowing that the pheromones would not completely work on her. She knew she wasn't strong enough to penetrate his heart from the back, but that was the only shot she had, so she took it. She also knew that she had about two and a half seconds before Mr. Not-So-Mysterious regained his composure and killed both her and Dani. With her good leg, she kicked him straight in his chest, flopping him backward onto the stake she had planted into his back, allowing the bodyweight of Mr. Not-So-Mysterious to finish the job. The stake punched through. He screamed, then exploded into dust. The silence that followed felt like a wound closing.

Although she had outsmarted him, she could not enjoy the moment enough to celebrate, as her risky ploy came with a price. The vampire's kiss had only exacerbated her wound, causing her suffering to increase exponentially. Every nerve burned. Her muscles spasmed. She wanted to lie down and disappear. She figured, at the rate she was losing blood, it wouldn't be long before the pain would subside, and she would join Dani in her unconscious slumber. The only difference? Dani would eventually wake. Kaitlin would not. Kaitlin rolled over onto her stomach. Her arms trembled as she pushed herself up to her knees. She could see the back of Middendorf's Café and knew Old Highway 51 was just past the parking lot on the other side. Time was short. Along with the noticeable loss in strength, she felt nauseous and was now sweating profusely. These are definitive symptoms of Hypovolemic Shock – extremely mild, but symptoms all the same. She pushed herself up, using only her arms and her left leg again, then bent down and hoisted Dani back to her shoulder. It was much harder this time. She gulped down some much-needed oxygen as she shifted Dani into as comfortable a position as she could find, and then she made her world small again.

"...Just... ...get to the road."

Her third mantra. Her third breath of hope. Just get to the road. Three hundred more feet… increasing the distance between them and the swamp and getting them that much closer to help.

CHAPTER 8

"*Just get to the road,*"

Kaitlin took that extra-painful first step over the tracks and pushed forward. Back on the beach, time hadn't mattered—only survival. Now, time was everything. She was dealing with a level of pain and fear that most people will never experience. It didn't matter how long it took, only that she made it. On this leg of the journey, things were much different. She had faced all her fears and conquered them. The pain was still there, even more so than before, but she had conditioned herself to take it. Time, however, was of ultimate importance. She had lost a great deal of blood, and there was no doubt that she was beginning to experience the symptoms.

"J-Just… J-Just… G-Get to the road," she whispered.

She staggered and stumbled over the uneven ground and through the extra-tall grass to find herself up against the back wall of Middendorf's. The place was long closed, but the scent of thinly fried catfish still lingered in the air, warm, nostalgic, cruel.

"J-J-Just get t-t-t-to the road."

She used the building as a crutch and leaned up against it until she made it to the front. She had the road in her sights; two-thirds of the journey was completed. She just needed to cross the barren parking lot in front of her, and the third of her four goals would be accomplished.

"J-Just get t-to the road," she whispered, but her body did not move. "Ahhw! …J-Just get to the road!" She yelled, trying to motivate herself, but her head pounded. The dizziness blurred everything. The world tilted, but she refused to fall.

She closed her eyes to center herself, then opened them extra wide and shook her head to clear her vision.

"Get to that r-road!" She cried as she pushed herself off the wall and stumbled forward. "D-Don't you s-stop! D-Don't s-stop, you get t-to that road!"

She wanted, ever so badly, something to lean on, just for a moment. Just a brief moment to catch her breath and clear her head, but there would be no stay for her, no assist, no relief. All she had left was her will. The will of a warrior who refused to give in to fear, who refused to give into pain. The will of a woman who refused to give in. She made it to the road, and as she stood there on the shoulder, literally on her last leg, pale and weak, her eyes barely open, it seemed as if her unrelenting perseverance had paid off. Far ahead, two headlights split the darkness. Her breath caught. Someone was coming.

The tiniest of smiles peeked through the sand, sweat, and dirt on Kaitlin's face as the lights got closer. The wind carried the sweet sound of a fast engine to Kaitlin's ears as tears of joy fell from her face. It was dark and there were no streetlights on this portion of the road, only the lights in the parking lot.

"Will they be able to see me?" Kaitlin wondered.

They had to. At this time of night, the chances of another vehicle coming down this road were a little shy of zero, and even though the freeway was less than two hundred feet away, it was raised up at least thirty feet off the ground for another mile. There was no fourth goal to achieve in this journey. This was the end of the road, right here, right now. She had made it this far. She could make it to the center of the road. Three more steps. She had to be seen.

"J-Just make it-t to the c-c-center of the road."

Make it, she did - right to the double yellows. She planted herself there, raised her free arm up, and waved it as if she was flagging the last taxi in the city. She would not leave this to chance and be missed. As the vehicle got close enough for the headlights to reflect off her body, she made sure that she would be heard as well.

"H-Help us, p-please! P-Please, help! He-e-elp!" She screamed, but the vehicle did not slow.

Instead, an angry horn was unleashed, seemingly canceling out her cries for mercy. Kaitlin was persistent with her pleas and insistent in her cries.

"Please! Please, help us!" she sobbed, voice cracking. "Stop! STOP!" she screamed until her throat tore as the vehicle blew past her, swerving to the shoulder of the road to avoid impact.

The partiers in the vehicle left an empty bottle of alcohol and a few choice words lingering in the air that does not bear repeating. The gust slammed into her like a punch. She crumpled, shielding Dani as her body smacked the asphalt. Again, she sacrificed her body for Dani by taking all of the force of the impact.

"STO-O-O-O-O-P-P!" She screamed until her lungs were depleted of air. She refilled them and screamed again. "OH, GOD, NO-O-O-O-O, NO, NO! PLE-E-EASE, SOMEBODY, PLE-E-EASE! HELP ME!!" She cried, expelling everything she had in her.

There was no mantra. No plan. Just a woman on the road, clutching a child and screaming in the dark.

CHAPTER 9

"W-Wake up. P-Please, w-wake up. I n-need you," she whispered, "I can't d-do this any m-more,.."

She shivered through her pleas; she was getting cold, especially limbs and extremities. The symptoms from her blood loss were getting worse. At this point, there were also no more tears to be shed. She had depleted herself of them as well. Even if she hadn't, there was nothing left to cry about, and she was just too tired. She just wanted to sleep. She closed her eyes and rocked back and forth, shivering in the early morning air.

"I-I-It's... O-Okay, baby… I-I-It's okay," she whispered. "Y-Y-You're gonna be j-j-just f-fine. J-Just f-fine… J-Just f-fine..."

Repeatedly, she whispered those two words into Dani's ear, hoping that she might deliver a subconscious message to the sleeping child, or perhaps it might act as a mantra for her when she woke. Only a semblance of the pain she had experienced earlier was present, and she was comfortable with it. She was comfortable with everything right now, so much so that she didn't hear the rattling engine. Didn't feel the headlights warming her back. The world arrived, but she was somewhere else. She didn't hear the squeaky sound of a door as it slowly opened or the deliberate footsteps over her left shoulder that followed, each step bringing fate closer and closer.

Maybe she did hear all that. Maybe she just didn't want to. After all, it could be some of Julien's minions who had come to fetch her home, or worse.

"So be it," she thought as a pair of legs walked past her, stopped, turned, and stooped down to face her.

A man knelt in front of her. Older, calm, unreadable. He didn't have many lines on his face, but he had a few around his eyes. She couldn't tell whether it was a look of anger or concern that he cast, so she didn't know whether to be frightened or not. It didn't really matter at this point, as she didn't have the energy either way. She saw his lips moving through her half-closed eyes, but his words were lost to her. She blinked a few times as if that would help, but she still could not hear what he was saying.

"Is he teasing me," she wondered, *"purposely moving his lips without making a sound, making it seem like I'm the one with the problem?"*

The thought of that made her angry. She had gone through enough tonight and was in no mood to be trifled with. She watched him as he stared at her leg, then shifted his focus to Dani. He reached for her, and that was enough to push Kaitlin over the edge.

"NO-O-O-O-O!" She screamed as she violently twisted and turned, clutching Dani tighter as she tried to scooch away from him.

Surprised by the sudden burst of emotion, he jerked his hand back.

"Whoa! Easy, child!" He said as he tried to settle her, but that just seemed to set her off more as she slapped at him with her free hand and tried to kick him with her good leg.

"GET AWAY! NO-O-O-O! DON'T TOUCH ME,--"

Her screams of anger began to transform into cries for help as the tears she had momentarily lost returned. The man fell backward onto his bum, horrified by what he saw before him.

"Dear God, what happened to this poor child?" He thought to himself.

"Okay. Okay," he said as he jerked his hands back and raised them next to his face. "It's okay. I won't touch her."

"No…" Kaitlin whispered. Screaming used up a lot of energy.

"I won't touch her," he reaffirmed.

He spoke in a calm, soothing voice and sat very still, trying not to provoke her, but Kaitlin didn't have much fight left in her anyway. Through that entire episode, she was only able to move about a foot.

"My name's Harland," he said, still holding his hands up. "You wanna tell me what yo' name is?"

Kaitlin lowered her head slightly and shook it, 'no.'

"Okay then. You don't have to," he said as he nodded reassurance to her. "Sweetie, you mind if I put my hands down? I don't know how long we gon' be here, and my arms is gettin' tired." Kaitlin nodded ever-so-slightly. "Thank you," he said as he slowly lowered his hands and let out a deep sigh of relief.

Harland was a big man, about six foot two, two hundred twenty pounds, and he had a welcoming smile to go along with that frame. It lit up the night when he shared it with her as he crossed his legs and got comfortable.

"Was on my way home when I saw ya'. Was out at Ol' Ms. Truman's place. Her mare was due, and I was there to make sure everythin' came out like it was supposed to," he chuckled. "That's when I heard about the train crashin' into the Ponchatoula Station. Heard on the news, there was a lot of casualties and thought maybe I'd head out that way and lend a hand if I could." He could tell from her body language that this bothered her a great deal. "I see from the debris in the lake that there'd been a pretty nasty accident out there, too. You wouldn't know anythin' 'bout that, would ya'?"

A tear fell from Kaitlin's eye. That was all the confirmation he needed.

"Okay, well… mighty obliged for the conversation, but uh,… Ponchatoula's another twenty minutes down the road here, so I guess I best be makin' my way."

He waited for Kaitlin to say something, but she just continued to stare at the ground, so he repeated himself, trying to be as transparent as he possibly could.

"Not exactly a doctor, but I am a damn good veterinarian, for sho'.

Been one for going on thirty years na' and, uh,... I got my kit in the truck and, well, I--"

"Help us... P-Please," Kaitlin whispered.

"Yes, ma'am, I'd like to, but I'm gon' need to come on over there to do so. Is that gon' be alright?" He asked.

Kaitlin nodded, and Harland crawled over to her. They were only a few feet apart, but he still moved in a manner that would not upset her.

"Now I have to say that I am concerned 'bout that little girl in yo' arms--"

"NO!"

"I'm not gon' touch her," Harland said as he threw his hands back up next to his face to ease Kaitlin.

"N-No!"

"Easy. I'm not gon' touch her... I was just sayin', I see that she's breathin' normally, and other than the fact that she's soakin' wet out in this night air, she appears to be fine. Good job," he commended her. Kaitlin didn't respond. "But I am concerned 'bout this leg of yours. Sweetie pie, I'm a damn good vet. I'll put my skills up 'gainst anyone in these parts, but I ain't quite good enough to do nothin' if you don't let me put my hands on that leg."

Kaitlin desperately wanted to respond to this man, she just didn't know how to anymore.

"Please, let me help you, sugar. It's bad."

Kaitlin finally grunted out a haggard groan and nodded.

"Okay. Na' this road's too dark to do anythin', and my headlights ain't good for nothin' but makin' shadows. I need to get you in that parkin' lot, underneath that light, 'kay?"

"I ca--, c-can't, make it--"

"I'm a pick you up and put you in my truck--"

"No."

"And take you over--"

"NO!"

"I'm sorry, but I ain't got time to argue with you no more."

Before she could protest again, Harland swept them up. Kaitlin screamed, not in fear, but in instinct, holding Dani even tighter. As

Harland ran to the back of his 1976 candy apple red Dodge Warlock pick-up truck. It was nearly a quarter of a century old, but it could still get the job done. He kicked the back gate open and gently slid Kaitlin and Dani far enough in so that they wouldn't fall out. Kaitlin found herself leaning up against a couple of five-gallon plastic containers filled with what seemed to be old cooking oil. A shotgun rested in its sleeve between the oil and the side of the truck.

Harland ran to the driver's side, jumped in, and without closing the door, shifted it into first and smoothly glided the truck into Middendorf's parking lot, right underneath the single light on the pole next to the building, an eighty-watt bulb about twenty-five feet up. Not ideal, but under these circumstances, it was the best he could ask for. He jumped out of the cab with a toolbox he used as a medical bag and a couple of clean blankets from the passenger seat. He plopped the blankets down next to Kaitlin and extended his hand.

"I need you to scooch down a little for me, darlin'."

Kaitlin grabbed his hand, and he gently pulled her onto the rear gate. Here, she could keep her right leg extended while dropping her left leg over the side and out of the way. He opened up a blanket and whipped it around her shoulders, then handed her another one for Dani.

"Let's get her warm, too. Wrap her up tight," he said. Kaitlin took the blanket and noticed she had some of the oil on her hand.

"It's just old, used canola oil," he said as he rummaged through the toolbox. "Believe it or not, that's what this ol' truck runs on," Harland grinned.

He snatched up a headlamp harness and a pair of spectacles and popped them on to properly examine her leg. Obviously, this man had seen a lot during his time, and it would take something special to surprise him.

"Holy– a gator and a vampire in one night?" He said in disbelief.

He looked to Kaitlin for confirmation, unable to believe what his eyes were telling him. Still incapable of holding eye contact with him, abashedly, she nodded as she continued to tuck a blanket around Dani.

"You need to get to a hospital. I gotta get you back to New Awlins--"

"No!" Kaitlin squealed.

"Na', sugar, you listen to me when I tell you this is serious--"

"They'll Kill me!" She screamed.

It seemed as if neither one of them believed she'd just said that out loud.

"I can't go back," she whispered under her breath.

"Little girl, I need you to tell me if you got somethin' to do with all the goings-on that happened back there tonight," he said.

Harland impatiently waited for a response. Kaitlin lifted her head, looked him straight in the eye, and gave him one.

"They'll kill us both," she whispered and lowered her head.

Harland was definitely perplexed by this girl, by this wound, by this whole night. He knew what a vampire bite looked like and didn't flinch when he saw one. He also knew trouble when he saw it, and this night, this wound, this girl, reeked of it. Part of him wanted to walk away, wash his hands of the whole mess, and get back to the safety of his world, but there was an innocence and vulnerability in Kaitlin's eyes that he could not shake. He reached into the toolbox and grabbed a bottle.

"Hydrogen peroxide," he said. "It'll clean it out real nice, without that 'set ya' hair on fire' pain of alcohol, but with a wound this size… ya' still gon' feel it a bit."

Kaitlin shrugged and nodded her permission. Harland emptied the bottle on her and watched as she grunted and squirmed. She let a few tears escape her eyes, but she did not cry out.

"…Judgin' from these marks, I'd say he was probably 'round… five, six feet?" Harland asked as he eyed Kaitlin closely. She had settled from the pain of the cleaning and was back to not responding. He didn't really expect her to.

"I'm talkin' 'bout the gator, by the way, not the vampire," he teased. "Yeah, he wasn't that big, but he sho' got ahold of you, didn't he? He wasn't expectin' you to fight back, though, huh? Don't expect that vampire did either." Harland grinned almost as if he was proud of her. "Either one of them get a piece of the little one?"

"No," she whispered.

Harland smiled. He was proud.

"Good. Next closest hospital's in Hammond. You okay with that one?"

"Yes," she said softly, still avoiding his eyes.

Harland nodded anyway.

"Thing is, we's a good thirty-five, forty minutes out, and you dun' lost a lot of blood. I'd say you lookin' at eight to… maybe twelve stitches, but…sugar, these wounds ain't gon' stop bleedin' on they own, and if you was to lose another thirty minutes worth of blood, I--"

"Go ahead… I can take it," she whispered.

"Darlin', I know you can. I just needed yo' permission."

Harland reached in the box and grabbed a fresh syringe and a small bottle. He could see it got Kaitlin a little excited, so he quashed it down before it got out of hand.

"This here's what we call a 'local' anesthesia, meanin' it's only gonna affect the area in which it is employed, you understand?"

Kaitlin relaxed and nodded.

"Problem is, I ain't got a lot. Wasn't really expectin' to do fieldwork tonight… I'll work as fast as I can, but,… well, you gon' feel a little bit more than either one of us wants you to. You should brace yourself."

Kaitlin looked up at him and really took in his eyes. Harland gave them to her without hesitation, then watched her as she gently laid Dani down next to her in the bed of the truck.

Harland was finally able to get a look at Dani. He smiled as he watched her scooch closer to Kaitlin before settling. He could tell that the child was okay, just sleeping, and didn't really want to be put down. Kaitlin brushed the hair from Dani's face, then braced herself as best she could before giving Harland a nod to begin. Harland nodded back and got to work. He moved from one stitch to the next with an adroit quickness that would have impressed any emergency room doctor. Kaitlin gnashed her teeth, clenched her fist, and dropped a dozen, or so tears, but she never let out as much as a pip. Nine stitches. Each one pulled a piece of her strength, but she didn't scream. Not once. Harland didn't quite know what to think of her. He just knew he liked her. He wrapped her leg, then carried both Kaitlin and Dani together around to the passenger side of the truck and sat them down.

"Pop your leg up," he said.

"Huh?"

She hesitated, unsure, but lifted her leg. He slowly closed the door as he guided her foot out of the open window.

"It'll get a little nippy once we get goin', but keepin' it elevated for the next twenty, thirty minutes will decrease the swellin' and the pain. Give you a little relief."

He balled up a blanket and slipped it under where her leg touched the door. He winked at her, walked back and closed the rear gate of the truck, then got into the driver's side. He tucked the blanket around her and Dani real nice so it wouldn't move. He turned on the radio, took hold of his sixteen-inch, double-bend shift lever, wrangled it into first gear, and took off down the road to Hammond. With the low hum of the radio and the soothing movement of the truck, Kaitlin realized how tired she really was, but with her leg out the window, it was difficult for her to hold Dani and find a comfortable spot to relax without bumping into Harland. She didn't want to lean up against him. She didn't feel right about it.

"I understand your position ain't ideal, but you can lean up against me if that'll give you some comfort," he said with a warmth we'd come to expect.

"No. I'm fine," she whispered.

"Okay."

Within minutes, her body gave in. She slumped against Harland, cheek resting on his shoulder, finally letting go.

CHAPTER 10

One thing will always hold true in these situations: vampires can never be trusted.

Back at the house, Tik sat in what had become her usual place at the head of Lucien's bed. Lucien slept peacefully now, but the room still pulsed with what had come before. Taq held his post as lookout. With a trained eye, he scanned the courtyard and surrounding area from the bedroom window. He scowled as headlights cut across the courtyard like blades. Trouble never came slow.

"Someone's coming," Taq said.

In an instant, Tik was by his side, and together they waited with a covetous curiosity as they gazed out the window. Below, Julien and Rayna exited the vehicle and made their way toward where the door used to be.

"Not one word," Tik said, low and lethal.

Taq's facial expression made it known that it was unwelcome, yet she stood there with an ever-growing impatience until he complied. He nodded without looking at her. That was enough for her, and she moved back to her spot on the bed, not noticing the sly smile that slid across his face. There was a fire that stoked inside that boy that needed to be extinguished, preferably by him, for his own good. He needed to be careful, on this night especially, that the wrong person didn't do it for him.

He watched the car as it pulled off toward the vampire lair around the side and wondered who of his comrades was driving the vehicle. Who of his friends was left. He heard two pairs of footsteps hit the stairs below and make their way to the top. He listened as they trudged the long hallway and, with perfect timing, he moved to the door and opened it as they arrived. Rayna entered first and moved around to take Tik's place at the head of the bed. Julien followed, stopping at the foot. They looked horrible. Their clothes were ripped and tattered, stained with dirt, swamp filth - and blood. That's twice in one night he had seen these two great ones bleed. Taq didn't understand how any of this was possible, and he liked it even less.

"How is he?" Rayna asked with a mother's concern that was not uncommon when it came to Lucien.

Everyone knew that he was her favorite. Maybe it was the fact that Camille never let her anywhere near Dani, or maybe it was something more.

"He's fine. Sleeping peacefully, finally," Tik said.

"What do you mean 'finally'?" Julien asked, neither accusatory nor angry.

"I-I-I mean he's... Before there was-- It was unnatural, ya' know? N-Now, he seems to be just... sleepin'. Normal."

Tik floundered her way through her painful response that seemed adequate enough for Julien. Rayna, however, was a completely different story. Tik could feel Rayna's eyes on her like the sun on a clear, hot day. Her heart pounded as she looked back and forth between Julien and her brother, but she did not dare take in Rayna's eyes. Julien nodded as he stared at his son. There was a sadness in him, and Taq couldn't tell if it was coming from Lucien's present situation or the chaos that had come from this night.

"Everything alright, sir?" Taq asked.

It was a simple question, perhaps a bit naive, but there was no malice or bitterness behind it. It was, however, enough to draw Rayna's glare from Tik to her ostentatious little brother.

"What?" Julien said as he turned to face him.

Most would have realized in this uncomfortable moment to just stop, to say no more, to throw a smoke bomb and disappear. Taq had that fire in him and it was being stoked. Tik had given him simple, specific instructions. She had used simple words to avoid them being misconstrued, and he'd nodded; confirmed that he understood when she said, "Not a word." Not. A. Word.

Taq uttered three. Perhaps she should have added the word "single" to her sentence. She would make a note to be more clear next time. If there was a next time.

"Sorry, sir, he was just concerned," Tik interjected before Taq could speak again. "We're both very sorry for your loss."

If vampires actually breathed, Tik would be holding her breath now, hoping both she and her brother would live to walk another night. Rayna didn't move. She didn't have to. Her silence hissed louder than any snarl.

"I'll be down in the study waiting for my father," he said to Rayna, never taking his eyes away from Taq.

Taq lowered his head, moved to the door, and opened it. Julien stopped at the door with his eyes still fixed on Taq.

"No matter what any of you think you hear,… no one comes down," Julien said, then looked to Rayna, "None of you."

The three of them listened as Julien moved down the hallway to the staircase. Tik let out a subtle, almost unnoticeable sigh of relief that was unmistakably premature. Rayna rose from the bed, her eyes fixed on Taq. She slowly moved toward him while directing all of her questions to Tik.

"Exactly, which loss was it that you were referring to?" Rayna asked.

Taq was confused. Rayna was looking at him, and perhaps she wanted him to answer. He thought about it for a quick second before he thought it best to finally take his older and much wiser sister's advice and remain silent.

"Ma'am?" Tik replied, also confused by the question.

"Whose – loss – were – you – sorry – for?" Rayna repeated, slower this time, so there could be no mistake.

She had made her way to the door, her eyes still locked on Taq. Under normal circumstances, no one would ever call a vampire timid. After dying once, the fear gene no longer existed within them, but Rayna had a unique way of bringing it back out. Taq was afraid to look at her, and although Tik was afraid to move, she knew if she didn't move her mouth real soon, one of them was going to die - again. This time, permanently.

"Camille, ma'am. I was--"

"How did you know that Camille was dead? And please, don't make me repeat myself this time."

Although incapable of it, Tik wanted to cry so very badly. She knew she had gotten herself into something, and Rayna was not going to give her an easy way out. Tik opened her mouth to answer but was cut off by Rayna as she interrupted her protégé.

"You've slowly become one of my favorites, Tikesha," Rayna said as she raised her hand and positioned her index finger directly in front of Taquan's left eye. "Please don't lie to me."

With fear in his eyes, Taq looked to Tik, who could do nothing but stare at her younger brother. It was always her job to protect him, and other than the night he was killed, and right now, she had done a fine job.

"Lucien told us," Tik whispered, thinking that would most likely be the last words she would ever speak. Rayna lowered her finger and turned to her.

"…When?"

"About an hour ago. He woke up screaming. Sat straight up in the bed and told us his momma had died. I ain't believe him at first. Just did my best to comfort him, but when Mr. Gerard walked in… the look on his face told me it was true."

Rayna's eyes flitted back and forth as she stared in Lucien's direction.

"…He say anything else?"

Taq looked at his sister, wondering if she would tell the truth about what really happened. He wondered if she should. Without hesitation, Tik looked straight into Rayna's eyes.

"No, ma'am. He collapsed in my arms and fell back to sleep. We tried to wake him, but… we couldn't."

Tik admired Ms. Rayna a great deal. In some respect, she looked at her as the mother she and Taq never had. She didn't want to lie to her; she didn't feel good about it, but one thing will always hold true in these situations: vampires can never be trusted. Rayna stared long and hard at Tik, and Tik held her stare like a champ.

"Taq, go on over to the lair and get Jimmy and whoever else is there to get over here and get the drapes back on these upstairs windows before dawn. I've lost enough tonight. Can't afford to lose any more of y'all over something as stupid as the sun."

"Yes, ma'am," Taq answered.

"And make sure y'all stay out of sight. Use the back staircase and the tunnel."

"Yes, ma'am."

"Tikesha, please join me in my shower. My back's full of silver slivers, and it won't heal. I need you to get them all out."

"What about Lucien?" Tik asked.

"Just get as much as you can. If he wakes, we'll get the rest out some other time."

"Yes, ma'am."

"Is he dead? The magic man - Y'all got him, right?" Taq asked.

Rayna's face could not hide the pure disdain she felt at the mere mention of his name. She inhaled deeply and exhaled, ever-so-slowly, as she pondered how to respond to what she felt was an intimate, personal question.

"I surely do hope so… Now move your ass and go do what I told you to!" Rayna said.

Taq jumped and Rayna snatched him by the arm.

"And you come get me the moment old man Gerard sets foot in this house."

"Yes, ma'am," Taq answered as Rayna stormed out.

In a flash, Tik was on Taq and hemmed him up against the wall by his collar. She wanted to punch him in the face but was afraid it might make too much noise.

"You ever disobey me again, I'll kill you myself," she whispered before she ejected him from the room.

53

CHAPTER 11

*H*arland Bisset, DVM

A siren shrieked past the old red truck, snapping Kaitlin awake.

"Easy. It's just a firetruck," Harland said in a comforting voice.

She was disoriented and confused from being woken so abruptly. More than startled, she was embarrassed, ashamed of how easily she'd folded into a stranger's shoulder.

"Sorry."

"Oh, you're fine," Harland reassured her.

She sat up and repositioned herself, which wasn't easy because her leg had fallen asleep. She gingerly pulled it back into the cab so as not to infringe upon Harland in that way again.

"Yeah, it's been about thirty minutes. I s'pose you can bring it in na'."

The question having been answered of how long she was out, her attention went back to the ever-sleeping beauty in her arms.

"Why won't she wake?" Kaitlin wondered.

"Wake up, baby," Kaitlin whispered in Dani's ear. "Come on, sweetie, please? You've got to wake up."

"She's not unconscious, she's just sleepin'," Harland said, reassuring her again. "If that's what you were wonderin'."

Kaitlin gave him a quizzical look. She was concerned and wanted to know more.

"She's moving," he replied. "She's been repositionin' and snugglin' and grabbin' up to you this entire time. I'd a been more than a little concerned if she wasn't."

Kaitlin took that in.

"She's just tired. Exhausted, probably. Whatever it was y'all been through," he said as he reached the outer perimeter of the train wreckage in Ponchatoula, "...must'ta... must'ta been a lot... for her."

They both looked onto the disaster area in awe as Harland drove by the plethora of police cars and emergency vehicles. The crash site was a mile and a half long and included many more casualties than the passengers of the train. The next ten minutes were spent in silence, neither wishing to comment on what they had just witnessed. As they pulled up to a red light, Kaitlin noticed a sign indicating that the Hammond Hospital was straight ahead. She also noticed that Harland seemed different after driving by the accident, almost as if he had left something there.

He hadn't noticed that the light had changed until the horn of the car behind him made him aware. Startled, he moved his foot off the clutch enough to make the truck lurch forward, almost stalling it out. Obviously, something was bothering him. He spotted a convenience store on the next block and pulled into it. He sat there for a moment with his eyes fixed on the dashboard and his brow furrowed as if he were searching for the answer to a math problem. He put the truck in park and turned it off.

"Sit tight. I'll be right back," he said without looking at her, then got out of the truck and entered the store.

Kaitlin looked at the steering wheel and noticed he had left the keys in the ignition. She thought about how easy it would be to just turn the ignition and leave, especially now with Harland acting this way. She hadn't known him long, but she knew him long enough to be concerned. He seemed distant and uncertain, and that just wasn't the Harland who sat with her in the middle of the road. She looked up and watched as he walked to the ATM machine to withdraw some cash. He never looked back at her while he waited for the machine to do its business. All this made her very uncomfortable, and she didn't know why. She watched him retrieve his money, grab two bottles of something from the refrigerated section, then stop and grab something else on his way to the register. Her anxiety grew with every step he took.

She wanted to leave and wished she had taken the vehicle when the chance was there, but that's not who she was. Even under these extreme circumstances, she couldn't bring herself to do it, and now it was too late as she watched him exit the store and get back into the truck. She fixed her eyes on a spot on the dashboard and focused on it as Harland sat motionless behind the wheel for another uncomfortable moment.

"Hmph," he grunted before he started the vehicle and put it in reverse.

He backed up a bit, deftly wrangled the odd shifter into first gear again, then pulled out of the lot without saying a word. It seemed like the longest three minutes of the night as they drove a few blocks down the street. The hospital was a madhouse. Police cars and ambulances were scattered about, with first responders running back and forth as they tried to help and direct as many people as they could. Harland pulled up as close as he could get to the emergency room, put the vehicle in park, and turned it off. Kaitlin was afraid, and she didn't know why. All she could do was stare at that single spot on the dashboard in front of her.

"...Usually what happens in situations like this is the police like to talk to all the survivors, to... try and get a clear picture of what happened," Harland said as he looked straight ahead to avoid eye contact with her. "They'll ask for names and addresses of where you was comin' from and where you was goin'. And they'll take that information and radio it to the police back in New Awlins. That way, they can contact people – loved ones or... others who may be... lookin' for somebody," he said as he turned his gaze to her.

She knew he was staring at her, but she could not bring herself to look back at him. Harland then grabbed the bag he purchased from the store and pulled out a bottle of Gatorade, and offered it to her. Kaitlin stared at the bottle for a few seconds before her confused eyes found his.

"You lost a lot of blood, and I'm guessin' that you probably ain't feelin' so good right about now. It's 'cuz your blood pressure dun' dropped way lower than it needs to be. You go in that hospital, first thing they gonna do after they check you out and admire my expert stitch work, is try and get you hydrated with some kinda isotonic, sodium chloride solution. Somethin' like this." Once more, he offered her to take the bottle, and this time, she did. "It'll start to get your hemoglobin levels and your blood pressure back up to where it needs to be. Unless you go to a hospital, you gon' need to drink a lot of this for the next few weeks."

He gave her a quick grin and a wink before he got out of the truck, put the bag in the driver's seat, and closed the door. He leaned in and continued the conversation through the rolled-down window.

"I'm a go inside and see if I can get somebody to take a look at you, even though there really ain't nothin' more they can do that ain't been done, hear me?" Kaitlin didn't respond.

"Now, it'll probably take me at least ten minutes to check in and find somebody and explain to 'em what happened to ya'. At LEAST ten minutes..." he emphasized. "I don't expect I'll see you or this truck when I return."

Kaitlin vehemently shook her head in protest.

"Harland, I would never steal your--"

"Sweet pea, if I'd a thought that, I'd've never picked you up. I've always had excellent instincts when it comes to judgin' people - it's a gift," he said as he tapped his temple with his index finger. "But after passin' by that accident and seein', first hand, the devastation and the complete disregard for human life,... I needed to know for sure whether you were a culprit of that insanity or a victim of it. That's why I pulled into the convenience store and left the keys. Had to give you a chance to prove me wrong."

"...I wanted to," she whispered painfully, ashamed to look at him.

It saddened Harland to see how the confession tormented her.

"Sweetie, every soul on this planet has inappropriate thoughts at one time or another. Morals is what keeps us from actin' on 'em, and as far as I can see, yours are just fine," he said with a proud smile. "Even if they weren't, you probably couldn't a' done it. This beat-up thing is nearly twenty-five years old, but trust me when I tell ya', it still got plenty-a-good miles left in it. Plenty. I don't drive it much. For Sunday mass or when I go callin' on the widow Baker, I put the top down on my mean, green, '95 Pontiac Firebird and let her eat up some street," he laughed, "but most times you'd find me drivin' my van. Dealin' with animals of all shapes and sizes it comes in handy. Got the magnetized placard on the sides: Harland Bisset, DVM - Animal Doctor." He beamed with pride. "Was headin' out to it after I got the call 'bout Ms. Truman's mare, and just before I got in, I looked over and saw the ol' red truck sittin' over there and,... for the life of me, I can't tell you why, but somethin' just pulled me to it," he said with a quizzical look on his face. "I grabbed my tool case and some blankets and hopped in. Keys was already in it; as you can see, I never take 'em out. Figure this the last vehicle a thief would think about stealin'. Even if they was that desperate, they'd be hard-pressed to get it to start. It's got a counterclockwise ignition cylinder on it. Means you gotta turn it backward to get it to start. If you get past that, you still gotta figure out how to get in first gear. The little diagram on the knob is just a distraction. Truth is, you gotta come off the clutch about halfway as you waggle the stick over to the left, then pull it down into first, not up. Goin' up ain't gonna get you nothin' but stalled out and swearin'.'"

He laughed, thinking about the ridiculousness of his design before being overcome with sadness.

"Me and my daughter pretty much rebuilt this whole truck durin' the summer of eighty-eight before she headed off to the marines. That's when we converted it to a hybrid. It runs on that canola oil in the back. It works best for biodiesel production. It ages slow and remains liquid, even in low temperatures." He smiled and winked at her again. "Go to any Chinese restaurant at the end of the night, hell, some of 'em will pay you to take it away for them. I promised I'd keep it tuned up and ready for her when she came back from the Desert Storm Operation. She was a mechanic. Did a full tour, and I can tell you there ain't a dad that was ever more proud than this one right here. A week before she was to receive her honorable discharge for her service, she was killed by a vampire while stationed at Camp Lejeune in Jacksonville, North Carolina. 'Course they said it was a snake, an Eastern Coral that had somehow snuck up and caught her right on the neck. Said she probably never saw him. Hmph... My little girl grew up playin' hide and seek in the bayous of Louisiana. Ain't no snake ever gonna sneak up on her. Sides, everybody knows Eastern Coral Snakes make their home in the Southern Carolinas, not the North... Been holdin' onto this truck for seven years... Never knew why until today."

"Harland, no, I--"

"I suspect she was a little younger than you when she was killed. I see a lot of her in you," Harland said with a lot of pride on his face. "Take good care of her, and she'll take good care of you," he said, patting the window frame with his hand.

Harland walked back and grabbed his toolbox, then moved up next to her on the passenger side of the truck.

"Harland,--"

"You go in that hospital, whatever or whoever it is that's chasin' you, will be here within an hour. Judging by what they did to that train, I don't think I'd like for you to be here when they arrive."

Kaitlin didn't know what to say. Harland made it easy for her.

"You can drive a stick, can't cha'?"

"...Yes."

Harland smiled as he tapped his temple. "Figured you could."

Harland gazed at Dani, who was clutching onto Kaitlin, sleeping peacefully on her shoulder.

"You ain't this child's momma, are you?"

"...No."

"Well... right or wrong, seems like you are now," he said, looking her square in the eye, "and lil' girl, if you gonna be her momma, then you got to BE her momma. Or don't. Hear me?"

Harland's words were heavy, and Kaitlin felt every bit of that weight. She nodded to him, and he nodded back, then headed for the door. Just before reaching it, he turned back and yelled to her.

"By the way, you might wanna check that bag fo' you toss it away!"

Kaitlin picked up the bag and opened it to find another bottle of hydrogen peroxide and three hundred dollars – the money he had taken out of the ATM. She looked up to protest, but the doorway was empty, like he'd never been there at all.

CHAPTER 12

hat was nothing was now something

Mist slithered up from the pavement, curling around The Trolley like a serpent before it vanished with a thunderous BOOM. It was either very, very late or very, very early, depending on your particular constitution, and the streets were desolate. As the mist dissipated, The Talisman was revealed, alone on a corner in downtown New Orleans. Some might say that "the early bird catches the worm." His particular constitution said it was early, and he had some fishing to do. He walked halfway down an alley, removed his glasses, and, without hesitation, popped both of his eyes from their sockets. He knelt, shook the eyes like dice between his palms, and rolled them across the alley's filth-slick stones. It brought a smile to his face as he remembered the good ol' days. He snapped his fingers, and the dice rolled into two full-grown Doberman Pinschers, who took off down the alley like they were chasing a jackrabbit. He placed his glasses back on his face, checked the time on his pocket watch, and vanished into the nighttime air as he walked after them, eager to pursue today's catch.

Meanwhile, outside the cave–

Hours passed as Tirin, Teddy, and Cree steadfastly raced against the never-ending threat from the east that the birth of every new day brings. Exhausted, their hands and fingers bloodied by the self-imposed, menial labor to which they had lowered themselves, they futilely strained to upheave and dislodge the granite rocks and boulders from the cave entrance. It seemed as if they were chasing their tails; with gravity running roughshod over the mountainous obstruction, every expulsion was canceled out and replaced two-fold by dirt and debris. Time was neither an ally nor a friend as the thick night grew thinner and deserted them a bit more with each failed attempt to gain access to the treasure within.

Perhaps it was just an abnormal sense of urgency that overtook them as they felt the surface temperature increase with every painful second that passed. Then, when that first ray of light broke free of the earth's grasp and escaped the horizon, the cave, the rubble, the promise of vengeance – all of it - was gone. Scattered away like smoke in sunlight. In their time, they had seen many things, but none of them had ever witnessed anything like this. The dawn had brought with it the promise of a new beginning and had taken the right of vengeance for their brothers and loved ones they had lost. There would be no second chance at dusk to redeem the failure of this night, for the cave would not offer them one. It would not show its façade again for another twenty-seven days, and not even an alpha could track down where in this swamp it would appear. The game was over. The cave had won.

Then, as the three battered warriors stood solemnly in the thick muck of the bayou with only their grief and the serene song of the cicadas to keep them company, the heartbreaking howl of a defeated alpha wolf was heard.

"AAAAAAAAAHHHHHHHHHHRRRRRRR!!!!!!"

Inside the cave–

A low, husky chuckle severed softly through silence. What was nothing was now something... A soft, muffled snicker dissected diligently through the dark. What was something was now more. From a chortle to a giggle. The intensity increased from a titter to a crow. The distance quickly closed as the volume steadily rose.

"A-A-A-HA-HA-HA-HA-HA-A-A!" Hagatha cackled.

'A whisper on the wind? A forgotten memory revived?' Jean wondered as he lay, helpless, in his comatose state.

It felt like a tower bell in his head. An ever-constant noise that bounced off his brain and echoed down his spine.

"It is just a dream," Jean thought.

"Some might say a nightmare," Hagatha giggled.

Jean was taken aback by the mysterious voice.

"What was--?... How did--?"

"What confuses you, my love?" Hagatha asked.

"No. This is,... not possible."

"Then imagine the possibilities," she giggled.

"This is a dream, I am unconscious."

"Unconscious has 'conscious' in the word. If the first is true, then the other is, too!" she laughed.

"Stop! I will not be baited by your whispers, witch."

"Some call them spells."

"Call them what you will. They have no influence over me," Jean said.

"In time, you may see things differently, my love."

This is nothing more than a distraction, Jean thought to himself. *"Heal,... Concentrate,... Heal,..."*

"Yes-s-s. Concentrate, my love. The deeper you go, in time, you shall see. The further you fall brings you closer to me."

"Your magic is long gone, hag. Your sorcery carries no weight here."

"Perhaps, but our joining will change all of that. Our union will be one for the ages."

"You are insane. I will not speak to you again."

"You need only listen. Listen as I sing my songs. Wrap my voice around your soul. Listen as I harden your heart as my songs take their toll," she cackled wildly.

"NO!"

"I claim this vessel as mine!" She shouted. *"I shall be reborn and grow more powerful than any being this world has ever known!"*

"I would never allow that to happen!"

"You cannot stop it, my lover, my love. My lover for life."

"You overestimate your power, witch!"

"You'll be the handle, I'll be the knife!" She sang.

"I will awaken in the morning and destroy this place and wipe away every foul remembrance of you."

"A-A-A-HA-HA-HA-HA-HA-A-A! I will feast upon your heartbreak after you discover there is no one to wake you. When you realize the hope you so pathetically embrace has abandoned you, my loins will become engorged! A-A-A-HA-HA-HA-HA!"

Then, her voice took a sinister turn. The playful tone was lost and replaced with something much more evil.

"How dare you challenge me, boy? I will spend the next century grinding your mind to meal! I will bend your feeble will until it breaks, and you succumb to every wanton wish and desire that falls from my lips!"

"Many have tried, but you will find my mind strong."

"Yes-s-s-s. You are strong," she said.

"You will not break me."

"So very strong... But I... Am... Patient... A-A-A-HA-HA-HA-HA-HA-A-A!"

CHAPTER 13

"*He's a girl, now. Look for her.*"

In the morning, Rayna entered Lucien's room in an absolutely stunning, form-fitting black dress that fell just below her fully defined, heart-shaped calves. She was a designer's dream because her body made everything look gorgeous, no matter the color, material, or cut. Even on this most unfortunate day, she looked as breathtaking as ever, albeit a bit more conservative than usual. Even though the long-sleeved dress held onto her body like high-performance tires on a winding road, it was one of the only dresses she owned without a slit in it to show off at least one of her perfectly proportioned legs. Its tight turtleneck hid both the ample cleavage she was known to display and the toned muscles of her tapered back, which was entirely the point of this ensemble.

Although Tik had removed a multitude of silver filings from her back, the method she was forced to use was not only painful beyond the tolerances of any normal person, it left Rayna's back bloodied and scarred and not at all pleasing to the eye. The slight cut on her face she received from Jean last night was nearly undetectable now, but even with her incredible regenerative powers, the damage he inflicted on her back would take more time to heal than anything she had ever been subjected to in her life, and they still weren't sure if Tik had removed them all. If she didn't, Rayna's back would not heal, and they would have to go through the entire process again. In time, the scars would heal and fade, but the memory of the pain that was caused last night would last a lifetime, which, for her, was a very long time.

Jimmy-Lee had joined Tik and Taq to comfort the slumbering prince of the Gerard fortune, who had finally awakened, but how does anyone comfort a child in a moment like this? Lucien hurled himself into Rayna's arms, and she caught him without flinching. Tears soaked her dress. Snot streaked her collar. She didn't move. Didn't speak. Just held him like it mattered more than anything else in the world. Rayna was the type of woman who, unless she offered you her hand to pay homage, generally didn't like to be touched. If you did so without prior authorization, you were most certainly going to die. Lucien had always been the exception to that rule. She let his tears and snot fall on her black dress without so much as a flinch. She didn't say a word. She just held him because that's what he needed from her right then.

"Momma's dead," he sobbed.

"I know. But I'm glad you're okay now."

"That man who took Momma threw sand on me, and when I woke up, she was dead!"

"I know, sugar, but you're alright now."

"Did he kill my momma?"

The hesitation in her response was minuscule. A small fraction of time that only a few others, outside of the ones in this room, would have been able to detect.

"...I'm not sure, but I think so."

"Why?! My momma never did nothin' to nobody! She would never hurt nobody! She liked people... She was always good to everyone. Why would he kill her?"

Rayna was only half-vampire, and that side was not present at this moment. The human side was, and it ached. She never imagined she could feel this way. She always wanted a child of her own, and it's not that it wasn't possible; she honestly wasn't sure one way or the other. It's just that the cost to even try for something that no one could say was truly achievable was much too high a price for her to pay. A tear fell from her face, closely followed by another.

"I don't know, sweetie. I don't know why bad things have to happen. I only know that when they do, we have to use them to become stronger than we were before they happened so that we can try and stop them from happening again."

Lucien nodded. In moments like this, when he was sad, he always played with his mother's necklace. He tugged at Rayna's turtleneck as if he were looking for it or something that might ease his pain.

"Did you find Dani?" he asked.

"I, ah... We think that your brother died last night, too."

Lucien shook his head as he continued to roll and unroll the material around her neck. Rayna's eyes furrowed, then made their way past him to Tik. Tik's heart skipped a beat. She wanted to run, but the sun was out. Where could she go?

"Sweetie, what do you mean?" Rayna asked. Lucien did not reply. "Did your momma tell you where Dani is?"

Again, Lucien shook his head no.

"Tik said you woke up and told her that your momma was dead."

Lucien nodded. "I like Tik. She's nice. She helped me."

"Yes, Tik is very, very nice-- Did anything else happen after that?" Rayna asked as her eyes switched back and forth between Tik and Taq.

Lucien continued to toy with Rayna's turtleneck, trying to get it just right.

"Sweetie, tell Ray-Ray what happened after you spoke with Momma... After she told you, she was dead... Luc?"

"I don't know," he replied softly. "I just remember when I woke up, Tik and Taq and Jimmy-Lee was here. Daddy's gonna find Dani, right?"

"...Yes. If he's out there, me and your daddy and Tirin will find him--"

"Her."

"What?"

"He's a girl now," he said. "You have to look for her."

Tik could see the anger growing in Rayna's eyes, and it petrified her.

"...How-- Why do you think Dani is a girl now, sweetie?"

"'Cuz she is."

"How do you know that?'

"I saw her the night Momma got hurt," Lucien said. He looked up and drew Rayna's eyes from Tik and Taq to him. "You saw her too, didn't you?" Lucien asked, eyes wide and unblinking. "Momma didn't want you to. She didn't want anybody to, but you did anyway, didn't you?"

Rayna didn't know why she felt embarrassed over the accusation, but she didn't like the feeling. She didn't like any of these feelings that had come to surface over the last few minutes.

"I don't know what I saw that night, baby. Everything was moving so fast. It was all very confusing," Rayna said, then kissed him on his forehead. She no longer wished to play this game. "But I do know that you need a bath, and Tik's gonna give you one, and then she's gonna get you dressed.

"We're gonna have to go some places today, and people are gonna be saying some things about your momma and Dani."

"What kind of things?"

"Things that may be hard for us to hear, but we're gonna all have to be strong and get through it as best we can. Okay?"

Lucien nodded and hugged her again, which made her smile. She kissed him again before she passed him off to Tik.

"Put him in a dark suit," Rayna said to Tik, who acknowledged with a nod. "Taq, stay with 'em. When he's ready, bring him down-stairs to me, then you two go to the lair and get some rest."

"Yes, ma'am," Tik and Taq responded simultaneously.

"Jimmy, you're with me."

Jimmy-Lee nodded and followed her out of the room. If she had been paying attention, she'd have seen the relief on Tik's and Taq's faces, but there were other unpleasant matters that needed to be addressed.

CHAPTER 14

"We are not humans! We do not wallow in the misery of our mistakes,"

Jimmy-Lee was the member Rayna trusted most of all her staff. He was the first vampire to whom she had turned in the Gerard household and had been on the payroll months before that auspicious night she and Julien met Tirin. If there was one person to whom the phrase "Vampires cannot be trusted" didn't apply, it would be him. She considered him to be more than just her "Number One"; he was her friend, and the feeling was mutual. He knew her better than anyone, even better than Julien and Tirin. He alone could tell by her gait, the cast she wore, and the tears she allowed to fall, that right now, she was anything but all right and he had a pretty good idea why.

"Beautiful dress you picked out, Boss. And you lookin' mighty fine in it this mornin'."

Jimmy knew how much Rayna adored compliments. For a woman who received as many as she did, one would think she would tire of them. They would be wrong in that assumption. She received everyone as if it were her first, and they always put a smile on her face.

"Thank you, Jimmy," she said softly.

When no smile breached her face as she started to descend the staircase, he knew things would only get worse when they reached the bottom. She stopped when her bare foot hit the last step. The ground floor was a mess from the previous night's carnage. Jimmy thought that her hesitation to leave the staircase was possibly because of that.

"Shall I go get your--" Jimmy started to say, but Rayna raised her hand and silenced him. Jimmy stood rigid, waiting for what was to come next. Every child hates it when their mom and dad fight. Even the tiniest altercations are stressful. This one was not going to be a tiny one. It had all the makings of the Grand Daddy of them all. Either way, it's not the child's fight, and the absolute worst thing anyone could do was to get involved. The last place Jimmy wanted to be right now was on this staircase, standing next to her, with Julien standing in the waiting area, looking out in the distance through the remnants of one of the large bay windows. He had his back to them, but he knew they were there.

He heard them walk down the stairs and stop, but did not turn to face them. He didn't even acknowledge their presence. He just stood there in silence, looking out at nothing, waiting for nothing. Or was he waiting for a fight? Jimmy didn't know the answer, but he knew that his boss was in a mood to give him one. He also knew that wouldn't be a very smart thing for her to do. The air between them was as thick as black smoke and just as toxic. Vampires can't breathe, and yet, Jimmy felt as if he were suffocating.

Julien didn't turn.

"What did you do with my father?"

"He's in the cellar." Rayna replied. "What would you have me do now?"

Julien let the silence stretch until it snapped.

"...Now you ask what I want..."

It felt like an eternity before the next words were said.

"Fine." She expelled, barely audible. Then, "Jimmy, go down and wrap him up nice and put him in a van after the sun goes down. We'll save the mortician a trip."

"Yes, ma'am--"

"Jimmy, I like you, but if you take one step off that landing, it will be your last," said Julien.

This is exactly where Jimmy didn't want to be – in the middle, yet somehow, when a third person is anywhere near a two-person argument, that's always where they end up. Jimmy froze like a statue in a museum, waiting for what was next.

"SHE wanted him down there, so leave him there until SHE decides what SHE wants to do with him."

"I put him down there on Mr. Jeffries orders--"

"DID HE ORDER YOU TO KILL HIM?!" Julien screamed as he finally turned to face her. All the sadness, anger, anguish, frustration, sorrow, grief, and heartbreak of last night was right here, right now. "'Cuz I know I sure as hell did not!"

"...Jimmy, go tell Tik we'll come up and get Lucien when we're ready."

"Y-Yes, ma'am," Jimmy whispered.

He took a single step up and waited to see if it came with any objection or the immediate loss of life. It did not. At this point, Julien and Rayna were so locked on each other that neither one of them even knew Jimmy was still there. He took advantage of the moment and proved them both right. Rayna stepped off the landing and fearlessly walked across the room toward Julien. He met her halfway.

"I asked you what you wanted me to do!" she shouted with a malignant tongue.

"I sure as fuck didn't want you to kill my father!"

"The mayor and the sheriff and his whole fucking hit squad had this house surrounded, and you picked that time to start a fuckin' fight?!"

"It was my fight! MINE! Not yours!"

"And how did you see it ending? Huh?! What was your next move AFTER he got away, 'cuz he was getting away! What were you gonna do then?!" Rayna flatly asked.

"I had it under control!"

"YOU'VE NEVER BEEN IN CONTROL OF ANYTHING WHEN IT COMES TO HIM! NOTHING!"

Julien's eyes blazed red as his hair moved wildly around him.

Rayna didn't flinch. She stood in front of him and looked right into the depth of his red eyes and waited.

"ENOUGH-H-H-H-H!" Tirin roared as he stood in what used to be the doorway, flanked by Teddy and Cree, his presence silencing even the ruin.

"...Is this what we do now?" Tirin asked with a calmness that this situation needed. "We kill each other for speaking the truth?"

"It's not the truth!... It's not the truth!! It's her truth, not mine!... Not mine!..." Julien hollered as the tears began to wash the red from his eyes, and his hair began to settle. "She killed him!" Then to Rayna. "You killed him... and it was supposed to be me." He dropped to his knees. The air cracked. "It was supposed to be me... AH-H-H-H-H-H!!!!"

Rayna reached out her hand and placed it on his head as tears poured down her face. She didn't know what to say, what to do. She didn't know how to fix this moment, so like with Lucien, she just held him and let him cry. He let it all out until there was nothing left, then he fell backward and sat there on the floor, broken and alone in a room full of people... or rather, malafecs.

"Do you want me to leave?" Rayna asked.

She didn't mean the room. There was a finality in the question that did not go unnoticed. Tirin looked at Julien and, with patience he alone possessed, waited for his response.

"I don't know... I don't know what I want anymore."

"I can't stay here like this, Julien. Walking on eggshells. Wondering if you'll ever forgive me for something that I honestly don't believe I need forgiveness for!" Rayna cried.

"You killed my father!" Julien yelled.

"He killed your wife! Your daughter! HE DID ALL THIS! Every-thing that happened last night was his doing!" She screamed. "I love you, but I won't apologize for what I did, so if you can't truly forgive me, then I have to leave because I can't stay here and see the resent-ment in your eyes every time you look at me."

Julien could not respond. Try as he might, he couldn't give her the reassurance she needed. All he could do was sit there and shake his head. She closed her eyes and sighed, then she walked over to Tirin, gave him a kiss, and headed for the stairs.

"He wouldn't have killed you, he loved you… but he damn sure would've killed me. And there wouldn't've been anything you could've done to stop him. I'll be out by the time you return from the press conference," she said before she ran upstairs.

Julien lowered his head. He thought that he had nothing left to cry about. He was wrong. She had been with him since he was ten years old. Outside of Camille, she was everything to him. Sometimes, even more than Camille was, which was always a problem. He knew she didn't want to go, and he didn't want her to. All he had to do was get up and stop her, tell her he wanted her to stay, and she would. Sometimes, that's the hardest thing in the world for a man, or warlock, to do. Tirin grunted a cue for Teddy and Cree to disappear, and they did. He walked over to Julien, sat down on the floor in front of him, and, like Rayna, let him cry.

"You know I don't want her to go," Julien said.

"Then stop her."

"I want to, but… I can't."

"Why?"

"She killed him, Tirin. She killed him right in front of me – right in front of me like he was nothing! Like--"

"And what were you going to do? What did you think the outcome of that fight, the fight you started, was going to be?"

"I was going to kill him for what he had done – for everything he had done!"

Tirin stared deep into his friend's eyes, searching for the answer.

"No… you wouldn't have."

"God Damn it,--"

"I looked. It was not there. It is not within you, my friend."

"You don't know--" Julien tried to yell.

"He would have killed Rayna. She is the only person he hated more than me. He would have killed her, and then he would have killed me for what my betas did to Cecil."

"No, I wouldn't have let,--"

"You couldn't have stopped him. Just like you couldn't stop him from killing Camille, and you had four years to do that."

"Yeah, I know! It's all my fault,--"

"It is ALL our fault!" Tirin roared. "Five years ago, you bestowed upon me the honor of protecting her. She was my sole responsibility, mine, and mine alone. And it was a privilege for me to do so. So many things I learned from watching that girl grow into the woman she came to be. Oftentimes, it was she who became a teacher to me. Then unknowingly, without provocation or necessity or cause,... she became... my friend," Tirin said, then exhaled slowly, trying to hold back his emotions. "But that friendship came with a cost. It tempered me in a way that... made it... difficult for me to fulfill my responsibility... both to you and to her. That is my failure, and it shall walk with me for the rest of my days... You are complicit as well, are you not?" He asked Rayna without looking at her.

Only Tirin could hear that she had come back down and had planted herself on the stairs.

"Your job was to see and to bring clarity into that which was unknown. To give us the answers to the questions that best served our purposes. She altered you as well, did she not?" Tirin asked in an accusatory manner. "YOU are supposed to be our first line of defense, not me!"

"I always tried to do that!" Rayna yelled.

"Then explain to me The Council's attack on our house, Kaitlin's betrayal, and how a single man, wielding that much power, CAN WALK INTO OUR LIVES AND DESTROY-R-R-R I-I-I-I-I-IT?!" he roared angrily, releasing all *his* pent up emotion.

"I DON'T KNOW!!" Rayna cried. "I'm an interpreter, Tirin, not a psychic."

"So Camille had no bearing on your interpretations?"

"...Are you implying that I held back? That I lied?!"

"It was no secret that you did not care for her like we did, and I can tell you with utmost certainty that she did not care for you."

"What are you saying?! You think I wanted this to happen?!"

"Tell me that you couldn't have done more?! That you did not allow your personal feeling to get in the way of the mission,"

"My people are DEAD! My friends are gone!--"

"That your incessant bickering wasn't counterproductive to the needs of our union!"

"I WAS DEFENDING MYSELF FROM HER! Not once did either of you think to do that for me!"

"A mother chooses not to argue with a daughter, not out of fear of losing, but because she possesses the maturity and the wisdom not to."

"I DID MY JOB!... I can only answer the questions asked of me."

"Then is it the question or person asking it that is to blame for our repeated failures? Enlighten us so that we may fix this miscarriage of justice here and now."

"It's not that simple, Tirin! The tiniest variance in sentence forma-tion could have bearing on the specifics of the outcome!"

"DENIAL-L-L-L! IT IS YOUR JOB TO PROMPT HIM TO ASK BETTER QUESTIONS! ...Or perhaps the wizard should have stepped out from behind the curtain and asked a few herself. Those variances could have saved lives."

The truth can be difficult to face. Rayna sat down on the stairs and buried her face in her hands. During that entire time, Tirin never took his eyes from Julien. Tirin now directed his words at him.

"If I am the blunt instrument, it is your hand that wields it. If she is the eyes, they are for your vision. It is your brain that controls this body and your heart that is responsible for its demise. She was your WIFE! He was your FATHER! And that... that little girl... that none of us got to know was your daughter!" Tirin said as a tear rolled down his face. "Your daughter..."

Julien could not look at him. Tirin gave him no choice.

"SHE TOLD YOU FOUR YEARS AGO!" He bellowed, indicating Rayna. "She has made some poor choices – we all have – but when have you ever known her to be wr-r-rong?!" He growled. "In a DAY, we all lost more than any being should be forced to lose in a lifetime. But we are not humans! We do not wallow in the misery of our mistakes, we stand up, and we F-I-I-I-I-IGHT!" He cried out. "...We fight... It is what makes us stronger than them. We three, together, FEAR-R-RLESS, acting as one, is a combination that is potent and unequaled, but we must ALL - every one of us - own up to our mistakes. Mourn our losses and let them make us stronger. We must forgive each other's failures, here and now, at this very moment. We must let them go, or we must walk away. There can be no other way."

Tirin jumped to his feet and looked down at Julien.

"I came here this morning to kill your father or die trying. She may have beaten me to it, but my intentions were clear. He has always been something that needed to be... exterminated. I apologize only for the fact that it was done too late."

Tirin offered his hand to Julien. "I forgive you, my friend. I forgive you both... Can you both forgive me?"

Julien looked up and, after a moment, took his hand, and Tirin pulled him up. Tirin then reached out his hand to Rayna. She walked over and took it. She reached out to Julien. He grasped her hand, then Tirin pulled them both into a tearful embrace.

"She brought out the best and the worst of us. Do not let her death stand for nothing. If we are to succeed, we must all be who we were meant to be – who we were born to be – or be nothing... RRRRA-A-A-A-A-HHH!"

He howled with a ferocity that had long been forgotten, and in the blink of an eye, he was gone. Julien and Rayna stood there holding each other's hands, both afraid to catch the other's eye.

"You were right, I... probably wouldn't have been able to stop him from... doing whatever he was going to do to you, but... I love you, Ray. You make me so God Damn mad all the time, but I do. Ain't nobody on this planet outside of Camille I love more, including him, but... he was my dad..."

Rayna hugged him and held him tight.

"I'm sorry, Julien, I truly am... I'm sorry."

"Tirin was right. He needed to go, and I wouldn't've been able to do it, so... It's gonna take me a little time, but don't leave, okay? I don't want you to go."

Rayna squeezed his hands and shook her head.

Julien hesitated, swallowed. "It's just gonna take some time."

"I've got time."

"...Then stay." Julien said. Rayna brushed a tear from her eye and nodded to him. Julien nodded back and headed for the stairs. "I'm a go see Lucien and lie down for a little bit before we go."

"One thing," she said and he turned back to her. "Today's gonna be a long day with all the stuff we need to do. If we're gonna get through it, you're gonna have to be--"

"Like him?"

"No, sweetie... Be better than him."

Julien thought for a second about what that really meant, then turned and walked up the stairs.

CHAPTER 15

H *ow To Be A Parent In Thirty Minutes Or Less*

Natchitoches, Louisiana

Kaitlin really was in no condition to drive. She managed to make it to the next city before she was forced to pull over. Her eyes just couldn't stay open any longer, and her leg was killing her. She stopped in what she thought was a safe area, huddled up with Dani under the blankets, and slept in the truck cab until the sun would no longer allow it. Dani stretched out her arms and yawned as if she had woken from the most rejuvenating slumber in history, oblivious to any of the perils the previous night had held. Kaitlin was overcome with both happiness and relief to see the young child wide awake and moving about.

"You're awake," Kaitlin whispered before she clutched Dani tight. "Do you feel okay?" Dani nodded. "Are you hungry?" Again, Dani nodded. "Me too. We'll find a drive-thru and get something before we get back on the road, okay?"

"Where are we going?" Dani asked.

Kaitlin realized she hadn't thought about that since the accident.

Originally, the train was just a means to get out of town quickly. A destination was never really decided. Jean was spontaneous and relied a lot on his great instincts to make decisions. If there was a plan, it went out the window when he did.

"...I don't know," she said, trying to hide the fear of uncertainty she was feeling. "Let's just get something to eat, and we'll figure it out after that."

Kaitlin started the truck and headed for the main drag in this forgotten old town. She found a local fast-food restaurant on the main street of the small town and limped in to use the bathroom and get cleaned up. That's when Dani first noticed Kaitlin's injury.

"What happened?"

Kaitlin was not ready to live through that night again, and there was no reason why Dani needed to know.

"I… got a little cut last night. It's fine," Kaitlin said.

"If Momma was here, she would heal it. Do you want me to try?"

"No, baby, that's too much for you. It's okay, it's fine."

After they cleaned up, they got some food to go and ate it in the truck. Kaitlin knew they couldn't afford to keep eating like this, so she found a grocery store and got some fruit, snacks, and other supplies for the road. She spotted a thrift store and took Dani inside to pick up a few things. For the most part, their clothes were dry at this point, but they were going to need a few changes. Dani was not the least bit happy about these 'new clothes' and she made sure Kaitlin knew about it.

"I don't like this store," Dani whispered way too loud.

"Okay, we'll just get a few things, and then we can leave," Kaitlin whispered back.

"But I don't want nothin' from here."

"Hush, Dani," said Kaitlin, trying to hide her embarrassment.

She pulled a shirt off the rack and held it up to Dani. Dani frowned and pushed it away.

"Eww. It smells funny."

"Dani, stop it. That's not nice."

"But I don't want it."

"Do you understand that we need to get you some different clothes?"

"I got lots of clothes at home."

"Well, we can't go there and get them, can we?"

They both stared at each other for a few seconds before Kaitlin took it upon herself and grabbed a few items that looked like they would fit. She took two steps toward the register, stopped, went back, grabbed Dani's hand, and pulled her. Dani was furious.

Outside, Dani sat in the truck with her bottom lip protruding just the right amount and her arms defiantly folded in front of her, the universal positions every child under the age of five uses to make their parents understand just how horrible they are at their job. Kaitlin tried her best to ignore the silent protest, as most parents do, to let the child know exactly how unimportant and insignificant their feelings are in the grand scheme of things. Unfortunately, in this case, as in most of this kind, both were working.

Dani had just lost her mother and was completely cut off from everyone she had ever called family. Now, she was being forced to live in a truck and wear someone else's musty old clothes. Kaitlin, at the ripe old age of twenty-five, had seemingly just become the adopted parent of a toddler with the mind of a twelve-year-old. There was no manual or book for 'How To Be A Parent In Thirty Minutes Or Less.' There was no template to follow, no experience to fall back on. She had nothing and she was alone, and on top of that, Dani was mad at her. Last night she had relied on Jean's words to help her make the world small and to focus. In all those cases, as extreme as they were, she at least had a goal to achieve, something pre-set for her to strive for. Today it seemed as if there were just too many thoughts and goals swirling around in her head. How could she possibly put all of her attention toward one? She didn't know why she started the truck because she had absolutely no idea where she was supposed to go and what she was supposed to do next. She only knew she couldn't stay here. Kaitlin put the truck in first, eased off the clutch, and it started to move.

"Dickory-Dock, make the truck stop."

The engine choked like it had swallowed something alive. The truck jolted, stalled.

Kaitlin blinked.

"You—What did you just—? Dani!"

"I want to go home."

"Oh my God! Don't do that! You hear me?... Do not do that again," Kaitlin said as she fiddled with the ignition and restarted the engine.

"Dickory-Dock, make the truck stop."

Once more, the truck jumped forward and slammed to a stop.

"Dani!"

"I want to go home!"

Passer bys could not help but take notice, which was the last thing Kaitlin wanted. They were supposed to blend in, become invisible, and get lost in the fabric of society. That was how they would escape. This was how they would get caught.

"Stop yelling, and keep your voice--"

"I want to go home now!"

Kaitlin was embarrassed, angry, and frightened all at once.

"Knock it off, young lady!" Kaitlin said before she caught herself and lowered her own voice. "And don't you dare stop this truck again, you hear me?"

"Then take me home! You take me home right now!"

"I mean it, Dani!" Kaitlin threatened as she went to restart the truck.

"Dickory-Dock--" Dani started before being grabbed by Kaitlin.

"DANI, stop it! You hear me?!"

"You're not my mom," Dani cried as she struggled with Kaitlin. "You can't tell me what to do!"

"Your mom is dead, and if you don't knock it off, we will be too!"

Dani angrily screamed as the red burst into her eyes. Kaitlin was horrified, scared beyond belief at the thought of what this little girl might do to her in this instance. Instinctively, she slapped Dani, and that seemed to horrify her even more. The red fell from Dani's eyes and was quickly replaced by tears. She couldn't believe Kaitlin had hit her, and neither could Kaitlin. They both stared at each other, crying, heartbroken at what the other had done.

"Don't you ever flash your eyes at me! EVER! Do you hear me?!" Kaitlin yelled. "Do you even know what that means when you do that? DO YOU?!"

"No!" Dani cried.

"It means that you are ready to fight! Ready to kill... Is that what you want? You want to kill me?"

"NO! I'm sorry!... I didn't-- want to hurt-- you-- I-- just-- want-- to go-- home!" She stammered.

Kaitlin grabbed her and held on tight.

"I know,... I do too... But we can't. Neither one of us can. They will kill us, sweetie... both of us. That's why your momma had to hide you for so long. I know you're scared, and... you're right, I'm not your mom. I'm sorry if I tried to be. I don't know what we are. All I know is all we got is each other, and if we don't help each other, we're not gonna make it. Okay?" Kaitlin asked tenderly.

Dani nodded as she sniffed, snorted, and exhaled.

"Why did my dad kill my mom?"

"Sweetie, I don't know that he did that--"

"He did! I saw him, he killed her!"

"Okay, listen to me. We don't know exactly what happened back there, so--"

"I hate him! I hate him!"

"Dani--"

A not-so-timid knock on the driver's side window startled them. A crowd of ten had gathered, and it seemed as if this gentleman had been elected to get to the bottom of whatever was going on here.

"Everythin' alright in there?" The man asked.

"Yes, sorry. We're fine, we just... needed a little cry, that's all. Thank you," Kaitlin said.

She was so embarrassed that she didn't want to look at him, and that made him want to look at her even more.

"Where y'all headed?"

"We're just passing through, okay?" Kaitlin said with some obvious irritation in her voice.

Whether she was driven by embarrassment or fear, she did not know, but either way, she knew she needed to get out of there right now, as she started the truck.

"I don't know. *Is* it okay?" He asked, returning Kaitlin's attitude with some of his own before he turned his attention to Dani. "Where yo' mama at, darlin'? She know where you at?"

This was getting out of hand. More people had started to gather as the rumblings grew louder. They weren't quite blocking the truck's exit, but they were definitely impeding a speedy getaway.

"Sir, would you please move? I told you we were fine."

"I'm talkin' to d'at little girl, right na'," he said defiantly. "Sweetheart, where yo' mama at?"

"Get out of the way!" Kaitlin yelled.

"Maybe you should get out d'at truck, and I mean right now!"

"Leave her alone!" Dani screamed.

Dani's eyes flared red from the sudden adrenaline rush, and if she had enough hair on her head, it'd be floating off the top of it. Around them, the crowd scrambled like animals before a storm while Kaitlin struggled with the new-fangled gear shifter she was still trying to master. The truck made a horrible wheezing sound causing one man to drop his phone before Kaitlin was able to slam the truck into gear and speed out of there. Dani blinked the red from her eyes, ashamed, already shrinking into herself. She was afraid of what she had just done and of what Kaitlin was going to do about it. Kaitlin got off the main drag as quickly as she could and headed north, steering clear of the main roads.

"...I'm sorry. I know I'm not supposed to do that no more, but I thought they was gonna to hurt you, and I got scared."

Kaitlin reached out her right hand toward Dani. Dani clasped onto it and held it tight.

"Thank you," said Kaitlin.

They drove in silence for the next thirty minutes. Kaitlin didn't know if someone had called the police or how they were going to react to Dani's mini-mactrouge. She only knew that if they kept having incidents like this, they weren't going to get very far.

CHAPTER 16

The moments that shape us

Julien descended the staircase with Lucien's small hand in his own. Both wore matching suits, clean, sharp lines over tired, heavy shoulders. One looked like the future. The other carried the past. Julien knelt down at the bottom of the staircase, careful not to let his knee touch the dirtied floor, and re-tied Lucien's matching black patent leather Oxfords before surveying his young protégé. As much as he wanted to smile at the handsome young picture in front of him, he could not, but the pride in his eyes could not be suppressed.

"It's not gonna be easy this morning. You gonna hear and see some difficult things. You gonna be okay?" Julien asked.

"Yes, Papa," Lucien solemnly replied.

For a brief moment, he seemed to ponder the question himself.

"Your grandpa never took me to places like this. He never let me see the truth of how things really were in this world. I only got his interpretations, which were, at times,... skewed."

Lucien's brow crinkled up.

"What's wrong?" Julien asked.

"What does 'skewed' mean?" Lucien asked.

"...Slanted. The way he saw things... wasn't necessarily the way things were." Lucien nodded, and Julien continued. "He meant well. Thought he was protecting me, but in reality, it left me unprepared on how to deal with situations that can alter the course of a young warlock's life. I don't ever want to do that to you. These moments, good and bad, easy and hard, are the moments that shape us into who we are going to be. Watch. Listen. Learn. The lessons that you take from them are the greatest gifts that a father can give to a son."

Lucien nodded his understanding. Julien embraced his brave little stoic, then kissed him on his forehead and adjusted his tiny suit and tie before sending him outside.

"Go outside to Rayna and Tirin. Tell 'em I'll be out in a minute."

"Yes, Papa."

Julien rose and watched the little man make his way across the rubble in the sitting room and out the space where the door used to be. Julien exhaled as he pinched the top part of the bridge of his nose between his eyes. He was tired, and it showed. The rest he had hoped to partake in earlier had been postponed by both the needs of his son and some unpleasant business affairs that needed to be handled personally by him before the press conference. That rest was going to have to wait. These are the moments that make us who we are.

Lucien found Rayna and Tirin in the courtyard, along with Teddy and Cree. Rayna had slipped into some black, peep-toe, stiletto ankle boots to match what she considered to be her conservative dress. Cree was in a long, black, sleeveless jumpsuit and some modest black casual heels. She looked very nice, with her hair pulled back in a tight pony-tail and some black onyx drop earrings to complete the ensemble. It was a rare occasion that Tirin allowed her to wear earrings or heels, but this was a special day.

Teddy cleaned up well, donning some black slacks, a shirt with a matching vest and tie, and a classic black fedora. It was no surprise when Tirin walked out from behind the car wearing black jeans and a black shirt, untucked but fitted. What was unexpected was that he had shoes on his feet – black boots with a single buckle on the side. It was his way of honoring Camille and Dane. Rayna swept Lucien up in her arms and planted a big kiss on him.

"Look how handsome you are," she said. "Where's your pops?"

"He said he'll be right out."

"How you holding up, big man?" Teddy asked as he walked by carrying an extra-large steamer trunk on his shoulder. Lucien nodded to him. "Good. Hang in there, buddy," he said as he placed it in the trunk of the sedan.

Cree came over with her arms outstretched, and Rayna passed Lucien off to her. She stared at him wistfully and he stared back, then wrapped his arms around her and gave her a good squeeze.

"Oh baby, I'm so sorry," Cree said, savoring the moment.

Tirin exhaled a gruff, sharp grunt. Cree sighed, then disengaged her hug and looked suspiciously into Lucien's eyes.

"Are you ready for this?" She asked.

Lucien gave her a single nod.

"Cree,--" Rayna warned, but too late.

Cree launched Lucien up in the air a good ten feet, and just as quickly, Tirin lept up, snatched him out of the air, and landed. Had it not been for his boots, he wouldn't have made a sound.

"Sorry, ma'am," Cree said in an abashed voice as she shrugged and pointed at Tirin.

Rayna glared at Tirin, knowing Cree was bound to do whatever he asked of her. Tirin glared back at Rayna in a very roguish, mischievous sort of way, then put his full attention on Lucien. It was the first time on this sorrowful morning that the boy allowed himself to smile. For a brief moment, Tirin had made him forget the previous night's tragedies. He quickly pushed it back down, embarrassed and angry that he had let it out.

"It is alright to feel something other than remorse. It does not take away from the events that have passed, nor does it belittle the ones we mourn. They are your feelings. Embrace them. To ignore them is to be dishonest, both to you and the ones you love."

Lucien nodded as a tear formed in his eye. For a second, he tried to hold it back, then looked up at Tirin, exhaled, and released it. Tirin nodded his approval to the young boy.

"Good. That is your lesson for the day," he said, delivering him back into Rayna's welcoming arms.

Julien exited the house with a black leather briefcase in his hand and scanned the fine-looking bunch before him with approving eyes.

"Alright. Let's go," he said as he walked toward the car.

"How you feel?" Rayna asked.

"I'm fine."

"You sure?"

"Rayna,--"

"Do me a favor, then."

"What?" He said with a tinge of impatience or perhaps exhaustion in his voice.

"Fix the house real quick before we go, please."

"I'll have some contractors come out and take a look--"

"Contractors?! That'll take months! We don't have time for that, Julien, just fix it."

"Now you know I can't be throwing magic around in broad daylight--"

"Who's gonna see? We're four hundred meters off the road, and our nearest neighbor's a mile away."

"Who's probably still freaking out after everything that happened last night!"

"So we're just gonna leave the place unguarded for a month? 'Cuz it's not safe for my vampires to walk around in there like this - sunlight coming through every hole and crevice."

"She's right. It isn't safe," Tirin added.

"Fine," Julien sighed.

He again pinched the bridge of his nose between his eyes, which garnered a concerned look from Rayna.

"Julien, you sure you're--"

Julien waved her off before she could start. He opened his mouth like he was about to speak until an idea popped into his head. He looked at Lucien and waved him forward. Rayna put him down, and he walked over to his father. Julien took his hand and knelt down next to him.

"You remember how you used to get mad and pout 'cuz your

momma was always making you do rhymes?" Julien asked. The corner of Lucien's mouth curled as he nodded.

"Ummhmm," Julien said before he turned to the busted house, and his eyes radiated red. "Et mandavero et præcepero spirituum et in umbra lucis, id restituere domum qui utitur nomine meo," he said in Latin as if it pained him and a golden pulse surged from his chest and rippled outward. Behind him, the house stirred. Dust trembled. Wood groaned. Stone clicked back into place. Julien exhaled deeply, then masked it with a breath as the red faded from his eyes. Lucien was so caught up in the way the house was magically putting itself back together that he didn't notice his father's brief moment of unsteadiness. Rayna did.

"Wow… How did you do that?" Lucien asked in awe.

"Rhymes are the foundation of everything we do. Thought Magic is the quickest, but it also requires a lot of energy. Energy that I just don't have right now," he said as he looked at Rayna.

Lucien had a bewildered look on his face.

"But… it didn't rhyme, did it?"

"No, not in English. Je commande les esprits dela luiere et de l'ombre, restaure cette maison qui porte mon nom. But it does in French. A good warlock has to be clever enough to find the quickest way and the most potent words to get the results he needs. Could I have made a rhyme in English? Yes, but it was quicker and ultimately more powerful in French - this time. Why? Certain languages have words that do not exist in English, and a spell is only as powerful as the words it's made of. It doesn't rhyme in Latin, it just gives it a boost. For beings like us, sometimes little things like that could be the difference between life and death. This is what your momma was trying to teach you."

"I understand… I miss her."

"I do, too."

Julien looked at him and smiled.

"You think the boy is ready to start in on some languages?" Julien asked Rayna.

"He's kinda young," Rayna replied with a playful uncertainty in her voice, garnering the sought-after yearning in Lucien's eyes, "but he has been doing well with the Latin alphabet."

Julien gave Lucien a stern look.

"It's not gonna be easy. You sure you can handle this?"

"I can do it, Papa."

"...Get him a tutor," he said to Rayna. "Get him started next week."

Rayna put on a proud smile as Julien stood up, grabbed Lucien's hand, and walked toward the car.

"Alright, let's get going. Today's not the day to be late."

Teddy and Cree held open the doors as Rayna, Julien, and Lucien got in the back. Tirin waited and watched with a curious eye as both Teddy and Cree moved to the passenger side up front.

"What are you doing?" Teddy said curiously.

"I... I'm sorry. I'm just used to getting in over here. Micah always drove," she said, showing her sadness.

"Cree," Tirin said, "the wheel is yours, now."

Cree lowered her head and nodded. Tirin let out a husky burst of a growl, and her posture changed. She raised her head with dignity, took in her sire's eyes, and nodded. Tirin beamed with pride and nodded back. Cree lowered her eyes out of respect but kept her head high and her shoulders back as she walked around to the driver's side and began her new responsibility as the driver for the Gerards.

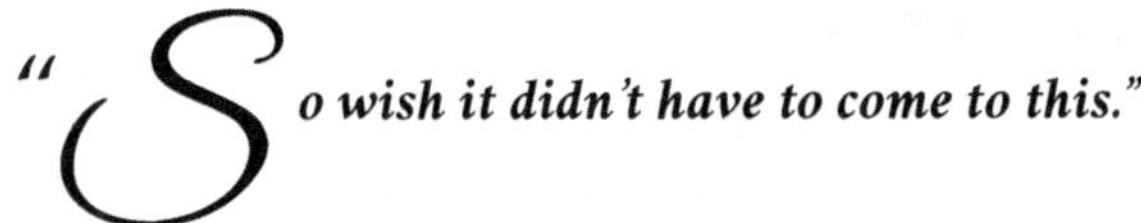

o wish it didn't have to come to this.

"Stop here," Julien said as Cree pulled the sedan to the curb in front of the New Orleans City Hall building.

The moment the tires kissed the curb, reporters surged forward, flashbulbs popping like miniature explosions in the humid morning haze. Tirin got out and held the door while he scanned the rooftops as his nose twitched furiously. He stopped and focused on a high-rise in the distance as Julien, Rayna, and Lucien exited the sedan. Tirin closed the door and bent down to the driver's side window.

"The Orleans Tower," he told Cree. "Find them."

The sedan pulled off, and Tirin bullied his way through the crowd with Julien, Rayna, and Lucien behind him. A deputy unlocked the door and escorted them to the elevator. Being Saturday, other than a small security detail for the press conference, the building was empty. Rayna exited the sixth-floor elevator with Lucien in her arms, where she found Mr. Jeffries from The Council waiting for them.

"Good morning, Mr. Jeffries," Rayna said as she put Lucien down.

Tirin and Julien walked past him down the hall. The only recognition Jeffries got from Julien was a supercilious stare. Jeffries smiled politely. It was enough for him that Julien was there. He was content with Rayna acting as proxy.

"I assume you've come prepared with suitable compensation packages for all parties?" Jeffries asked.

"I'm sure the mayor and local law enforcement will be quite pleased with our offerings," Rayna answered.

"Excellent," Jeffries said, handing Rayna a large manila envelope, "perhaps you could be good enough to pass this updated dossier to your employer to look over before the press conference. Once he's thoroughly finished pouting, that is."

Rayna winced as Julien stopped and turned back to Jeffries. Lucien looked up at Mr. Jeffries, then at his father, then back at Jeffries, taking note of the tension between them.

"Does it have anything different to say about my daughter?" Julien asked.

"Why would it? I don't believe anything has changed since our discussion earlier this morning, has it?"

Julien looked at Rayna, then turned away and continued down the hall without answering Jeffries. Lucien stood there and continued to stare. He wasn't quite sure why, but he knew he didn't like him. Perhaps it was because he talked like the black man on the train.

"I'll take a quick read and pass on any pertinent information," Rayna whispered as she grabbed Lucien's hand. "Come on, Buck."

Lucien continued to look back at Jeffries as Rayna pulled him down the hall, leaving Jeffries standing there with a questioning look on his face. Tirin was met at the door of the private meeting room by two of the sheriff's heavily armed deputies, who stood guard outside. They didn't say anything, but their condescending stare spoke volumes, and Tirin was hearing every word.

"Easy," Julien said to Tirin. "They're just window dressing. The good stuff's inside. Go on."

Tirin brushed by the two guards and opened the door. Rayna and Lucien entered, followed by Julien and Mr. Jeffries. Inside, Mayor Kelvins was seated in the middle of the conference table, facing them as they approached. The Chief of Police, Leroy Collier, a black gentleman in his late forties, was seated to the left of the mayor. Leroy was a good friend to the Gerard family, not only to Barrett but to Julien and Rayna as well.

Mr. Jeffries walked around the table and sat next to Leroy while Sheriff Bailey stood off to the right, leaning against the large window, looking as inhospitable as ever. It was clear that after last night's unpleasantries, neither he nor the mayor felt inclined to greet Julien and his entourage in the formal manner with handshakes and salutations. Leroy, however, rose from his seat and gave them a proper welcome. Rayna offered her hands, and he gladly took them, planting a kiss on each one. He then knelt down to eye level with Lucien.

"You must be Lucien. My name's Leroy."

Leroy offered his hand, and Lucien took it.

"Nice to meet you, Leroy."

"Nice to finally meet you, young man. I want you to know how sorry I am for what you're going through. I only met your momma once, but that was enough to see how special a person she truly was. She will be greatly missed."

"Thank you," Lucien said sadly.

Leroy nodded and then rose to Julien. They looked at each other a moment before they embraced. Leroy was a big man, and he hugged Julien tight as they both tried to contain their emotions. He released Julien and looked deep into his eyes.

"Son, I've known you your whole life. When you ready, you come see me and let's you and me talk about what really happened. Okay?" Leroy said in a hushed voice.

Julien nodded as he wiped a tear away from his eye. Leroy looked at Tirin. They also knew each other well. Leroy gave him a nod, and Tirin nodded back; their respect for each other was mutual.

"You wanna cry too, Leroy, or can we get on with this so-called 'meetin'?" Sheriff Bailey asked.

Bailey and Leroy were not the best of buddies. Leroy stopped on the way to his chair, ready and willing for a confrontation with the sheriff.

"Why don't you try and show some compassion, Bailey? Especially on a day like this," Leroy said.

"Oh, I do. For all the humans that died."

"Alright, you two, enough," Mayor Kelvins ordered.

Leroy reluctantly followed the command of his boss and sat down, but the sheriff was not compelled to do so.

"You know, Kelvins, sometimes I think you forget that you don't have that type o' authority over me."

"This here's my city, Bailey--"

"And it's my county, Mayor. And I'm gettin' a little tired of malafecs thinkin' they runnin' shit 'round here."

"Sheriff Bailey, please," Rayna exhaled. "I was truly hoping that we could all be a little more hospitable this morning. Especially in front of the child."

Rayna placed herself on the table near the sheriff, hoping that she might distract him enough to de-escalate the volatile situation.

"I like you, Ms. Rayna, but I will never understand why you choose to make a home and work with these... things."

"Maybe 'cuz she's one of 'em, you nitwit, now sit down and shut up!" Mayor Kelvins said angrily.

"Say what 'na?" Sheriff Bailey said, truly perplexed by the mayor's statement. Rayna smiled and winked at him.

"See, this is part of the reason why I wanted you to come along," Julien said to Lucien as he seated him on the table top. "So you could see, first hand, what most humans truly think of us."

"Momma always said that most humans were good," Lucien said.

"Eh. That 'most' part is one of the few things your momma and I disagreed on," Julien said as he winked at Leroy and opened his brief-case. "Gentlemen, let me begin by saying how truly sorry I am for all the events that occurred last night."

Julien pulled two checks and three different-sized envelopes out of his briefcase as he spoke. He placed them on the table, positioning them in a specific order, with the checks faced down. There was no pride in the gesture, only the hollow weight of obligation wrapped in velvet guilt.

"My family aired its dirty laundry in the street. I hope that this will help with the repavement."

Julien pushed one of the checks over to the mayor.

"This is for last night. It should have never happened, and I'm truly sorry that it did. This is just the beginning of the restitutions I plan on making over the next few years for this city. I hope it is agreeable to you."

Kelvins picked up the check and looked at it a good while. His eyes told everyone in the room that it was more than agreeable. Next, Julien pushed one of the envelopes toward Leroy.

"Leroy, I know you and my father came up together and, uhm…"

It seemed as if Julien might be overtaken by emotion at this moment. Lucien grabbed his father's hand to comfort him. He looked up at his father, and a tear rolled down his cheek. Lucien then looked over to Tirin, who nodded proudly to him. Rayna was also proud, but she was also not used to the magnitude of the emotions this little boy was putting her through. She turned her head to not give herself away as Julien brushed the tear from his son's face and found the strength to continue.

"I'm so sorry for the way things went down yesterday, and I will come by next week and explain it all to you. Afterward, well… I hope you can find it in your heart to do business with me like you did with him."

Leroy blinked twice, then tucked the envelope away like it held the weight of history. "You come on by when you're ready, son," he said, his voice cracked with restraint.

"Thank you," Julien said with the utmost respect and sincerity. "Leroy, I'm wondering if you could give us a few minutes before the mayor and I join you out there."

Leroy got the hint.

"Mayor?..." Leroy asked. He was his boss, after all.

Kelvins nodded, and Leroy excused himself from the table. Julien waited for the sound of the closed door before he continued. There were two envelopes and a check still on the table. Julien stared at Mayor Kelvins for a few good seconds, then turned his head and attention to Bailey, who looked back at Julien with as much contempt in his eyes as they could hold.

"Hmph," Julien smirked as he picked up the thicker envelope. "This was for him," he said to the mayor, referring to Bailey. The sheriff clenched his teeth as Julien put the envelope back into his briefcase. "But I don't think he'll be needing it now," Julien said as he lowered his head.

Rayna didn't move, but her eyes shifted toward the sheriff like storm clouds gathering at the horizon.

"So wish it didn't have to come to this," Rayna sighed.

Sheriff Bailey looked at her, then his eyes shifted to Tirin, who raised his right hand as talons sprouted from his fingertips.

"Mr. Gerard!" Mr. Jeffries called out.

"Julien, you best stop that boy if you care for him!" Kelvins stated.

Bailey's lips parted ever-so-slightly to allow more oxygen into his lungs, which was depleting at a faster rate due to his steadily increasing heartbeat. He kept looking over his shoulder out the window, like he was expecting someone or, perhaps, something to save him from this predicament. Sadly or happily, depending on your preferences, his expectations would not be met.

usiness in the bayou

The sheriff kept glancing out the window.

"Why you keep looking out that window, Sheriff?" Julien finally asked, not with curiosity, but with a hint of something else.

"You son of a bitch, what'd you do?" Bailey asked as his anger started to push courage out of his mouth.

Lucien had no idea what was going on, but was captivated by the drama of it as Tirin took another step and extended his arm, allowing the talons to scratch along the wall as he inched closer. Sheriff Bailey had a look of confusion etched over his face, not by what Tirin was doing but by the fact that he was doing it and none of his people had stopped it. He angrily grabbed the walkie-talkie mic that was clipped to his tie.

"MACK!" He yelled. "What the fu--" .

"Mack's indisposed right now," Cree's sultry voice said through the walkie-talkie, "but Randy's waiting on pins and needles. Literally."

Cree giggled through Randy's cries in the background. All the blood seemed to fall right out of Bailey's face. Tirin let out a low, sustained growl as he moved closer. Before Bailey could speak again, Teddy's voice came over the walkie.

"I wish I could say the same about Tracey and Bobby," Teddy said as he opened the door, entered the room, and tossed both of their walkie-talkies into the corner. "But I can't," he finished with an angry tone.

Tirin took another step. Bailey foolishly tried to draw his gun, and Julien's eyes flashed red.

"Gun ut calor in infernis arderet," Julien chimed.

Both Lucien and Mr. Jeffries looked at Julien, then at Bailey.

Bailey howled and dropped the smoking pistol. Lucien's eyes widened. "That," Julien said calmly, "is why we study our rhymes."

"MR. GERARD!" An angry Jeffries yelled.

"Calidior, calidior, et flammas in tumorem convertendum," Julien continued, ignoring Mr. Jeffries's plea as the gun began to smoke and bubble. "Calidior, calidior, adolebitque et quell!"

The gun melted into a molten glob on the floor before it evaporated, leaving only a stain behind. Julien's eyes faded back to normal.

"Wow!" Lucien cheered. "That was a good one!"

"This is just another example of how important incantation magic is and why you need to keep up on your rhymes," Julien said to Lucien as if he were commenting on a verse of poetry.

Lucien heard his father's lecture and repeatedly nodded his understanding, but his attention was focused on Sheriff Bailey and what was to come next.

"Mr. Gerard! I must insist that you stop this immediately!" Mr. Jeffries demanded.

"Stop what? I haven't done anything."

"Mayor! Do somethi--" Bailey yelled.

In a flash, Tirin zoomed over to Bailey, grabbed him by the neck, and raised him up off the ground with one arm. Julien looked at the mayor, who seemed as if he might explode as he glared at Julien.

"Don't worry, he's not gonna hurt him. Yet," Julien reassured Kelvins. "But you have to admit his attitude was becoming a bit distracting," Julien then said to Tirin, "Set him down, please."

With her foot, Rayna pushed out a chair from under the table, and

Tirin slammed Baily down in it. Rayna hopped off the table, and Tirin shoved the chair and Bailey back into the table. Bailey tried to scream, and Tirin squeezed his throat a little bit more than what was needed to silence him. Rayna sighed as Bailey struggled to breathe, so she balled up a piece of paper from Mr. Jeffries's dossier, which did not go unnoticed by Mr. Jeffries.

"Say, 'Ahh,' please," she asked Bailey nicely.

He didn't feel inclined to comply, so she perched herself back on the table next to him, pinched his nose and slipped the paper in when he gasped.

"Let him go," she ordered Tirin, who instantly released Bailey's throat. Bailey sucked in all the air he could before Rayna stuffed the piece of paper deep into the back of his mouth. "Now, hush."

Bailey made a futile attempt to struggle before Tirin grabbed him from behind the neck with his clawed hand and stifled it, applying just enough pressure to let Bailey know the talons were there but careful not to break his skin.

"Be-e-e stil-l-l-l," Tirin whispered. Bailey complied.

The mayor was livid. Both he and Mr. Jeffries had had enough of whatever the hell it was that was going on in this 'reconciliation' meeting.

"Now, getting back to our business," Julien said as he re-opened his briefcase.

"Just what the hell you think you doin', boy?" asked Mayor Kelvins.

"I'm sorry?" Julien said, not understanding the question.

"You think you can just walk up in here, kill four deputies and just-_"

"Kill?" Julien interrupted. "We haven't killed anyone, Mr. Mayor. Not today, anyway," he said as he eyed Bailey.

"Don't you play games with me, boy," Mayor Kelvins said.

"Teddy, you didn't kill those two deputies outside, did you?"

"No, sir."

"Then where the hell are they?!" Kelvins yelled.

"They're tied up right now," Teddy answered.

"Tirin, did Cree kill those other two?" Julien asked.

Tirin grunted. Rayna snatched the microphone off Bailey's tie and called out to Cree.

"Cree, sweetie..."

"Yes, Ms. Rayna?"

"You didn't happen to kill those two deputies, did you?"

"No, ma'am. Both are alive and kicking," she responded. A loud thud, followed by a painful groan, was heard. "Well... They're both alive. I'm kinda the one doing the kicking."

Rayna looked over her shoulder at the mayor and Julien.

"Cree, you can come on back when you're ready."

"I need to hear it from him, ma'am," Cree said.

Rayna rolled her eyes as she held the mic in Tirin's direction.

"Clean up. Then bring the trunk," Tirin said. "Teddy, go help her."

Teddy exited the room. Bailey's eyes opened up about as wide as they could when he heard the word "trunk." Rayna released a deep sigh.

"I did hope we didn't have to use it, but you're just not being very nice," Rayna whispered.

"Mr. Gerard, please, I must insist--" Mr. Jeffries tried to say.

"I dun' had about enough of your 'insists' for one day, sir. This isn't London. Your 'insists' don't carry that kinda weight over here," Julien said with just enough attitude in his voice to let everyone know that things were about to get serious. Except, maybe, for Rayna and Tirin. For them, this was fun.

"He's not O positive," Rayna whispered just loud enough to distract Julien from his next task.

"He's as white as the paper you stuffed in his mouth," Tirin said with a gruff whisper.

"Now that's just plain racist, Tirin."

"It's not racist, he is white."

"So's Teddy."

"And Teddy's O positive," Tirin said, proving his point.

"That's so ridiculous," Rayna said. "Fine. I'll bet you five hundred dollars that--"

"Can you two just... keep it down over there for one minute? Please?" Julien said through clenched teeth.

Rayna and Tirin quieted themselves momentarily, anyway. There was one check and one envelope left on the table. Julien took a calming breath then pushed the envelope toward the mayor. He then sat down and waited for Kelvins' response. By appearances alone, Kelvins could see that there was a substantial difference in width between the envelope in front of him, the one that Leroy took, and the one that was to be for the sheriff. He made no attempt to hide the contemptuous scowl on his face as he picked it up.

"It's a bit light, boy. Don't you think?" Kelvins said.

Julien shrugged whimsically, then said, "Open it."

Kelvins opened the envelope and turned it upside down. Nothing. If this was a joke, Mr. Jeffries was not the least bit amused, and neither was Mayor Kelvins.

"Is this some kind of sick joke--" Jeffries tried to say.

"Why, is it funny to you?" Julien said, cutting him off.

Jeffries tightened up as Julien pulled a ledger out of the briefcase and dropped it on the table.

"I found this this morning. Say what you want about my father, but the man kept receipts.

"You not tryin' to blackmail me, are you, boy? 'Cuz--"

"If I was, that last check wouldn't still be on the table. But we'll get to that in a minute," Julien said as he opened the ledger. "My father has supplemented your income on a monthly basis for the past six years, solely for the privilege of letting Rayna clean up your city and letting you take the credit for it. Every week, I have her and her people sweep through the streets and 'take care of' the transients, addicts, low-level criminals, and thugs so that you don't have to. It keeps your city clean and your tourists safe, and it replenishes our ranks when needed. Because of that, it seems like you should be paying me."

"Now you wait just a Goddamn minute,--"

"What'd you call my father?"

"--What?!"

"Let me help out with this one. Long as I can remember, I've only ever heard you call him 'Mr. Gerard' or 'Barrett.'"

"What in the red hell are you talkin' about, boy?!"

"I'm talking about respect. From last night all the way up to right now, I've been putting a 'Mr.' in front of that title of yours. During that same time period, you seemed to have misplaced the one that goes with mine."

Kelvins stared at Julien, confused as to the meaning.

"How many times he dun' called me boy?" Julien asked Rayna.

"Five," Rayna sighed.

"Alright, God Damn it, fine. Julien--"

"My friends call me Julien, and we ain't there yet."

"You trying to go to war with me, boy?"

"Six," Rayna interjected.

"Absolutely not, mister – Mayor. I'm trying to start a relationship with you, sir. You had one with my father, a good one, but you and me..." Julien shook his head. "But I'm willing to try and establish one right now if you are."

"But, you could beat him in a war, couldn't you, Papa?" Lucien interrupted.

Julien stopped what he was doing and took the time to turn this into a teachable moment.

"Yes, I could. But it's not about me and him, son. If it was, I probably would've killed him already for the blatant disrespect he's shown us, but – and this is the main reason why I wanted you to be here today – so you could see first hand. I don't want to fight with Mayor Kelvins. I don't want to fight with anyone, really. Despite what some militant warlocks will tell you, the hard truth is a war with the humans is a war we cannot win. If we could, Mr. Jefferies, over there, and his Council buddies would've done that a long time ago." Jefferies seethed as he eyed Julien. "The fact is, there's just too many of them, and they are too powerful, even though most of them don't even know it. We all need to learn how to live together, son – humans and malafecs, in peace. I don't know, maybe one day, we will, but until that day comes... well, we gotta do business like this, in the shadows, and stay hidden from all but a select few."

Julien could tell that his son didn't understand something by the tiny furrow in his brow.

"What is it?" Julien asked.

"Why him and not him?" Lucien asked, pointing at Bailey.

"His hatred toward me is too strong to make way for anything else," Julien said of the sheriff. "His," Julien indicated the mayor, " is not. Finding humans like him is essential for our survival and eventual peace. They hold our anonymity, and we hold something very dear to them: money. This is what capitalism is. Don't you agree, Mr. Mayor?"

"I do, but the weight of this envelope is not making me feel very benevolent."

"I understand. Unfortunately, that's not gonna get settled today, but if you call my office Monday morning and make an appointment with my assistant for someday next week, I'm sure me, you and Ms. Rayna can sit down and figure some ways to get that envelope filled again. Hopefully, this last check here will tide you over 'til we can work all that out."

Kelvins picked up the check, and it seemed to make him more unhappy than he was when he picked up the envelope. The check was dated and made out to him and has the word "one" written on the dollar line and the number "one" in the amount box.

"One dollar?" Kelvins said with a dangerous smile on his face.

"I'm prepared to put up to six zeros after that one."

"What you say, 'na?"

"It just depends on how much you think he's worth," Julien replied, indicating the sheriff.

"Excuse me?!"

"You know I can't let him live after what he's done. How much is a man's life worth to you?"

"Julien, you just can't--" Kelvins tried to say.

"We ain't friends yet, remember? Now it's down to five zeros. If I were you, I'd really think about my next words before I said 'em."

The mayor choked down his anger and took a moment.

"Mister Gerard," he said through his teeth.

"Yes, Mr. Mayor?"

"If the sheriff and four of his deputies go missing in one day, that precious anonymity you so desire may be in jeopardy."

"They won't. The four deputies will take a few days off before they come in and resign."

"And just why would they do that?"

"Because they received a higher paying job in the private sector working security for me. Before this day is through, my associate, Mr. Tirin, with a little help from his pal, the moon, will make them an offer that they just cannot refuse," Julien said, then to Tirin, "How long 'til the full moon?"

"Eight days," said Tirin.

"Expect their resignations on Wednesday."

"Uh-huh. And I suppose the sheriff's gonna get that same offer?"

"Those two," indicating Rayna and Tirin, "are still, annoyingly, trying to work that out."

During the entire negotiation, Rayna and Tirin had been in a constant argument about how the sheriff would meet his demise. Lucien had been paying close attention to that as well.

"Make him a vampire, Ray, Ray!" Lucien shouted.

"I would, baby, but I just don't feel like A positive blood right now," Rayna whined.

"But Tirin said he was O positive."

"Tirin's wrong, baby."

"I will take that bet!" Tirin responded.

Julien shook his head at Tirin.

"Either way," Julien continued, "after a few - very long, painful days - it's probably not gonna work out, and he and I will agree to part ways. Indefinitely."

Kelvins flinched from Bailey's muffled scream as Tirin sank the talon of his index finger into the sheriff's shoulder like he was dipping his finger into a glass of milk. Rayna bent down and bit into the other side of his neck as Tirin sampled the blood on his finger. Tirin then angrily growled from the result.

"Oh God," Rayna said as she gagged. "It's just as bitter as he is."

"How does she always know?!" Tirin roared.

"Why you keep bettin' with her?" Julien said, then looked at his watch. "Sorry to press you, Mr. Mayor, but we really need to wrap this up. I'm gonna have to put you on the clock. Every five seconds, you lose another zero, starting now. Five, four, three,--"

"Alright, God Damn it, Fine! Just sign it… Please."

"…Please, what?"

"…Mister Gerard," Kelvins forced through his lips.

Julien smiled, then filled out the check and signed it.

"And that's how it's done," Julien said to Lucien as he picked him up and headed for the door.

Kelvins angrily followed close behind him, not wishing to see any more of Bailey's demise. Mr. Jeffries, however, was not satisfied as he rushed to catch up.

"Mr. Gerard, I can assure you my report will not be laudatory, and my superiors will not be pleased," Jeffries threatened.

Cree opened the door, and Teddy entered with the trunk on his shoulder. Cree strained to hold in her laugh as she held open the door for them.

"Good morning, Mr. Mayor," Cree smiled.

Kelvins looked back at the mess that was Sheriff Bailey, shook his head, and exited. Julien and Jeffries followed him into the hallway. Cree closed the door behind them. Her laugh, as well as the other's laughs, could be heard on the other side of the door as Julien finished up his business with Mr. Jeffries.

"Thank you, but we're fine now, Mr. Jeffries," Julien said as he stopped and turned to him. "You can go on back to London. Your services here are no longer needed. See, this is how we do business in the bayou, and if you and your superiors don't like it, y'all can kick rocks, or pound sand, or whatever it is that you British people do. But stay out of my business. And stay out of New Awlins," Julien said as he turned and walked down the hall.

Lucien waved him goodbye over his father's shoulder.

CHAPTER 19

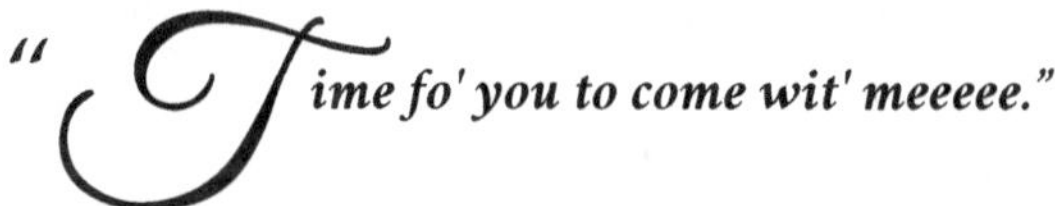

"*Time fo' you to come wit' meeeee.*"

Cotton Valley, Louisiana

The sun sat high in the sky and let its rays fall down on top of an old abandoned farmhouse. The ol' red pick-up truck and its two new inhabitants had just pulled off the road and stopped in front of the deserted dump to put some canola oil into the tank. After the early morning fiasco, Kaitlin laid some good rubber on that road, trying to put as much distance between her and that town as possible. Twenty more minutes and they'd be done with Louisiana and into the good state of Arkansas, and after all the events that had transpired over the last twenty-four hours, it was about nineteen minutes too long. Kaitlin knew that the tank had more than enough fuel to make it to the border and then some, but unfortunately, her pint-sized partner, with her tightly crossed legs, could not. There was a boarded-up old well along the side of the house that was more than big enough to hide someone looking for a little privacy. This was about as good a place as any.

"I can't go here!" Dani whined as she fidgeted in her seat.

"There's nothing else for miles!" Kaitlin pleaded, exiting the truck. "Now, come on."

Dani tentatively got out of the truck. She didn't like it at all. She was trying to be a trooper, but it seemed as if every hour, something new was being dropped on her that was worse than the last. She took Kaitlin's hand and began to walk toward the well before she snatched her hand away and stopped.

Even after everything, Dani still thought like a child. "There's no toilet paper!" she cried, drawing a battle line only a toddler could draw.

"Dani--"

"My mom said we always had to use toilet paper!"

It seemed as if they were well on their way to their next big blowout until a clear and constant growl was heard behind them. They turned and saw two Dobermans sitting fifty yards away, watching them. The dogs didn't bark. Didn't move. Then, without warning, they collapsed into eyeballs, rolling and blinking on the grass like something from a fever dream. Both girls gasped but weren't really scared. They had seen more than enough frightening things over their lifetimes, and this just wasn't one of them - until The Talisman walked around the corner. He stooped down, picked up the eyes, removed his glasses, and popped them in their sockets one by one, then returned the glasses to his face. He checked his watch, then looked at his prize and smiled before he extended his hand to her.

"Come, child. Time fo' you to come wit' meeeee," he said in the most non-threatening voice he could offer her.

Kaitlin took a step and inserted herself between Dani and The Talisman. He tilted his head as if he were puzzled by the move. Many had tried to mount a defense against him, and many had failed, using much more aggressive tactics than planting themselves between him and his prize. He found this… curious. He then waved two fingers and sent Kaitlin flying across the yard. She landed in the bed of the truck - HARD. She didn't get up.

"NO!" Dani screamed as her eyes flamed red.

❄

Meanwhile, at the press conference-

The mayor had just finished his briefing and was about to turn over the podium to Julien when Lucien, who was seated next to his father, suddenly felt violently ill. He had only experienced this particular feeling once – earlier this morning, and he was scared because he wasn't ready to feel it again.

"I need to go to the bathroom," he whispered to his father.

"Didn't I ask you before we came out here?" Julien whispered. "Now you're gonna have to wait. This won't take--"

"I can't. I need to go bad," Lucien interrupted.

He hopped out of his seat and ran for the door.

"Lucien!" Julien shouted in a loud, whispered tone just as the mayor had introduced him.

Julien looked at the crowd, then took a step to follow after his son. Lucien stopped at the door and turned back to Julien.

"No! I can go by myself! It's just right here, I'll be right back!" Lucien shouted loud enough for the entire room to hear. Julien simmered in his embarrassment for a second, then turned to the podium and addressed the reporters.

"Sorry. Kids," he said, then started his part of the briefing.

At the exact moment Lucien tried to run into a stall in the restroom, Dani's power surged, and Lucien collapsed and fell to the floor. Their pain was synced, two sparks on a wire, flaring miles apart. His hair began to float, and when he lifted his head up, his eyes were blood red.

Back at the well, Dani pulled from her Qi, just like the man on the train had taught her. She summoned an energy blast from her soul and tossed it at The Talisman. It bounced off of him like a crumpled piece of paper. She whimpered, but she was her mother's daughter; she was a fighter, and she was not ready to give up. She strained as she formed the biggest energy blast her little body could muster and launched it at him with everything she had. He caught it in his hand, popped it in his mouth, and spit it at her. It exploded on the ground in front of her.

Petrified, her eyes faded to normal as her tears washed the red away, and she wet her pants as he took a step toward her. Just then, Kaitlin popped up with the shotgun Harland had left in the back. This was one gift from Harland she had hoped she would never have to use, but fortunately, she was a country girl and knew how to use it if necessary. She racked the shotgun with shaking hands, took aim, and prayed her instinct was enough. She fired a single round, and her aim was true, but it really didn't matter. The Talisman raised his hand, and the bullet bounced off of it. He didn't break his stride or even look at her. He did point his finger in her direction as a warning, though. She would not get another.

With an unsuited defiance, she cocked the gun and took aim again as The Talisman moved toward the fossilized little girl. His stride took him over the loose boards of the well. Kaitlin shifted her aim and fired at the boards. They instantly gave way to his weight, but he caught hold of the sides and struggled to hold himself up.

In the restroom, Lucien pulled himself up to the sink and, with tears in his eyes, tried again. He grunted in agony as his eyes ignited red. He squeezed the countertop, and his hair began to float off his head. He fought to contain any and all noise, but he could not.

"Aa-a-a-a-h-h-h-h!" He screamed. It was not loud enough for his father in the press conference next door to hear, but there was one who could. Five floors above, down the hall, behind a closed door, Tirin heard his cry.

"Lucien…" Tirin whispered.

"What?" Rayna asked with much concern. "What is it?!"

Tirin jetted out of the room and was gone before she finished her sentence. He followed the voice to the first floor, where it echoed around, making it difficult for him to pinpoint an exact location, so he zipped in and out of the three restrooms on the floor until he found Lucien huddled over the sink, nursing a bloody nose.

"What happened?" Tirin growled, ready to kill anyone or anything that might have done this. Lucien looked up from the sink and gasped.

"I fell."

Cotton Valley, Louisiana - One minute earlier

The boards instantly gave way to The Talisman's weight, but he caught hold of the sides and struggled to hold himself up. No one was more surprised than Dani when the red glow returned to her eyes, and even though her buzz-cut hair was not long enough to float, it tingled her head. She was surprised by how fast she drew and released an energy blast - almost as if she was being controlled. She launched it, and it hit the well like a stick of dynamite. The blast struck like thunder. The boards splintered and shattered skyward as The Talisman plummeted to the emptiness below. Dani fell out of mactrouge, into a state of shock.

"Dani, get in the truck!" Kaitlin screamed. "DANI!"

Dani didn't move; she just stood there, tears falling down her face. Kaitlin crawled out of the truck to get her. Her leg was bleeding again, nothing like before, but the hard landing had done some damage to the wound. She limped over to the still-frozen little girl.

"Baby, you okay?! Huh?! What is it?!" Kaitlin asked as she patted Dani down, checking her body for wounds.

"Talk to me, WHAT'S WRONG?!"

Dani's cry turned into a full-on wail. Kaitlin knew that The Talisman was anything but dead, and they needed to get out of there fast.

"Come on, we can't stay here."

Kaitlin grabbed Dani's arm, and Dani yanked it away.

"Dani, we gotta go!"

"I can't!"

"WHY?!"

"BECAUSE I PEED ON MYSELF!" She wailed.

It wasn't just the terror. It was the shame. She was embarrassed and everything else that a nearly four-year-old girl could be in this moment. She didn't want to do this anymore. She wanted her old life back, even if it meant she had to be a boy again. A part of her knew that life was gone, but after all, she was still only a month shy of four, and that part of her didn't. Suddenly, the ground began to quake and shake beneath them.

"COME ON!" Kaitlin yelled.

"NO!" Dani screamed.

Kaitlin picked Dani up and got to the truck as fast as her bruised body could take her, with Dani fighting her every step of the way. She got to the truck and deposited the screaming child into the passenger seat. She fired up the ol' red truck and took off just as the well exploded upward, like a geyser, spewing water everywhere. Two unusually large droplets hit the ground and exploded into the Dobermans, who took off in pursuit of the truck. Kaitlin watched in the rear-view mirror as the Dobermans faded from her sight, and the truck accelerated over a hill and down the road.

CHAPTER 20

𝒜n imperfection in the ring

Hagatha cackled long and hard.

"Wake up, wake up, my prince-to-be. Wake up my prince and play with me-e-e-e-e."

"Be silent, crone!" Jean thought.

"For two hundred years, I was silent. My whispers went unanswered. Until they were heard by you."

"I heard no such calling! Now you flatter yourself an enchantress? HA! Any power you possessed died long ago--"

"Did you not see me in your dream, my love? Hmmm? I most certainly saw you," Hagatha cackled over Jean's silence. *"My lover, my love, my lover for life; forever together as man and wife,"* she sang.

Day after day, she talked and laughed, and night after night, she laughed and talked. She picked at his brain and challenged his mind at every turn, never allowing him more than a moment of peace. Jean realized that if the ranger had not woken him by now, it was because he was unable to. He also knew that if he could not somehow find a

111

way to shield his mind from this onslaught, she would eventually break him down. She pressed against the walls of his mind like rising water, seeping into every crack. Sooner or later, she would flood him; sift so deep into his soul that her essence, her very being, would infuse with his, and then two would become one. His mind was strong, but she had an eternity to play with it. There was only one person who could save him. So he drifted away to the past and found her.

June 1992

    7 years earlier

Nineteen-year-old Kaitlin Morrison peeked her head out of the cabin door in Port-au-Prince, Haiti. Neither the humidity nor the ninety-seven-degree temperature had the slightest effect on the Tulane University student. She had grown up in a sub-tropical climate on the coast of Mississippi and was used to it. This being her first trip out of the country, she was a bit light-headed from the adrenaline rush she was experiencing and nearly tripped as she descended the airstair. Prior to this, her biggest trip was the ninety-minute drive from her home in Gulfport to her dormitory at Tulane. Her heart raced from the anticipation and excitement of the adventure waiting for her on the other side of the terminal. She had volunteered for an outreach program where she would spend her sophomore summer teaching English to the children at the monastery in Boucan Carre. Not only would it look good next to the bachelor's degree in education she was pursuing, but the chance to travel and see the world in exchange for doing something she loved was an opportunity she could not resist.

The interior of the Port-au-Prince International Airport was exactly what she had expected it to be. It didn't have the extravagances like the airports in Dallas and Miami that she had flown through to get here, but she didn't mind. It was very utilitarian, nothing out of the ordinary, exactly what one would expect from a third-world country. She had been looking forward to this trip for months and had prepared herself fully. Everything was covered, from travel down to the living conditions, so that there would be nothing to surprise her or remove that patented smile from her face... except, maybe her panties and other personal items sprawled out on the baggage turn-stile, spinning around on display for anyone who cared to see. A couple of local children took the opportunity to make a game out of this humiliating misfortune by using her underthings as hats and scarves, while a few of the older ones rifled through the contents of the opened bag in search of things of more value.

"Hey! That's my stuff!" Kaitlin yelled as she ran toward them.

The three of them scattered like roaches do when the kitchen light is turned on, scurrying out of every exit the terminal had to offer.

"Somebody stop them!" She yelled.

As is the case in most instances of this nature, no one heard her plea for help, at least they pretended not to, save for one. A tall man in his early thirties took on the role of knight in shining armor. He had just entered the terminal as one of the older boys plowed into him while trying to make a clean escape. The man apprehended the young culprit and dragged him back to the scene of the crime as Kaitlin tried to gather what was left of her belongings.

"Shame on you! What'cha 'tink ya' doin'?!" The man scolded the boy, who couldn't be a day over ten years old.

"We just playin', sir," said the boy, who gave up the futile struggle against the much bigger man.

"You should know betta'. Apologize to da' lady."

"Uhm... sorry, ma'am," the boy said, trying to look as innocent as a guilty little boy could.

He handed Kaitlin the pouch of toiletries he had lifted and lowered his head in shame. Kaitlin's embarrassment seemed to temper her anger, leaving nothing but frustration as she took the bag from the child's hand.

"Na' git ya' behind home fo' I call da' constable. GIT!" The man ordered as he smacked the young boy on his backside. The boy did not hesitate to make a speedy exit. "And tell your friends to do da' same!"

"Thank you for your help," Kaitlin said, still embarrassed. "I appreciate it."

"I'm so sorry, ma'am. Hope ya' don't 'tink everyone in Haiti is as bad as all d'at."

"No... I'm just--" she started as the man started running around the turnstile, gathering up her things. "Oh, no, you don't have to--"

She released a frustration-filled exhale as he returned with everything that was left.

"Thank you," she said.

She was so flustered by the entire affair that she couldn't even look at him.

"You American, yes?"

"Yes," she said as she continued to re-pack her bag.

"Yes! We get a lot of tourists down here, but never durin' hurricane season. What brings ya' to our island d'is time a year?"

"I, uhm, I'm teaching English this summer to the children at the monastery in Boucan Carre."

"Da' Sacred Heart Mission?"

That brought her attention out of her bag and back to him.

"Yes. You know of it?"

"I am from Boucan Carre!" The man said as he pointed at himself. "MICHAEL CAREW! I was raised in da' orphanage d'ere! Come! My cab is just outside. I will take ya' d'ere as a favor to da' monks. Free of charge, of course."

Kaitlin politely shook her head no.

"Thanks for the offer, but there's supposed to be someone named Jean here to--"

As Michael reached down to help her up, he accidentally, on purpose, ran the ring finger of his other hand across her arm. An imperfection in the ring left her with a tiny cut. It was just a scratch. A nothing mark. But her blood soaked into the metal like ink on old parchment.

"Ouch!"

"Ohh! So sorry, ma'am."

Kaitlin checked her arm and saw the mark. It couldn't have been more than a quarter of an inch long. Michael took out a handkerchief and gently dabbed at the blood.

"It's okay. It's just a scratch," Kaitlin said.

"You were speakin' of Jean Laveau, yes?"

"Yes!" Kaitlin seemed both surprised and relieved that he knew him. "He's supposed to meet me here and escort me back to the mission."

"I see," Michael said.

He seemed almost disappointed, and Kaitlin picked up on it.

"What?" she asked, wanting to know more.

"No, it's nothin'. I know Jean. He is a good man and works very closely with the monks..."

"And?..." Kaitlin asked.

She knew there was something more, and she wanted to know. Michael gave in with a sigh.

"He has no car, and he is constantly runnin' behind. He was to escort you on da' bus, yes?" Michael asked. Kaitlin nodded.

"Yes. Which it appears he has missed, and d'ere will not be

anodder' for hours. Please. You will come to Boucan Carre wit' me. To ride da' bus alone would not be safe for a young woman such as yourself."

Kaitlin was exasperated by this whole situation, and she just wanted it to be over. She looked around the terminal and saw that it was quickly depleting itself of people by the second. She looked toward all the exit doors and saw no one was entering them. She agreed with what Michael said about riding the bus alone, and she didn't feel very good about staying here by herself either.

"Are you sure? I don't want to be a burden. If you have work to do,--"

"Please! You are no burden. It would be a pleasure," Michael said as he bowed his head to her.

"...Okay."

"Excellent! Come, my cab is jus' dis' way," he said as he led her toward the door. "I will have you in Boucan Carre before nightfall. What kind of music do you like? I have CD's of all kinds..."

With much discretion, Michael discarded the soiled handkerchief in a trash canister as he escorted Kaitlin out of the terminal into the bustling, busy streets of Port-Au-Prince. It seemed her new adventure had just begun.

Back in the terminal, a hand reached inside the trash canister and plucked the bloodstained handkerchief, like it were a precious thing. A thing it had been waiting a very long time for.

CHAPTER 21

"$\mathcal{A}$*scream will only bring them here quicker."*

Haiti

June 1992

Boucan Carre is roughly eighty kilometers from the airport in Port-Au-Prince. Eighty kilometers. That's all it was supposed to be. But in Haiti, where roads buckle under storms and memories of a forgotten occupation, distance is never just distance. Most of their roads were built between World Wars One and Two. Now, only about a thousand kilometers of paved roads exist. Most had been ravaged by the harsh climate, and many stretches either needed extensive maintenance or were no longer passable. With no street signs or accurate maps available, what should have been a little more than an hour had taken twice that time. The detours, dead ends, and long winding roads, along with Michael's incessant talking and blaring rap music, had taken a toll on Kaitlin. She had no idea where she was or where she was going, and she was beginning to believe that he didn't, either.

It had been a long, sweaty ride, with her only relief coming from the hot breeze generated by her rolled-down window. The sun's rapid

117

descent from the sky was matched only by Kaitlin's rising concern. Just then, Michael pulled into a long-abandoned gas station and cut off the engine.

"Wh-Why are we stopping?" Kaitlin asked, trying not to show any fear and doing a pretty good job at it.

"Water break, ma'am. It's been a long trip," Michael said as he exited the car. "I apologize for da' discomfort, but don't cha' worry. Boucan Carre is just over da' next hill," he pointed as he walked away.

"Okay, well, can't we just wait until… we…"

Kaitlin stopped, as Michael had already disappeared around the back of the station. A deep sigh of frustration escaped her lungs as she wiped the sweat from her brow and exited the car to stretch her legs.

"*It had been a long trip,*" she thought as she leaned up against the vehicle and surveyed her surroundings. There was nothing but the road, mountains, and an abandoned gas station in the middle of nowhere, straight out of every traveler's nightmare. Only the tropes had teeth here. "*What a strange place for a gas station,*" she thought. "*No wonder it was abandoned. Who would ever come out here?*" The tiniest frown descended on her face as she was made uncomfortable by her own thoughts.

"Michael?" she called out, showing no distress in her voice. "I really would like to get there before nightfall… Michael?"

She eyed the uninviting station and, against every impulse in her body, slowly began to move toward it.

"…Michael? Is everything okay?…"

A loud howl was heard off in the distance to her right, then dead silence. There were no birds or frogs; there was nothing. She looked into the dense jungle, hoping that howl was nothing more than a stray dog in search of food, until the howl was heard again. This time closer. It made her uneasy. It also made her think that perhaps it would be better if she waited inside the station, which seemed so much more inviting than a few moments ago. She turned to run inside and hit something solid. A man. Standing where there'd been nothing seconds before. No sound. No warning. Only a twenty-two-year-old Jean Laveau, who was, somehow, standing right there. He caught her in his arms and muffled her imminent scream.

"Shhhhh. A scream will only bring them here quicker."

He removed his hand from her mouth, turned her around, and walked her back toward the cab.

"Mich,--"

"Gone. Probably making his way through the Central Plateau by now--" he said as he stuck his head inside the cab window and released a sigh of frustration over his discovery. "And he took the keys."

"He took the k,--"

Jean pulled her away from the car toward the road.

"We will have to continue on foot. Come," he said as he dragged her along behind him for a few steps before she yanked away.

"Wait a minute! Who are you? And how'd you get out here, anyway? We haven't passed anyone for hours," she said as she stopped and folded her arms in front of her in defiance. "I'm not going anywhere with you until you tell me who you are and where Michael is. Michae,--!"

Jean grabbed Kaitlin as she tried to call out to Michael and quickly covered her mouth with his hand. They briefly struggled until another howl momentarily froze them. This one was louder and closer than the one before.

"Perhaps you'd like to wait here and ask them?" He whispered before he uncovered her mouth and tried to pull her down the road. Their struggle escalated into a scuffle, as Jean found himself on the defensive. He ducked and feinted Kaitlin's never-ending barrage of slaps and blows.

She wasn't fighting him out of fear. For some reason, she didn't appear to be afraid of him – she was angry.

"Get away from--! Ouch!" She yelled as he tried to grab her again. "Get off of me-- LET GO!"

The two of them tussled for a short moment before Jean turned her around and got hold of her from behind in a very compromising position that Kaitlin was none too thrilled to be in.

"Let me go! HEL-L-L-P!"

Jean was exasperated with this young woman and again muffled her scream.

"I am Jean Laveau. The man you were SUPPOSED to be waiting for at the airport," he whispered through clenched teeth.

"Jean Laveau?" Kaitlin said in an inaudible, muffled voice.

Jean immediately released her, turned her around, and glared at her. She glared back at him with every bit of insolence she could muster. Jean re-grabbed her and continued down the road with her in tow.

"...You were late," she said with an indignance that seemed appropriate under the present circumstances.

"Your plane was early," he corrected her. "Besides, didn't your mother ever tell you not to travel with strangers?"

"It's 'talk'; never 'talk' to strangers, not 'travel,'" she corrected him.

"Ah. Thank you, and congratulations," he said with just enough sarcasm in his voice to piss her off even more. "Now you have done both."

Another howl. They were closing in. Jean stopped and turned back to Kaitlin. He was frustrated and did not try to hide it. He knew that it would be futile to continue walking and that it was time to deploy other methods.

"You can run, yes?" He asked.

"What? Why?"

His eyes scanned over her entire body in a way that made her feel violated. He grabbed her arm and focused on her cut.

"Michael, he did this to you?" He asked as he released her and pulled a tiny vial out of the pouch around his waist.

"Yes," she said. Jean sighed and shook his head. "It was an acci,--"

With neither provocation nor permission, Jean ripped a piece of her top off at the sleeve and swiped the ripped cloth down her arm, gathering as much sweat and blood as he could. Her blood was already claimed. Jean knew it. She didn't. The cloth he stole wasn't just fabric, it was a binding. A mark undone.

"WHAT THE HELL?!" Kaitlin yelled.

She was appalled. She wasn't sure of anything right now other than the fact that she did not like him. So that there was no question to that fact, she slapped him across the face. He sighed again, touched his finger to his mouth to check for blood, then continued with his task.

"You have been marked," he said, indicating the cut.

"This is how they have been tracking you."

"Who?! What are you talking a,--"

Again, without her permission and to her dismay, he poured the contents of the vial onto the wound.

"OOOWWW!"

It burned. She screamed, and Jean moved when she tried to hit him. He danced around and avoided her while he looked for the right-sized stone to complete his task.

"He finds naïve, unsuspecting, innocents,--"

"Naïve?!"

"People who will not be missed,--"

"NAÏVE?!"

Jean picked up a stone and wrapped the bloodstained cloth around it, avoiding Kaitlin's wrath as best he could. With her blood bound to it, he flung the stone like a curse in reverse, one predator chasing a false scent.

"And they pay him for it."

"You keep saying 'they' and 'them'. WHO?! WHO ARE YOU TALKING ABOU--?!"

"LYCANS! In human form, but still just as dangerous. What did you think that was? A dog?"

"...You're kidding me!"

A bloodcurdling roar was heard. Jean looked at Kaitlin as if to say, 'Does that sound like I'm kidding?'. Two miles. One sun. And the last light dying fast. If she didn't move now, she'd be moving in pieces.

"Run as fast as you can, and stay on the road. DO NOT GO INTO THE BRUSH. The outskirts of town are two miles over that hill. Be quick. You must reach it before nightfall," he warned.

"Why, because they turn into big, hairy wolves at night?"

The sarcasm in Kaitlin's response was lost on Jean as he looked to the sky to check the sun's position. He knew they didn't have a lot of time. He hoped it was enough.

"There are creatures far worse than lycans who travel these woods at night. Go," he said in a hushed voice.

"But what about my suitcase,--"

"RUN." He emphasized.

Kaitlin was angry that she had been abandoned and played for a fool by Michael and perhaps by this man, as well. She wasn't quite convinced he really was Jean Laveau, but either way, she definitely didn't believe any of the nonsense he had just spewed out. Lycans? Werewolves? Really?! She didn't believe in this kind of stuff. She had no idea what was out there, but the urgency in his voice and the grave look on his face convinced her that whatever it was, it was bad. She started a casual jog down the road until a soft growl was heard. It emanated from the thick brush on the left side of the road and lingered in the air just long enough to frighten her into wishing she hadn't chased Jean, or whoever that man was, away. She looked back, and he was gone. Like mist. Like memory. Like magic. All that remained was the warning echo in her head.

"...Jean?..."

A violent commotion was heard in the dense brush just off the road where the growl had come from.

"RUN!!!!" Jean's voice called out.

This time, she did.

CHAPTER 22

aybe Dani would be better off without her.

Neosho, Missouri
July 15, 1999

Kaitlin and Dani were both still pretty shaken up after their bout with The Talisman. They didn't speak. Didn't stop. Just kept going, mile after mile, all the way through the state of Arkansas without stopping. Just a brief break to grab some take-out from a Chinese place and fill the tank with canola oil. The restaurant was more than happy to give them all the old oil they could carry, then they got right back on the road. It was a quiet trip for the tanned Thelma and tiny Louise. It seemed neither one of them had much to say to the other. Dani kept her eyes out the passenger-side window, and Kaitlin kept hers on the road. When the sun finally punched the clock on this extremely long day, they found themselves in Neosho, Missouri, a beautiful town thirty minutes south of Joplin. It was the perfect place to stop for the night, seeing how they didn't know where they were going, anyway.

From there, it was a coin toss; they could either go west and skim across the top of Oklahoma or the bottom of Kansas, or they could continue to travel north and intermix themselves deeper into the state of Missouri. Hopefully, an answer would present itself tomorrow. Tonight, they just needed a shower and some sleep – in a bed. They parked the ol' red truck at the Best Western off of I-49 and Kaitlin got Dani into the shower, then took one herself. It was a long, hot one, and somewhere in the middle of it, she found herself balled up on the shower floor crying. After everything that had happened to her over the last forty-eight hours, she hadn't had time to process, let alone mourn, the loss of her best friend and the loss of the love of her life. Both of them were taken from her in what now seemed to be the most random of acts.

It had happened so fast she could barely remember it now. All she could see was the two of them crashing through that window and being swallowed up by the night. It was inconceivable for her to believe that she would never see either of them again. Now they were gone, and she was alone. Obviously, Julien blamed her for everything that had happened, and she wondered if all this was her fault.

"How many lives were lost that night because I sent off a simple letter? How many of them were once my friend?"

Her head pounded, her right leg throbbed, her body was bruised, and her heart was badly broken. On top of all that, there was a nearly four-year-old girl in the next room who hated her. She needed a mother, and right now, Kaitlin felt she wasn't doing an adequate job of being one. She didn't know how, and frankly, she wasn't sure if she wanted to learn. It may have even crossed her mind once or twice that maybe Dani would be better off without her. She had no idea where to go, what to do, or what was to become of them. How in the world was she going to support this child when, at this moment, she couldn't even support herself? This motel was a luxury that they really couldn't afford. Kaitlin knew that, and she was beating herself up because she did it anyway.

"Did I do this for her or for me?"

She tortured herself over that question, and she honestly didn't know what the answer was. All she knew was that there were no answers lingering around the shower floor. She came out of the bathroom and was both relieved and surprised that Dani was still there. Dani lay in her twin bed with her eyes fixed on the ceiling above her. Kaitlin came over to tuck her in, and Dani turned away.

"…Goodnight," Kaitlin said with a faint and fragile voice.

No response was given. Kaitlin got in her bed, turned out the light, and, as quietly as she possibly could, cried herself to sleep.

Each morning brings with it a day filled with endless possibilities, and this morning was no exception. It seemed at some point during the night, Dani had escaped her own bed and snuggled up next to Kaitlin in hers. It also seemed as if Kaitlin didn't mind one bit.

"Good morning," Kaitlin whispered.

Dani yawned and stretched her tiny limbs as she rolled over to face Kaitlin.

"Good morning," Dani whispered as she wrapped her arms around Kaitlin and buried her head underneath Kaitlin's chin.

Those two little words from that little girl meant the world to Kaitlin.

"I had a bad dream," Dani said.

"Oh, I'm sorry, honey. You want to tell me about it?"

"It was about Jean," Dani said as Kaitlin tightened up. "He was in pain. I wanted to help but… I didn't know how." Dani's eyes shimmered with something deeper than a dream. Kaitlin's gut twisted. It wasn't just a child's story. It was a tether. "We have to help him."

As happy as Kaitlin was that Dani was once again talking to her, the topic of conversation was a painful reminder of the sadness in Kaitlin's heart.

"It's just a dream, baby. Jean's… Jean's gone. Like your mother."

"I don't think so. I can feel him," Dani said as she shook her head.

Kaitlin wasn't emotionally ready for this conversation, so she steered Dani away from it.

"You look like you're hungry," Kaitlin said. Dani nodded in agreement. "Come on. Let's go get something to eat."

They got dressed and walked across the parking lot to grab a quick breakfast at the local Denny's before they got on the road. On the door was a flyer stating that the Indigo Sky Casino was holding interviews this morning at ten for all jobs. It was just fifteen minutes down the road, across the Oklahoma border and Kaitlin did find this town to be very charming. Perhaps they would stay here for a while.

That very same morning, Rayna sat yoga-style on the veranda with her usual carafe of specially-mixed Bloody Marys at her side as she soaked in the morning sun. If not for the two-inch high stack of paperwork in front of the scantily clad diva, this would be considered the perfect morning for her. Her eyes flitted across each and every document, spending more time on some than others as Tirin charged through the veranda door. He paced the length of the porch and back, then trudged it again and again until Rayna was annoyed enough to deal with him.

"Good morning, Tirin," she sighed. "Is there something I can do for you?"

"Did you speak with Lucien about yesterday?" He asked with a gruffness in his voice that was not unusual to her.

Rayna continued to scan the document as she entertained Tirin.

"The entire day? Or do you want to narrow it down to a,--"

"You find this funny?"

"Tirin, the boy said he fell."

"You know that injury was not caused by a fall."

"I know that sometimes dirty, icky things happen to little boys in bathrooms. Big boys, too, for that matter."

"This is serious!"

"What would you have me do?" She asked. "He told you he fell; he told me he fell. When asked by Teddy and Cree, he said he fell, and when asked for the fourth time by his father – He. Said. He. Fell. Whatever truly happened in that bathroom is a conundrum that none of us will ever know if he doesn't…" Something on this particular document grabbed her attention, and held it.

"What?" Tirin asked.

"Where is he?"

"Lucien?"

"Julien!"

"In the study."

Rayna jumped up and swung on a robe as she marched into the house with Tirin on her heels. As they barged into the study, Julien's annoyance over the interruption was quickly outweighed by his embarrassment over Rayna's attire, or lack thereof.

"Jesus Christ, Ray, how many times I gotta tell you,--"

"I found her," Rayna said. "She's alive."

Rayna slapped the document on Julien's desk and closed and tied up her robe as she moved to the map. Julien picked it up and tried to make sense of it.

"What is this?" Julien asked.

"Police incident report. I've got a copy of every one made in the last thirty-six hours across the entire state. That one's from a small little nowhere place right outside the Natchitoches Parish," she said as she stuck a pin in the map. "Seems there was a commotion caused by a black woman with a little white girl."

"Shit, Ray, that could be anybody."

"How many 'anybody's' you know got red eyes?"

Rayna had their full attention now.

"It's a ways off the main highway, and trust me, she'd have wanted to get out there as quick as possible."

Rayna had always kept just about everyone and everything at a distance. She didn't allow things to get personal. Julien could see that, for some reason, this seemed personal.

"You seem to be very familiar with this place."

"I was born in Natchitoches." She said softly, like the name itself had teeth. Neither Julien nor Tirin said a word. It was the first time she'd let the past slip through.

"You always said you were born in New Awlins,--"

"This isn't about me, Julien, it's about your daughter. Now, do you wanna try to get her back or not?"

"I do," Lucien said as he walked into the room in his p.j.'s and 'Dragon Tales' slippers.

"Good morning, young man," Julien said.

"Good morning," Lucien replied to everyone.

"You feel better this morning, Buck?" Rayna asked as she swept him up.

"I'm fine," he said. "We gonna get her back, aren't we, Papa?" Lucien didn't ask like a child. He stated it, like a boy who believed in something bigger than fear.

Julien thought about it before answering.

"That was twenty-four hours ago, Ray. We have no way of,--"

"She'd have gone north to Shreveport," Rayna said. "We can start there."

"It was still twenty-four hours ago. Unless she stayed there, which would be stupid, how do,--"

"It's a chance, Julien. Maybe we get there, and Tirin picks up a scent, maybe she makes another mistake, maybe I find another incident on the way, I don't know. It's a chance. That's all I can give you. It's up to you whether or not you want to take it."

Julien looked into his son's eyes as he pondered it. Lucien had Camille's eyes. He remembered that Dani had his. That made for an easy decision.

"You think you can get yourself dressed?" Julien asked.

"I always dress myself," Lucien frowned.

"Well, then, let's move. The plane will be prepped and ready in an hour."

"Katie just tried to help Momma, Papa. Now she's helpin' Dani. Don't be too mad at her, 'kay?"

Julien met his son's gaze. Camille's eyes stared back. He didn't need any more reasons.

"Alright," Julien said. "Let's go."

CHAPTER 23

"*If you truly want to go, this is the only way to get there.*"

Julien and the crew took the jet to Shreveport, and on their way, Rayna found another incident involving a well that had exploded on an abandoned farm in Cotton Valley. Two limos pulled up to the old farmhouse. Teddy and Tirin hopped out of the first limo and started to survey the grounds. The three vampires in the back stayed inside the car. They had day gear on, but unless they were needed, there was no reason to put them at risk. Cree pulled up the second limo with Tik in her day gear riding shotgun and Julien, Rayna, and Lucien in the back. Cree jumped out of the front and joined Tirin and Teddy as Julien, Rayna, and Lucien exited the rear. Lucien ran straight to the well and knelt next to it.

"Papa, over here!" Lucien yelled. His voice didn't just call, it led.

Julien and Rayna followed the young warlock over to the well, which had been plugged and reboarded as Tirin and Teddy sniffed out the area. Lucien walked over to the road and pointed some tracks out to Cree, who took off and followed them down until she was out of sight.

"The Talisman was here," Tirin said.

"What?! Why is he involved in this? God damn it!" Julien yelled.

"Easy, Julien, let them finish," Rayna said.

"The blood we found was Kaitlin's, not Dani's, but..." Teddy said, then hesitated.

"...What?!" Julien asked.

"Dani urinated here," Tirin finished. "We can't tell if it was before, during, or after the confrontation. It is, however, within the battle zone."

"Is she alive or dead?" Julien asked.

"I don't know."

"Fuck, Tirin!"

"I don't know what this man does."

"He takes their souls, and if he did, the body would not remain on this earth," Rayna said.

"She's alive, Papa."

"And how do you know that?"

Lucien became very self-conscious as they all looked at him, waiting for his answer. He measured his response carefully – as carefully as an almost four-year-old could.

"Because,... I would feel it if she wasn't."

Cree came running back from up the road where Lucien had pointed.

"The tire tracks over there tore out of here and left some burnt rubber on the road out there," Cree pointed. "I followed that scent about a quarter of a mile before I lost it."

Tirin took off down the road. He would be able to follow the scent further.

"Papa, we're wasting time!"

"Hold on, Luc,--"

"She's alive, and they went that way! We gotta go now!"

"Lucien!" Julien yelled.

Startled by his father's tone, Lucien silenced himself. Rayna didn't care for the dejected look on the young boy's face caused by Julien's inappropriate tone.

"He's just a boy, Julien," she admonished.

Julien grimaced and turned away. Rayna picked Lucien up as Tirin zipped back over to them.

"She's alive," Tirin said as he took a breath. "I picked up her scent as far as a mile up the road."

"This road goes straight 'til you hit Sarepta," Tik added as she brought Rayna a map from the car. "Then there's a few different options."

"We need to stop this Talisman first," Julien said.

"I don't know that we can," Rayna said.

"Un-fucking-acceptable, Ray. Try again."

"What do you want me to say?"

"You know where he is?... Yes or no?!"

"Maybe! But, Julien, think about,--"

"Then let's go there."

"We're really close, Papa. I think we can catch up if,--"

"We're more than a day behind, son. We can fool around, chasin' our tails, and end up with nothing, or we can stop this thing that's trying to kill her."

"Gotta say I agree with Luc. We may never get an opportunity like this again," Rayna said.

"I guess you and I have different definitions of the word 'opportunity.' I want The Talisman, and I want him now," Julien said. Then, to everyone, "Let's move!"

Julien signaled everyone back to the cars.

"We can't get there that way!" Rayna shouted.

Everyone stopped and looked back at her. She let out a deep sigh as she shook her head. She ramped up the dramatics to let Julien and everyone else know that she was not for this before she gave in to his demands.

"Did you bring your coins?" Rayna asked.

Rayna already knew the answer to that question, so she deserved the irascible look she received from Julien. No warlock traveled without coins. Gold was currency. It was contract. It's an unwritten rule learned at a very young age. Even Lucien cast a perplexed frown on his face by the absurdity of the question. Aware of her mistake, Rayna rephrased her query.

"I meant, how many did you bring?"

"Cree! My pouch, please," Julien ordered without looking at her, not noticing her look to Tirin for permission. Tirin nodded, and Cree darted to the car and zipped back with a fist-sized purple pouch in her hand.

"Thank you," Julien said as she handed it to him.

He walked over to Rayna and gave it to her. She opened the pouch and took out a single gold coin, and held it in front of him.

"Gonna need a little boost," she said as she closed her eyes and concentrated.

Julien grabbed her hand, closed his eyes, and when he opened them, they were blood red. The others watched with great interest and scrutiny. They had all seen a great many things, but none of them, Julien included, had any idea what was going on. Then, an eerie, all-too-familiar mist rose up from the ground. Teddy jumped, momentarily startled by the unnatural apparition, then he immediately lowered his eyes in shame. He didn't need to look up to see the malice in his sire's eyes. He flinched. A faux pas that, whether it be today or tomorrow, he would pay a stiff price for. Tirin took a step toward Teddy until the 'BOOM!' was heard. Tirin swiveled around to see The Trolley approach from seemingly nowhere. It stopped in front of Julien and Rayna, and the doors hissed open. Julien didn't know what to think as he temporarily put his anger on the back burner.

"Now what?" he asked, unsure of his next move.

"If you truly want to go, this is the only way to get there, but I strongly advise against this," she said as she looked over to Tirin.

Julien stepped onto the Trolley, disregarding her advice and ignoring the coin box. One of those mistakes he would immediately be made aware of. A deep, foghorn-sounding alarm split the air like divine punishment—loud, brutal, and unmistakably earned. They all covered their ears from the deafening sound that would not stop until Julien stumbled back down the steps.

"What the fuck?!" he yelled in Rayna's direction, trying to recover from the disorientation caused by the horn.

"It's not free, Julien! You have to pay!" She yelled, referring to the coins. "And it's an expensive trip." Then, she muttered to herself, "in more ways than one."

Julien gathered his composure and snatched a coin from her hand, leaving her the pouch.

"Take who you think we'll need."

Rayna nodded and kissed Lucien on the cheek.

"Sweetie, you're gonna have to stay here,--"

"No, he comes," Julien said, overriding her.

"Julien, don't." Rayna's voice dropped. "You bring him into this, there's no walking him back."

Julien took Lucien from her arms and snatched the coin pouch out of her hand.

"He comes. Get who you need," he said and then walked onto The Trolley.

Julien dropped two coins in the box, tossed the pouch down to Rayna, and walked to the back of The Trolley. Rayna was hot, but she knew at least one of them needed to keep their cool if they were to survive this.

"Tik, Taq, with me," she called out as she waved Tirin over.

"My betas?" Tirin asked.

"They should stay. See if they can uncover anything else. Maybe they can pinpoint which way they went after Sarepta," Rayna said.

Tirin nodded and grunted the command to Teddy and Cree.

"Wyatt!" Rayna shouted to one of the vampires in the car. "You and Lester stay with the cars and assist Teddy and Cree if needed." Then she whispered something only Tirin could hear. "Be ready."

"For?" Tirin asked.

"...Whatever's at the end of this mist," she said with an uncommon concern.

It put Tirin on point, and that's exactly what she hoped it would do. She put a faux smile on her face as she climbed onto The Trolley. She threw down three coins and watched the others enter, then threw in one for herself. The driver was as cordial as usual and smiled as he tipped his hat, then waited with his usual patience until she found the right seat and got comfortable. Lucien ran to her, and she swept him up and sat him down in the seat next to her. They played Patty Cake as Tik and Taq watched from the seat behind. Lucien clapped along as if the world wasn't folding in around them. Rayna kept pace, but her eyes never left the mist outside the window. Julien sat alone in the very back, where The Talisman usually sits.

He appeared to be deep in thought, but he was focused. Tirin stood by himself in front of Rayna and Lucien with his eyes locked on the driver. The driver caught Tirin's opposing stare in the rearview mirror as he checked to see if everyone was settled. He acknowledged Tirin with a smile and nod. Tirin didn't offer him as much as a blink, but that was of no concern to the driver. The fares had been paid. All that was left for him was the drive. He pulled the whistle twice, and the door hissed closed as the mist rose up and engulfed The Trolley. Then, with a thunderous *'BOOM!'*, it was gone.

<h1 style="text-align:center">CHAPTER 24</h1>

The slow-moving mist exploded out of a crack of lightning, with The Trolley in its wake. It screeched to a stop on the other side of the street, a few doors down from The Fat Lady. Funny how it never seemed to stop in the same spot, as if there might be some other destination hidden within this secluded borough. They all exited the transport and took in their surroundings except for Julien, who kept his eye on the mechanical monster as it backed into the mist, then with a *'BOOM!'* disappeared, sucking the mist away with it. He seemed amused by the oddity until the *'BANG! BANG!'* of the heavy bolts unlocking echoed through the street. His eyes flashed red as he turned, expecting some wanted adversity. Instead, they watched the heavy metal door with the rusty hinges as it squealed open and stopped, waiting for someone, or something, to enter. Julien's eyes settled to normal.

"I guess that must be the place," he said.

He could *just* hear the music coming from within, and it put an incongruous smile on his face and a tap in his step. There was a very distinct whimsicality about him now that Rayna did not like. Julien started for the door. Rayna doesn't often show how fast she really is, but she used every bit of speed in her possession to zip around in front of him and block his way.

"Julien, listen to me," she said with an earnestness not often displayed. "This may look like New Awlins, but trust me when I tell ya', it ain't. You need to calm yourself."

"I am calm. Don't I look calm?" Julien said in a manner that Rayna did not, for one second, believe.

"Julien,--"

"I just want to have a conversation with the man, Ray. That's all. Come on," he said as he stepped around her and crossed the street. "They've got music playing, and you know how you love to dance."

She threw her head back and tried to release all the frustration she had pent up in her body, but a single exhale was nowhere near enough, so she stopped Tirin and tried to pass some along to him.

"You, of all people, should understand the danger we are in," she whispered. "You need to talk to him 'cuz he sure in three hells ain't listening to me."

"And what is it you would have me say?"

"Y'all know I can hear you, right?" Julien said as he continued toward the door. "The acoustics in this place are AMAZING!" He yelled up in the air, allowing the words to bounce off the buildings and echo down the street.

Tirin growled under his breath as he walked around Rayna in pursuit of Julien. Rayna felt as if she had lost complete control of this situation, but in truth, never at one point did she have it. So, she focused on the one person she could control - Lucien.

"Come here, Buck," she said, and he ran to her.

For anyone who was paying attention to the boy, it was obvious that he did not wish to be there either. None of them knew, but Tirin was not the only one who had engaged The Talisman.

"I want to go home," Lucien whined.

"I know, baby. I do, too," Rayna said.

She tried to comfort him as he rested his head on her shoulder, but it's difficult to comfort someone when you're not comfortable yourself.

"You two can take that stuff off," Rayna said to Tik and Taq. "There's no sun here."

They tentatively pulled off their hoods and gloves to find that it was true.

"Wow! This is pretty cool!" Taq laughed.

"I know," said Tik. "Feels good to be able to walk in the sun again."

"Sweetie, I don't know what that is," Rayna said, pointing upward, "but I promise you it ain't the sun."

When Julien arrived at the door, our favorite Doorman was there to greet him. Julien sized him up and was not impressed.

"Is this him?" Julien asked Tirin.

"No," Tirin said as he inserted himself between the two of them.

"You have business here, sir?" The Doorman asked Julien.

"I do. Sounds like a lot of other people do, as well?" Julien said, referring to the revelry below.

"No more than any other day," The Doorman stated.

"Is it a private party, or may my friends and I join in these festivities?"

The Doorman stepped aside and let Tirin and Julien enter, but Rayna's approach was impeded by the mountainous man.

"No kids," he stated in a tone that took negotiation completely off the table.

Rayna's eyes narrowed, but before Julien and Tirin could even think about doing anything to aid her cause...

"Tik. Taq." She commanded, and one breath later, the wall had a new decoration: 300 pounds of doorman and two vampire escorts. With her path no longer obstructed, she entered The Fat Lady with Lucien in her arms.

"What do you want us to do with him?" Tik asked

"Keep him company. We won't be long," she ordered as she walked down the stairs.

Tirin and Julien followed her down. Once Rayna's foot came off the landing and hit the bottom floor, the place went silent, and everyone in the joint had their eyes on her, or was it Lucien? D nearly broke a glass trying to get over to them, and the usually pleasant fellow was unusually unpleasant.

"How many places like this, you know, allows kids?" D said as he walked up on Rayna.

Rayna was not used to people breaching her personal space, but before she or Tirin could do anything they all would most definitely regret, Julien put a comforting hand on Tirin's shoulder. It halted whatever the alpha's next move was going to be, and then Julien stepped by him and moved to Rayna's aid.

"I don't know," Julien said. "Exactly what kinda place is this?"

D figured Julien was in charge, so D stepped to him.

"Mister, you don't know, you don't need to be here."

Julien stepped in and closed that distance a little more.

"Oh, I do if The Talisman is here."

The crowd gasped. This just wasn't right. This was not the protocol, and everyone in the room was more than a little uncomfortable, except for Julien and D, who seemed just fine up in each other's faces. Tirin, on the other hand, had had enough. He wasn't cool with D's close proximity to Julien, and he was ready to do something about it until Rayna took another stab at trying to control the situation.

"JD, why don't you let me do the talking from this point on? Please?" she politely asked as she saddled up next to them with a gold coin between her fingertips.

Neither Julien nor D was about to back down, but the sight of the coin in his peripheral definitely caught D's attention.

"Uhm, excuse me, sweetie. We jus', ahh, here for da' show?" she stammered, unsure if she was using the proper phraseology.

With his eyes still on Julien, "...We might have a table for ya', ma'am, but,--" D tried to say before Rayna interrupted as she produced another gold coin.

"That booth, right there, looks awfully nice."

With much reluctance, D's eyes shifted from Julien to the coins. The rest of his body would soon follow suit; after all, business was business. He displayed a definite change in attitude toward her after he took the coins.

"That's a private booth, ma'am. It only seats two," he politely stated before he and his previous attitude turned back to Julien.

"And we still don't allow no kids up in here," he said with a finality that was nonnegotiable.

Julien saw that Rayna's way was working. He had a chip comfortably resting on his shoulder, but he had no quarrel with this man. He was saving himself for another. So, he decided to take another approach.

"Rayna, take Luc and wait outside, please," Julien said with a transparent calmness.

"Julien, maybe I should be the one who,--"

"Take Lucien and wait outside, please," he restated in a very specific manner, letting her know that this request was actually not a request at all.

Rayna stared at Julien for a brief moment. Not out of anger but concern. She knew to argue with him now would be pointless, so she turned and walked up the stairs with Lucien.

"Tirin, why don't you go with her?"

"I'll stay," Tirin said with a certainty that most would neither question nor object.

Julien seemed torn and considered the positives of having an alpha with Tirin's gifts at his side in the coming moments. There was only one negative, and it came with a price that Julien was unwilling to pay. It was the only thing that could pull his eyes away from D right now as he turned to face his friend. Tirin's eyes, however, were still locked on the happy-go-lucky Maitre D.

"I really need you to look after Rayna and Luc. To make sure they're safe," Julien whispered.

"We both know that Rayna is more than capable of looking after herself."

"Yeah, but I still need you to look after Luc. Until I get back, YOU'RE responsible for him. No other."

Tirin's eyes ripped away from D to Julien, and a soft, sustained growl escaped through his lips. He was angry, and at that point, everyone in that room knew it. He didn't appreciate Julien's tactics. With a single word, Julien had released Tirin from his duty to protect him and placed the onus of Lucien's life in his hands. It was the only thing Julien could have done, shy of killing him, to make him leave. Honor is a lycan's blood, his dignity. Julien knew Tirin would not jeopardize the integrity of those beliefs, not even for him. Tirin slowly walked up to the landing before he whipped around and, again, scanned the entire room. His eyes made contact with every single person, and then he locked them on Julien. Julien smiled and winked at his friend. Tirin roared as if he was trying to tear down the room with it, then in a blink, he was gone.

"Right this way, Boss," D said, picking up his normal demeanor as if nothing had happened.

Julien followed him to the booth and saddled in nicely.

"You drinkin'?" D asked.

Julien didn't even bother to look at him, let alone answer. D shrugged and placed the old, beat-up tin cup on the other side of the booth and closed the curtains. Julien sat there and waited with no expectation of what was to come. If he did have some, I'm sure they wouldn't have been anywhere near what he saw. A hand, followed by an arm, pulled itself out of the shadowy side of the darkened booth. He watched in awe as the rest of the body began to reveal itself, leaving some parts partially shaded. The hand reached into the cup and grabbed - nothing. The Talisman leaned forward as half of his face oozed into the light.

"What is thisssss?"

Julien could do nothing but stare at the atrocity before him as he tried to gather his thoughts. Sometimes, expectations are necessary. They help one avoid situations like this and usually give way to a plan.

Outside, Tirin paced in front of the closed door like a caged animal waiting for dinner. Rayna stood by the curb, flanked by Tik and Taq. She bounced Lucien in her arms like a pro while she whispered and mumbled questions to herself as she skillfully handled her tarot cards. With each question, a card was flipped. Although this was Tik and Taq's first outing with the A team, the tension that exuded from both

Rayna and Tirin made them feel as if things were not going as planned. Their feelings were confirmed when a certain card appeared from the deck and silenced Rayna's questions. She gasped as if it took her breath away.

"Tirin...." she said with a cracked voice, then, "TIRIN!"

"WHAT?!" Tirin yelled.

"I think you should move away from that d,--"

BOOM! The Fat Lady exploded in glass and brick, vomiting fire and magic. The door came flying off its hinges and just missed the agile alpha, who skillfully dove out of the way. Julien emerged through the dust and smoke, his hair flying wildly and his eyes glowing red, as The Fat Lady tumbled down behind him. His eyes faded to normal as he approached the others.

"We're done here. Call that trolly thing and,--"

Behind him, the building mysteriously began to rise up from the ground like a Phoenix, putting itself back together, brick by brick.

"Papa!" Lucien screamed.

Julien turned in time to see the roof reform and land perfectly back into place. Lucien had witnessed his father's prowess the other day when he magically restored their home to its previous luster. The spell was effective and precise, but it was slow-moving. This building had put itself back together in a fraction of that time. They all stared in awe as the door hurled past them and flipped onto the hinges. A split second later, the knob turned, the door swung open, and The Talisman came striding through, angry and with a purpose.

Julien re-energized himself and threw up a force field just as the Talisman raised his hand and released a powerful, sustained blast. It hit Julien like a freight train and knocked him backward. Without the force field to protect him, he would have been pulverized. Tirin leaped and caught him in midair, but the blast was so powerful it sent them both flying twenty feet backward. Tirin transformed into full alpha mid-flight as he cradled Julien. He completed his transformation just as the force slammed them into a lamppost. Severely bent, the post teetered over and crashed to the ground. The impact left both Julien and Tirin unconscious as Tirin's body transformed back to its human state. The Talisman moved in to finish them as Tik and Taq zoomed in to attack.

"STOP!" Rayna ordered, and fortunately, they obeyed. "Don't. Move." She said as her mind raced to find a solution. "Uhm, ex-excuse me, Mr. Talisman?" She said as she searched her purse for the coin pouch.

Rayna was known for the quickness of her computer-like mind. Never was there a time when it needed to be quicker.

"Got a job here for ya."

"Don't need a job. Got one," he said as he continued toward Julien.

"Okay,--" she stalled as she tried to produce the coin. Well, then,--" she said as she finally retrieved a coin from her purse. "How 'bout I hire you?... P-Please?"

Without even looking, The Talisman could feel the coins pull on his body, and he stopped just a few strides shy of his destination.

"Please. There's no pay there."

She mustered a fragile smile as he turned back to her, and she quickly produced a second gold coin as he approached. Now that she alone had his full attention, what would she do with it?

"For your trouble," she said, indicating the two coins. "Please. Take 'em."

Afraid to look at him, Lucien buried his head in Rayna's shoulder. The Talisman took the coins and placed them in his breast pocket. They crackled and sizzled, and when they stopped, he opened his pocket watch and waited. For the first time in her life, she knew what it meant to be scared as his ominous stare pierced her half-human soul.

"Someone dies nowww. Whoooooo?..."

His tone sent a shiver through her body. She squeezed Lucien tighter as he cried. Her mind had always been her greatest weapon, and for the first time, it seemed as if it had failed her. Her witty lines and hypnotic smile could not bail her out of this quandary, and the more she searched for a solution, the more obvious it became that there wasn't one.

"Two coins, twoooo deaths. I won't ask againnnnn."

Rayna stood there like a little girl who had just been busted by her father. She sighed heavily as she tried, unsuccessfully, to swallow her tears, then painfully pointed to Tik and Taq. Tik was horrified, but more than anything, she was truly hurt.

"Ms. Rayna," Tik gasped.

"I'm so sorry!" Rayna cried.

The Talisman snapped his watch closed and stamped his staff on the ground. The snake heads came alive as he turned to his task. Rayna closed her eyes and squeezed Lucien, more for herself this time than for him. I wish I could say Tik and Taq put up a good fight, but their screams and pleas said something else. Then, silence. Rayna opened her eyes to find The Talisman looming over her and Lucien with an odious glare in his eyes.

"Any get in waaay of Talisman, fall preeey to Talisman."

Once more, he raised his staff and slammed it to the ground with a thunderous blow. The snake eyes glimmered, and The Trolley rolled up next to them with the doors open.

"Take your friends and goooo..." he ordered. Rayna nodded submissively. "Never return here againnnn..."

He turned and strode back into The Fat Lady as the mist began to rise.

CHAPTER 25

*M*alcolm Terrence

The mist dissipated, giving no sign that it was ever there as The Trolley jetted off, on its way to collect its next fare. Julien was conscious but still very groggy from his run-in with The Talisman. He had to be escorted to the cars with one arm over Tirin's shoulder and the other over Rayna's, all the while being subjected to a severe tongue lashing from her. Normally, he would have shut her down by now, but in his present condition, he could do nothing but listen. She was angry. Tik and Taq were much more than two of her guards; they were like her children, and there was absolutely no reason for them to die like that. Again, Julien's stubborn selfishness was the cause of lives lost, and she had been continually forcing that into his already-aching head since they had boarded The Trolley. Lucien walked close behind, trying not to lose contact with Rayna. Julien said he wanted him to learn firsthand. Well, the young heir had received a full day of schooling. Unfortunately, his day was not over yet. Not even a second had passed since The Trolley's departure before the naked alpha's nose became inflamed.

"NO-O-O-O!!" He roared.

He charged forward, and as his right foot hit the ground - *SNAP!* His ankle was ensnared in a bear trap. He roared as the intense pain radiated through his body. Reflex caused him to take another step to stabilize and support his body and alleviate the pressure on his right foot. *SNAP!* The left had suffered the same fate. Both ankles were now ensnared in bear traps. The pain took his voice and gave it back as a howl heard for miles. Rayna dropped Julien to try and aid Tirin in any way she could, but from nowhere, a steel lasso wrapped around her body and pinned her arms to her side as a steel noose caught her around the neck and tightened. It pulled her up, forcing her on the very tips of her toes to avoid strangulation. Dazed, Julien stumbled to his feet and frantically looked in every direction for the hidden attacker.

He knew only another warlock was capable of such wizardry, but who in their right mind would dare challenge a Gerard? Before that question could be answered, he was jolted with a force that seemed to send a continuous electrical current through his body. It forced him to his knees as he quivered, paralyzed from the searing pain. Two chains simultaneously dropped from the sky and attached themselves around Tirin's wrists, then recoiled, stretching his body to its limit. Lucien was horrified. His tiny eyes sparkled red, and his hair floated wildly around his shoulders. He desperately wanted to help, and even though he had amassed this incredible power, he had no idea how to use it.

"Papa, tell me what to do!" He screamed. "Please, just tell me, and I will!"

"Outstanding!" came the strangely familiar British voice behind him, measured, amused, and entirely in control. "He can't right now, but I will."

The voice startled Lucien out of his mactrouge. He stopped screaming, but his tears had no end. He knew the voice came from behind him, but the child was too afraid to turn around and look.

"It's okay, child, no one will hurt you."

Lucien called upon all the courage in his body to help him turn and face this monster. He sniffed and snorted in rhythm, nearly causing himself to hyperventilate as he turned around to see what was waiting for him. To his surprise, nothing but the barren field, the old abandoned farmhouse, and the wind. He blinked rapidly to hold back his tears, and with every involuntary eye closing, the opening seemed to make things clearer. Thirty feet in front of him, a malevolent band of malafecs resolved into the open field, as if pulled from some dark dominion by the mist itself. Piece by piece, they appeared, dressed in violence. Lucien got a good look at them all, but his eyes became focused on the man in the middle. His strange voice was familiar, but that face; he could never forget that face. It was the man he had seen through his sister's eyes on the train. With his momma's help, they had saved Dani from him, but his momma was not here now.

Next to the leader was a mountain of a man. He was scary-looking and seemed to be very angry. His eyes were for Tirin and Tirin alone. Lucien knew he was an alpha. Lucien assumed the three men and two women to the angry man's right were his betas. They had Teddy and Cree gagged and on their knees. Lucien wanted to cry again because it looked like they had beaten them up pretty good, but he held it in. To the left of the leader stood four strong men, hidden in hoods, wearing gloves. He knew what they were. The leader took a few steps forward, stooped down, removed his sunglasses, and bid Lucien to him.

"Come here, child," he said with a smile on his face.

Julien, Rayna, and Tirin all struggled to call out to Lucien, but the three of them were in more pain than any of them had ever been subjected to. It was everything they could do to breathe and remain conscious at the moment. Besides, what could they tell him that would help in this situation?

"It's alright," the man assured Lucien with his sincere, albeit sinister smile. "Come. You will not be harmed. I promise."

Lucien bravely walked to the leader, trying not to hear the painful, futile struggles of the three behind him.

"What's your name?"

"...Lucien."

"Hello, Lucien. My name is Malcolm Terrence." Malcolm offered his hand, and Lucien shook it. "Nice to meet you. I'm one of the representatives for The Council in the Southeast region. I think you met an associate of mine, a – Mr. Jeffries?"

Lucien nodded as he began to well up again.

"Please don't kill my papa. Please."

"Shh, shh, shh, now. No need for all that," Malcolm said in an attempt to comfort the boy. "I have no intention of killing your father. However, he and his friends have broken quite a few rules, and that, quite simply, cannot be tolerated. They've been naughty; now they must be punished. Do you understand?"

Lucien closed his eyes to suppress the tears and nodded. Malcolm smiled at him with true admiration.

"You're almost four years old, aren't you?"

"...I'll be... four in two weeks," Lucien snorted out.

"Full mactrouge at age four," Malcolm said as he furrowed his brow and studied the boy in a manner that would make any parent uncomfortable. "You shouldn't be able to do that for at least another couple of years... Who taught you how?"

Lucien was uncomfortable with the question. He had suspected it was one of the gifts he had unwillingly received from his mother, but he wasn't really sure. Even if he was, this man would be the last person he would tell. So he shrugged his shoulders and left it at that.

"You and your sister. Descendants of Esmerelda," he smirked with a hint of reverence. "Forged in blood and brilliance—reborn to haunt our future."

He signaled with his finger, and two of the hooded guards behind him stepped up and flanked him.

"This is Winston, and his name is Royce. They may look scary, but,--"

"They're vampires," Lucien said.

"Very good! You'll need to stay here with them while my associate and I have a few words with your father. And you won't be afraid, will you?

"...No," Lucien said as he shook his head.

"Excellent," Malcolm said. He stood up and left his pleasantness down with Lucien. "Bryson," he called out.

The alpha stepped forward, and he and Malcolm walked over to their three bound guests. Malcolm surveyed the three of them individually. Tirin was covered in sweat and panting heavily, but even now, Malcolm saw in his eyes everything he needed to know. This one was defiant to the end. He smirked and moved on. He didn't even glance at Julien as he walked past him to Rayna. By this point, her eyes were barely open, and her breathing was slow and encumbered. He smiled as he admired every inch of her phenomenal physique. His eyes twinkled red as he raised his right hand, with his index finger touching his thumb. He slowly separated them - unravelling her bindings like a man unwrapping a gift before his eyes faded back to normal. It loosened the noose and allowed her to take in more air. He left a wink and his smile with her as he turned and moved to Julien. Malcolm was all business now as he looked down at Julien's paralyzed body. Julien looked as if he were having a seizure as his body continuously jerked and twitched from the constant pain. Bryson had no interest in Rayna or Julien. He planted himself in front of Tirin and held his stare while Malcolm stooped down. He wanted Julien to see him.

"Levi dolor prohibere," Malcolm whispered, and again his eyes twinkled red before they faded. It eased Julien's pain - a bit.

He wanted to make certain that Julien understood him completely.

"Despite my recommendation, the Council has seen fit to pardon you. The Gerards have always gotten preferential treatment. Given your ancestor's contributions to our growth as a whole, this has always been... acceptable, I suppose. Until now. Your father's deeds alone have created countless opportunities for our kind and helped embed us deeper into the fibers of society. You? You have done nothing to increase your family's wealth. Your blatant disregard for our customs is insulting, and I, for one, will not allow an arrogant, ungrateful child to jeopardize our race's existence because he FELL IN LOVE WITH A WITCH!... OUR LAWS ARE NOT OPEN TO INTERPRETATION!" he yelled with a hostility that seemed to surprise Bryson, whose eyes wandered from Tirin to Malcolm for a brief second before Malcolm calmed himself. "...They have been put in place for a reason, and YOU do not get to pick which ones you choose to follow. For years, someone has wiped your nose and cleaned your messes. Apparently, now, that has fallen to me."

Malcolm stared at Julien with suspicious eyes. He stood up and surveyed his surroundings. Something bothered him.

"What are you doing out here?" he asked.

The Trolley is not exclusively a 'warlock thing'; it's a 'New Orleans thing,' rooted in voodoo and black magic. Locals in the know were familiar with it, but to someone outside of this area, it would be viewed as nothing more than a flashy, unnecessary use of magic. Even Julien was unaware of its existence until today, so he gave him nothing but a cold, angry stare.

"Lucien?!" Malcolm called out, his eyes still anchored on Julien, expecting him to give something away.

"Yes?!" Lucien answered.

"You leave him out of this," Julien whispered through gritted teeth.

"You put him in it by bringing him here," Malcolm smiled as he turned to the young boy. "One last question, and then you and your father and his friends are free to go."

"Luc,--" Julien tried to call out, but Malcolm, with his hands behind his back, clenched his fist and increased Julien's pain while shutting him up.

"What exactly were you looking for out here?" Malcolm asked with the smile and demeanor of the Cheshire Cat.

"Kaitlin took Dani… We were trying to find him and bring him-- her home."

Malcolm unclenched his fist, and Julien was released from the added pain. He didn't necessarily do it for that reason. He was actually stunned by this new revelation.

"Is it possible? Could it be possible?" he thought. "...Extraordinary..." he whispered to himself.

He seemed almost proud she had escaped him, then regained his composure and turned back to Julien.

"You're done here. GO HOME. Mourn; bury your family - all of them. A costly scenario has been put in place to try and erase some of the damage you have done. You WILL follow it to the letter."

"What about Neely?" Bryson growled, his eyes still fixed on Tirin. "And Tyre-e-e-e-e."

"Ah, yes..." Malcolm said. He had forgotten about that, as was evident by the severe change in his disposition. "Felix Neely was an invaluable aid whose knowledge and loyalty can never be replaced. He was also my friend," Malcolm said as his eyes raced back and forth between the three of them. "Tyree was the alpha assigned to your wife, who worked hand and hand with Felix. To this date, Felix's body has not been found. Not a trace. Tyree's body was, minus his head... An unsanctioned killing of a council member – even a human one – is punishable by death."

Malcolm studied the three of them, waiting for a response he knew he would not receive.

"Release this one to me," Bryson said of Tirin. "We both know it was him."

"Personally, I believe all three of them had a hand in it, but without proof, retaliation is not allowed. You know this."

"So we are to do nothing, then?! They killed two of our brothers, and we are to just let them go?!"

"We're not savages, Bryson," Malcolm replied with more than a little irritation in his voice. "The Council had given me explicit orders: he, the alpha, and... this exquisite creature were to be disciplined for the malfeasance they had conducted over the past week. We have done that, and then some, I might add. My dissension of their verdict on the Neely matter was noted and disregarded. Anything more I do here at this time would be considered insubordination. They are to live... for now, anyway."

Malcolm stewed over his own words as he glared at the three of them with distasteful eyes. He was particularly perturbed by Julien. The arrogant, smug look on his face was more than Malcolm could stomach. Then something sinister came to him as his brow unfurrowed and the corners of his mouth turned up.

"However, The Council gave no such decree as pertaining to them," Malcolm said as he turned to Teddy and Cree.

"Give them to me," Bryson said as he turned away from Tirin for the first time.

Malcolm could see the anxiety and anguish he had caused, and it gave him much satisfaction.

"As you wish," Malcolm said.

Tirin was enraged as Malcolm and Bryson walked back to the others. Bryson barked out a few commands, and both Teddy and Cree were unbound and brought to their feet.

"NO-O-O! NO-O-O-O! Tirin yelled. "It was me! I killed them! Fight ME-E-E-E-E-E!"

"Wh-Wh… but you said you would let us go! You said!" Lucien cried.

Malcolm bent down to him.

"I said I would let *them* go," Malcolm said, indicating Julien, Rayna, and Tirin.

"And I will keep that promise, but this is a lesson your father never learned. Because of that, he could never teach it to you. There are always consequences to one's actions. We'll use this as a teaching moment. Royce," he said to his vampire. "Hold him up so he can see - everything."

 *ou should be proud to witness his excellent display!"*

Royce lifted Lucien like a trophy, angling his tiny frame toward the bloodshed that was to come. Lucien's screams shattered the air. There would be no turning away. Julien, Rayna, and Tirin screamed out their protests, but they could do nothing to stop what was about to happen. Bryson ripped off his shirt and glared at Teddy and Cree with an antipathy they did not deserve. His fight was with Tirin, but since he was not allowed to do that, these two were an unsatisfying substitute. Neither of them had any chance whatsoever of even hurting Bryson. A beta versus a Council alpha wasn't a fight—it was ritual slaughter. Even if Teddy and Cree fought him together, you would have to consider it a win if one of them was lucky enough to inflict a scratch on his body. Bryson knew this, everyone did. Bryson's only solace was knowing that Tirin would feel every ounce of their suffering, and he planned on making it monumental.

"Which one of you dies first?" Bryson growled.

Both Teddy and Cree bravely stepped forward.

"NO! RUN! RUN-N-N!" Tirin yelled, but he knew neither would.

No beta would. Teddy growled at Cree, forcing her to step back. She wanted to argue, but knew she couldn't. He was Tirin's new number one now. She had no choice but to follow his orders, so she stepped back.

"Give him a weapon," Bryson ordered, and one of his betas stepped forward and planted a five-foot-long spear next to Teddy. "Let's see if the little pup can at least make it entertaining."

Teddy picked up the spear and tossed it away, then spat at Bryson's feet. Bryson growled and bid him forward. Teddy charged the hulking killer with a superbly controlled hostility. His skill and form were breathtaking, and he still couldn't even lay a finger on Bryson as the big man effortlessly bobbed, weaved, and stepped out of the way of impending blows. The others laughed as they watched the humiliating display.

"This one is well-trained," Bryson barked. "Kudos."

Alphas don't do sarcasm, so the compliment was true. Then, like water, Bryson feinted to the right and, stepped in and delivered a thunderous blow to Teddy's midsection, knocking Teddy backward and off his feet. Teddy landed on his stomach and threw up blood. Cree screamed and tried to help her brother, but the other betas grabbed and held her. Teddy struggled to his feet as blood dripped from his mouth.

"Teddy, no-o-o," Tirin cried. "No."

Teddy heard the pleas of his master, but he would not yield. Bryson raised his hands as the talons grew from his fingertips.

"Only the left," he growled as he placed his right hand behind his back.

His crew cheered him on as he bid Teddy forward. Teddy charged and achieved the same result as before. He swung for gold but struck nothing but air. Bryson swung and connected his left hand to Teddy's head. His talons swept across Teddy's face like claws on clay. Skin parted. Blood sprayed. One eye went dark. Lucien screamed and struggled to break free of the vampire holding him.

"You dishonor him with your tears, boy." Bryson barked. "You should be proud to witness his excellent display!" Then he turned to his betas, "I was wrong! This one is no pup! He is an excellent fighter!"

The crew howled and barked their appreciation and respect for Teddy as he struggled to rise once more. Bryson shook his head.

"You have proven yourself. You need not rise again."

Teddy was a mess. He could barely see as the blood from his face poured through his remaining eye. He raised his head to Cree and mustered a final smile for her. With pride, she smiled back and nodded her respect as tears poured from her eyes. He then looked to the screaming Lucien and gave his young master a smile and a wink, although, with only one eye, it was difficult to differentiate from a blink. Most would not have been able to tell, but Lucien knew. Finally, Teddy turned to his sire, who could do nothing but look back at him as the tears streamed down his face. Teddy nodded to his master and mouthed the words, "Thank you." He was proud to have served him and thankful for Tirin saving his life all those years ago. Then Tirin said two words that no one, especially him, would have ever thought he would say.

"Stay down... STAY. DOWN." Tirin ordered his new number one.

It was an order that Teddy could not take.

"For my flinch," Teddy whispered as he stumbled to his feet.

Bryson smiled and nodded his respect to the brave beta, then bid him forward one final time. Teddy charged as best he could. At this point, he was moving about as fast as an above-average human. Bryson stood his ground and let him land a blow, a strike across the big man's face. Out of respect, he gave him that one, but no more. Bryson blocked Teddy's next swing, then pummeled him with ten successive blows. He hit him so fast that Teddy could not fall to the ground until he stopped. Then Bryson looked at Tirin with unadulterated rancor, raised his left foot, and stamped down and crushed Teddy's skull, never taking his eyes off Tirin. Tirin roared until all the air in his lungs was depleted. Then Bryson turned to Cree.

"Release her," Bryson ordered. "Let's see what this one's made of."

One of the betas grabbed the spear and planted it in the ground in front of Cree. She picked it up, twirled it in her hands a few times, and took a defensive stance. She obviously knew how to use it.

"Let's speed this one up a bit, shall we?" Malcolm said with a yawn. "I'd like to be done with this before nightfall."

Bryson ignored Malcolm's whining. This was a matter of honor, and like Teddy, she would be given an opportunity to prove if she was worthy of it. Julien struggled to raise his head. He had seen Cree work a staff before and knew what she was capable of if given a chance. He was going to try and give her one. The pain was so intense it took everything he had to focus and concentrate as Bryson readied himself for Cree.

"Gravabimur. Vinctorum catenis in terram," Julien whispered over and over. Blood trickled from his nose, but he could not make his eyes red.

Cree feinted a charge, then extended the spear and spun around to the betas behind her. She sliced through the neck of one of them, leaving his head dangling on his shoulder as his body fell to the ground. She was able to catch a second one in the neck with her swing, but not as clean as the first. He grabbed his neck as blood spewed out and gagged as he fell. The other three were able to react in time to avoid her fatal swing as she completed her turn and charged toward Bryson. Malcolm rolled his eyes from the amateurish error of the betas and looked to Bryson, who was reeling from the effect of the first beta's death. Cree stabbed the spear into the ground and catapulted herself into the alpha. She kicked him in the face and sent him flying backward. He landed on his back, tumbled over and with amazing agility, rolled up to his feet. He dabbed at his face with his hand and found blood on his fingers, coming from his nose. The other three betas encircled Cree and prepared themselves for battle as Bryson let out a barbarically vicious roar that made the three betas retreat back into formation.

"NO! SHE'S MI-I-I-I-INE!" Bryson yelled with a ferocity that even made the vampires flinch.

"THEN COME ON!" Cree yelled back.

She did not flinch as she glared into his eyes. Malcolm laughed out loud from the blatant show of disrespect. This was the kind of entertainment he had hoped for. He was so enthralled by this battle that he did not notice Julien's whisperings, nor did he notice the red as it began to flicker into his eyes. With his hands at his side, Bryson's talons grew, and he charged Cree with an inhuman savagery. Cree's footwork was nimble, and her skill set was complex as she wielded that spear like it was an extension of her arm. She blocked and parried all of Bryson's blows but was still forced to give ground to the speed and raw power he possessed. They both knew she could not withstand an onslaught of this caliber for much longer. Just then, Bryson struck the spear and broke it in two, and without missing a beat, Cree adjusted and held a now baton-length stick in her left hand and a baton-length stick with a razor-sharp spearhead in her right.

She changed her stance and bid him forward just as the ever-chanting Julien had stabilized the red in his eyes. Bryson leaped forward to finish her, and Cree ducked under and turned her body as she sliced the spearhead along the back of Bryson's knee, severing the tendon. The betas were in almost as much shock as Bryson was. The smile fell from Malcolm's face.

"AGAIN!!" Tirin yelled. "AGAI-I-IN!!"

Bryson pushed himself up using only his good leg and hopped around to face Cree as she charged. He swung, and she popped his arm with the stick, blocking it, then sliced through his stomach with the spearhead and opened him up.

"This is not possible." Malcolm thought. He turned to Julien and saw his eyes red and his lips moving. *"He's doing this."*

Malcolm's eyes beamed red. He clenched his fists, causing Julien an exorbitant amount of pain, and the red instantly fell out of Julien's eyes as he screamed.

"Satis," Malcolm snapped and thrust his hand outward. His voice wasn't loud, but it broke the battlefield.

With a flick, he stole her air, her flight, her fight. Cree's body flew across the field as if she had been smacked by a giant hand. She crashed to the ground fifty feet away, and it was everything she could do to maintain consciousness.

"Get her," Malcolm ordered the three vampires, "and bring her to me."

Malcolm glared at the mess that was Bryson. Another ten seconds and Cree would have finished him.

"Get him on the bus," he ordered the betas, who carefully picked him up and loaded him on the vehicle as Malcolm faced off with Julien again.

The lead vampire put Lucien down and followed Malcolm as the other two vampires dragged Cree over.

"Well played, Mr. Gerard," Malcolm seethed. "Bravo."

"What do you want to do with her?" the lead vampire asked.

"Leave her. She fought well."

"But it was rigged! He cheated!" the lead vampire yelled.

"Yes, but she was unaware of it. She fought with honor and skill. I will not punish her for that," Malcolm said. "Besides, someone needs to drive them home."

The other two vampires discarded Cree like refuse, bones barely holding together. Lucien ran to her as Malcolm glared at Julien with a particular revulsion.

"If you're lucky, Mr. Gerard, you will never see me again."

"...I wanna see you again," Julien struggled to say.

"Hmph," Malcolm smirked. "If I ever find one shred of evidence that you had anything to do with Felix Neely's untimely disappearance, you will get your wish."

With a quick, striking gesture, he blew up Julien's second limo. Lucien jumped, startled by the unexpected explosion. He stared at Malcolm with a particular glare of his own as he watched them leave. A second later, Julien, Tirin, and Rayna were released from their respective entanglements and collapsed. Malcolm left the grand impression that he had intended. One that a particular little warlock boy would never forget.

CHAPTER 27

*"*There's no such thing as werewolves."

"My lover, my love, my body to be, wake up and share your mind with me," Hagatha whispered, but Jean would not allow her to break his thoughts. *"Mmmm. So pretty is this one that dominates your dreams... Kaitlin-n-n-n,"* Hagatha cackled. *"I wonder if she tastes as good as she looks? Should we boil her in a pot of broth with vegetables?... Hmm?"*

Jean had managed to sink himself into a deep, meditative sleep. He refused to play this witch's game, but his silence only drew her rage, and she increased the intensity of her efforts.

"Or perhaps I will stuff an apple in her mouth, then make you skewer her with a spit and roast her like a suckling pig over an open fire! You will be forced to turn her for hours until her eyes explode and her skin is crispy! We will sing campfire songs through her screams! And once she is done, you will serve me a plate of roast Kaitlin and watch as I feast on your lovely wench for supper!"

Jean's body twitched from the pain, but he held onto the dream.

June 1992

Kaitlin reached the top of the hill and stopped to catch her breath. She could see the village below, but for some reason, the road took a quarter of a mile bend to the right as it descended. If she were to continue straight through the jungle, it would save her at least ten minutes, and she was very tired. She took some deep breaths as she stared into the bush. The air beneath the jungle canopy clung to her skin. It was thick and not the least bit inviting, but neither was the seemingly never-ending bend in the road before her. She leaped off the road and dashed deep into the brush. The dense canopy allowed only fifteen percent of what little light was left, making it seem like she had entered into a different world. THIS WAS A MISTAKE. She was scared; every impulse in her body told her that she shouldn't be there, and just as she was about to turn back, a low, sustained growl was heard. She froze. She hoped that maybe if she didn't move, whatever it was would just go away.

"There's no such thing as werewolves," she repeated to herself as she slowly turned around.

A hundred feet away, high above, on a tree branch, crouched like a jungle panther, a shirtless, black male in his early twenties, watched her without a blink in his eye.

"Keep tellin' ya-self d'at, sista," he said to her.

"How could he hear me?" Kaitlin thought. *"No one could. I barely,--"* Her thought was interrupted by a female voice behind her.

Kaitlin turned to see a black female in her late twenties walking toward her.

"Him tell ya' to stay on da' road for a reason, sista. Prolly shoulda listened."

Unnoticed by Kaitlin, Jean slipped from the shadows like a blade from its sheath, placing himself between Kaitlin and the danger behind her in the tree. The female stopped at the sight of him. Jean put his hand on Kaitlin's shoulder, letting her know that he was there. It startled her.

"AHH!--" she screamed, then, "Where did you,--"

"This part of the road is intermittently sprinkled with silver filings," he said, not taking his eyes off the female. He knew she was the more dangerous of the two. "They would not have risked it for you."

"She's been marked, Houngan! This one belongs to us!" the female yelled with an antipathy that Kaitlin did not understand.

The female took a step closer, and Jean moved in front of Kaitlin, shielding her from the imminent attack. The male leaped out of the tree to counter Jean's move and began to slowly circle around, putting himself between them and the village as the aggressive female held her ground in the front.

"I cannot let you have her, Medjine."

"You know this woman,--" Kaitlin tried to say, but was cut off.

"You cannot stop us all and protect her!" Medjine said.

Jean could feel the presence of the male behind him, but seemed more concerned with Medjine.

"All?" Jean said as he mockingly looked around. "Perhaps I only need to stop you."

Medjine paused. She was alarmed by the comment and nodded to the male for confirmation. The male let out a boisterous, sustained howl. Kaitlin, now back-to-back with Jean, cringed from the sound and grabbed hold of Jean as she watched the male, whose eyes were locked on her. Both Medjine and the male became anxious when the call was not answered. A wry smile formed on Jean's face as he shrugged his shoulders at Medjine. He had hoped that would be enough to make her back down, but the anger that bubbled in her eyes told him otherwise.

"On my word. Toward the village," Jean whispered.

"But, he's,--"

"I know," Jean said as his eyes, unbeknownst to Kaitlin, blazed into a warm cerulean blue. "This time, trust me."

For Kaitlin, this moment seemed like an eternity, and the silence was pure torture. Her heart was beating so fast in her chest she was afraid she would pass out before the word was given. Jean was calm and cool. It was as if he had done this hundreds of times before. His patience was outer-worldly as he stood there, motionless, his now cerulean-blue eyes focused only on Medjine.

"...RRR-R-A-A-A-R-R!" Medjine roared.

"NOW!!!" Jean yelled.

This time, Kaitlin listened to him. Despite her better judgment, she took off straight toward the male. Jean spun from left to right and released an array of tiny energy blasts. Medjine was agile enough to avoid the charges while she simultaneously slashed and eluded all the snaking vines and branches attacking her. Jean continued his spin as the male leaped toward Kaitlin. Jean waved his right hand in a backhanded motion, and as if the tree was a part of him, it swung a thick branch and smacked the male, sending him flying out of Kaitlin's path. He landed hard against the trunk of another tree, and before he could rise, thick, thorny vines snaked out from the tree and wrapped themselves around his torso and legs. He howled from the pain and submitted.

Kaitlin was shocked; she'd never witnessed anything remotely close to this. She stopped running and looked back at Jean and saw him spin around just in time to avoid what would have been a lethal blow from Medjine's razor-sharp nails. Kaitlin watched as Medjine attacked Jean with superhuman speed. She squinted in disbelief, trying to look at what seemed to be a blur. Jean ducked, bobbed, and weaved as he danced in and out of shadows to avoid her. Medjine continued to back Jean up with her aggression until he hit her in the chest with the energized palm of his hand and knocked her backward. She rolled to her feet and leaped toward him. She faked a dive at Jean, veered midair, and used the trunk as a launchpad, aiming straight for Kaitlin. Jean jabbed his energized hands in the air, and two sharp branches jetted out of the tree behind Kaitlin and caught Medjine in mid-air, impaling her through both shoulders. Medjine let loose a shrilling howl as she squirmed and dangled in front of Kaitlin, writhing in pain. The nausea was the first thing Kaitlin noticed, followed swiftly by a chill as her blood pressure dropped below normal levels. The air became thick, making it difficult for her to swallow. Her hearing was somehow diminished, and her sight grew blurry, as a dark veil fell over her eyes. Her eyelids now seemed much too heavy to hold up and began to fall just as the jungle started to twirl, and her body gave way to gravity.

he Midnight Man

Haiti

June 1992

Kaitlin woke to a hot stripe of sunlight cutting across her face. For a moment, she couldn't tell if she was dreaming, dying, or just late.

"Where am I? What time is it? Am I still dreaming?" Kaitlin had all of these questions and a few more when she first opened her eyes to find herself in a strange room she had never been in before, with a silver-haired stranger seated beside her, with his hands folded in his lap like a patient ghost.

She jolted upright, heart racing, at the sight of this older gentleman in his mid-fifties.

"Easy, easy now. It's all right," he tried to reassure her. "You're safe."

"Where am I?! Who are you?!" Kaitlin asked with much apprehension, her anxiety level at an all-time high.

"The Sacred Heart Mission. I am Father Arron. We spoke to each other on the phone. Remember?"

Kaitlin lunged for the monk and wrapped her arms around him.

"Oh my God, Father," she cried. "What happened to me?"

"Breathe, child. Breathe..." he said as he held her and let her cry. "Seems your first day with us has been an eventful one."

Kaitlin looked up from the monk's shoulder and was startled to see Jean leaning against the doorway. She pushed away from Father Arron and fell back onto the bed.

"Were you injured?" Jean asked.

She stared at him, afraid to speak. All she could do was shake her head no. Jean sensed her fear and, not wishing to agitate her any further, nodded with a diffident smile and quietly slipped out of the room.

"...That man, he... he saved my life," she said in a way that made it difficult to see exactly how she felt about that.

"He's been known to do that on occasion," said Arron.

"I don't understand how he... These people were chasing me, but..." she said, trying desperately to keep her composure.

"They moved like... I've never seen people move like that. Like... like..."

"Like animals?"

Kaitlin looked at him, not believing what she just heard, as tears filled her eyes.

"It's shocking at first, I know. It's almost like... going to sleep and waking up the next morning, only to find out that the world you knew no longer existed. That, in fact, it never really did."

"So, then, they were werewolves?" she asked as she wiped the tears away.

"Well, lycans, actually," he corrected. "In human form. They change their outward appearance during the light of the full moon to some-thing closer to what you would consider to be a werewolf, but... they have adapted so much over the centuries that, even in their human form, they are almost just as fast and just as strong in the non-full moon hours as they are in their demon form."

"Then the man who saved me, Jean Laveau?" Kaitlin asked. "He's a... a demon?"

Father Arron couldn't help but smile at Kaitlin's innocence.

"No, child. I assure you, he is as human as both you and I."

"But... the way he moved. He was just as quick as they were."

Father Arron breathed out a chuckle.

"My dear, if that were true, he'd have been killed a long time ago."

Kaitlin didn't understand Father Arron's joke. He offered her his hand, and she took it. As he helped her up, she noticed her suitcases in the corner of the room.

"He went back for them after he brought you here," Arron said as he folded his arm around hers and escorted her through the mission.

They walked down the corridor to the courtyard, where they found Jean reading bedtime stories to some of the orphans. She was confused. It was strange for her to see him in this light, but at the same time, she was comforted by it. He looked up from the book, and she caught his eyes from across the courtyard. In that brief moment, she saw him, and it seemed as if neither one of them wanted that moment to end. He smiled, then refocused himself back into the children's story. As Father Arron guided Kaitlin back to her room, he began a story that would not only change her perception of the world but perhaps of Jean as well.

"Demons have preyed upon man since the dawn of time," Arron said. "They, not us, are at the top of the food chain. What keeps the balance of power in our favor is that certain individuals - certain holy men from around the world have been bestowed with a powerful gift. God has given them the power to battle and vanquish these creatures. A tribal witch doctor in Central Africa, A mystic shaman from the mountains of Peru, A secret society of Catholic priests throughout Europe, A rabbi in the concrete jungle of Manhattan. These, and dozens more from around the world, are our protectors. They fight what we cannot. They seek out and hunt what we run away from. They are what demons fear at night. He is a Houngan. A Boku prince. A Voodoo Priest of the highest order. He has trained his entire life to fight for those who cannot fight for themselves, and he would die before he would allow any harm to fall upon us. His name is Jean Laveau, or as some like to call him, 'The Midnight Man.'"

Father Arron looked deep into Kaitlin's eyes for a moment, then nodded as he smiled.

"What?" Kaitlin asked.

"Just checking to see if you were going to be alright," Arron said.

"You can tell that by looking into my eyes?"

"The eyes are the window to one's soul, my dear. You can always find a person's truth in them… if you choose to look." He smiled. "Get some sleep. Tomorrow is a new day."

The next day was, in fact, a new day, as Father Arron had predicted. Despite her asperous entrance into this new world, she could not remember a time when she had experienced a more peaceful sleep. To be woken by the quiet song of a single bird outside her window and a beam of warm light that had found its way through the curtains was astonishing to her. She couldn't remember the last time that she had been woken by anything other than an alarm clock, and the smell emanating from those fascinatingly fragrant flowers on her bedside table was intoxicating. She just wanted to lay and let it soak all over her. Then the moment was ruined, as she remembered she had forgotten to set an alarm clock. She had no idea what time it was. Being Sunday, her first day of teaching would not start until tomorrow, but;

"What of breakfast? Where do I go? What was the protocol?" Just then, a beautiful church bell rang ceremoniously from the courtyard. *"What was that bell for? What does it mean?"* These questions and more spun around in her head as her heart began to race.

She jumped out of bed and ran into her bathroom, where she was reminded that she was in a third-world country. She had prepared herself for that, even the low to no water pressure for the shower, but no amount of preparation would ever get you ready for the ice-cold water that comes out of it. The first splash hit like an ice cube to the spine, so much for paradise. She made a significant effort to clean herself and get out of there as quickly as she could. As she wrapped a towel around her body, more for warmth than to dry herself, she was startled by a knock at the door.

"One second, please!" She yelled as she shivered and shuffled into the next room to open the door.

She cracked it open and was surprised to see Jean Laveau and two teenage boys with a very large, heavy-duty, covered cooking pot at their feet. Whatever was inside was obviously hot, as both boys wore heavy oven mitts for protection.

"Good morning, Ms. Morrison," Jean said.

"Bonjour, ma'am," the boys said in unison.

"Uhhh, hi? Good morning,--" Kaitlin said.

"This is Emmanuel and his brother Wilson," Jean said. "Go ahead, boys, hurry. It looks as if she is in need."

The two boys shuffled past a bewildered Kaitlin into the room with the big pot. She turned to Jean.

"They are here to fill your tank with hot water. Although it seems you have chosen to forgo this modest luxury of ours," Jean said.

He couldn't help but grin at the shivering beauty.

"I forgot to set my clock, and when I heard the church bell,--"

"The first bell is your clock, as there are no outlets in this room. It will ring every morning at seven a.m.."

"Oh."

"The next bell is breakfast. Forty-five minutes after the first, then again at nine for school or, on this day, for church. There is a bell schedule on your desk."

"Oh, I,--" Kaitlin started, but was interrupted by the boys.

They had finished their task and shuffled back into the room with the giant pot in tow.

"Excuse us, ma'am," they said as they squeezed past her and exited the room.

"Thank you!" Kaitlin called out after them.

"They will bring you hot water every morning shortly after the first bell," Jean said.

"You probably should have stopped them. As you so sarcastically pointed out, I chose to forgo that luxury this morning."

Kaitlin did not flinch as Jean reached out and gently ran his two middle fingers from her hairline, backward, over the top of her head. He revealed the excess soapsuds to her as he rubbed his thumb over the two fingers.

"Well," he said with a coy grin, "you still have thirty minutes before the next bell. You may wish to indulge."

Jean bowed his head to her, then caught her eyes before he turned away and moved down the hall. Kaitlin ran her fingers through her hair and was gifted a handful of the sticky, oily substance known as soap. An exasperating sigh passed through her lungs as she closed her eyes and shook her head. She wasn't quite sure what she thought of this man - yet.

"Oh, wait!" she called out, stopping him before he rounded the corner. "Where is breakfast, by the way?"

"Did you not get the tour?"

"No. Yesterday was a bit,--"

"Yes. I was there. If it is to your liking, I will come and collect you shortly after the next bell."

"Uh, yes-- I mean, that would be fine. Thank you."

Jean smiled, bowed his head again, and left. She closed the door and took his advice, and indulged in the soothing, hot water.

CHAPTER 29

*E*xpand the width of your possibilities

Haiti

June 1992

Shortly after the next bell, there was a knock on her door. She opened it to find a very different Jean Laveau. He wore a comfortable pair of loosely-fitted white, khaki slacks and a matching white short-sleeved guayabera shirt. She, in her white floral print summer dress, hadn't planned to match—but neither could ignore the similarities.

"He looks very nice," she thought, and she wasn't sure why that surprised her.

"I… didn't know what to wear," Kaitlin said. "I hope this is appropriate. If not, I can,--"

"No, it is… quite lovely. You look… very nice, actually."

Kaitlin cast a dubious glare his way as she closed the door.

"Wow. That almost seemed like a compliment, Mr. Laveau," she said as she moved past him down the hall.

"…Almost?" A confused Jean whispered to himself as he walked after her.

Once in the courtyard, Jean gave her the abridged tour of the five-building complex before they entered the mess hall, where they were immediately greeted by the robust Father Tanzi. He was a boisterous mountain of a man with a harsh, gruff exterior, but his heart was more than big enough to fill his rotund size. He was in charge of feeding the village, and he took great pride in it.

"Brother Laveau!" Father Tanzi boomed in his deep, resonant voice. "Who is this lovely creature you have blessed my dining room with this morning?"

"Father, allow me to introduce you to Ms. Kaitlin Morrison, our new English teacher. Kaitlin; Father Tanzi."

"Good morning, Father, nice to meet you."

"Good morning, my dear!" He smiled. "I hope your sleep was more peaceful than your arrival into our tiny pocket of the world."

"Honestly, I can't remember having a more peaceful sleep than I did last night."

"Ah!" Father Tanzi chuckled. "The Arabians! Excellent!"

"I'm sorry?" Kaitlin asked.

"The Arabian Jasmine!" He bellowed. "A rare flower found only in the northeastern mountains. One of the most fragrant flowers in the world! Known to induce a most peaceful sleep. Brother Laveau thought you might fancy them and gathered a bunch and had them put in your room before you arrived."

"That was,... very thoughtful, Mr. Laveau. Thank you. They are quite beautiful."

"Please, it is just Jean," Jean said.

"Thank you, 'Just Jean,'" Kaitlin responded.

"No, no. I meant it is just,--"

"Jean. That's what I said - Just Jean, right?"

"No, you misunderstand. My name is,--"

"I'm *just* joking – Jean."

Jean looked at her curiously before a smile overtook his face.

"It was very funny," Jean chuckled—lightly at first, then openly.

The sound drew glances. It had been a long time. Father Tanzi's smile widened as he took Kaitlin in.

"Why don't you get her a plate, Brother Laveau?"

"Yes, of course. Excuse me."

Jean headed for the buffet as Father Tanzi walked Kaitlin to her table.

"Did I say something wrong?"

"On the contrary, my dear. You seemed to have said something right," Tanzi said as he sat next to her. Kaitlin gave him a quizzical look. "You made him laugh."

"It was just a stupid joke."

"Perhaps, but he hasn't laughed out loud in over ten years," Tanzi said with a suspicious smile set upon his face. "Do you like chai tea, my dear?"

All of Father Tanzi's questions seemed to come off as an interrogation, but this particular one lit up Kaitlin's eyes.

"Are you kidding? It's my favorite. I've been longing for one since I got off the plane yesterday."

There was a devilish hint in Tanzi's eye that somehow seemed fitting. Then, without warning, he lashed out at Jean as he returned with two plates of food.

"Why didn't you tell me this one liked chai?" he asked.

"I-I did not,--"

"AMEEL!" he called out to someone across the room. "CHAI!"

As Father Tanzi rose from the table, a tall, slender man approached. Father Morelli was several years Tanzi's senior, but his spirit was ageless, and his wit was as quick as a country mouse.

"She hasn't been here a full day, and already you're subjecting her to those dried-out, burnt leaves of yours?" Father Morelli said. "Hasn't the poor girl been through enough?"

"Pay this one no heed. My chai is world-renowned," Tanzi replied as he walked off.

"So is turpentine, but we don't wish to drink that either," Morelli said.

"I heard that!" Tanzi shouted from a distance.

"I swear that man's ears are as big as the rest of him," Morelli whispered as he looked to Jean for an introduction.

"Oh, excuse me," Jean said as he swallowed the food in his mouth. "Kaitlin Morrison, I present to you, Father Morelli."

"Good morning, Father. So nice to meet you."

"The pleasure is all mine, I assure you. I apologize for yesterday's unpleasantries. I'm just thankful Brother Laveau was able to… make things right? Hmm?" he said as he looked to Jean.

"Yes, Father," Jean replied.

"Good. Well done. I don't know what we'd do here without him," he said with pride as Father Tanzi returned.

He placed a cup in front of Kaitlin, then carefully poured the tea himself.

"It's important that it's poured gently into the cup, so as to not break down the components of the tea," Tanzi said as Morelli rolled his eyes.

It seemed as if everyone's attention was again on Kaitlin as they waited for her to sample Father Tanzi's brew. The room quieted like a courtroom awaiting a verdict. Even the children paused mid-bite in anticipation of this, most important tasting.

"Oh my goodness, this is delicious!" Kaitlin said.

Father Tanzi was a passionate man who took great pride in everything he did. It brought him much happiness that people enjoyed his food, but the chai was personal. He didn't have the luxury of pulling leaves from a jar on the shelf. Everything was made from scratch, and these leaves were grown in his personal garden.

"I'm sure you are aware of the effect your smile has on others," Tanzi said, not trying to hold in his emotion. "Today, it honors and warms my heart."

"Mm. Well said, Father," Morelli added with the utmost sincerity. "I hope it honors me equally, if not a tiny bit more, after you taste my tea this evening."

"It is an insult that you even call that watered-down soup tea. It is no match for a delicacy such as this," Tanzi declared.

"Brother Laveau, you've had them both. What is your opinion?" Morelli asked.

A question all of Haiti was interested in.

"Ah…" Jean murmured as he tried to ingest the forkful of food he had just placed in his mouth. "I am,… but a simple man. I do not know that I have the knowledge or the awareness to decipher the difference in such matters. I can only say that they both bring happiness to my mouth," Jean replied. "Ms. Morrison, on the other hand, seems to have tasted many more samples than myself. Perhaps she would be a more capable connoisseur for your contest."

Kaitlin gave Jean a look that he pretended very hard not to see.

"An excellent idea!" said Morelli. "Jean, you'll see that she's placed at our table tonight?"

"Of course, Father."

"Excellent! Now, if you'll excuse me. We must prepare ourselves for this morning's services."

Both Morelli and Tanzi excused themselves, leaving Jean and Kaitlin alone.

"Thanks a lot!" she admonished Jean. "How am I supposed to make that decision?"

"Judiciously," Jean laughed again.

Kaitlin took notice this time.

"*Hmph. Twice in one day*", she thought.

"You know, I can see why everyone makes such a big deal about you laughing." Jean looked at her, not understanding her meaning. "You have a great laugh; it… really opens up your face."

"…Thank you, Ms. Morrison… That almost seemed like a compliment."

"Almost," she said with a smile. "You know, if I'm to call you Jean, it seems only fair that you call me Kaitlin."

"'Just' Kaitlin?" he said as he took in her eyes, and they both laughed.

"Yes. Just Kaitlin. Or Kate,… if you like."

Later that day, Jean took 'Just Kaitlin' and several children on a hike before dinner. There, at the top of the hill, reaching up for the sun, lay a bed of Arabian Jasmine's. Kaitlin seemed unnaturally drawn to them.

"They're so beautiful," she said as she inhaled the bunch, then closed her eyes and teetered. "Ouu. Strange. I feel a little dizzy. They really are very strong. Are you sure they're safe?"

"Absolutely. I have slept with them since I was a child."

"Really?"

"Yes, and it would make me very happy if you did as well." Kaitlin furrowed her brow. "No, not with me, I meant the flowers. To sleep with the flow,--"

"Yes, I understand. Why?"

"The fragrance is strong and reminiscent of the pheromones given off by vampires before they attack. They are the creatures I was referring to when I said there were worse things in the woods at night than lycans. Building up an immunity to them could one day save your life."

"Hmph. And I thought you were just giving a girl some flowers," she said as she looked into his eyes.

"Well, they are very beautiful, as well. Perhaps you might consider it a, how do you say? A two-for-one?"

They both laughed.

"By the way, how did you find me?" she asked. Now, it was Jean's turn to furrow his brow. "Yesterday. We hadn't seen or passed any vehicles for hours. How'd you find me?"

"What would you say if I told you I changed into a giant raven that flew above the treetops?"

"I'd probably say that was impossible, and I'd think you were trying to pull my leg again."

"Many things in life seem impossible, Kaitlin. In those moments, I would ask you to, perhaps, expand the width of your possibilities."

The thought resonated deep within Kaitlin and pushed a smile onto her face. In two sentences, Jean had taken "limits" from her perspective and replaced them with "limitless." Soon after, they headed back for the village, as dinner was approaching and Kaitlin had a contest to judge. It turned out Father Morelli's chai, although completely different in texture and consistency, was equally as good as Father Tanzi's.

This left Kaitlin with an impossible decision until she found Jean's thoughtful eyes across the room and remembered his quote.

"The only real way to decide is with time," Kaitlin said. "Taste, consistency, and character, over the long haul." She smiled. "I'll judge at the end of summer."

This temporarily took her off the hot seat and ensured her a generous supply of chai for the coming weeks. She expanded the width of her possibilities. When she returned to her room for the evening, a fresh bouquet of Arabian Jasmines was waiting for her. The next morning, Kaitlin had skipped breakfast for some reason. Jean went to check on her and saw her struggling to pick up a stack of textbooks she had dropped in the courtyard. He rushed over to help her and found her frazzled and completely out of sorts.

"Are you all right?" he asked.

"No. I'm lost. I missed breakfast, and I don't know what I'm doing. I have three classes to teach with kids who all have different levels of understanding, and I don't even know if they'll understand me."

"I do."

"I'm not teaching you. You're not there."

"I will be. For as long as you need me to be."

Kaitlin found a calmness in his eyes that seemed to say everything was going to be all right. It was soothing, and she welcomed it as they picked up the books and he walked her to the classroom.

"I'm sorry. I just feel a bit overwhelmed this morning."

"There is no need for an apology. Everyone becomes overwhelmed at some point."

"Even you?" she asked.

Jean laughed.

"Yeah, well, you just don't seem like the type of person who gets overwhelmed easily."

"Hmph," he smiled. "The world is a big place, Kaitlin Morrison. Sometimes, to survive it, we must find a way to make it small. Do not focus on the number of classes you have today. Narrow your perspective and see only the one. Set that as your goal and accomplish it. Then move to the next."

She realized that they were standing outside the door to the classroom. She looked into his eyes and found the strength to enter it.

"Bonjour, Madam Morrison!" The class rang out in unison.

Jean was ready to translate, but found it was not needed, as Kaitlin understood.

"Bon maten, klas. An Anglè sa ye, 'Good morning, class,'" she said slowly. "Ou ka eseye, 'Good morn-ning class'?"

In unison, the class said, "Good morn-ning, class."

"GOOD!" Kaitlin said happily. "Trè bien. Now,..."

She went on for several minutes before she even noticed Jean was gone. Over the next several days, they spent what seemed like all of their free time together, talking, learning from each other, and laughing. Lots and lots of laughing. In a matter of days, they had become the best of friends. One night after dinner, he walked her back to her room.

"...I do not understand how they can call it football if they do not use their feet," Jean said as they reached her door.

"They do!" Kaitlin laughed. "Just not all the time."

She opened the door and turned to him.

"Hey. I haven't seen you in any of my classes the last few days, Mr. Laveau. Have you become tired of me?"

"I can assure you, Ms. Morrison, that is not the case."

Kaitlin gazed into his eyes, waiting for a response.

"Then what is it?" she asked.

"I said I would be there for as long as you needed me. You no longer need me."

"...I can assure you, Mr. Laveau, that is not the case."

She rose onto her toes. He met her there, arms circling her waist.

Their lips touched, soft as jasmine petals, just as the door closed behind them. That was the night when Kaitlin Morrison and Jean Laveau became more than friends.

CHAPTER 30

"*Your offensive skill is impressive, but unless you improve your defense, the floor will always be your friend.*"

New Orleans, Louisiana

July 4, 2006

A month shy of his tenth birthday, Lucien was well on his way to becoming a most proficient practitioner of magical mastery. He snapped his fingers and ignited a flame in his hand. He marveled at his achievement for a few seconds before he moved the firecracker in his other hand to the flame. He watched the fuse burn down to an uncomfortably short level before his eyes flamed red. It seemed as if he had frozen the fuse, but no warlock, or witch for that matter, has the power to stop time. He had simply slowed it down to a point where it seemed as if it wasn't moving.

He tossed it over the balcony as his eyes faded to normal, and it exploded. He took another, tossed it up high, snapped his fingers, and created a flame, then, with a puff of breath, blew the flame toward the firecracker. His aim was true; the flame hit the firecracker in mid-air, and it exploded. He was quite pleased with himself, as was Rayna, who watched him like a proud mom. He had become very adept with his studies at such a young age. Jimmy Lee entered the room, but because the balcony door was open, he could not go any further. Sunset was looming, and there was enough light in the room to give him pause.

"Excuse me,… ma'am?" he called. He couldn't see her, but he knew she was out there.

"What is it, Jimmy?" Rayna called back.

"Bossman wants you in the study."

"I'll be right there! Thank you!" Rayna said, then to Lucien, "Come on, bub. Probably almost time for us to go, anyway."

Lucien took the rest of the pack and launched it over the balcony as far as he could. He snapped the fingers on both hands and threw the flames with laser-like precision at the pack and exploded it.

"Wow! Did you see that?!" Lucien asked with the jubilance of someone who was nearly ten years old.

"I sure did," Rayna said as she walked in the room with Lucien on her heels. "You are becoming quite the little warlock, aren't you?"

"You think I'll be as good as Papa?"

"Nope," she said in the most aloof and indifferent voice she could muster.

Lucien's face, shoulders, arms, practically his entire body, drooped.

"I think you're gonna be a whole lot better," she smiled as she grabbed hold and tickled him until he couldn't stand it any longer. "But you may not make it to your daddy's age if you don't learn how to close doors." She turned him around to the balcony door he had left open and swatted him on the butt. "You trying to blow my vampires up like those firecrackers?"

Lucien ran and closed the balcony door, then ran and caught up with Rayna as they playfully traversed down the long hallway to the stairs. He raced her to the bottom and won, as she always let him, then busted into his father's study. Rayna followed him in and closed the doors behind her. Tirin was already there, standing with his arms folded across his chest. It was difficult to tell if he was angry or bored. Either way, his demeanor changed when Lucien entered the room. He dropped down to Lucien's level and put up his fists. Lucien jumped into a fighting stance and immediately started swinging and throwing punches, good punches, and even though not a single one got through Tirin's defense, anyone could see that this boy was skilled. After a multitude of punches had been thrown and blocked, Tirin thrust his palm into Lucien's chest and knocked him back a few steps before he fell on his bottom. Tirin grabbed him and hoisted him up above his head.

"Your offensive skill is impressive, but unless you improve your defense, the floor will always be your friend," Tirin whispered to him before he set him down.

Rayna was not happy with that particular lesson. Tirin did not care.

"You could let him win once in a while," she said as she tried, unsuccessfully, to hide her displeasure from him.

"Or, if you stop fighting all his battles for him, he may learn to win on his own."

Tirin knew Rayna's eyes were fixed on him, and again, Tirin didn't care. She knew, but she let her eyes stay with him a while longer anyway before she turned and focused on the business at hand. Her brow furrowed as her head tilted to the side.

"What's going on here?" she whispered.

Tirin's sigh turned into a low, sustained growl. Whatever it was, he wasn't happy about it. Julien stood in front of a map of the United States on the wall next to the desk. He impatiently listened with folded arms as the short, mousy man in front of him, a Mr. Endicot, painstakingly explained his theory on how to track Kaitlin and Dani. The map had about fifty red and blue flags pinned in different cities, with the red flags only placed where a blue flag had already existed. Rayna's eyes began to flit as she tried to make sense of this mess. Lucien gave up after a good ten seconds, and Tirin was just waiting for the signal to kill him.

"Dad, it's gettin' dark. The fireworks gonna start soon," Lucien interrupted. He had already had his fill of this fool.

"Alright, alright," Julien mumbled. "We got time. Go pee and get a jacket. It gets chilly down by the river."

Lucien could barely hold in his excitement as he sprinted out of the room. Any amount of time he got to spend with his father was always special to him, but over the last few years, that time had declined much more than either of them would have liked. The mousy man continued as Julien, Tirin, and Rayna watched.

"So, Mr. Gerard," Mr. Endicot said. "To capsulize, using the formula I've come up with, we're certain, give or take six percent, that we can not only predict Ms. Morrison's next move but tell you exactly where she will be moving to. Within a thirty-two-mile radius... give or take."

"Rayna?..." Julien sighed. Rayna just shrugged her shoulders. "Go on," Julien said to the man.

"Very good. Now her tendency, to this point, has been moving from a small city to big, then big, big - small; big, big - small; small, small; small - BIG; then small, big; sm--"

"Where's she at now?!" Julien interrupted.

"Uhhh, well, according to my calculations, we're ninety-four percent certain that she's... here," Mr. Endicot said as he stuck a blue flag into the map. "Hanover, Pennsylvania. Or, within thirty-two miles of,--"

"What about The Talisman?" Julien asked.

"Welllll, our calculations on him aren't as accurate as the ones we have for Ms. Morrison, but we do feel,--"

"Is he gonna show up or not?!" Julien yelled.

"Uhhh, n-no. N-No, sir. We don't feel that the, uhm, Talisman,--"

"Tirin, get an eight-man team and have the jet prepped and ready to go in an hour."

Tirin nodded and then looked to Rayna.

"I'll need three vampires," Tirin said to Rayna. "And I'll take the deputies and leave Cree with you, but she will need to change on this night."

Rayna nodded. Tirin knew she was upset by this, and he knew why, but orders were orders. He lingered a moment and then zipped out of the room.

"Well, uhm, yes. Well, thank you for seeing me... Mr. Gerard. And, uh,... Ms. Rayna had mentioned there would be a generous, uh, stipend for,--"

"You're coming with us," Julien said as he moved to the desk to grab some things.

"Me?! Uh, no. No, no, no, no. I don't, uh, I'm not a,--"

"You stand by your work, sir?" Julien asked with a very serious look on his face.

Tirin zipped back into the room and stood uncomfortably close to the man.

"Well, yes, but,--"

"Ninety-four percent, right?"

"Uhhh, yes, but,--"

"Good. 'Cuz if she isn't there, only six percent of you is coming back," Julien stated, then looked at Tirin. "Take him."

Tirin grabbed Mr. Endicot by his arm and escorted him out. Julien continued to pack up some papers, trying his best to pretend Rayna's glare didn't bother him.

"You got something to say?" he asked without looking up.

"What about the fireworks show?"

"...We'll have to catch the next one."

"Julien, you promised him."

"Rayna, if there's even a ten percent chance my child is there,--"

"There's a hundred percent chance your child is here! And he needs his daddy to stop,--"

Rayna silenced herself when she noticed Lucien was standing in the doorway. Julien glared at her as if it were her fault before he approached his visibly upset son.

"...You're not gonna go?" Lucien asked, dejected.

Julien paused. He knew Lucien was disappointed, and he needed a moment to try and find the right words to make him understand.

"Son, I'm... I'm trying to bring your little sister home to us, where she belongs. You understand that, right?" Julien said. Lucien nodded yes, but the true answer was no. "Rayna'll take you. So you'll still get to see the show." Then to Rayna, "get him anythin' he wants."

"I always do," she replied, an unnecessary dig that Rayna felt was necessary.

"I'll be back tomorrow. Maybe we'll go out on the boat, okay?" he asked. Lucien nodded. "Okay. Good," Julien said as he kissed his son on the forehead. "Y'all have fun, na'."

Julien exited the room without looking at Rayna. He felt guilty enough. Rayna moved over to Lucien and rubbed his head. It had somehow become her job to raise the spirits of the crestfallen boy, and, like with everything else she does, she had become quite good at it.

"Come on, Buck. After da' show, we'll get a sundae."

"...Banana split?"

"Oooh. Tough negotiator you are. Let me get my stuff."

She exited the room as Lucien stood in the doorway, simmering. He walked over to the map and studied it a quick second before he closed his eyes and concentrated.

"Lucien, honey, you comin'?" Rayna called out from the other room.

Lucien's eyes opened, gleaming red. He flicked his finger at the map - soft, deliberate - then his eyes faded back to normal.

"Coming!" He called out as he ran out of the room.

He had magically pinned a blue flag into the map where none had been placed before: Tomah, Wisconsin.

CHAPTER 31

The Gateway to Cranberry Country

Tomah, Wisconsin

July 4, 2006

Bang! Snap! Pop! A string of firecrackers exploded as five mischievous children tore across the gravel lot of the Daybreak Motel like outlaws on the run. Two of them donned Native American Indian costumes. The other three were in shorts and tank tops with moccasins and feathered headdresses, and all had their faces painted in some festive way. They sprinted across the parking lot, screaming and giggling before they disappeared between buildings 'D' and 'F.' Kaitlin hopped out of the ol' red truck with her list of apartments and mobile homes for rent in her hand. She and Dani had been 'living,' if that's what you want to call it, in this motel for nearly a month. She'd been working night shifts at a competing motel as a housekeeper and had just procured a couple of shifts as a server in a local restaurant downtown. All in all, they were doing pretty good, and they hadn't had an unpleasant episode in nearly three months. Maybe it was over? Maybe everyone had given up and decided to leave them alone. Either way, it was time to get out of this motel and try to put some stability in their lives. She grabbed two bags of groceries from the back and climbed the stairs to the second floor. When she got to her room, she was not surprised to find the door unlocked; she was miffed by it.

"That girl," she mumbled to herself as she pushed open the door.

She stepped in as the door slammed shut behind her and saw that the place was an absolute mess. The chairs were turned over, and the seat cushions had been ripped. The lights on the nightstand were on the floor, and the bedsheets were scattered around the room. Coming home to this would give anyone anxiety. It should come as no surprise that she dropped her grocery bags on the floor, but it wasn't because of the ripped cushions or the scattered bedsheets. It was because of the paw prints that were on them.

"Oh my god," she exhaled. "Dani..."

She opened the door, and The Talisman was there. His hand clamped her throat before breath or scream could escape.

"Any get in waaaay of Talisman..."

He whispered his warning to her and smiled as he released her. She fell backward into the room, gasping for air as the door swung shut. She paused for a second, afraid, then jumped up and reopened the door. He was gone. She ran out onto the landing and saw the Dobermans racing across the parking lot. In the distance, she saw the county fair - where Dani was. She raced down the stairs to the ol' red truck and took off toward the fairgrounds.

'WELCOME TO CRANBERRY COUNTRY - TOMAH!'

The large banner hung high above the fairgrounds, ushering in hundreds of people of all ages as they wandered around the commemorative carnival, enjoying the rides and many activities. Six playfully naughty children ran into a gigantic playpen looking for something to get into. A nearly ten-year-old Dani was one of them. They came upon a slight, small-boned man, dressed in a round cranberry costume with a black bodysuit underneath and a yellow baseball cap, which read, "Berry The Cranberry." He was handing out flyers next to a wooden statue of Chief Tomah, the Native American the city was named after.

"Fifteen percent off any cranberry products! Tell 'em Chief Tomah sent you and take twenty!" Berry The Cranberry, shouted with much enthusiasm as he handed out his flyers. "Here ya' go. Thanks! Fifteen percent off any,--"

Berry was interrupted by the barrage of cranberries the children had just pelted him with.

"Hey!" Berry shouted with an unimpressive anger. "You kids better knock it off or you're gonna get it!"

They laughed, then pelted him again.

"I mean it!" Berry declared before being assaulted one final time.

The mighty cranberry had fallen. Berry T. Cranberry fled his post, routed by sugar-high hooligans wielding actual berries. They immediately took his place next to the statue of Chief Tomah and proclaimed it as their own. Spoils of their victory.

"Ladies and gentlemen, the fair will be closing one hour early this evening so we can all enjoy the Fireworks Spectacular over Lake Tomah! Happy Fourth of July from the Gateway to Cranberry Country! Once again, the fair will be closing sixty minutes early,--" an overly exuberant voice announced over the loudspeaker.

"Come on, let's go down to the lake!" the 'Wannabe Leader' of the bunch suggested.

"No, we got plenty of time for that," the 'Actual Leader' overruled. "Let's go see the sideshows!"

"Yeah! Let's go see the wolfman!" the 'Cheer Leader' ratified.

Then, of course, everyone else jumped on board – all but one.

"No, come on, guys. Let's just go to the lake," Dani said.

Dani was the new kid, so she didn't really have a lot of pull. Actually, she didn't have any, but the boys thought she was really cute, so they let her tag along.

"Awwww! Dani's scared!" Actual Leader teased.

He was one of the boys who thought she was cute, so he didn't go too hard on her.

"I'm not scared. I just think it's stupid. You do know he's not real, right?" Dani said. She did not think he was cute, so she came at him pretty strong.

"How do you know, new girl? You ever seen a real wolfman before?" Actual Leader asked.

He didn't appreciate being spoken to in that tone, and he was letting her know. Dani stared at him. She didn't blink.

"No," she lied. And then she let it go.

She was, in fact, the new girl, and she actually liked some of these kids, so she backed off without making a scene. The leader took that as a personal victory.

"That's what I thought," the Actual Leader stated as he glared at her.

"Alright, come on, let's go then," Wannabe Leader called out, thinking he was saving Dani from any potential embarrassment.

Dani did think *he* was cute, so she smiled at him and let him believe he had actually saved her. Then, to her complete surprise and consternation, Cheer Leader slyly slid his arm around Dani's shoulder.

"Don't worry, babe, you can sit next to me," he said, trying to be as macho as he possibly could. "I'll protect you."

"Eewww!!" the other two girls in the group said in unison.

They all laughed as Dani wiggled away from him.

"No, thank you," Dani said.

"Suit yourself, babe," Cheer Leader said, doing his best to disguise the anguish of pre-teen rejection.

Dani didn't mean to hurt his feelings. She didn't want to hurt anybody's feelings. She just wanted what all, almost-ten-year-olds want: friends. The group laughed and darted toward the sideshows, swallowed by the noise and light. Dani followed, slow at first. Something in her gut told her not to. But she followed.

CHAPTER 32

The sideshows

Sideshows have been around for hundreds of years. In their earliest beginnings, they were basically anything that could draw a crowd. Over time, they evolved into wild stunts that personified a particular sort of peril or pitfall - like outlining a person's body with knives thrown from an inadequate distance; blindfolded, of course. Or shooting a bottle off of someone's head, over your shoulder, while looking through a mirror. Danger and excitement, that's what drew the crowds. It also cost a few amateur daredevils their lives. At the turn of the twentieth century, sideshows took a distasteful twist to exploiting human oddities and deformities. "Freak shows," as some would call them. These shows were eventually outlawed, which was widely protested by the performers themselves. The very laws that were put in place to protect them, sadly, caused their demise. Nowadays, sideshows have become a novelty, a comical parody of themselves, using actors to portray the daredevils and freaks of the past. Everyone knows they are no longer real and that the particular element of danger that made these shows mesmerizing, no longer existed in these, almost abandoned, set off to the side, shows.

On the eastern outskirts of the fairgrounds, inside a compact compartment attached to the west side of the main tent, a husky fellow, just south of his forties, sat quietly in this makeshift dressing room as he worked a conspicuously challenging crossword. The Ringmaster's robust voice could easily be heard through the closed curtain that separated the adjoining tents as he captivated the modest crowd of mostly children and a few teetering drunks, with stories of his unheralded exploits and undocumented travels to exotic destinations around the world.

"Buck up, Petey! Last show tonight!" Whispered an exuberant young stagehand as he poked his head through the flaps of the tent.

"Yeah, yeah," Petey mumbled.

"Come on, man, you got a few out there! Get into it!" The young man said as he popped his head out of the tent and disappeared, extremely disappointed with Petey's enthusiasm, or lack thereof.

However disinterested Petey appeared to be, he was first and fore-most, a professional. He could hear the Ringmaster clearly. He knew his cues, and he knew where he had to be and when he had to be there, and right now, all he wanted to do was complete another line of his provocative puzzle in peace. A few seconds later, the tent flaps opened and closed, but instead of being followed by the annoyingly upbeat voice of the young stagehand, a soft, rolling growl was heard.

"Knock it off, Mick!" Petey snarled. He was irritated by the constant interruptions, and he intended to make sure Mick under-stood that. "Listen, kid, I don't need you to,--"

Petey stopped himself as he looked up into the mirror and saw someone who was not Mick. This seemed to irritate him even more. There are rules of conduct. You don't just walk into someone's private tent unannounced. Before Petey could tell the stranger a thing or two about manners, the stranger pounced on him with an unnatural quickness and snatched a bite-sized chunk out of his neck, silencing him - permanently. The stranger then stood there and watched Petey as he convulsed and choked on his own blood. Then he watched him die. It took longer than Petey, or anyone in his place, should ever have to suffer through. The stranger didn't seem to have an opinion on that one way or the other as he turned his attention and his sporadically spasmodic sniffer to the Ringmaster's voice, and the oddity that awaited him on the other side of the curtain.

In the main tent, Dani and the other kids sat in the bleachers and listened intently as the Ringmaster spun his treacherous tale. The Cheer Leader, once again, tried to slip his arm around Dani's shoulder. This time, she administered a far-from-gentle squeeze to his hand. He opened his mouth about as wide as his face would allow and mouthed an 'AH-H-W-W!' without making a noise. Dani released him, and he withdrew his unwelcomed appendage and placed his hand in his lap. Dani withheld the grin from her face, so as not to embarrass him, as he discreetly massaged his hand in silence. There would not be a third attempt.

"—Time was of the essence, as our food supply was nearly depleted," the Ringmaster continued. "I, myself, led the expedition as we frantically tracked the boy-wolf. Day and night, night and day, we tirelessly traveled, from the shores of the Black Sea all the way through the hills of the Carpathian Mountains! It was there, on a cold and wintery night, after forty-three days of battling both starvation and the elements unleashed on us by God himself, that we found him. Quick as the Devil, he was. He killed two of my men in seconds, before I, myself, stepped forward and clamped the chains on his hairy wrists! AND THAT IS HOW HE WILL BE PRESENTED TO YOU TONIGHT! Bound in tempered steel, encased behind these solid iron bars - ten leagues thick! Ladies and gentlemen! Boys and girls! I give you - TRAJAN DRAGOS! THE HU-MAN WO-O-OLF!"

The curtain opened to a weak smattering of applause, only to reveal the stranger, standing alone, chained, in a cell. His nose twitched rhythmically as he raised his head, and when his eyes opened, they gravitated straight to Dani and stopped. Dani gasped, and not because of the chains. It was the, more than familiar nose twitch and the feeling of danger that came with it.

The other kids, however, didn't seem to be impressed with this particular presentation of 'The Wolfman'.

"He doesn't look as good as the last guy," The Actual Leader complained.

The Ringmaster seemed to have a problem with him, as well.

"Hey. Where's Petey?" He whispered out of the side of his mouth. "And who the hell are you?"

Those words broke the stranger's strange fixation with Dani as he turned both his attention and his intention to the Ringmaster.

"Clamped the chains on yourself, did you?" asked the irritated stranger.

"Oh, my God, no. Get outta there!!" Dani screamed.

"Chill out, New Girl, he'll be fine. Geeze!" Said The Actual Leader as he shook his head, disappointed at her fortitude.

"It's okay, Dani,--" The Wannabe Leader added, trying to calm her.

Dani was in firm disagreement with that assessment.

"RUN!" She screamed as two shadows slipped into the tent's edge. Malcolm's eyes lit with anticipation. Bryson's with disdain.

"Ah. Just in time. I was afraid we missed it," Malcolm said with a mischievous fascination.

Just then, the stranger started to scream as the bolts in the shackles around his wrists began to explode out of their hinges as he morphed and transformed. The only reason the Ringmaster wasn't scared was because he couldn't believe what he was witnessing. Dani both believed and understood, and she was going crazy over it.

"Get outta there, Mister! Run!! RUN!!!" She continued to scream, but no one was listening to her.

Now that the man was fully transformed into his bestial form, he could have easily pushed the rigged door down, but he wanted to prove a point, so he bent the bars open and ripped the door off the hinges. The kids, however, still weren't buying it. They booed and laughed, drowning out Dani's cries, until the beta leapt out of the cell toward the Ringmaster and bit him in the throat. Once the blood began to spew from his neck, the boos and laughter magically turned into screams as the kids, and drunks climbed over each other to get out of there. The tent was cleared in a matter of seconds, except for Dani, who hadn't noticed Malcolm and Bryson - yet. Her eyes were fixed on that beta, and his were fixed on her. Malcolm was on pins and needles as he took a seat in the opposite bleachers and readied himself for this part of the show.

"Alright, then. Let's see if our girl has learned more than nursery rhymes," Malcolm smiled.

Bryson exhaled a frustration-filled growl. He didn't understand Malcolm's dangerous fascination with this child, and he most certainly didn't like it. He would have ended her himself, but Malcolm would not allow it. He wanted to see how Bryson's beta handled his business, and so far, he seemed more than worthy enough to complete the assignment.

One thousand, one hundred and twenty-nine miles away, Lucien was lucky enough to be escorted by two of the prettiest and, no doubt, toughest women in town. Rayna and Cree bracketed the young warlock as they wandered along the riverfront at Algiers Point. In a few short minutes, thousands of partygoers would witness fourteen thousand glitter-filled rockets light up the sky above the Mississippi. It was difficult to tell who was more excited between Lucien and Cree as they stumbled upon a funnel cake booth.

"Ouu. You can't have fireworks without funnel cake," Cree gasped.

With much enthusiasm, Lucien nodded in agreement as he stuffed the last bite of his burger into his mouth. Rayna rolled her eyes and exhaled her way toward the booth. Lucien and Cree smiled, but the smile on the proficient practitioner's face was fleeting. Over the last six years, he had mastered a little bit of control over the unwanted gift bestowed upon him by his mother. He was no longer a victim to it, more like a participant in it, and as his body and mind grew, the pain it inflicted on him decreased. Whenever Dani mactrouged – full or half – Lucien was psychically yanked into it and could see through her eyes. His job was to assess the threat, implement the power given to him by Camille and vanquish it. Simple. The twins were quite formidable when they worked together, although Dani didn't actually know that they were. That was the problem. She mistook Lucien's voice in her head as her own thoughts - her conscience, and when they were out of sync, the mental and physical strain that Lucien exuded was, at times, too much for his body and mind to take.

Lucien loved his sister. Even if he hadn't been plagued with the power bestowed upon him by his mother, he still would have done anything he could to protect her, but sometimes he just wanted to be a kid – like now. What he failed to understand is that she felt the very same way. When Dani hit full mactrouge, his head buzzed like static as their bond lit up—vision, sensation, instinct—flowing both ways. He winced and let the tiniest grunt escape his mouth, which, unfortunately, didn't go unnoticed by his malafec escorts due to their heightened senses.

"What's wrong?" Cree asked.

Rayna was in the funnel cake line, twenty feet away. She couldn't hear Lucien with the noise from the crowd around her, but she could hear Cree. She swiveled around to check on Luc and saw him pop down, out of her view.

"Nothin'," Luc said. "Just gotta tie my shoe."

Rayna looked to Cree, who shook her head and mouthed, *"Tying his shoe."* Rayna nodded and turned away. At almost ten years old, Lucien Gerard was fluent in four languages, yet he pretended as if no one had ever taught him to tie a shoe. He fumbled with the laces as he surmised his sister's situation.

"Malcolm," Lucien thought.

"—On the fourth of July," Dani finished.

One thought. Two minds.

"Look at that," Malcolm whispered to Bryson. "Full mactrouge. Amazing."

Bryson was not the least bit impressed as Malcolm looked on with great anticipation. His beta charged, and Dani launched a series of tiny blasts that kept him off balance. Lucien knew that wasn't going to be enough. He blinked, and his eyes turned red for a quick second before falling back to normal. It boosted Dani's next blast, and as he pushed himself up from his shoe, he discreetly adjusted her trajectory, and Dani's blast nailed the beta. It wasn't enough to kill him, but it hurt him pretty good as he fell and crashed through the stands.

Malcolm winced, as did Bryson, but for different reasons. Bryson felt the pain of his beta - all of it.

Back in New Orleans, the fireworks were just about to begin.

"Look, Luc, it's startin'," Cree said.

Lucien turned toward the lake and moved in front of Cree so she couldn't see his face as he continued to concentrate and monitor his sister. He was happy he hadn't had to do very much, but he also knew it was far from over.

"It's not over. Stay aware and watch your back for the--" Lucien's thought was interrupted.

It hinted to Dani that she should be fearful of an ambush from a hidden vampire, so she immediately leapt over where the beta had crashed through the bleachers, toward the center of the tent.

"--Vampire," Lucien finished his thought. *"NO, don't jump!"* But that thought was too late.

A vampire tackled Dani in mid-air, and they both crashed to the ground. He picked her up by her neck and squeezed. She scratched and clawed at him, but he was way too strong for her to do any kind of damage that way. Her hair fell to her shoulders as the red in her eyes began to flicker, and with that, Lucien's connection was beginning to close. He had to act quickly. If she fell out of mactrouge completely, the connection would be broken and he wouldn't be able to help her. He faked a sneeze, and the red popped into his eyes again, but this time he needed to hold it longer, so he kept himself bent over with his hand covering his nose.

"I need a tissue!" he mumbled, trying to buy some time as he held the red in both his and Dani's eyes.

He knew Cree didn't have a tissue, but he wasn't expecting the busy-body next to her to pull a box out of her suitcase of a purse.

"Here you are, young man," Mrs. Busy-Body said.

"Thank you!" Lucien replied.

He grabbed a few tissues and started to fake-clean his nose. He had to act fast, in more ways than one, as the vampire had shown his teeth and was pulling Dani in to finish her. With added pain, he increased his concentration, and with a thought, several pieces of splintered wood from the shattered bleachers rose up and flew toward Dani and the vampire. They lodged themselves deep into the vampire's back and legs. The vampire dropped Dani, and she laid on the tent floor as she gasped for air.

"Mag-nificent," Malcolm whispered to himself.

For the first time, Luc and Dani both saw Malcolm, and that was the motivation that Dani needed.

"You all right, young man?" Mrs. Busy-Body asked. "You need some more?"

"No, thank you, ma'am," Lucien said cordially, as he popped his head up with normal eyes. "Thank you!" he shouted.

"You're welcome, dear!" Mrs. Busy-Body shouted back.

The fireworks were revving up, and things were getting loud, and Malcolm was there. This was far from over. He looked over his shoulder to check on Rayna. She had reached the front of the line, and they were sprinkling a generous amount of powdered sugar on his funnel cake. He didn't have much time.

"Come on! You can do this!" He thought.

Dani shifted into full mactrouge again as her hair lifted off her shoulders. The anger and frustration inside her erupted out through a powerful scream, followed by a burst of energy that sent the vampire flying backward. He quickly regained his footing and readied himself for another run as Dani locked eyes and focused on a jagged, wooden tent post. It shivered, lifted, and hurtled through the air. One second later, the vampire exploded into dust. Malcolm applauded with sincere zeal for her effort.

"Truly magnificent, my dear," Malcolm said as the injured beta erupted from the wooden bleachers and leapt toward her again.

Before Lucien could blink, two gunshots were heard, and the beta fell to the ground, dead. He morphed back into his naked human form as Kaitlin ran over to Dani with a gun in her hand. Malcolm was not at all happy by this. Lucien, however, was momentarily relieved. Kaitlin had saved the day, temporarily, anyway, and he didn't have to risk revealing himself to the crowd to do it. Now the problem became who was going to save Kaitlin.

CHAPTER 33

That's what big brothers do

"FOUL!" Malcolm cried out. He snapped his fingers, and the gun flew from Kaitlin's grasp, into Malcolm's hand before she could fire it again. He held it in front of Bryson, who was recovering from his beta's death. The gun pushed the alpha to become even more enraged after he smelled the fumes.

"Silver-r-r-r-r," Bryson growled.

"I wish to never have the pleasure of seeing her pretty face again," Malcolm said.

"No one will," Bryson said as he rose.

Bryson was interrupted when the canvas above them screamed as it tore. Wind rushed in as the entire tent collapsed, one wall at a time —until all that remained was sky... and The Talisman.

Dani gasped. Her knees buckled and she wet herself as she fell out of mactrouge. The connection was lost, and there was nothing Lucien could do to help her. Malcolm stopped Bryson from interfering. He did not know of The Talisman or what he was capable of, but he was very interested to find out. Kaitlin tried to pull Dani away, and The Talisman thrust his hand in Kaitlin's direction, sending her flying backward. She landed awkwardly on her back as The Talisman strode toward Dani, who seemed to be in shock.

Back in New Orleans, Lucien was in a panic. He felt helpless, angry and scared. He was supposed to be there for her, to help her, and he had failed. His eyes began to well up.

"No! She'll find a way! She'll find a way and I have to be ready! But what am I gonna do?" he thought.

What was he going to do? There were no bathrooms for him to hide in. Even if there were, how would he get there? He had no chance of outrunning either of the two females with him. There was only one thing he could do. He had faith that his sister would somehow re-establish the connection, and when she did, he needed to be ready. He turned to Cree with tears in his eyes, and the smile swiftly fell from her face.

"What's wrong?!" Cree said.

"Get me out of here," Lucien begged, chest heaving. "Now." He whispered.

His tears weren't from pain—they were from failure. He'd lost her. And he needed to get her back before it was too late.

"RAYNA!" Cree roared.

Rayna dropped the funnel cake and pushed through the crowd in seconds.

"Get me outta here,--" Lucien cried as he doubled over. When he came up, his eyes were blood red. "NOW!"

Rayna scooped him up and pushed his head in her chest to hide the red in his eyes.

"Make a hole and get us to the car as easy as we can without making a scene," Rayna ordered Cree.

With this many people around, they couldn't just take off. People would get hurt, and they would be exposed, and that was not acceptable. Cree opened a path through the crowd as fast as she could, with Rayna on her heels. She didn't hurt anyone, but when she moved someone, they stayed moved.

At the fair, Bryson was none too happy to be sidelined by Malcolm.

"Why did you stop me?!"

"Lycans," Malcolm said as he shook his head. "Always so anxious to rush into a fight. Why don't we see what this player can do before we engage, hmmm?" Malcolm said, then, "Come on, little one..." Malcolm whispered. "Get up."

"Fight! Fight, God damn it! FIGHT!" Kaitlin screamed as she tried to fight off her pain and get up.

Malcolm looked at Kaitlin, then twirled his index finger in a winding motion and flicked a tiny energy jolt at Dani. It was enough to snap her out of shock and back into the fight. Her eyes flared back to red. She didn't understand why, but something inside her had snapped into place—like someone had turned the lights back on. Flames burst into her palms without thought. This time, she didn't question them.

Rayna and Cree had escaped the crowd and made it to the street. As soon as they rounded a corner and felt reasonably safe, Rayna kicked off her heels.

"Follow me!" She ordered Cree, and they jetted off to the cover of a nearby park.

Just as Rayna laid Lucien down, he convulsed and screamed, then went into full mactrouge. He looked like he was in serious pain as his body tensed and tightened.

"What's wrong with him?!" Cree cried out.

"I don't know, but I don't think we should disturb him," Rayna said. "Do a quick sweep. Make sure no one's around."

"Okay, but I kinda have to change," Cree said, seemingly embarrassed by the fact. "I can't hold it off much longer."

Rayna sighed, then nodded to Cree.

"Go. Check the area, but stay out of sight. Then meet us back at the house when you can."

Cree nodded, then painfully burst out of her clothes, into her bestial form. She took a few extra deep breaths, then jetted off.

Lucien knew the only chance they had was if he took control, and as painful as that was for him, he did it anyway.

Dani jumped up and snapped her fingers, as Lucien did earlier at the house, and her hands flamed up. This seemed to surprise her more than it did Malcolm. She thrust her hands in the Talisman's direction and created a barrier of fire between them.

"Goood," Malcolm commended her.

The Talisman, not at all dissuaded by this, inhaled and sucked in all the flames and blew them back toward her, creating a flamethrower-like beam of fire. She screamed and instinctively raised her arms, creating a force field to block it. She then spun around as she collected it and slingshotted it back at him. It hit him like a sledgehammer. He barreled into a carnival booth, and it burst into flames. That was all she had, all both of them had, as Dani fell to the ground. A second later, The Talisman exploded out of the flames. He smoldered as his singed clothes repaired themselves and he strode her way.

"This is absolutely amazing. And you wanted to fight that," Malcolm said to Bryson, who did not respond.

"No more play, girl. Been chasin' you far too long. It's time for you to come wit' meee-- Uhhnnn!"

Kaitlin staggered, battered, bloody, and furious. She grabbed a nearby tow hook and rammed it into his back with every ounce of rage she had left. The Talisman was shocked, as was Malcolm and the crowd watching. The Talisman turned and snatched Kaitlin by her throat.

"Uh-Oh," Malcolm said, completely unsympathetic to Kaitlin's predicament.

"...Fall preeeey to Talisman..." he said, completing his warning from earlier.

The Talisman removed his glasses, and his eyes began to swirl.

"...D-Dani...The chain,--" Kaitlin gasped.

The hook was connected to a long, thick chain attached to a giant tractor. Both Dani and Lucien concentrated as her hair floated off her shoulders. Fascinated, Malcolm looked on. Dani quivered from the strain, which quickly built into a scream, and magically the machine started and shifted into gear. The tractor plowed deep into the cranberry marsh next to the tent and snatched The Talisman along with it. He released Kaitlin as the tractor dragged him behind it and submerged him deep into the marsh. A line of blood fell from Dani's nostril as her hair settled, and the blue came back to her eyes just before they closed, and she fell to the ground. Kaitlin crawled over to her and picked her up. She looked to where Malcolm was, but he was gone. She took Dani and made her way through the mumbling crowd of onlookers as fast as she could manage. Malcolm and Bryson watched from the crowd.

"Let me go after them," Bryson asked.

"...No. She's earned this day." He said with pride.

Moments later, the Dobermans drudged out of the cranberry marsh. The crowd backed away from them as they shook themselves off. Malcolm discreetly flashed his eyes red. Not even Bryson knew. The dogs began to sneeze uncontrollably. Disoriented, they barked and snapped at each other a bit before taking off in the opposite direction of Dani and Kaitlin. Malcolm smiled as he and Bryson moved off and disappeared in the crowd as the Dobermans raced across the fairgrounds.

It was early morning when Lucien woke up and found himself at home, in his bed, with Rayna and Cree hovering over him.

"Tell me you're okay," Rayna said.

"…I'm okay," he answered like someone who thought they were about to get in trouble would.

"Good. Now tell me what's going on."

Lucien considered himself to be an excellent liar when he needed to be. A gift he had inherited from his grandfather, but he knew against Rayna, he didn't have a chance, so he told her almost everything. He figured if he gave her a few good tidbits of truth, he might be able to get a few 'lies by omission' past her.

"I told you guys I could feel Dani's presence sometimes. I didn't tell you that I could feel her pain."

"Why?" Rayna asked as her brow wrinkled.

"'Cuz if I did, I was afraid you guys would try and stop me from helpin' her."

"Help her do what, Luc?" Cree asked.

"Fight. She was gettin' attacked by Malcolm and The Talisman," he said as tears started to fall from his eyes.

"You saw this?" asked Rayna.

"Yes."

"What about your dad and Tirin?"

"I don't know. All I can see is what she sees, and only when she's in mactrouge. I see it in my head. I saw Malcolm, and then I saw The Talisman."

"Go call Tirin," Rayna said to Cree. "Find out if they were attacked and if they're all right."

"NO!" Lucien cried. "If dad finds out, he'll stop me, and I can't stop! She needs me! She's out there all alone, and I'm the only one who can help her!"

"Baby, I can't lie to Tirin, you know that," Cree said.

"Don't lie, just don't tell him what he doesn't ask," Rayna said.

"What?!" Cree said.

Cree was shocked that Rayna would even ask her to do such a thing because Rayna knew what Tirin would do if he found out, and they both knew he would eventually find out.

"Say I was concerned," Rayna said. "I read the cards and saw something strange. I asked you to call and verify. All those things are true, are they not?"

"Yes, but,--"

"Then that's all that needs to be said. FOR NOW," she emphasized.

Cree sighed. She didn't like this at all, but for Lucien's sake, she complied.

"Fine. But when he asks, and he will, I'll tell him everything, and he's not going to be happy with either of us," Cree said before she zipped out of the room.

Rayna liked Cree a lot, and she felt bad about putting her in that situation, knowing that eventually she would be disciplined for it. She was also proud that she was willing to take the impending discipline for the young man lying in this bed.

"Cree just did a very big thing for you. So did I, because eventually all this comes back to me. Why does this need to be a secret?"

"...Long time ago, before I knew Dani was a girl, I thought Momma liked him more than she liked me, and it made me sad. Then one day she told me the reason why she spent more time with Dani was because she needed to protect him because he wasn't as strong as me. Then she told me that it was my job to look after him and protect him when she was gone," he said as tears fell from his eyes. "'Cuz... 'Cuz that's what big brothers do. So that's what I'm gonna do."

Rayna hugged him so hard she was afraid she might break him, but she was so proud of him and didn't want to let go.

"You keep right on protecting her, you hear me?" Rayna said.

"Yes, ma'am," Lucien said.

"And I'll make sure that no one ever stops you."

She kissed him on the cheek, and they sat there and stared at each other for a moment.

"You sure you're all right, Buck?" she asked. He nodded. "You hungry?"

"No. I'm just tired."

"Mm. Magic comes with a cost." She said, almost to herself. "Get some rest. We'll talk later."

She kissed him again, turned off the light and closed the door as she left the room. Halfway down the hall, she met Cree.

"Wherever that was, they weren't there. They're on their way back," Cree said. "Minus Mr. Endicot."

"Did Lucien come up?"

"...No, but it's just a matter of time. You know how much he loves Luc, and he's still never let the bathroom incident, from the courthouse, go. He knows Luc's hiding something, and he'll never stop searching until he finds out what it is."

"I know," Rayna said. "Neither will I."

Rayna walked away as Cree stood there for a moment, confused.

"I thought you just did," Cree thought.

CHAPTER 34

"**N**one that I have faced are more difficult to kill."

Hagatha's venom laced every word, as she continued to weave through Jean's subconscious like coiled smoke.

"You think you can hide behind this one forever?! HA! When we are one, my love, my lover, my lover for life and free from this prison; free of strife,... I will scour the world for this one, and know that when I find her, lover,... I will TAKE MY TIME! Her torture will last one day longer than yours! AHH-HA-HA-HA-HA-HA-HAAAA!"

Jean didn't speak. Couldn't. His meditative dreamscape trembled as her laughter scraped across his mind. A single tear slipped down his cheek.

Haiti

July 1992

On the first Saturday of every month, the outreach program that supports the Boucan Carre Mission, allotted for the hour-long trip to the marketplace in Beau Pere. The trip to the giant bazaar featured hundreds of shops and tents selling everything from exotic edibles to textiles and handmade jewelry. It was written into the schedule, not only as a means to collect needed supplies, but also as an enjoyable, entertaining reward for the hard work and diligence put in by both the mission staff and students. It was a fun getaway that everyone looked forward to every month, and Jean was no exception. He had told Kaitlin about this day weeks in advance and couldn't wait to share the magical marketplace with her. All was well until Kaitlin spotted the male and female lycan, Medjine, who had hunted her shortly after she had arrived in Haiti just over a month ago. Kaitlin froze as Medjine and the male, along with three others she had not seen before, stared her down from across the street. She unconsciously dropped a piece of fruit, which tipped Jean off that something was wrong. Jean followed Kaitlin's eyes and found the five betas to be the cause of the bruised fruit and Kaitlin's spiked anxiety. Not only were they alive, but none of them had any noticeable injuries.

"Kaitlin,--" Jean tried to say.

"But, I-I... I saw you... kill them," Kaitlin whispered.

"Their tissues have the power to regenerate at a highly accelerated rate. There are more powerful malafecs, but none that I have faced are more difficult to... kill."

That was not exactly what Kaitlin wanted or needed to hear.

"...I want to go."

"You need not fear. They will not harm you. Not here," Jean said as he stared them down.

As Kaitlin turned, she bumped into yet another unpleasant surprise: her much-too-helpful guide, Michael. He was donning a pricey piece of custom jewelry, obvious spoils from his dirty dealings. He seemed more surprised to see her than the reverse. The fear and anxiety Kaitlin was experiencing was displaced with an acrimonious umbrage that was more than deserving.

"You!" Kaitlin exclaimed.

"M-Ma'am, I-I-I--" Michael stuttered before being silenced by Jean grabbing him by the neck.

Jean switched the position and maneuvered Michael into a chokehold, and squeezed.

"Jean, what are you doing?!" Kaitlin said as she watched Michael struggle.

"This is an example of the lowest form of human life," Jean explained as a crowd had begun to form.

"Jean, let him go. Stop it! You're killing him!" Kaitlin yelled.

"He does not deserve to live," Jean said as he stared at the five betas and tightened the chokehold on Michael.

The betas hated Jean and wanted to come to Michael's aid. Medjine growled, and the other four readied themselves as the crowd backed away, giving them space. Jean's eyes ignited, and he smiled, daring them to come forward. With reluctance, the betas backed down, all but Medjine. She stood her ground, her hate-filled eyes locked on Jean.

"Jean... Please..." Kaitlin begged, then placed her hand on his arm.

Jean was so locked in his own rage that he nearly forgot she was there. He shot a look her way and saw the fear in her eyes. He also saw compassion, something he had forgotten a long time ago. It settled him and brought him back from the bitter place he had built for himself. His eyes faded to normal, and he let Michael go. Michael dropped to his knees, gasping and coughing, trying to intake as much air as he could. Medjine defiantly stepped forward and helped Michael up, then spat at Jean's feet.

"Ya' time draws near, Priest," she said to Jean before turning to Kaitlin. "And I will take great pleasure in watchin' what 'appens to you."

She snapped at Kaitlin, making her jump, and Jean's eyes flashed blue, causing Medjine a great deal of pain. The female beta tried to scream, but was magically silenced by Jean. She fell to her knees and huddled up on the ground. All this hostility and violence was too much for Kaitlin. It was not who she was, and even though some of it was for her benefit, she did not approve. She fought through the crowd and ran away. Jean's eyes faded to normal, and Medjine was released from her pain. He looked down at her and Michael, then found the eyes of the other four in the crowd. It was more than obvious, the special hate they carried for him, and if they didn't know before, it was made clear on this day that the feeling was mutual. He turned and ran after Kaitlin.

205

CHAPTER 35

$\mathcal{H}$*azel*

Haiti

July 1992

Nearly a mile away from Jean and Kaitlin, in a quiet shop on the outskirts of the bazaar, Father Arron had accomplished all his clerical duties, gathered all the necessary supplies on his list, and placed all the mandatory orders for next month. He was now free to explore the hidden wonders of the marketplace. Yet something clung to the back of his thoughts. A presence. It created a subtle tension that seemed to follow him throughout the marketplace like a shadow waiting in the crowd. Arron was an avid chess player, and by far, the best in the mission. He organized a chess club and held tournaments after classes up until the dinner bell, and happily taught the game to anyone who was interested in learning. For years, he had wanted to learn how to play the Tridimensional chess game, made famous by the old 'Star Trek' television show, but had never been able to get his hands on one. Earlier in the day, he had overheard that there was an antique shop in the marketplace that might have procured a set, completely intact and in good condition. A hard-to-believe rumor for this part of the world, but anyone acquainted with the good father knew that those were the type of breadcrumbs he would follow every time. The disappointment that followed as the shop owner shook his head 'no' was quickly masked by a presence he had not felt in a very long time. The shop owner's look gave nothing away. It was one of, neither fear nor excitement, neither anger nor sadness. If anything, it was a wonder. The bell on the door had not rung. No one could recall it even being opened, yet someone else was there. Arron did not wish to turn around, he was compelled to by the very presence he had felt traveling with him the entire day. Behind him stood a tall, strong, beautiful, black Haitian woman in her early twenties with a radiant smile that could almost rival Kaitlin's, if not for the hunger that loomed just below the surface.

"Hello, Father. Rememba' me?" the woman whispered.

...He did. In her eyes, he saw a memory that had haunted him for nearly eleven years. The memory of a scared twelve-year-old girl, taken from her bed at the Sacred Heart Mission by an angry mob. He saw her dragged into the street like a bag that was too heavy to carry. He saw her gagged so that her cries could not be heard, and bound so she could not run away. He saw her tossed into a cage like a rabid animal, and then he saw her look at him as he stood in the crowd - watching. She saw him watch as they hoisted her cage onto a cart and wheeled her through the gates of the mission. Her muffled cries went unanswered as she begged him for help with tear-filled eyes, and as the gate closed behind her, she saw him turn away. She watched him the entire time because he was the one who was supposed to protect her, and she watched him do nothing.

"Hazel..." Arron whispered, not realizing he had said her name out loud.

She smiled at the acknowledgment.

"I tol' ya' he'd rememba' me," she said to the huge Haitian man in his late twenties who had entered from the back of the shop unnoticed. "I was his favorite."

The large man moved to her side with his eyes locked on Arron.

"I t'ink ya' know my friend, Holton," she giggled. "Him rememba' you."

Holton let out a soft growl as the shop owner timidly reached for the shotgun under the counter.

"Shotgun be no good to ya', Mr. Owner Man. It just piss 'em off."

The owner backed away from the counter and raised his hands.

"We... I... thought you were dead," Arron stammered.

"Usually what 'appens when ya' toss a twelve-year-old girl off a cliff," she said.

"Hazel, you falling off that cliff eleven years ago,--"

"TOSSED, Father," she emphasized. "Like a sack a' yams."

Arron did not dispute Hazel's claim. He couldn't.

"You were afraid of me?" Hazel asked, her voice a mash-up of anger, sadness, confusion and pain.

"No! I-- I never thought you were... You were supposed to be held!" Arron said, releasing all the pent-up emotion with it. "That's all! For your safety as well as the village's. I swear. But... the people panicked and,--"

"Ya' said nothin'. D'ey listen to ya', Father. They'd a done anythin' ya' asked. And ya' just... turned away," she said as a tear ran down her face.

Arron lowered his head because she was right. He wasn't afraid, perhaps he should have been, but he wasn't. He was ashamed. Hazel extended her hand, and Arron reached out and grabbed it.

"I forgive ya', Father," she said. "'Cuz if not fo' d'at night, I wouldn't be da' woman I am today."

Her eyes illuminated red, and she squeezed.

"So I come back to t'ank each an' everyone a ya' personally."

Arron couldn't break free of her grip as the pain became unbearable.

"What about da' houngan?" Holton growled.

"Mmmm, Laveau..." Hazel smiled. "Him I missed most of all. D'at smile and d'em pretty, blue, glowin' eyes-s-s...."

Arron dropped to his knees, and Hazel pulled his hand closer. She squeezed until his wrist popped and his hand peeled open like a blossom under duress.

"Did ya' know he was my first kiss, Father? Hmm? Him tell ya' d'at? Ohhhh, da' times we had." She smiled as she burned a message on his palm with her glowing fingernail. "Me an' him got some catchin' up to do. Maybe you tell 'em come see me tonight, huh?"

Arron began to scream as smoke started to come from his hand.

"'Dis' my address. You tell'em, Hazel say to come on by. I'll be waitin' for him," she said with a sinister smile.

She released Arron's hand, and he fell to the ground, unconscious.

"Oh-h-h-h. This one I li-i-ike... Show me more," Hagatha whispered.

CHAPTER 36

The Coffee Table

Haiti

July 1992

"She's angry. She blames me, and rightfully so. I abandoned her because of my ignorance and fear," Arron said as Jean bandaged his hand.

"No, Father. I am the one she is angry with. The message was for me… I will go to her," Jean said.

There was an unusual solemnness in his voice and disposition that was completely missed by Father Arron.

"Absolutely not! She was not your responsibility then, and she is definitely not now."

"Why?"

"She's a witch, Jean—full-grown and fully awakened. We have no choice but to wait for help."

"From whom? The Council?"

"YES! She is as much their problem as she is ours."

"So you would call upon one evil to destroy another?"

"It's not that simple, Jean, and you know it!" Arron said, his frustration and fear getting the better of him. "Do not twist my words and turn them against me!"

"What is it you think they can do that I cannot? That I will not?" Jean asked in the most earnest way.

Arron looked at Jean and stopped. Only now did he detect his solemn disposition. Only now could he see the pain in his eyes.

"...What is necessary," Arron said with as much empathy and compassion as he could.

"Hazel died eleven years ago. The woman who revealed herself to you today is someone that I do not know."

"On the contrary, my son. She is a woman you know all too well, and now that woman is a full-grown witch."

"All the more reason I must deal with this swiftly, before others are hurt."

"Jean, listen to me,--" Arron started, but did not finish.

Jean's emotions had finally gotten the better of him, and he could hold them no longer.

"She was innocent, Father!... She did nothing eleven years ago but copy me!... We were playing a game. I revealed my magic and was deemed a voodoo priest of the highest order. She revealed hers and was condemned for it. This is not The Council's mess to clean. It is mine. The evil present here now is because I... because I did nothing. Because I was afraid to stop it. I cannot afford to make that mistake again."

Jean headed for the door.

"She has the alpha, Holton with her," Arron said in a pain-filled voice. He hoped if nothing else, that would stop Jean. "You remember your last encounter with him?" Jean did not respond. "I cannot put you at risk again."

"I am here to be put at risk, Father... It is all that I am here for."

"*All?*" Arron said as he shook his head, not trying to hide the bitter taste caused by Jean's choice of words. "Oh, Jean. There are so many who would disagree with that."

"I cannot hide from this. I have to face her, Father. You know she will not rest until I do."

"They are the most powerful demons on this planet. I don't know that… I do not know that you will be enough."

"…If I do not return by sunrise, you should contact The Council. They may be your only hope."

Father Arron embraced Jean and held him tight. He did not want to let him go, for fear he may not ever see him again.

"Listen to me and listen well. If you do not release this guilt you harbor, you will not be able to fight her, and you will die." Jean struggled with Arron's words. "What happened to that girl eleven years ago was not your fault. Nor is it your fault what she has become…"

Father Arron blessed Jean and broke down. Jean set him down and kissed him on the forehead before he exited the room. Kaitlin was waiting in the hallway. She had heard everything. They stared at each other for what seemed like a lifetime, but neither knew what to say.

"Kaitlin,--"

"You know how we're always arguing over who makes better chai tea, Father Tanzi or Father Morelli?" she interrupted.

"…Yes."

"Well, I never told you, but there's this coffee house in New Orleans called The Coffee Table. You know, like a coffee table, but it's an analogy for,--"

"I understand."

"Anyway, no disrespect to Father Tanzi or Father Morelli, but the chai at this place is unbelievable. You really need to taste it. I mean, I don't think we can have a truly objective discussion on chai tea unless all the samples have been tasted. Right?"

Jean nodded, then Kaitlin's eyes fell to the floor, and she asked the question she had intended to ask from the beginning.

"Did you love her?"

"…A long time ago,… yes."

"And now?…" she asked as she found his eyes.

Jean so badly wanted to say yes. He thought it might relieve some of the guilt that he was harboring if he could, but as he stared back into Kaitlin's eyes, all he could see was the love he had for her. It pained him to shake his head no.

"So I was thinking; my job here will be over in a few weeks, and I'll be going back home, and I thought, maybe you might like to go - with me - to The Coffee Table - in New Orleans - to try the tea."

"...I would like that very much."

"Then it's a date?"

"...It is," he said softly, holding her gaze a moment longer.

"Good. Because if you say you're going to come to New Orleans with me, that's like a promise and holy men never break promises, right?... Right?" She asked as the tears began to flow.

Jean embraced her and held her tight. He hoped it was a promise he could keep.

CHAPTER 37

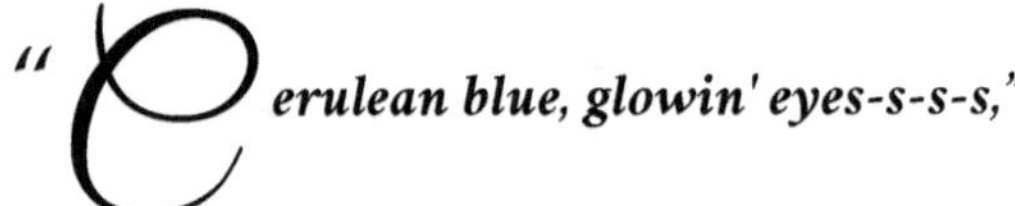

Haiti

July 1992

The moon was large, but not quite full, as it sat just above the mountain tops off in the horizon. It lit up the night and created a clear path through the dense growth of the Central Plateau and enabled the large black raven to easily spot the well-lit shack on the shore of a small pond in the distance. The large bird landed in a tree, and a now-human Jean jumped out of it onto the outskirts of a field of waist-high grass and foliage. He sensed danger in front of him and stopped.

"Bonjour, Jean. I knew you'd come. Even if ya' are eleven years late."

"…Show yourself to me."

Through the tall grass, Jean saw Hazel come out of the pond next to the shack naked. She was silhouetted and partially blocked by the large leaves and vegetation between them. She took her time as she dried her wet body while she spoke to him.

"Is my adult form not desirable to ya'?" Hazel asked. "Or do you now prefer one d'at is soft'a, weak'a, like da' American whore ya' masquerade around wit'? D'ey tell me she is very pretty."

"Tell your friends to show themselves, Hazel. I heard the vampires from three hundred feet away, and the stench of the lycans is almost unbearable."

Hazel laughed—a sharp, guttural sound—and suddenly, the tall grass rustled as shadowy figures rose one by one, their silhouettes multiplying until twenty bodies loomed before him. Hazel tied a sarong around her waist and pulled a small tank top over her head as she stepped out of the shadows. She was very beautiful, but no amount of beauty could hide the evil that now resided in her.

"Oh, Jean. You always knew how to make me laugh," she smiled. Then, her tone changed to something more serious. "Aller!" she ordered. "Now!... Leave us."

There was an unmistakable malice in her words that Jean took note of as, one by one, the bodies dropped down below the grass. He watched as the tall grass folded and unfolded as they moved out of the field, taking great care to keep their distance from him - all but one. He moved straight toward Jean and stopped about ten feet in front of him, and rose up so tall, it seemed as if he could touch the sky. It was Holton, the alpha. Jean's eyes blazed blue, and his hands energized.

"Hol-ton; STOP," Hazel commanded, and he obeyed.

"You have trained your dog well," Jean said.

"Careful, luv'a. For him, d'is personal," Hazel warned.

"Want 'em to know," Holton demanded. "Want to see his face when he knows."

Hazel sighed. "Very well."

"MEDJINE!" Holton bellowed.

The grass behind Holton folded and unfolded itself toward Jean. Medjine popped up and stood next to Holton. The growl that exuded from her breath was full of hate and came from a place deep within her loins. It was accompanied by a stare that held equal weight and followed by a spit in his direction that carried enough malignance to destroy an entire village.

"She is my mate, Houngan!" Holton said. "Tonight, you alone pay fo' da' pain you 'ave caused her! Medjine, go-o-o."

Medjine roared, then ducked down and disappeared into the grass as Holton moved forward, toward Jean.

"Hol-ton..." Hazel calmly warned.

"And my price is da' blood of da' ones you love most," Holton said as he continued to move toward Jean. "No one touches da' girl! SHE'S MI-I-I-INE, RHA-A-A-R-RR!!"

"The mission," Jean gasped as Holton transformed into his bestial form.

Holton charged. Jean spun out of the way, then readied himself for battle, but Holton had disappeared into the night. Jean glanced back to where Hazel was, but she was gone. He turned to pursue the others only to find Hazel right in front of him. The cerulean blue fell from his eyes.

"Hazel, please. Do not do this."

"I waited fo' ya'. I waited fo' ya' to come an' rescue me. Even as I fell from 'da sky, I still believed ya' would come," she said as the tears fell from her face. "An' ya' never did... WHY?"

"I am sorry I failed you... I truly am," Jean said with tears in his eyes. "Let your anger and vengeance be for me. Do not punish them for the failures of a boy who was not brave enough to fight for the girl he loved."

"'D'ey murdered d'at girl, Jean. I cannot forgive d'em fo' d'at."

"Hazel, please... You know I cannot let you do this."

"D'en ya' 'ave to kill me to stop it."

Jean vehemently shook his head no.

"I love you, Jean... but if ya' don't... d'en, I'll kill you."

He could see how much it pained her to say that, and she could see how much it pained him to hear it.

"Hazel, let me help you."

"IT'S TOO LATE NOW!" She screamed. " Da' little girl is dead, an' da' woman d'at took her place... She's bad. Kill me. If ya' don't,... I cannot stop her from killin' ya'."

Jean wanted to reach out and pull her into his arms and hold her tight enough to make both their pains go away. Hazel wished that he would, but that moment, like so many others in life, was fleeting. It flickered and floated away until it was gone. Hazel blinked, and her brown eyes turned red.

"DO IT!" she screamed. "KILL ME! DO IT, OR I'LL KILL YA'!"

Father Arron was right. He could not do what was necessary. He threw a weak energy blast in her direction. It was not meant to hurt her, only distract her as he leaped into the air and turned into the large raven. Hazel blocked the blast, then leaped up and grabbed the bird, and they both fell to the ground. She landed on top of the re-transformed Jean and pinned him. Her skin took on a dark green tint, and her hair rose up and floated wildly around her. This is what she had become. Jean screamed as her nails grew into sharp talons that pierced his arms as she held him down. Unable to free himself, he transformed into hundreds of beetles that engulfed Hazel. She screamed and leaped into the air, hovered a few feet above the ground, and violently spun around, sending the beetles flying off of her. As they came back together, she exhaled a stream of fire on them, and they scattered and reformed behind her as Jean, with his clothes still smoldering from the flames.

Hazel turned to engage him, and long blades of grass rose up and snatched her to the ground. They snaked around her body and face, squeezing her to her limits, then pulled her under the soil. The ground began to shake, then a violent explosion ejected her from the earth and sent a wave of flames radiating out of her that torched the field. Jean threw up a force field to protect himself, then, with a forceful wave, overflowed the pond into the field, eradicating the flames. Hazel hovered in the air above the ground.

Her rage pulsed through the air, warping the grass around her with radiant heat as her body began to glow like a furnace stoked with fury. She opened her mouth and released a blood-curdling, sustained scream that disoriented Jean. He staggered about in pain as blood began to drip from his nose and ears, and he fell to his knees. With one last effort, he slammed his charged hands together, and it created a thunderous sonic '*BOOM!*' that canceled out the shrill and knocked Hazel to the ground.

She was back up before he could gather himself, and a brutal, high-speed, hand-to-hand battle ensued. Jean was on his heels as she punched, kicked, and slashed at him with a speed that was equal to his. He released close-range energy bombs that she skillfully deflected, and she was relentless. With her combination of speed and strength, he found himself incapable of sustaining a suitable defense for her onslaught. Inevitably, she wore him down. Exhausted, he stumbled and dropped his guard. It was only for a second, but one second for a witch can be an awfully long time. "She toyed with him, each strike more vicious than the last—slashes that burned, fists that cracked bone, the punishment unrelenting." Jean tried to defend himself, but she was too strong. Finally, she hit him with a monstrous combination that knocked him off his feet, then caught him in mid-air with a powerful Qi blast that sent him violently to the ground. Bloodied and badly beaten, his Qi began to flicker as the blue glow faded from his eyes and hands. She charged herself and sent a sustained energy blast as Jean melted into a shadow and disappeared.

"Erabam-merket-feliza-radun-YA-A-A-A!" she yelled with a hateful tongue.

The incantation caused the sky to rumble as the wind wildly raced about. Clouds formed and blocked out the luminous moon, eliminating the contrasting shadows, leaving only darkness in its wake. A soft rain began to fall as lightning flashed throughout the sky. In those brief moments of light, a battered and bloody Jean was revealed behind her, on his hands and knees. He did not attempt to rise. He knew he didn't have the strength within him to do so. Hazel smiled with an earned confidence as she turned to face him and, highlighted by the illumination from the streaking bolts of lightning, she began to transform. The tall, strong frame she had presented to him was just a facade, an image of the woman she thought she might have become. She screamed in pain as her spine curved forward, and her shoulders scrunched tightly together, forcing a well-defined bulge in her upper back to protrude. It sat heavy on her left shoulder, and the weight of it seemed more than her once 5'9" frame could bear as she leaned considerably to that side. Her long neck had shriveled and tilted forward, almost horizontal to the ground. She winced as she forced her head up and twisted her chin to the right so that her left eye, the only one that remained, could see. The red glow faded from the hate-filled eye as it did her gnarled hands and partially paralyzed fingers. This grotesque form—this shell of pain and vengeance—was now her only truth. She stepped toward him with her right leg, dragging her busted left leg and twisted foot behind her. A laborious task that she seemed to have become accustomed to. Within each flash of lightning, she flickered, back and forth, from the tall, strong woman he had been in love with, the woman whom he had empathized with moments ago, to the grotesque creature who had become nothing more than a vessel, filled of anger and hate; a container for evil.

"You see me? You see what they did to me?" She asked him in a withered, raspy voice. "What,… you did to me."

Jean closed his eyes, but his tears squeezed through. It pained him to look at her. Not because of what she had become but because of the guilt he harbored for letting it happen.

"Hazel--"

"No, not yet, luv'a. Not gonna kill ya' yet. Gonna keep ya' alive awhile. Be a good boy and stay alive fo' meeeee."

Jean opened his eyes, his breath steady now, his gaze sharp with newfound focus. Hazel didn't notice that he was becoming rhythmically in sync with the wind. He was becoming in-tune with the elements, and as his focus grew, so did the storm.

"Want ya' to hear how d'ey raped your precious village and tortured d'at American whore; Want you to smell her blood on Holton's fingers. I want ya' to beg to die - like I did; layin', broken at da' bottom of d'at ravine - waitin' fo' ya' to come."

He raised his head as the rain increased, and his eyes radiated cerulean blue. Hazel's smile widened as she showed him the talons on her right hand.

"Oooooohh. I always liked those cerulean blue, glowin' eyessss…… Let me 'ave one."

In an instant, her hands and eyes pulsed back to red, and she charged. Jean raised his right arm to the sky, and like a lightning rod, he was struck simultaneously by several bolts. Using his body as a conduit, he redirected the energy down his torso through his outstretched left arm to her. The pain was unfathomable, and the scream he produced testified to that. He fought to hold on and to sustain the incredible energy that flowed through his body. Hazel's scream matched his as she fought to withstand it. It was an eternity's worth of torture that lasted a mere three seconds. Three seconds that one of them would never forget. "When the smoke cleared, all that remained of Hazel were charred fragments—unrecognizable, save for the haunting echo of the woman she once was." Next to her, Jean's body lay lifeless on the ground. The gentle rain from the fading storm was just enough to keep him awake as he floated in and out of consciousness.

Then he remembered, *"The Mission..."*

The raven flew perilously low over the trees to the mission. He didn't have the strength to get to his normal flying height. It was obvious that a large battle had taken place and that there were many casualties on both sides. Inside the confines of the mission walls, the raven crashed to the ground and transformed into Jean. It was everything he could do to get up, and it was probably unwise given the shape he was in, but he needed to find Kaitlin.

"...Kaitlin!... KAITLIN!" Jean screamed as he wandered around as if he were lost.

He stumbled upon Father Arron on the ground in front of the church. Jean turned him over to find his arm was broken, and he was bleeding from a wound to his head.

"I tried to stop them, but-- Awhh!... I'm sorry."

"Wh-where is she?..."

Arron looked to the church. Jean dragged him to a bench in the courtyard and propped him up before he went inside. He opened the door of the tiny church, and his head began to spin.

"Oh, God, no,--"

Suddenly, there didn't seem to be enough air in the world to support his breathing as his chest tightened. An unconscious Kaitlin was bound to the giant cross above the altar. A pool of blood had gathered on the floor beneath her from two very precise cuts to her lower abdominal region. He struggled to move forward, but the air became thin, his vision became blurred, and his battered body was more than his legs could carry. He collapsed on the floor in front of her, and unconsciousness took him away.

"YOU..." Hagatha exhaled as if what she had just seen in his mind had injured her in some way. *"You killed my sister,"* Hagatha exhaled. *"MUR-DERER-R-R-R-R-A-A-A-A-A-A-A-A-A-A- A!!"*

The scream seemed to puncture Jean's head and pierce his eardrums as his catatonic body quivered. It was followed by a welcomed and much-needed silence. For several moments, all he heard was her haggard breathing. It sounded as if she was in pain, or maybe,... as if she was crying. Then she whispered to him, devoid of all emotion:

"They will invent new words to describe the pain I'm going to inflict on you... I'm going to rip you apart slowly, then make great haste in putting you back together for the sheer joy of ripping you apart again. Pray to whatever God you worship; hitherto, forever, you are denied the pleasure of death, Jean Laveau. From now until the end of time,... YOU. ARE. MINE."

Hagatha remained silent for a very long time. Years might have passed before she spoke to him again. Jean did not know. She left him alone to reflect on Hazel's memory, and that may have been the worst thing she could have done to him.

<h1 style="text-align:center">CHAPTER 38</h1>

*M*r. Perfect

Dale City, Virginia
May 2012

If more people saw the butcher's section behind the grocery store, there likely wouldn't be one. Fifteen-year-old Dani hopscotched her way over the small pools of blood on her way to the time clock next to the office to punch out. She didn't mind the blood; she had seen more than her share in her fifteen years, she just didn't want it on her white tennis shoes. She removed her apron as Mr. Johnson, the store manager, came out of the office with her paycheck in hand.

"Here you go, young lady," the manager said.

"Thanks, Mr. Johnson," Dani smiled.

She was genuinely happy. Not just because she was being given money, as every teenager smiles when they receive it, whether it be in the form of cash or check, but for some reason, it makes it more special when you earn it.

"Dani, you know Patti Lynn's goin' on maternity leave next week.

Well, Al and I talked it over, and we thought you'd be the best person to replace her on register three," Mr. Johnson said.

"Seriously?" Dani replied, trying to hold in her excitement.

"You'd have to join the union, and you'd get the worst shifts being the new girl, but you'd be makin' at least five hundred dollars more a week with overtime."

If Dani's eyes opened any wider, they would have fallen out of her head.

"Oh my God!" she squealed. "Thank you, Mr. Johnson!"

"No, thank you," he said with earnest sincerity and gratitude. "You're the best employee we have. You never complain. Don't think you've been late once in eighteen months, and all the customers love you. You keep on, and next year, we'll be promoting you to my job."

Dani beamed with pride as Mr. Johnson walked off. It meant the world to her for him to say those things. She released her ponytail and gave her head a good shake as she exited the back of the store, looking more like her mother than Kaitlin would be comfortable with. Another employee came out shortly after she did. Eighteen-year-old Austin James, with his perfect smile and perfect hair that seemed to never need to be combed. He was just a tad too good-looking for his own good, but to Dani, he was, well, perfect.

"Hey, Dani! Wait up!" Austin called and then ran after her as a car full of high school girls drove by.

"HEY, AUSTIN!" they screamed.

Austin flashed his perfect smile, oblivious to the effect it had—not just on the girls, but on Dani's suddenly racing heart.

"You need a ride?" one of the girls asked.

"Naw, I'm good. Thanks, though."

All the girls seemed to puff out their bottom lip and pout as they continued on their way, disappointed and even a bit confused that Mr. Perfect would rather walk with some no-name underclassman than ride with them. Dani also seemed shocked by this interesting turn of events. So much so that it actually made her a little uncomfortable. She dropped her gaze like she was facing down an alpha wolf. Funny thing was, Dani never bowed to lycans—but this boy? He rattled her.

"Hey, Austin," Dani forced out of her throat.

"Congrats on the promo. That's huge," Austin said.

"Thanks," she nodded with a cracked smile as a bonus.

"I just hope they let you off for the Senior Prom," Mr. Perfect said slyly.

"I'm not going to the prom, Austin. I'm just a sophomore."

"That doesn't matter as long as your date is a senior… Like me."

There it was. The reason behind his perfectly timed exit. The reason he rushed after her with every perfect hair in place. The reason he perfectly avoided a car full of teenage co-eds. He had planned this perfectly, and Dani had no idea what to do. At fifteen years old, she had fought and defeated more creatures, been on the winning side of more fights, seen more blood, both hers and others, than she would care to remember. She had survived all that to be made so nervous that she thought she might actually puke because an eighteen-year-old human boy asked her out. She said nothing. Her voice had vanished—lost somewhere between her stomach and her throat. Her gross motor skills were in overdrive, though, and working well outside of her control as she began to walk at a pace much faster than her body wished to go. It made it seem as if she was trying to get away from him. Austin sped up and jumped in front of her in an attempt to force her to stop. It worked. Dani stopped but found herself unable to look up at him. She wanted to. She tried to, but her body wasn't really listening to her demands right now. She was flustered and having a difficult time breathing. Right now, her only goal was to not pass out.

"I know it's kinda last minute, but, well, you're not really the easiest person in the world to talk to. Ya' know?"

Talk?! In the past year, she had actually attended a school on a regular basis; walked through busy hallways; eaten lunch in a cafeteria – with other people. Those were huge accomplishments for her. To actually talk to someone? She was gonna need another year to cross that one off her bucket list.

"Austin, I-I-I--"

"Wait. Let me do this right and make it official: Dani, would you be my date to the prom?" he asked perfectly.

Dani's head popped up, and she made eye contact with him. A mistake, because now she couldn't stop looking at him. She was certain that he could see her shivering. He could probably hear her knees knocking together. Her mouth wanted to say, "YES!" but her body shook her head no.

"I-I don't think I,... I can't,--"

"Please."

"You... You can go with any girl you want, Austin."

"I hope that's true, 'cuz I really want to go with you."

The perfect response, of course. How could she say no? She couldn't even stop looking at that perfect smile on his perfect face. As she sank into his perfect eyes, she wondered if this was how vampires entranced their prey—helpless, breathless, willing. She had completely forgotten why she was fighting against it. When she finally got home, Kaitlin reminded her.

"It's too dangerous!" Kaitlin said in a rather loud voice.

"We've been here almost two years! We've never gone this long before! Maybe it's over."

"You know better than that."

"Well, if that's true, then it's even more important that I go."

"Dani,--"

"All my life, all I wanted was to feel normal. Go to school, kiss a boy... We have friends here. Good jobs. People like us. Please, Kate? If I'm gonna die, then let me at least live once. Please?"

Kaitlin was right. It was too dangerous. It wasn't over, and it never would be, but Dani was right as well. She knew she was on borrowed time, but she had more than earned a shot at a normal life, even if it was only an illusion. "Kaitlin knew it was a mistake—and still, she couldn't bring herself to say no. Because no parent could look in their child's eyes and steal their only chance at a dream."

icture-Perfect

On the night of the prom, Austin showed up at Dani's doorstep in a brand new, blackberry pearl Dodge Challenger. It was his pop's, but for tonight, it was all his. Dani had asked to meet him at the venue—less about convenience, more about shame. No one needed to see where she lived. Not tonight, but Austin insisted that he pick her up, and he wouldn't take no for an answer. Partly because he wanted to show off the car, but mostly because it was the gentlemanly thing to do. To Dani's surprise, he wasn't taken aback by the fact that they rented a small trailer in a trailer park at all. He genuinely thought it was kinda cool; he genuinely thought *she* was kinda cool. The perfect kid was full of surprises. He sat down at the pull-down kitchen table and talked to Kaitlin for fifteen minutes while Dani finished getting ready. He actually had a real conversation with her – about literature, of all things. Even with her guarded instincts, Kaitlin couldn't help but be impressed by the young man. He was polite, engaging, passionate about his future, and well,… Perfect.

As they go, prom dresses aren't cheap, and Dani and Kaitlin really didn't have time to save up for one, so alternative measures needed to be employed. Normally, Kaitlin would never allow Dani to use her magic on such frivolities, but this wasn't just a dance. It was a once-in-a-lifetime moment that would never come again. A special dress was definitely required. When Dani stepped out, the room fell still. She wore a cobalt blue, sheer-bodice ball gown with a thigh-high split —elegant, bold, and powerful. Rayna would've smiled.

It was all Kaitlin could do to hold back her tears. She gasped, and two slipped out.

Dani looked so much more like Camille's sister than her daughter. Her long, curly, dark brown hair fell off her shoulders onto her back in the exact fashion that Camille's used to. If not for Dani's blue eyes, they could've been twins. For the first time, Austin seemed out of sorts. He nearly spilled his glass of water as he stood up when Dani entered the room. Many things he expected when he asked Dani to the prom. For her to look like this was not one of them. Normally, she did her best to hide her looks so as not to stick out; to just blend in, but on this night, in that dress, with her hair that way, the only place she'd blend in would be on a runway in Milan.

"Y-You look amazing," Austin said in a way that made Dani uncomfortable because she knew he really meant it.

Dani was used to receiving bruises, not compliments, so she didn't really know how to take them. Throw a right hook at her, she was fine, but in this moment, she wanted to turn around and go back into the bedroom. Since fleeing was not an option, she looked to Kaitlin for help.

"He's right. You do," Kaitlin nodded, then quickly gathered herself. "Alright, you two, let's get some pictures."

Kaitlin grabbed the disposable camera she had purchased from the drugstore earlier that day and saved Dani by breaking the nervous tension both she and Austin were experiencing.

"Oh, wait!" Austin said.

He ran out to the car, and there, in the passenger seat, rested the missing piece. He rushed back in with an azure-dyed Phalaenopsis orchid corsage.

"Now I'm ready," he said confidently.

Austin was back to being perfect again and had somehow managed to pick the perfect corsage, but who would expect anything less from him? He slid the corsage on Dani's wrist, and it fit - perfectly. 'SNAP' Kaitlin took the perfect picture and with that, Dani's picture-perfect night had begun. She embraced Kaitlin at the door, and the two of them stared at each other with dubious smiles on their faces. Neither of them believed they were actually doing this.

"Thank you," Dani said as she wiped a tear off of Kaitlin's cheek.

"Promise me you'll have fun," Kaitlin said.

Dani shrugged and offered Kaitlin a semi-panicked smile.

"I promise she will," Austin said perfectly. "And don't worry, Ms. Morrison. I'll have her home by one-thirt--"

"Twelve o'clock," Kaitlin interrupted.

"Ah, twelve o'clock," Austin nodded with a playfully perfect smirk, "and not a minute after."

Dani walked over to the car and reached for the door handle.

"Wait!" Austin called out with a little more volume in his voice than he had hoped for. "Sorry," he said at the level he was shooting for the previous time. "You need to let me do that kinda stuff for the rest of the night. Just doors and chairs and stuff, okay?"

Dani nodded, a little embarrassed by the faux pas. This was gonna take some getting used to for her. Austin opened the door, grabbed her hand, and slid her in. Dani bit her bottom lip, trying to tame the smile that insisted on breaking free. She wasn't used to joy arriving without consequence. It made no sense to her, and she had no idea why, but she liked how that felt. She liked everything that was happening right now, and, most importantly, she liked him – a lot. He was perfect, after all. When they pulled up to the auditorium, Austin nearly broke his ankle trying to get around the car and open the door for Dani before she did. He failed, but she remembered and closed it back and waited for him to do it.

"I'm sorry," she said with a sheepish grin.

"It's okay," Austin laughed.

He extended his hand to her, and she took it and held on tight. She could hear the muffled music above as they ascended the stairs to the venue, with every step bringing more clarity to the sounds and more anxiety to her. She squeezed his hand. His touch seemed to calm her nerves, but she had to contain her strength to make sure she didn't actually break it by the time they reached the top.

"You ready for this?" Austin smiled as he placed his hand on the door.

"…I don't know," Dani whispered.

Not even The Talisman had her this shaken. At least with him, she knew what to expect—fear, fight, survival. This? This was uncharted. Austin laughed, then he found her eyes and smiled.

"You'll be fine. Trust me."

For some reason, she did. Austin opened the door and led her into a magical world, the likes of which she had never before seen.

"Welcome to the Two Thousand and Twelve Senior Prom," Austin said.

Everyone and everything looked beautiful: the people, the decorations, the lights. For one night, they had converted the event dining room at The Potomac Science Center into heaven. The room was darkened and lit only by the constantly-moving stars, planets, and galaxies displayed onto the walls, floor, and ceiling by eighteen projectors, synced up and controlled by three laptop computers. It felt as if they were actually moving through space. Each round table for six had two orbs on it, each eight inches in diameter, providing additional lighting along with keeping the theme of the night intact. The DJ booth was a comet, elevated above the dance floor. Even Austin was blown away by the display. He knew what the theme was, but he had no idea it would turn out like this. Dani was so caught up in the spectacle she had forgotten how nervous she was. She didn't notice the gaggle of students who had flocked over to meet with them until Austin interrupted her dream with an introduction.

"Dani, this is everyone. Everyone,… meet Dani."

Dani was petrified. She had dreamed about this very moment every night for the past week. Nightmares, really. She'd imagined every version of disaster—his friends ignoring her, the girls whispering, the boys laughing, the night ending with her alone at a table for six, then the long, humiliating walk across the room to the door while the entire room whispered and giggled behind her.

The imagination of a fifteen-year-old can be a dangerous gift if not used properly. Not once did she ever dare to dream that they might actually - like her. That the girls would love her dress and ask her where she got it from, then be in awe when she told them she had made it herself. Not once did she envision that the boys would find her to be witty and have a great sense of humor, and compliment her on her great laugh. That each one of them might actually want a turn dancing with her, so they might get to know her better. Lost in the dark delusion of this being the worst night of her life, she never once gave breath that it may be her best.

The girls did, indeed, compliment her dress; the boys loved her laugh, and she spent most of the night dancing, talking, and making new friends. She was the belle of the ball, and no one was more proud of that than the perfect guy who brought her. No matter how much fun she was having or who she was talking to, she couldn't help but look for his eyes, wherever he was, and when she found them, he always had a perfect smile waiting for her. She didn't know what this feeling was that she felt every time she looked at him because she had never experienced it before, but whatever it was, she felt it was real.

She tasted foods well beyond her and Kaitlin's budget, and there was a chocolate fountain for dessert; a fountain that actually spewed warm chocolate. She learned how to line dance, took group and individual pictures with everyone to memorialize the occasion, and as this most incredible night grew long in the tooth, lost herself in Austin's arms as the DJ played the last song of the night: "Set Fire To The Rain" by Adele. The perfect song for a perfect night. One she would never forget.

CHAPTER 40

"*ou taste REALLY good,*"

Three cars were parked in a secluded little clearing overlooking Headly Run Creek, a not-so-secret make-out spot three miles outside of Dale City. Everyone who grew up in the area was familiar with Headly Run for various reasons, whether it was hiking, fishing, or a summer picnic with family and friends. These six teenagers, however, weren't up there that night to test out their fly-fishing technique. The prom guests at Austin and Dani's table were testing the waters in other ways. Two of them had gone for a quiet moonlight stroll through the trees east of the tiny clearing to practice their "breathing techniques" in private. The other two were conducting a science experiment in their car to see if they could figure out a way to make the temperature inside the car warmer than the temperature outside of it. Judging from the thick condensation on the windows, it would appear their experiment had been a successful one. At the top of the clearing was a broken-down, four-foot-high stone wall overlooking the creek. Austin sat on the wall with his back to the creek, while Dani stood next to him, staring down into the water.

"Are you cold?" Austin asked. "'Cuz we could sit in the car if you,--"

"No! I mean... Thanks... I'm fine," Dani replied.

Dani was everything but fine. She knew what this place was—everyone did—but now that she was here, standing on the edge of one of those moments, she felt like she'd forgotten the steps to a dance she'd never learned. She had no idea what she was supposed to do... Practice the weird and uncomfortable noises she was hearing from the two kids behind the tree line, or get back in the car and blow air on the windows to make them fog up. She'd had such a beautiful night up to this point, and she was freaking out because she didn't want to ruin it now. Right then, Austin leaned in to kiss her. As much as she wanted to, it caught her off guard, and she leaned away from him. Off-balance, Austin hopped off of the wall. Dani felt horrible. She could tell that Austin was embarrassed, and that was not at all her intention.

"I'm sorry,--" Dani tried to say.

"Sorry," said Austin, cutting her off.

"I'm just,--"

"No, I shouldn't have tried to,--"

Both of them were trying so hard to apologize that neither one was hearing the other.

"I never kissed a boy before."

Austin heard that. He immediately stopped talking and listened.

"I, I don't know how," Dani said.

She didn't understand why, but saying that was one of the hardest things she's ever done. Someday, she may understand that it was also one of the bravest.

"I'm sorry," she said. "Sorry for ruining your night."

Dani turned away from him. She felt humiliated and wanted to cry. Austin never gave her that chance. He placed his hand on her arm and turned her back to face him.

"You really need to stop apologizing for being you," he said. "I, for one, kinda like who you are."

"You don't know who I am, Austin. If you did, you probably wouldn't want to."

It hurt him to hear her say that. It turned his perfect smile upside down and brought a great sadness over him.

"What happened to you, Dani? What could someone do to make you like this?" he asked. "Whatever it was, you need to find a way to let it go, 'cuz it's killing you. You need to learn how to like yourself again. I need for you to dig you, as much as I dig you."

Dani smiled. That may have been the nicest thing anyone had ever said to her. A single tear rolled down her face, and Austin closed the small distance between them and brushed it away. He left his thumb on her cheek as he cupped her face in his palm and laid his fingers on the nape of her neck. Dani began to tremble, but she did not resist.

"Tilt your head up a bit," he instructed her. "Right there. Good. Now close your eyes and stick your tongue out."

Dani's face crinkled, puzzled by the request.

"Just try it," he smiled. His smile was enough to make her comply. "Now place your lips on your tongue; top lip touching the top side of your tongue, bottom lip touching the bottom," he asked; she complied. "Now, pull your tongue back into your mouth without closing it or letting your lips touch," he asked; she complied. "Perfect."

Austin gently kissed her—soft but sure. Just long enough to make her heart stutter and her fear forget itself, then he released her and backed up a step. They stared at each other, both full of astonishment at what had just taken place.

"Oh my, God, your lips are so soft," Dani whispered.

"You taste REALLY good," Austin gasped.

I think it's safe to say that neither one of them had expected such a prodigious result. It's also pretty safe to assume that neither one of them, at that moment, expected a vampire to leap over the wall and land on Austin's back, but that happened, too. The collision knocked Dani to the ground, and in an instant, the vampire locked up with Austin and sunk his teeth deep into his neck. Most of the time, vampires are extremely careful when they drink. They want to do their business and be off, leaving as little indication or evidence behind that they were ever there. This wasn't one of those times. This vampire brutally ripped and shredded Austin's neck like a rabid animal, lapping up as much of the blood as he could. He held his hand over Austin's mouth, muffling his screams, then sadistically twisted Austin's head, forcing the blood to spray out of Austin's neck, onto Dani's face. Dani sat there on the ground in shock, covered in Austin's blood.

Another girl's scream was heard as two more vampires dragged the couple in the woods back into the glade, and two other vampires dragged the third couple out of their car. The vampires held the kids at bay, facing Dani as they screamed and laughed at them while they intermittently fed off of them. Finally, Austin's vampire released him, and Austin's limp body fell forward into Dani's arms. The vampire then let out a long, raucous burp.

"Damn. You taste really good too, dude!" he said as he busted out laughing.

Dani didn't move. She just sat there with Austin in her arms. "She rocked him, back and forth, blood soaking into her dress. Her lips moved, but no sound came. There were no words for this." A sixth vampire, a woman, advanced from the woods and B-lined it straight over to Dani. She was different from the others; all business and a bit of an attitude to boot. Obviously, she was in charge of this little raiding party and was not here to bandy about.

"This is her?" she asked with skepticism flowing from her face. "This is the witch?"

"Yeah, this is the little bitch," Austin's killer said as he licked blood off of his hands and fingers.

"She's just a little freakin' girl," the leader said with her skepticism quickly turning to disgust. "I can't believe he sent all of us here for this." She knelt down to gather a better assessment of Dani. "My God, she's fucking hyperventilating."

"Yeah, I think she's gonna pass out," Austin's killer said.

"...Un-fucking-believable," the leader said as she shook her head.

She exhaled her frustration, then stood up to address her crew.

"Hey... HEY! Listen up, Jack-asses! We were sent here for witch blood, not that shit. Get rid of them, and let's fucking feast on this bitch and get the hell out of h,--"

Like lightning, Dani grabbed the leader's wrist and snapped it to the bone. The leader screamed from the pain of the compound fracture, and as she squirmed to get away from Dani's vice-like grip, some of her blood accidentally dripped onto Austin. Dani yanked her in close, grabbed her with both hands, and slung her into Austin's killer, knocking him down. The other vampires, using the other kids as shields, began to close in on Dani as she gently laid Austin's head on the ground and rose to face them.

"Kill this fucking,--" the leader screamed until she saw Dani's eyes flash red and watched her hair as it rose up off her shoulders. "Oh, shit!"

CHAPTER 41

New Orleans, Louisiana
May 2012

Although he was compared to his father much more than he liked, Lucien and Julien Gerard were two very different individuals, mainly because of their upbringing. Believe it or not, Julien was a street kid, well on his way to becoming a first-rate thug, just like his father. Barrett didn't want that, so at age twelve, he sent him off to the best private school money could buy and enacted 'special' means to keep him there. As an adult, Julien resented that. He felt he had been babied and kept in the dark on too many things, so he vowed he would not make the same mistake with his son. No posh, private schools, no babying. He wanted to keep it real with his son, and at fifteen years old, Lucien was anything but a baby. He dropped out of school, much to his father's dismay, and not because he wasn't smart enough. It was because he was too smart. He was every bit as brilliant as his father was, he just showed it in different ways.

Julien was a wannabe thug, turned book-smart businessman. Lucien was a street-smart shark, and the sky was the limit for what he'd turn out to be. He was fluent in six languages, and there was absolutely nothing he couldn't do with a computer keyboard at his fingertips. Like his father, he learned it on his own without the use of magic, but also like Julien, when it came to his sorcery, he was a deftly skilled artist, second to none. Perhaps he was more like his father than he knew. From a very young age, all warlocks are taught the importance of assembling a crew that is loyal to them. A laborious task that could take many years to complete, but a warlock is only as good as the malafecs he walks with and in most cases, they walk with their crew for life. Lucien's crew was comprised of two sibling vampires and a young, male alpha. The tandem team of Alvin and his sister Opal, both forever fly in their mid-twenties, and a nineteen-year-old alpha wolf named Mason, or "Mace" to the few who could call him that and survive.

This particular crew, on this particular night, could be found hustling pool at a local joint called Malaffections, a magically, mystical place that was accessible to both humans and malafecs. It was the type of place where you could get, or do just about anything you wanted, if you could pay for it, and the use of magic, of any kind, was strictly forbidden. Lucien never needed to use his magic for these kinds of things. He was just that good of a pool player. At fifteen, technically, he shouldn't even be allowed in the joint, but when your father is the majority owner, it's pretty hard to keep you out. The minority owner, Mademoiselle Phee, a terribly attractive and mysterious woman in her late thirties, wasn't at all crazy about the kids hanging out in her ultra-private club, but Lucien never caused her any trouble and, strangely, Mace actually lived there. He had a room all to himself on the third floor of the recently renovated, obscenely opulent, bordello-styled hotel.

The arcanely alluring Mademoiselle Phee was obviously more than a landlord to the young alpha, but neither he, nor she felt inclined to go into detail about their relationship, so Lucien never pried. All that mattered was that, both he and Lucien had free rein of the place, allowing them to enjoy all the little perks that this hedonistic hangout had to offer. Tonight, it was billiards. Nine-ball was Lucien's game and he was one shot away from winning when he received a long-distance 'call' from his little sister. Lucien had near-perfect control over the gift. As long as he wasn't taking over her body, tapping in from a distance caused him no harm. He mostly stayed out of Dani's mind. She didn't need him—not usually, anyway. He checked on her from time to time, to see where she was and how she was doing, but for the most part, he respected her privacy and stayed out of her personal affairs. Plus, he realized that she was generally strong enough to take care of herself now. This call felt different. He didn't know why, but it was. Lucien pulled back from the table with a concerned cast, then, with a focused urgency, began to break down his cue. Opal saw the look on his face and gave the ever-flirting Alvin a nudge, then garnered Mace's attention. Mace never watched Lucien. His eyes were always on everyone else.

"What's up player?" Alvin asked with a playful tone.

"It's Dani."

That was all they needed to hear. Unlike his family, the three of them knew what he did for his sister, so they understood the urgency of the moment.

"Sorry... I gotta go," Lucien said to his opponent.

"The fuck you do! That's my mutha' fuckin' money on the table," said his rather large and angry opponent.

Mace was normally a pretty quiet and laid-back kind of dude. The tall, gangly teenager never looked for trouble, but if it happened to show up, he was more than willing to handle it. He may look unassuming, but to assume that he was skittish about a confrontation would probably be the last assumption you'd ever make.

"I don't know that that type of language is necessary, sir," Mace said with his calm, soft-spoken voice, but his eyes said something different.

Normally, Lucien would let this little scenario play out, but his sister needed him, and neither he nor Mace wanted to cause a scene in Mademoiselle Phee's place, so he put a stop to it before it got started.

"No disrespect, friend," Lucien said. "I scratch. The money and the game are yours. We'll run it back some other time. Cool?"

Seeing as how he was losing horribly and was moments away from receiving a humiliating ass-whooping, with both his reputation and his money saved, the large man wisely let it go. Lucien broke down his stick, and he and his comrades quickly headed for the door, where Mademoiselle Phee was waiting for them. She had witnessed what just happened and was concerned.

"You okay, kid?" Mademoiselle Phee asked.

"Yeah, Phoenix, I'm good," Lucien responded.

Mace lowered his head as a soft, sigh-growl escaped his lips.

"You call me Phoenix in public one more time, you won't be."

"...Sorry."

"Now, what's up?" Mademoiselle Phee again asked.

She'd known him since he was a little kid, so she knew him well enough to know something was bothering him.

"Honestly, Phee, I ain't feelin' very good. Think I need to lie down fo' a minute," he said. "You mind if I get a room upstairs? Of course, I'll pay for it and,--"

"Come on," she said, with no intention of taking his money. Then, "did you eat?" She asked Mace.

"No, Ma'am, not yet," Mace said as he shook his head.

Mace was a very respectful dude, but he was always unusually respectful toward Mademoiselle Phee. Everyone knew this, but no one knew why. Phee tapped her tiny earpiece and spoke into the microphone on the side of her face.

"Raquel, find a table for Mason and his two friends. I'm sending them your way." P said, before nodding to Mason. "Go."

"Thank you, Ma'am," Alvin said, speaking for both he and Opal.

Mademoiselle Phee nodded and waved them into the dining room, then took Lucien up the service elevator to her private quarters.

"You need anything else?"

"For you not to tell my father?" Lucien asked, with a timid undertone.

"...Tell him what?" Phee asked, then closed the door.

Lucien sat down in her easy chair and closed his eyes. He concen-

trated as he assessed his sister's situation. Then a wave of anger overtook him that rose the hair up off his head.

"You care about your friends, bitch? DO YOU?!" the leader screamed
as she held her broken wrist. "She fucking blinks, rip every last one of
them to shreds."

Dani didn't blink, but Lucien did. Lightning flashed throughout
the sky, and a violent wind kicked up. Dani looked at the leader and
saw the fear in her eyes as the powerful wind held her and everyone
else prisoner in their own bodies. Lucien flicked his fingers, and
targeted energy blasts exploded from Dani's body toward the
vampires holding her friends. The blasts dislodged the vampires from
their prey and knocked them clear of the kids they were holding.
Then Lucien let his sister go to work.

"*Go get 'em,*" he thought.

That's what she heard, and that's what she did. Her eyes shifted to
a small branch on a nearby tree. It was more than adequate for her
purposes. She clenched her fist, and it snapped off the tree and flew
toward her, finding a home in her right hand. With accelerated speed,
she dusted through the violent assailants, save for two: the leader and
the killer. She stopped right in front of them in silence. Her chest
pulsated in and out from all the energy she had just expelled, and she
stared at them in a way that was very uncharacteristic of her. She had
evil in her eyes.

"Look, kid, we can work somethin' out. Huh?" Austin's killer said.
"We can just tell The Council that,--"

That's all Dani needed to know. She released the stake, and as it
fell:

"Push," Dani said, and the stake accelerated into the killer's foot,
and he screamed. Then she whispered, "Profunde."

The stake buried itself deeper and pierced through his foot,
pinning him to the ground. His screams were lost as Dani turned her
focus to the leader. Dani snatched her by the neck and lifted her until
her feet no longer touched the ground.

"Tell Malcolm, next time, I want my lesson from him," Dani said, then dropped the leader like the trash she was. "Dis potentia."

As the leader fell, a force grabbed hold of her and flung her into the forest like she had been shot out of a cannon. Her screams were silenced by the loud thud of her body as it smacked into a tree. No human would have survived the trauma of that collision, but she wasn't human. She would have been badly hurt, crippled, and her suffering would have continued for days, if not weeks, but the message would be delivered. Austin's killer would not be that lucky. Dani stared at him as the tears fell from her eyes and washed the red away. Lucien's connection was cut. He could no longer see, but he could feel her pain and see the thoughts in her head. He was powerful enough to re-establish a connection if he wanted to, but he knew she didn't need him anymore. So he just sat there and stayed with her in the only way he could.

"I wish I were strong enough to bring you back... just to kill you again. Every day... Because that's what you did to me!"

She punched him in his chest so hard that her hand ruptured his heart and broke a piece of the stone wall behind him. He disintegrated into dust, and she fell to her knees and sobbed until the rage got the best of her and she unleashed a deafening scream.

"Why?! WHHHHHHHHY?!!!"

It was so loud that the other kids were forced to cover their ears as the vibrations blasted a chunk out of the stone wall and sent it crashing into the creek below. She sat there a moment before she crawled over to Austin's body and, as gently as she could, scooped him up in her arms. She stood up and turned to see her friends, or what used to be her friends, on the ground with their ears still covered by their hands. She looked into each one of their eyes and saw the same thing: fear. And she thought her heart couldn't break any more. She had just saved them, and in doing so, became their worst nightmare. She carried Austin's body past them and placed him in the backseat of his car, then walked out of the glade and disappeared.

Lucien opened his eyes, and the tears came. Not from pain. Not from powerlessness. But from knowing this time, he couldn't protect her from the cost.

"I'm sorry, Sis," he whispered to himself, knowing she couldn't hear him.

CHAPTER 42

*I*mperfect

Dale City, Virginia
May 2012

It had been three days since the closed-casket funeral that she could not attend. She and Kaitlin had packed up and disappeared within an hour of Austin's death... Murder. They had grown skilled at vanishing under the cover of night. The trick was simple; Never fully unpack. Never have anything of real value that you can't keep on your person at all times, and... Never fall in love. There had been collateral damage in the past, innocent lives had been lost, but never anything like this. They had learned to keep their heads down, to be quiet, to not get involved and to keep everyone at a distance. Dani had broken every single one of those rules. Selfishly, she looked up, talked to people, made friends and fell in love, and because of that, she felt just as responsible for Austin's death as the vampire who took his life. In the past, they had always been a mystery; no one really knew who they were. From time to time, they would be mentioned on the local news or make a brief appearance in a headline on page three of the local paper, but it was always as 'young girl,' or 'two strangers,' or something of that nature. Today was the first day that her face was plastered on the news – a picture from the school yearbook that Kaitlin had always specifically told her NOT to take. Dani had always listened, except for this one time. They had never been anyplace this long. She liked it here, and people liked her. It was just a stupid high school picture. Who would care? What harm could it be? Now the sheriff was looking for her for question-ing. Austin was a very popular boy; his parents wanted answers, and the sheriff was determined to get them. He had questioned the other four kids who were present that night, and they all told the exact same story: that they had been attacked by a band of vampires – they all had the bite marks to prove it - and that Dani had saved them.

Knowing the friends she'd made that night stood by her gave her a fragile sense of solace. They hadn't turned on her, and they were appreciative of what she had done. More importantly, they didn't see her as a monster. The problem lied in *how* she saved them. That threw away the very little credibility the kids had. No one wanted to believe a story about vampires and witches, so it got turned into a teenage satanic ritual that got out of hand, and now the new girl and her black mom were the prime suspects in the murder of a local high school hero. Sometimes the best place to go when everyone is looking for you is no place. With all the helicopters and traffic cams and their faces plastered on the local news, Kaitlin knew that if they ran, the ol' red truck wouldn't get them very far. They drove the truck about a mile into the woods, and Dani camouflaged it magically, but Kaitlin knew that it was only a temporary fix. They couldn't run, but they couldn't stay here, either. If this wasn't resolved soon, this local story would turn into a national one, and once it reached Louisiana, their odyssey would be over. They might have a day before Julien arrived in town, and although they could probably hide from the local police, Tirin would hunt them down within a few hours. They had one shot to clean this up, but it was risky, and the clock was ticking. You never know what to expect when you open someone's eyes to the truth. Some will thank you for it. Others will curse you.

Sheriff Merl Talbert was on the phone in his office when the truth came through his door.

"Alright, lemme finish up here and I'll be home in an hour…" Talbert said over the phone. "I love you too. Bye."

He hung up the phone and was startled to find Dani sitting in the chair in front of him.

"What the,--!"

"Hello, Sheriff," Dani said.

"How the hell you get in here?"

"You know who I am, right?"

"I know who you are, and I'm gon' ask you one more time, how,--"

"Sheriff, we don't have a lot of time, and I know you have more pertinent questions to ask me than how I snuck into your office."

"…Alright then," Talbert said. He was a no-nonsense kind of guy, so he got right to it, "Did you kill the James boy?"

"No, and I think you already know that."

"Then why'd you run?" He asked her flat out.

She paused a moment before she answered.

"It seemed easier at the time."

"Easier than what? Telling the truth?"

Dani nodded.

"Most people don't want to hear the truth," she said.

"I'm the sheriff, Ms. Morrison. I ain't most people."

"Your daughter was one of the girls up there with us," Dani said. "What did she say?"

"Right now I'm more interested in what you have to say."

"It's gonna be pretty much the same thing."

"Fine, you wanna play this, I'll ask you like I asked her; With all this killin' goin' on, how come the only body we could find was the James boy?"

"When vampires die they turn to dust."

"How convenient."

"And four kids getting bitten in the neck by snakes and calling it a satanic ritual isn't?"

"Don't you sass me, little girl. 'Cuz I ain't the one on trial here. You wanna talk about vampires and witches, and yet ain't nobody offered up an ounce of evidence or a shred of proof! You don't like my story? Prove yours. You 'posed to be some, big-time, vampire killin' witch, right? Prove it!"

"I'm not a big-time witch, Sheriff. I'm probably not even a very good one, but I did come here to offer you some proof. I'm just afraid of what happens after that."

"Why's that?"

"Most people find it a bit unsettling."

"Thought we already agreed, I ain't most people?"

Dani sighs deeply, then, "My eyes will turn red and my hair will go crazy and float off my shoulders and head. You say you'll be okay with that. I know that you won't. You'll probably get so scared that you'll pull your gun, which will scare me and force me to take it away from you. Then you'll freak out and scream, and everybody out there will be running in here. Then we'll have a situation on our hands, and neither one of us wants that. I know I don't."

"Little girl, I ain't never screamed in my whole life. You think you can clear all this up? Then please, be my guest, 'cuz I'm gonna need all the help I can,--"

"Before Talbert could finish his sentence, Dani slipped into full mactrouge. Right on cue—he jumped up and pulled his gun."

"Venio!" Dani cried out, and the gun ripped out of Talbert's hand and flew into hers.

Dani fell out of mactrouge and sat quietly, looking down at the floor. She was embarrassed and afraid of what was next. Talbert stood at his desk in silence, trying to make sense of what just happened.

"...You okay?" Dani asked after a good ten seconds or so. Talbert nodded. "You want your gun back?" Talbert nodded once more. "You still want to shoot me?" Talbert shook his head. "Okay... Can you just,-- maybe sit down, 'cuz you're making me super nervous right now."

Talbert nodded and sat down as Dani got up and put the gun on his desk. He picked it up and awkwardly tried to holster it while seated, as Dani sat back down and crossed her legs yoga style in the chair. Neither one of them knew what to do next.

"...Sheriff,--"

"Why'd them vampires want to kill Austin?"

That question made her want to cry. She paused, gathered herself and held it back.

"Because he was with me… They were after me."

"Vampires and witches don't get along or somethin'?"

"Sheriff, we don't have time for this--"

"MAKE - TIME. You want me to help you? Help me make sense of this, because somehow, I gotta figure out a way to explain it."

Again, she sighed and tried to hold back her tears. This time it didn't work. "Three hundred years ago, a group of warlocks decided that witches were too dangerous to live after a certain age, so they hooked up with vampires and lycans – that's a werewolf, in case you didn't know, but I wouldn't call them that to their face. They're called The Council of Warlocks. They made my daddy kill my mom when I was four," she said as tears streamed down her face. "I was an anomaly, I guess,… a mistake, because, for whatever reason, they wanted me dead then, too. Katie, the woman you think is my mom, raised me and gave me her last name so I didn't have to use mine. They've been hunting us ever since, and if you don't let us go, they'll come back with more, and they'll kill whoever they have to, to make sure no one knows I ever existed. And because you put that picture on the air, my father and his people may already be on their way here. I don't know what his plans are for me, but I know he'll kill Katie without question. And there's something else that's been chasing me, and I can't even begin to explain that. Please,…" she cried, "lift the blockade and let us go!"

The sheriff nodded.

"Thank you," Dani said. "Now I need you to rush me to the cemetery. It's already dark, and we don't have much time."

"Time for what?"

Dani closed her eyes and shook her head. It killed her to say this.

"They turned Austin into a vampire, and if I don't stop him, he's gonna rise up and wreak havoc on this entire town."

Ten minutes later, Sheriff Talbert and Dani pulled up next to the ol' red truck outside of the cemetery, where Kaitlin was waiting for them. Dani jumped out, full of anxiety over what needed to be done.

"Evening, Ms. Morrison. Your girl here gave me a hell of a story--"

"Did he awaken?!" Dani interrupted.

"No, but it's close," Kaitlin said. "Are we free to go after this, Sheriff?"

"Yeah. We took care of that, but you still may get a few stops 'cuz of this ol' red truck here."

"Dani, change the color," Kaitlin said.

"I gotta get in there!--"

"You have time. Change the color, please."

Dani moved to the truck, placed her hand on the hood and popped into mactrouge.

"Soren yi; something old, Soren yi; something new. Soren change this color red to blue."

From where her hand touched the hood, a blue color ran through the truck like water and enveloped it. The sheriff could do nothing but shake his head in awe. Kaitlin reluctantly handed Dani a stake.

"Sweetie, I can--" Kaitlin tried to say.

"No. I have to," Dani said. "Come on, Sheriff."

Dani started to climb over the wall as Talbert awkwardly looked at Kaitlin. He was very uncomfortable with what was about to happen.

"I don't… Is this really necessary?" He asked.

"The first place he'll go is home," Kaitlin said.

Talbert turned and started to climb the wall. Dani had already scaled it, but Talbert was having a difficult time, so she gave him a magical little boost. Much to his disliking, he was lifted over the brick wall and set down on the other side a little harder than either one of them would have liked.

"You couldn't land me no softer than that!" He yelled.

"Sorry!"

"JE-SUS!--"

"I'M SORRY!" a discombobulated Dani said.

She was trying to hold it together, but was genuinely flustered over the entire situation. She helped him up, and they walked in silence over to the grave. Every step the sheriff took made him that much more uneasy about what was to come. He didn't realize that Dani had those same feelings, two-fold.

"Stay hidden," Dani said as they reached the grave. "If he sees you, he'll come after you, and that gun won't do you any good."

"You sure you're okay?" He asked.

He never got a response, but he didn't need one. Deep down, he knew she wasn't. Dani sat on the ground up against a large gravestone and solemnly watched over Austin's grave, waiting. The sheriff didn't question or bother her about how long this was supposed to take or any nonsense like that. He just waited with her. Twenty minutes later, to the sheriff's horror, the earth above Austin's grave began to move. A hand erupted through the soil, closely followed by another, then they clawed their way up. The head followed, with the torso not far behind. It was like witnessing a birth as they watched Austin pull himself out of the ground. Like any creature, being birthed is hard work, and the first thing they want to do when it's over, is eat. Austin sensed someone behind him, and he whipped around to see Dani seated calmly on the ground against a gravestone. She stood up with a smile propped on her mouth underneath her grief-filled eyes. Austin smiled back as he slowly walked toward her.

"Don't be afraid," he whispered.

"I'm not," Dani said.

"I'm not gonna hurt you."

"I know."

He stopped in front of her, and they both took each other in. In a way, they were both glad they got to see each other one last time.

"Could you-- Just,... Tilt your head back, and close your eyes for me one more time."

A tear rolled down Dani's face, but she complied with a nod.

"Yeah. Just like that... Perfect."

He showed his teeth and, as he moved in to "kiss" her, she brought a stake up through the bottom of his rib cage and punctured his heart. The last image she saw of his face was one of heartbreak, and then he was gone. She dropped the stake and stood there, quivering in the breeze. The sheriff walked over and held her.

Dani and Talbert climbed over the high stone wall of the cemetery and jumped to the ground. Kaitlin stood there in the shadows, waiting for them. Dani walked straight into her welcoming arms and burst into tears. There was nothing for Kaitlin to say. She could only imagine how difficult that task must have been, so she just held her and let her cry in peace.

"I uh,… already put the word out, but,… I'll make it very clear to everyone here that y'all are good people and never did anything wrong."

Kaitlin nodded, and as the sheriff turned to leave, the sound of a can being kicked broke the imperfect moment. They glanced down the street and saw a tall, dark shadowy figure.

"No!" Dani screamed, terrified of what was approaching.

The sheriff pulled his gun, afraid of whatever it was Dani thought was coming. Then an old black hobo moved into the light of the streetlamp and scampered across the street. He seemed to be more afraid of them than she was of him. Kaitlin exhaled her relief. Neither one of them was in any condition to do battle with The Talisman tonight. Then a low rumble echoed across the sky, and Dani's body stiffened. Something inside her broke loose. Kaitlin turned to find Dani with a freshly wet stain in her jeans between her legs, and she was hyperventilating in what looked to be a most unhealthy way. Kaitlin took a step to grab her, and Dani's hair began to float as her eyes faded red. This time, her hands also took on the red hue and began to glow. Energy seemed to be amassing in her body, with Dani having no control of it. It looked as if it would break her apart, and there was nothing Kaitlin could do to stop it. Talbert didn't know what to do. He was scared, and he had a gun in his hand.

"NO, DON'T SHOOT HER!" Kaitlin screamed as she threw herself in front of him.

"A-A-A-A-A-A-W-W-W-W-W-W!!!!!!!!" Dani screamed.

As her scream tore through the night, a blast of pure red energy erupted from her like a detonation, punching through the clouds and darkness alike. The force blew out all the streetlights and knocked both Kaitlin and Talbert to the ground. Then, just as quickly as it had started, it was over. Car alarms and barking dogs were heard off in the darkened distance. The sound of sirens followed shortly after. The only light for blocks was Dani's still-glowing body. She stood there shivering with a vacant, far-off look on her face. Kaitlin had never seen this before and was noticeably afraid. Talbert was too. He carefully holstered his gun, but kept his hand on it.

"Dani?..." Kaitlin said.

Dani didn't answer. Kaitlin rose to her feet and, with extreme caution, moved over to Dani as Talbert watched. She gently touched her shoulder, then slowly and delicately pulled her into an embrace. Dani began to cry. She didn't know what was happening to her. Neither did Kaitlin. And that was the most terrifying part of all.

Her hair settled and fell to her shoulders, and the red washed away from her eyes. Kaitlin nodded to Talbert that it was okay. He stared at them a moment, then took his hand off his gun.

"Come on baby," Kaitlin whispered. "We have to go."

Talbert nodded in agreement, then watched as Kaitlin put Dani in the Ol' Red, now Blue Truck, and drove away.

CHAPTER 43

She saw more darkness in him than in that unlit corner of the room.

Hagatha had been quiet for some time. Jean didn't know how long; he had lost all awareness of time. Days, months, perhaps even years had passed since he last heard her whispers, but his senses were keen. He knew she was still there, so he remained vigilant, and his thoughts were steadfast and fixed.

Haiti

July 1992

Kaitlin lay, unconscious, in the hospital bed. Jean, all bandaged up, knelt at her bedside, deep in prayer. Father Arron limped into the room, his arm in a sling. He also lowered his head and prayed. The village had sustained more casualties than at any time in recent memory. No one man, woman or child had escaped this battle unscathed, although the consequences for some seemed much higher than for others.

"She lost a great deal of blood, but she has a strong will to live,"

Arron said with a solemn tone. "There were, however,... complications... She was six weeks pregnant." Jean closed his eyes, but it did not stop his tears from falling. "The incisions were precise. Deliberate, and..."

Arron's pause was, perhaps, too long, but for him to say these next words was just as painful as it would be for Jean to receive them.

"She will never be able to have children again... I'm so sorry, my son."

Jean clung to the bedpost, his fingers white-knuckled, as if holding on could somehow tether him to hope. He sat there and cried silently, not daring to break the fragile quiet of her rest.

Once Hagatha saw Kaitlin's loss in Jean's dream and felt the weight of his pain, her self-imposed silence ended. A soft giggle fell out of her mouth. It multiplied in both volume and length as it grew into a chuckle, then turned into a deep, uninhibited laugh. Not the normal, sinister cackle she had exuded in the past, but an actual belly-shaking, button-busting laugh. It flourished and amplified until it reached a fever pitch and continued, without pause, for quite some time.

Several hours later, Jean was asleep in the chair next to Kaitlin's bed. A sudden gasp escaped her lips as pain woke her, and Jean, startled from sleep, found her watching him with a weak, forgiving smile. He moved to the bed and knelt at her side. She ran her fingers across his bandages and the bruises on his face. She was happy that he was alive.

"You came back to me," she said.

Jean didn't know if he had the strength to tell her as the tears began to pour from his eyes. Instead, she cradled his face gently.

"Shhhh. It's okay. We're okay."

He didn't have to tell her. She already knew. Somehow, that made it worse.

August 1992

Three weeks later, Kaitlin sat on her bed in her room with her two packed suitcases next to her. Her time in Boucan Carre had come to an end, and she was scheduled to leave for home in the morning. Jean had promised to join her, but she was worried that something inside of him may have changed. Jean stood at the window with his back to her, soberly staring down at the people in the courtyard. Both the children and the adults moved about as if everything was back to normal. They seemed to have forgotten the tragic events of three weeks ago. Even Kaitlin wanted to move on and let it go, but Jean clung to it like a wound that refused to close.

"I don't care about them, Jean. I just want to go home," Kaitlin said.

"We will. After they pay for what they have done," Jean said, devoid of all emotion.

He seemed cold and detached from everything, including her.

"And then what? One of them seeks revenge for what you do? It never ends this way."

"It will tonight."

"Jean, please,... Please, don't do this," she pleaded. "Don't go. Please! Stay with me and let's leave this place tonight."

"We cannot leave at night. It's too dangerous, you know that."

He moved away from the window and knelt before her, placing her hands in his.

"Do not worry; we will soon sip chai tea at a coffee table on Bourbon Street," he said with a smile. "I will return to you this night and we shall leave together in the morning... I promise."

He kissed her, then walked over to a shadowy corner near the window. When she turned back, she saw more darkness in him than in that unlit corner of the room. He closed his eyes and stepped into the shadows—letting the darkness swallow him whole.

CHAPTER 44

he Lost Soul

Haiti

August 1992

It is a fact that in every place where large populations of malafecs exist, there will be a place, or places, that cater to them. Basic supply and demand, or in this case, demand and supply. That is how the integration between humans and malafecs began. To say that all malafecs are bad would be equivalent to saying that all humans are good, and we all know that's just not true. For some malafecs, it is enough to just exist, and they like doing so in peace. There are places all over the world where they can go to eat and drink what they like and be with who they wish to be with, sans harassment or judgment, as long as they can pay for it. Haiti is no exception. The tiny island has one of the lowest ratios of humans-to-malafecs in the world. A place like that would obviously have a big demand, and Jean Laveau knew one of the places that was always available to meet it.

Five miles northwest of Boucan Carre, there was a seedy bar on the outskirts of Beau Pere. The locals called it, 'L'âme Perdue'; The Lost Soul. A few humans had free range and could come and go as they pleased, and then there was Jean Laveau. The moment he entered the place it went silent. As he moved through the room, a few malafecs growled or stared him down, but most dared not cross his path. Most. A large vampire seemed to take exception to his being there and stepped in front of him.

"You think you can just walk up in,--" the vampire tried to say.

Jean never gave him the opportunity to finish. With incredible speed, he drew a stake from his coat, staked the imbecile and replaced the stake without breaking his stride. At that point, several malafecs thought it would be a good time to exit the bar. They all either knew Jean or knew of him. Whether they cared for him or not, they had respect for him and what he was capable of.

In the back corner, five malafecs circled a table—varied, wary, and silent. One female beta sat among them. Medjine. She didn't turn, but she knew he was there. He stopped behind her chair, and the other malafecs at the table got up and moved away. Jean walked around to face her and sat in the now-empty seat next to her. She knew why he was there; she knew what she had done, and she was scared, but she was a lycan. She would show him no fear and be defiant to the end. Jean stared at her hands, then shifted his eyes to hers and stayed with them much longer than any normal man should.

"Her wounds were too small for someone with hands the size of your boyfriend's," Jean said.

Medjine said nothing, then her lips curled into a smile as six brave betas, probably from her pack, surrounded the table. They were nearly undetectable. Nearly. Jean didn't care about them. His eyes never wavered from hers. His lack of concern uncurled the smile from her lips, leaving apprehension and uncertainty in its wake.

"Holton gonna rip ya' to shreds, Houngan," Medjine tried to say with as much pleasure and contempt as she could muster. "He'll be here in a minute."

"That will be fifty seconds too late for you."

The cerulean blue hue faded into Jean's eyes as the six lycans surrounding the table charged. Jean's hand swept from his coat. Silver rods flew—pencil-thin and deadly—piercing the air like thrown light. Six of them found a home in each of the lycans. Two more found their way into two random malafecs who were a little too close to business that didn't concern them. Fortunately, one was a vampire. He survived. The others fell to the floor. Medjine was enraged. She roared as loud as she could, then rose up to attack. Jean struck her square in the chest. Her breath caught, her eyes widened—and then her body went limp, collapsing over the table's edge. As she fell, a retractable silver stake in Jean's coat sleeve was revealed. He removed it from his wrist, took off his coat, sat back down, folded his arms across his chest and waited. He didn't have to wait long before a monstrous roar was heard off in the distance; then again, this time closer. Like roaches, the malafecs began to scatter out of the room as another roar was heard. The ceiling lights began to swing, and the corrugated walls on the shack vibrated and shook. Seconds later, a huge lycan crashed through the door like a wrecking ball, splintering it. He stopped when he saw Jean seated next to Medjine's dead body. He surveyed the room to find all six of his betas scattered on the floor. His bellowing roar nearly shook the shack to the ground, and still Jean did not move. The huge alpha transformed down into Holton, except for the long, razor-sharp talons on his huge fingers. Now, Jean stood. He stepped over Medjine's body and challenged the hulking man by holding his glare. Like all alphas, Holton is patient, even in anger. He slowly circled Jean, studying him, looking for the slightest flinch.

"No one gonna save ya' d'is time, boy. Gonna kill ya', then I'm gonna kill every man, woman and child in d'at mission. 'Cept 'in d'at gir-r-rl. Got other plans, now, for her-r-r-r."

Jean extended a silver stake and took a defensive stance as his eyes and hands glowed blue.

"You will have to step over my dead body first."

"D'at's da' plan," Holton nodded.

In a blur, Holton streaked across the floor toward Jean. For a creature of his size, his agility was incredible. He was somehow able to avoid the stake and most of the perfectly-timed energy blasts. Jean was no less impressive. He matched Holton's speed and intensity step for step, avoiding his razor-sharp talons, but having to eat a few of the monstrous blows from his fists. Then Holton began to change, at will, from beast to his human form to try and gain any advantage in this war. They laid waste to the bar and, eventually, to each other. In the end, a single ceiling light flickered as it swung. On one pass, it revealed shattered wreckage. On the next, Jean's bloodied form slumped over Holton's massive corpse. Jean pushed himself off Holton and fell to the floor. He lay there, on his back, watching the ceiling light swing. It was hypnotic. His eyes faded to normal, and his lids grew heavy from the rhythmic sound it made, but this was not the place for consciousness to be lost. He clutched the wound from an errant talon he caught in his side and staggered to his feet. Then he froze; his body tensed, and his eyes reignited with a low, cerulean blue hue. He was no longer alone. Vampires. He felt their eyes all around him, closing in from every direction. He reached for his pouch of trinkets, but it was gone – ripped from his belt during the battle. He was surrounded, weakened, and badly injured. Not even he could defeat them like this. Then, from the black void where the door had once stood, Michael emerged—calm, silent, and smiling.

"Au revoir, Laveau," Michael smirked.

The air was stale and musty in this room, so Michael's words hung there a little longer as the stealthy assassins skillfully stalked Jean without making the slightest of sounds. All that was heard was that single ceiling light as it swung back and forth, creating a dizzying array of shadows as the bulb flickered off and on.

"*The light,*" he thought.

Jean blinked, and the blue in his eyes illuminated as two broken chair legs flew into his hands. Like a ghost, he flickered and flashed in and out of the shadows and dusted every single vampire in the room. He reappeared, disoriented and dizzy, painfully sucking air into his burning lungs as the light swung back and forth above him. The swinging light should've been the only sound other than that which came from him, but there was something else. DRIP. DRIP. DRIP. It was almost deafening as it echoed in his ears.

"What is that?" he wondered.

He looked down and saw blood dripping from the stake in his left hand.

"Impossible!"

Jean swung around to find Michael slumped on the ground, clutching his chest, fighting to hold onto his last breaths. All Jean could do was watch, until Michael's chest moved no more. Some might say it was an unfortunate mistake, that it didn't matter because Michael was bad. Some would be right, but it was a mistake that Jean was not allowed to make, and good or bad, it was still murder. Jean fell to his knees and lowered his head in shame as the thunder rumbled in the distance.

A storm was coming.

A heavy rain drenched the Boucan Carre compound the next morning. Kaitlin had fallen asleep on the bed in the same spot she had sat the night before. The door opened, and Father Arron entered and sat next to her. He whispered something to her and Kaitlin burst into tears. He cradled her in his arms and held her tight as the rain pounded on her window.

The storm had arrived.

Jean's dream had turned into a dream he wished to dream no more. Some call those nightmares. When he brought himself out of the self-induced dream state, he found the ground in Hagatha's cave had become moist. The local forecast had predicted that there would be severe flooding throughout the southern Louisiana area. Water seeped up from the earth all around him and began to trickle into the cave.

The level rapidly rose around Jean's body, and just as it was about to overtake him, he became buoyant.

"*AH-HA-HA-HA-HA-A-A-A!*" Hagatha cackled.

Then the storm took him away.

CHAPTER 45

"*How stupid are you?*"

The hard, violent rain pelted Jean's partially decayed body as he floated beyond the limits of the cave.

"Wake up, my lover, my love, my blitheful delight; your bride awaits on this auspicious night. AH-HA-HA-HA-HA-A--"

Suddenly, Hagatha stopped her lurid laughter as if she had somehow been interrupted; as if her privacy had been invaded.

"...No. No, this is not for you. Get out! GET O-O-OUT! Leave us! HE'S M-I-I-INE!"

A flash of light opened up in a cloud, and a single rod of lightning escaped. It crackled as it slashed a path to the ground and exploded – *BOOM!*

Willard, New Mexico
July 2017

Twenty-year-old Dani jolted upright, heart racing, breath ragged. The truck's interior slowly came into focus, the rain hammering against the windows grounding her in reality. She stayed still, unsure if she really was awake—or still inside one of the many nightmares she had over the years that involved Jean Laveau. She sat straight up in the passenger seat of the ol' red, now blue truck. She remained very still, as if she were afraid to move. It's always disorienting coming out of a nightmare, but this one was different. It felt like she was pushed. She found comfort in the rhythmic sound of the hard rain that pelted the truck, and her body relaxed, and she folded herself into the back cushion of the pick-up. As she adjusted the rear-view mirror to check her hair, she noticed a large sign on the street that told her they were in someplace called, "Willard, NM." She didn't care. She was more concerned about her hair. She was frustrated and a bit angry that it wasn't quite as long as her mother's was at her age.

She pushed the mirror back and turned to see that Kaitlin had just about finished up in the motel office. Then her gaze met the clerk's through the rain-speckled window. He was about her age, maybe a little older, and his nostrils flared ever-so-slightly every time Kaitlin lowered her head. A beta. Dani turned away and sighed. Kaitlin exited the office and ran to the truck to avoid getting soaked in the rain.

"Okay, Sleeping Beauty, we're all set, and don't think you're gonna stay up all night, either."

"I don't think we'll be stayin' here very long."

Kaitlin looked back inside and saw the guy, on the phone, staring at them.

"Damn it!... Why can't you get these feelings before I pay?" Kaitlin said as they pulled off toward their room.

Thirty minutes later, a key was heard engaging the lock of their darkened room. The door flew open, and someone rushed in and dove onto the bed. Dani, seated comfortably in a chair next to the night table, flicked on the light to find the beta from the office had just destroyed an innocent pillow.

"How stupid are you?" Dani asked, just as two vampires walked into the room.

"How stupid are *you*?" asked Beta Boy.

Dani broke off the arm of the chair and, with a quickness that surprised the young man, staked the two vampires before they could move. She then tossed the stake away and bid the office guy to come forward.

"Come on, Beta Boy. Let's see what you got."

It was obvious from the expression on his face that he thought things might have gone differently, but he was a beta, and he wasn't about to back down. Plus, he didn't really care for being called "Beta Boy." He leaped off the bed and attacked her with an impressive skill and quickness that didn't suit his goofy exterior. The only thing more impressive than him was her. She didn't have her mother's polish or power—yet. But Dani could fight. And that, she did better than most. Dani was a street fighter, and the girl could flat-out throw down. Even Tirin would've been impressed. She tossed Beta Boy around the room like a rag doll, and she wasn't even breathing hard. She sent him barreling into the far wall, and as the demoralized dunce slid to the floor, four shots were fired in his direction. Dani's eyes gleamed red, and although her hair wasn't quite as long as her mother's was at this age, it was more than long enough to beautifully rise up off of her shoulders.

"STOP!" Dani ordered.

When Beta Boy opened his eyes, he found that the four bullets had done just that. Or, at least, they appeared to be. They were actually just moving extremely slow. Either way, they had him pinned up against that wall, and he couldn't move without risking injury or death. His eyes found Dani across the room in full mactrouge, with her arms extended toward him. It was as if she were in a tug of war with the bullets; holding them back, stopping them from reaching their destination, but from the surprised, strained look on her face, it seemed as if this was much more of a task than she thought it would be. She struggled to breathe through her tightly clenched teeth, and her flexed arms and hands quivered from the stress this ambitious endeavor had unexpectedly put on her body. He glanced just to the right of Dani and saw Kaitlin standing in the bathroom doorway with a towel around her wet body and a gun in her steady hand.

"What're you… doing?" Dani strained to say. "I-I got… this."

In full mactrouge, Dani was an intimidating sight, but this was old news to Kaitlin now. The strain on Dani's face and the tremor in her limbs, however, was not.

"What are *you* doing? Are you okay?" A concerned Kaitlin asked.

Dani didn't answer. Holding these bullets at bay was hard enough. Talking only made it that much more difficult.

"Dani? What's wrong? Why are you trembling?"

"Because this… Harder… than… I… th-thought…"

"Then stop it… LET THEM GO!"

"…I-I-I… don't want him dead," she blurted out, losing just a sliver of control. Enough to make the bullets lurch forward the tiniest bit. Barely noticeable to the human eye, but to Beta Boy, it was harrowing as one of the bullets was uncomfortably close to his chest.

"If-If I get a say in this,--" Beta Boy tried to insert his unwanted opinion into the conversation and was severely admonished for it.

"You don't!" Kaitlin snapped, the exhaustion in her voice betraying just how close she was to her limit.

"…K-K-Kait,… p-please…" Dani begged.

Kaitlin was incensed. It had been a very long, irritating day on the road. She was hot and sweaty and more than a little agitated by this unwelcomed interruption. All she wanted was to relax in a cool, peaceful shower, to help wash away the 450 miles she had put on the Ol' Red, now Blue Truck today, and then a warm, cozy bed to help her forget about it. She didn't know what was going on between these two and at this late hour, after this type of day, she wasn't interested in drawing it out. She seethed as she angrily marched across the room to Beta Boy, stamping a trail of wet footprints on the carpet, behind her. Then stooped down to his level so he could see her eyes. She wanted to make sure he understood her completely.

"You think you're fast?" She asked Beta Boy.

He did, actually, but he could also see from the expression on her face and the irritation in her eyes that the question was most likely rhetorical, and it would probably be in his best interests if he didn't respond. He was right. Kaitlin placed her right index finger on the trigger and positioned the gun about an inch away from his head.

"Try me." Kaitlin retorted as if she truly wanted him to.

Then, with her left index finger, she reluctantly changed the trajectory of the four serendipitously slow silver bullets to a much less lethal path. Dani released a haggard exhale as she painfully fell out of mactrouge, and the bullets instantly ruptured and splintered the wall within millimeters of multiple parts of Beta Boy's body. Kaitlin didn't flinch. The gun in her hand was steady as her finger rested, heavy on the trigger. For a second, it crossed Beta Boy's mind to take Kaitlin up on the offer to 'try her'. Dani was still sucking air, trying to recover, and that might be all the time he needed to escape, or attempt something worse, but when he looked into Kaitlin's eyes, he thought better of it. They could have killed him, but they chose not to. He was alive. Whatever plans they had for him were probably better than the alternative.

"Now, what's this about?" Kaitlin asked.

The question wasn't directed to anyone in particular, but the tone in her voice indicated that someone had better answer her fairly quickly. Beta Boy shrugged. He didn't know and was just as curious as Kaitlin was. Dani took a deep, calming breath as she reset herself and walked over to them.

"Thanks," she said to Kaitlin, "I can handle it from here."

Dani reached out, grabbed him by his throat and squeezed. She didn't have the energy to mactrouge, but she didn't need to for him. Kaitlin lowered the gun as Dani lifted him up by his neck so that his toes were just touching the floor, making it very difficult for him to breath.

"Handle what?" Kaitlin asked, not trying to hide the growing annoyance in her tone. "It *was* handled until you got in the way."

"I wanted to talk to Beta Boy before--"

"TALK?!" Both Dani and Beta Boy winced from the fury in her voice. "It's after midnight!"

"Well, we were gonna have to leave anyway--"

"Stop fooling around and finish this!" Kaitlin ordered as she marched back toward the bathroom. "NOW, DANIELLE!"

Kaitlin slammed the bathroom door closed and restarted the shower. Dani knew that whenever Kaitlin called her 'Danielle,' she was serious.

"She gets really grumpy when she's tired," Dani whispered.

"Look,--" Beta Boy tried to say, but Dani squeezed a little harder on his neck, cutting him off.

"You get to be killed by me another day. You're too much of a buffoon to be from The Council, so you go back and tell my father he can stop chasing me. Tell him I'm coming home."

Dani threw Beta Boy out the door and watched him run off.

Kaitlin had heard the entire conversation through the bathroom door. Dani was right. She was grumpy, and now she was also concerned. Twenty minutes later, Dani shielded herself from the pouring rain as she ran out of the front office with the money from the register - all of the money. She hopped into the driver's seat and to her surprise, Kaitlin was not pleased.

"What? We didn't even stay here," Dani pleaded.

"The room only cost sixty dollars," Kaitlin said softly. She was tired, and her patience with this night was long gone.

"I figured the rest is for pain and sufferi--"

Kaitlin snatched the money out of Dani's hand, pocketed the sixty bucks for the room and exited the car. Dani flinched when she slammed the door.

"Yeah, she's definitely tired," Dani thought.

She sighed and shook her head as she watched Kaitlin put the rest of the money back into the register, then walk out and re-enter the car.

"Go," Kaitlin said.

Dani wanted to protest and thought seriously about it for all of one second before she put the Ol' Red, now Blue, into first gear and wisely, did what she was told.

CHAPTER 46

Santa Rosa, New Mexico

Dani drove for another ninety minutes while Kaitlin slept in what appeared to be a most uncomfortable position, but after sixteen years, the ol' red, now blue truck was like an old easy chair that they both just folded into. They ended up in a city that the original Route 66 ran through back in the day: Santa Rosa, New Mexico. It was nice; clean, with around three thousand people who were mostly tourists. It was what Kaitlin and Dani considered to be an 'in-between' place. They'd be good here for a week or two, and then they'd move on. They slept through the morning and found a busy little diner near the motel to sample the cutting-edge cuisine the city was known for.

"I'll start off with a margarita,--" Dani told the waitress.

"No, she won't," Kaitlin corrected.

"--And can you make it a Cadillac, please?" Dani continued.

"Two lemonades," Kaitlin said, "and how are the enchiladas?"

"Go for the rojas. They are the best in town," the young waitress replied.

"Perfect. Two chicken enchiladas rojas and make one extra picante, please."

"Got it. Be right back," the waitress said as she moved off.

"She was totally gonna give me that margarita," Dani exclaimed.

"No I wasn't," the waitress called out as she went into the kitchen.

"So unfair," Dani pouted. "You do know I'm gonna be twenty-one next week, right?"

"Yeah. About that… I heard what you said to that boy last night."

This particular topic seemed to puncture the perkiness in Dani's upbeat posture as she powerfully expelled all the air in her body and slouched back into the booth.

"Can we just not do this now?" Dani asked.

"What I've been trying to tell you is you don't have to do it at all."

"He killed my mom, Kate."

"You don't know that."

"I saw him do it."

"You've told me how your mother died, and I've always believed you… but not once have you said you saw your father do it… Did you?"

"It was an energy blast. Who else could have thrown it?"

"Barrett, Cecil? I don't know. It's a very good question, and since he is your father, don't you think that's reason enough for you to be sure?" Kaitlin asked.

"I'll never understand why you always defend him, especially when you know what he'll do to you."

The waitress returned and set their lemonades on the table.

"Your order will be right out," said the waitress as she moved to help another customer.

"…I'm not defending him," said Kaitlin, "and this isn't about me. You're the one I'm worried about."

"I don't know why. You know I can handle myself."

"I'm not talking about that, and you know it."

Dani stared into her lemonade as the somberness of the conversation seemed to catch up with her.

"…I'm fine."

"After all we've been through, neither one of us is "fine." We need to take some time and--"

"It's been sixteen years! How much more time do we need?"

"Well, we definitely need time to process the other event that supposedly is going to happen in about a week."

"Jesus! I'm not going to just suddenly become this evil demon and hurt people!" Dani said in an angry tone and a bit louder than she, Kaitlin, and a few other patrons would have liked.

"I know that," Kaitlin said through clenched teeth. Then, with all the restraint she could muster, "Now keep... your voice... DOWN." They both took a breath and tried to de-escalate the conversation down a notch or three before Kaitlin continued. "I didn't believe it about your mother, and I certainly don't believe it about you, but the fact is, you are going to go through something, and we don't know what that is. You could be happy, you could be sad, you could finally get off the ground, or you could become ill – I don't know, but whatever it is, you and I should be focusing on that, instead of trying to fulfill some ridiculous prophecy."

"My mother hid me for almost four years so that I could fulfill that 'ridiculous' prophecy," Dani said sharply.

"Your mother hid you so that you could live!" Kaitlin fired back.

They seemed to be in a fierce competition on who could cause the most distress to the patrons within earshot of them. Right now, it was a tie as the waitress inch over with their food in hand. The timing was perfect, as it forced them to put the conversation on hold and gave them both a chance to calm down. It had become heated, and neither one of them wanted that.

"Who gets the picante?" The waitress asked with a diffidence she hadn't shown before.

"Me," they both said in unison.

They looked at each other and laughed. It released a lot of tension between them, the waitress, and the other customers.

"You can just put them down, and we'll split it up," Kaitlin said.

"Alright," said the waitress as she placed the plates on the table. "This one's the picante. Can I get you anything else?"

"Shot of tequila?" Dani asked.

The return of Dani's waggish rhetoric eased the waitress's mind and took away any tension left hovering over the table.

"Kiddo, if you can't tell that we don't have a bar, you probably shouldn't be drinking," the waitress said with a smile and a wink.

Dani forwarded a sheepish smile and a shoulder shrug.

"We're good right now, thank you," Kaitlin said as the waitress moved off. Then to Dani, "You're in control of your destiny, sweetie. No one else."

"But what if I'm not, Kate? What if I'm just a rat on a wheel?"

"Then jump off the wheel, Dani. Break it. Burn it down if you have to."

Just then, Dani gasped as if she had just been hit. She was out of breath, and her face became flush.

"What's wrong?" Kaitlin asked with great concern.

Dani looked up at the television screen on the wall across the room. The news was on, but there was no sound.

"Excuse me," she called out to the waitress, "could you turn that up, please?"

The waitress pulled the remote from her apron and tapped the volume up.

"Look..." Dani said, pointing to the screen as the news anchor's words played like a slow drumbeat in her ears.

"--The body of an adult male and the skeletal remains of another were found early this morning deep within the bayou of the New Orleans area. Authorities believe that heavy rains and flooding over the past week unearthed the waterlogged body. Investigators are unsure why the one male has remained relatively intact, but,--"

"Oh my God..." Dani whispered. "It's him..."

"Who?"

"Jean,"

"WHAT?!" Kaitlin said, unable to keep her voice down.

"It's him. I can feel it. And... And--"

CHAPTER 47

"--He's alive," Rayna said after she flipped over a tarot card.

New Orleans, Louisiana

July 2017

Her tone was usually unbiased in her readings, and as much as she tried to hide it, everyone could tell that she was more than a little agitated by that particular card. Julien, now forty-two, lurched in his chair behind the desk at Gerard Enterprises, straddling a fine line between shock and fury. He wasn't quite sure which way he wanted to go, but it was beginning to look more and more like anger was winning out. Tirin seemed unfazed, as usual, but his eyes somehow found their way from whatever was so interesting outside the window he was staring through to her. Serena held a taut grimace on her face. The one-time personal assistant slash receptionist, now V.P. slash campaign manager, had come a long way in sixteen years. She was actually two years older than Julien, but somehow, with all the stress she endured in that office, even with her face all scrunched together, she still managed to look younger than him. Lucien sat quietly on the sofa under a "Gerard for Governor" banner. He wore a façade of indifference like someone would their favorite sweatshirt, but underneath, he raged. All in all, the room was tighter than a jar of peanut butter at a squirrel convention. The next words uttered from anyone in that room needed to be prudent and carefully weighed.

"You said he was dead," Julien said in a most imprudent way.

"I never said he was dead,--" Rayna tried to explain.

"I asked you, point-blank, in the swamp!"

"You asked me what I saw, and I told you, 'nothin'.'"

"YOU TOLD ME HE WAS DEAD!" Julien yelled.

"'DEAD' is somethin'. 'Nothin'' is nothing, is it not?"

Rayna could feel Julien's glare from across the room, but she couldn't pull her eyes away from that card. She kept looking at it as if, any minute, she expected it to change as the news anchor finished her report on the television.

"--Both bodies are being transferred to the hospital at The Louisiana State University Medical Building for further,--"

Julien turned the television off with the remote as Rayna flipped another card.

"And he's not alone," Rayna said. She seemed confused by her own cards as she flipped over another and then another. "Oh my," she said as she flipped over one more. "This cannot be true."

"What now?" Julien asked as he tried to buffer his anger.

"The… Old One seems to be with him; I-In him."

"Who?" Julien asked as his eyes widened. Rayna would not respond with her name. "You're fuckin' kiddin', right?" Rayna would neither respond nor look up at him. She just continued to stare at the cards.

"I don't give a fuck, YOU get him back here. NOW."

It wasn't the tone that brought her eyes away from the cards to Julien. It was the task. She was embarrassed that she was to be used in such a manner. Her eyes twitched around the room to find everyone staring at her. All but Lucien. His eyes were locked on his father. For him, it wasn't about the task. It was about the tone. He didn't like the way his father had spoken to her. He never liked the way Julien spoke to her and Lucien looked like he was about to let him know it.

"So, am I to be punished? Like a child?" Rayna asked.

"This is no punishment,--"

"Then explain!" she yelled.

"Since when do I explain myself to you?!"

"Since when am I ordered to attend to such things?!"

"You attend to whatever the hell I tell you to attend to!!"

Lucien had had his fill of this and Tirin wasn't really digging it either. They both knew better than to get themselves in the middle of one of their knock-down drag outs, but someone had to put a stop to this.

"--What about yo' daughter?" Lucien said, beating Tirin to the punch and hoping to put an end to this incessant bickering. "If that broadcast was national, then wherever she is, she's probably on her way d'ere now."

"Now, how the hell would you know that? Huh?! I thought you said you didn't know where she was!" Julien yelled.

"I don't!" Lucien answered with equal force. "I can only see when she fights, for the 'umpteenth' thousand time, but I feel what she feels and for whatever perverted reason, she got strong feelin's for him."

Julien glared at Rayna for confirmation. She glared back with unrivaled defiance before she flipped another tarot and read the mystical card.

"Hmph," she grunted as her eyes shifted to Lucien. "She will try to help him." Then, in as nasty a way as she could, "So, what are your orders now?"

"You know what, Rayna? Fuck you! You get me six bodies, and I'll go do it, my Goddamn self!"

"Oh, no, no, no, no, you can't do that, sir," Serena said, stepping into a situation she most definitely would have been better off staying out of.

"Dying next week's not fast enough for you, huh?" Rayna said.

"Don't start that shit with me, Ray," Julien warned.

Rayna swept up the cards and threw them across the room.

"Then why do you even ask for my readings if you refuse to listen to anything they say?!"

"TO HELL WITH YOUR GOD DAMN READINGS!!" Julien yelled as he erupted out of his chair.

"SIR!" Serena interjected.

Everyone, including Serena, was astonished by that outburst. Even Tirin raised his head in wonderment.

"...JD... Excuse me, but... No. You don't get to say that. Not this time. Every time you've gone against her, there have been consequences, monumental casualties that have changed the lives of everyone in this room," Serena said. "This time is no different, other than the fact that YOU will be the casualty. I mean, she's never been wrong. Has she?" Serena scanned the room for an answer. No one gave one. "Because if she has, then,--"

"What do you want me to do, Serena? Kill my daughter? Hmm?" Julien asked in a contemptuous voice. Serena lowered her head. "Is that what y'all asking me to do?... IS IT?!" He shouted.

"No! We're asking you to not be so fucking pig-headed and use that magnificent brain of yours to try and think of a way around it!" Rayna yelled. "No one here wants Dani killed, but in five days, for whatever reason, she's gonna want to kill you."

"It's because she thinks you killed Mom," Lucien said, waiting for his father to deny it.

The statement seemed to penetrate Julien's impenetrable defenses as he stumbled backward into his chair. For twenty-one years, he had quietly wondered how he could be cursed with such an abhorrent prognostication. He never allowed himself to believe it because he couldn't, for the life of him, imagine why any daughter would want to take their father's life – until just now. There was a growing pain in his chest as it tightened around his heart. He thought he might have a heart attack, and he welcomed it. He closed his eyes, hoping he may never have to open them again, and he might not have had to if it wasn't for Lucien's next question that ripped through his soul like a reaper's scythe.

"Did ya'?" asked Lucien.

It's amazing how two three-letter words could hold so much venom and hatred.

"Luc, I told you—" Rayna began.

"Naw," Lucien ordered. He seemed to be becoming more and more like his father everyday. "Let him answer. I know what you said. But fo' years it's confused me why my brother felt so much love fo' one, and why my sister felt so much hatred fo' da' other. ...Why she hate you, Pop?"

Of all the things Julien Gerard had gone through in his life, only two events were more painful to him than this one.

"...She probably does think I killed your mother," Julien said as he turned to his son, "and from her perspective... she'd be right. Your mother hid Dani because she didn't trust I'd do what was necessary to protect her. Or either of them. And as I tried so hard to prove her wrong..."

There was a long pause between his next words. Sixteen years long.

"...She jumped in front of me during the battle with Laveau and I...... I have to live with that for the rest of my life. Even if that's only 'til Wednesday."

Lucien shook his head. He was angry and sad. He felt everything and nothing at the same time. He wanted to cry, but refused to do so here. He wanted to leave the room, but couldn't find two legs to stand up on, so he stayed seated and turned his head away.

"Julien... There has to be a way to,--" Rayna tried to say.

"There's not. Humans may have control of their destiny, but malafecs tied to a prophecy are bound to that prophecy. We're like rats on a wheel; we can run, but we ain't going nowhere."

"That's just a stupid myth," Rayna said with a pained look on her face. "You don't believe in that any more than I do!"

"None of us do," Tirin added.

"Well maybe I do, maybe I don't, but what I do know is that for the last sixteen years she was raised like a human, by a human. I'm hoping Kaitlin's influence might deter her from her malfeasant, malafecian thoughts."

"And you're putting your life on that?" Rayna asked.

"That's all I can do without hurting her, and I'll die before I hurt another member of my family. Simple as that."

"Julien,--" Rayna pleaded.

"You send the best you got to bring Laveau back here, and you tell 'em I don't want one hair on my daughter's head touched. We clear?"

Rayna was so furious with him that her eyes filled with tears. Angry tears. She had to close them so they wouldn't fall out.

"Fine," she forced herself to say. "I'll need Cree to lead the team in case they do run into her. She's the only one who might be able to recognize her."

Julien looked to Tirin.

"You shall have her and Randy as well," he nodded.

"Then it's settled… Thank you," Julien said to all of them before he got up and left the room without saying anything more to his son.

Perhaps he was embarrassed or ashamed by what had just transpired between them. Whatever the reason, the self-consciousness he felt stopped him from noticing the dilation in Lucien's eyes and the grim, pained look on his face. He may have asked Luc if he was okay or if anything was wrong. It would have given Lucien the opportunity to tell him the truth. Whether or not he would have told his father that the all-too-familiar and unwelcome feeling he was experiencing was a painful harbinger that signified imminent danger for his sister, was a decision he would have had to make in that moment.

In this moment, he masked the pain in his head and the overwhelming emotions he was experiencing and excused himself as he left the room. He couldn't afford to wait for the elevator, so he took the stairs down to the next floor and ducked into the bathroom. He fell over the sink and winced as he released an arduous breath, and his hair began to float around his shoulders. He had learned to control these feelings and the pain had become minimal. Dani was much stronger now, so he didn't have to expel that much of his own energy. Except for when one particular foe presented himself to her.

CHAPTER 48

What followed would be neither polite nor respectful.

Santa Rosa, New Mexico

Five minutes earlier

The enchilada rojas were more than formidable at this Santa Rosa spot. It would have been nice to stay for a week or two and sample some more of the commendable cuisine of the city, but time waits for no wo-man.

"You know, you don't have to go if you don't want to. I can do it," Dani said.

"What are you talking about?" Kaitlin asked.

"If we get a motel near the Texas border, I can just drive in and get him and bring him back in a day."

"You think I'd let you go into Louisiana alone?"

"L.S.U. is only an hour outside of New Orleans. I just don't want you to be,--"

"Stop. We stay together – always. You understand?" Kaitlin said. Dani nodded, embarrassed that she'd even posed the question. "Come on, let's go."

"Pick me up in the front," Dani said as she crawled out of the booth. "I'm gonna grab a paper."

"Okay."

Kaitlin headed for the back door as Dani exited the front of the restaurant, where three newspaper dispensers awaited. She threw some change into the machine and grabbed a paper. As she had gotten older, her intuitive powers had increased dramatically. Witches are known to develop what's called a "third eye," where they are so in-tune with their instincts, they can actually see danger moments before it happens. It didn't matter whether it was Lucien's instincts or hers, something forced Dani to raise her eyes off that newspaper and when she did, she saw two Dobermans sitting across the street, staring at her. She exhaled so fast she forgot that it was usually followed by an immediate inhale, and panic set in. A truck passed—and when it cleared, The Talisman was standing there. He adjusted his glasses, checked his watch, then snapped it shut. Dani was frozen over with fear.

Back in New Orleans, Lucien needed to act.

"No," he exhaled as quietly as possible. "Don't you fuckin' freeze on me. Get into mactrouge, Dani. Move!"

The Talisman tipped his hat and nodded to Dani. Whether it was a polite greeting or a sign of respect was irrelevant, because what followed would be neither polite nor respectful. He tapped his cane on the ground and the snake heads came alive, and just like she'd always done since she was nearly four years old, she wet herself. He raised his hand and beckoned her to come. She gathered what little composure she had left and illuminated her eyes red as her hair came alive.

Good girl, Lucien thought. Already in full mactrouge, he braced for the agony of joining her fight from afar. "Now let's kick this son-of-a-bitch's ass once and for,--" "AWWWHHH!" he cried out and held his head, then collapsed to the floor.

The Talisman snatched his hand back and a powerful force yanked Dani toward him. Her momentum halted only when she slammed into the row of newspaper machines. His perplexed face wrinkled as he released her and she fell to the ground. Once more, he extended his hand and yanked it back with more force than the first time, and again, Dani's body slammed into the machines. Frustrated with that outcome, The Talisman thrust his hand outward and the force lifted Dani up and slammed her into the brick wall behind her. She collapsed to the ground, bloodied, as her eyes flickered and faded to normal.

Lucien was on the bathroom floor writhing in pain. He reached up, grasped hold of the sink and pulled himself to his knees as he fought to hold onto full mactrouge.

"Dani-- Stay… Stay awake… St-Stay… awake…" he whispered. "I… I can't.… help you, if you, pa-pass out."

Tears began to fall into the sink, along with the blood from his nose. He was losing her and he couldn't do anything to stop it. He was barely holding on himself and expelling everything he had just to keep her from passing out. His body began to tremble as his eyes flickered, but he would not cut the connection between them and he would not fall from mactrouge - no matter what the cost.

Dani was on the brink. The Talisman stepped off the curb and strode toward her. He stopped in the street just in front of her, with only the newspaper machines between them. With a sharp gesture, he parted and flattened the metal machines like aluminum cans and created a clear path between them.

"Been a while, girrrl. Been busy. But it yo' time now. Noowwww ya' come wit'--"

Kaitlin slammed into The Talisman with all the speed the ol' truck could muster. He must've flown thirty feet in the air before he hit the ground in the middle of the busy intersection at the corner. As he rose, a speeding semi screeched to a halt, but not before it smacked him into an oncoming vehicle, which then crashed into a parked car, burying him in the carnage. Dani was in bad shape. So was Lucien, but he was thankful that Kaitlin had shown up when she did and he was able to release from his sister. Kaitlin jumped out of the steaming pick-up and ran over to Dani. She was bleeding from her face and the back of her head. Kaitlin struggled to get her to her feet.

"Come on. Come on, baby, I can't carry you! You gotta walk!"

Kaitlin put Dani's arm around her shoulder and took a few steps toward the truck before being stopped by a familiar bark coming from the wreckage. Kaitlin turned and saw movement. Something was struggling to get free.

"It's leaking!" someone yelled. "It's leaking gas! We gotta get that guy outta there!"

The man driving the car that hit The Talisman was unconscious and the parked car that he crashed into was badly leaking gas. They were one electrical spark away from a catastrophe as panic filled the street. The driver from the semi limped over and tried to get the man out, but the door was stuck. He frantically called for help as he tried to pull the man out through the window. All the while, the Dobermans were clawing through the wreckage and breaking free. Kaitlin propped the wobbly witch up against the truck and called for her assistance.

"Dani... DANI!" Kaitlin emphasized and Dani opened her eyes. "Sweetie, you gotta blow up that car."

"W-What?" A disoriented Dani whispered. "No… There's too-- too many peop,--"

"Baby, he's coming. You gotta blow it up."

"But there's a man… in the car,--"

"Then get him out, just--"

Kaitlin saw one dog's head pop up from the wreckage with the other's right behind. Both of the dogs barked and growled as they struggled to break free. Kaitlin shook Dani to keep her awake.

"Do it! Do it!!" Kaitlin screamed.

"No, I can't,… I don't know how," Dani cried.

"Yes, you do!

"No!"

"He's gonna kill us if you don't blow it up!!"

"I can't,-- I CAN'T!!

Dani was losing it, so Kaitlin slapped her, praying it might ground her.

"DO IT, GOD DAMN IT!! DO IT NOW!!"

Left with no choice, Lucien took full control of Dani. He popped into full Mactrouge, assessed the situation, and executed. Then he screamed like he never did before from the pain it caused him.

Dani came alive and inflated into full mactrouge. With incredible speed and accuracy, she shot a fiery blast from her eyes, slicing past Kaitlin's head and striking the gas tank on the parked car. It exploded just as the dogs broke free. Simultaneously, she encapsulated the two men at the car in a force field. The massive explosion sent them flying fifty feet away, but she was able to catch and guide them safely to the ground. Kaitlin released a deep sigh of relief, knowing that the men were safe and no one was injured. She turned to find Dani trembling, hyperventilating, her gaze unfocused—as if she didn't recognize where she was. As her hair settled and the red faded from her eyes, a line of blood fell from each nostril.

"Katie?… I don't know what's… H-Happening to… m-m,--"

Dani collapsed in Kaitlin's arms. Kaitlin slid her into the passenger side and ran around and jumped into the driver's seat as the sirens from the fire trucks and ambulances closed in. The ol' truck was badly damaged from the collision and Kaitlin struggled to pop it into first gear. She was so upset over what she had just put Dani through that it made it difficult for her to drive as her hands shook and tears gushed out of her eyes.

"DAMN IT!" she screamed as she pounded the steering wheel with her fists several times.

She took a much-needed breath to center herself, then again grabbed hold of the sixteen-inch, double-bend, shift lever and wrangled it into first gear. The truck made about as much noise as it ever did as it wheezed and struggled to get up to speed, but it hadn't let them down in sixteen years and it wasn't about to today. It sputtered down Route 66, to the outskirts of town. A few moments later, to the astonishment of the crowd, two burnt Dobermans limped out of the flames, snapping at anyone who dared get in their way.

CHAPTER 49

Lucien was seated on the floor against the wall in the executive bathroom at Gerard Industries and he didn't look like he wanted to get up any time soon. His hair, soaking wet from a mixture of sweat and water, dripped onto his shoulders. Add in the blood from his runny nose and he looked as if he was the sole survivor of some type of natural disaster that happened only within the confines of this restroom.

He took some deep breaths as he prepared himself for the strenuous ascent to a standing position. As he sat there in deep contemplation of what might be the easiest way to accomplish that lofty goal, the door opened and Tirin walked in. At that point, Lucien decided that perhaps it would be best if he just stayed where he was for a while longer. Tirin glanced in his direction, then walked over to the urinal. Lucien exhaled as he rested his head against the wall and waited for the tongue-lashing he assumed he was about to receive.

Depending on the situation, twelve seconds can be either a very long or very short time. Tirin stood at the urinal in silence as he handled his business for twelve *long* seconds. When he was done, he put everything back where it was supposed to go, made some minor adjustments for comfort, zipped up and flushed, then swiveled around and moved to the sink.

He turned the water on without even looking at Luc, who was seated on the floor right next to it. Instead, he focused on the task of washing his hands. He was an alpha, after all, and they put complete focus on everything they do. A good eighteen seconds later, he grabbed a towel from the basket of clean towels, unfolded it and aggressively maneuvered it over his hands for a complete and proper dry. By this point, it's safe to say that Lucien was more than a little pissed – no pun intended. He felt like Tirin was going out of his way to ignore him. When you see someone you know sitting on the floor in the executive bathroom, soaking wet and bleeding, it usually leads to a question or two: *"You okay?" "Everything all right?" "Can I fucking get you something?"* To show even the tiniest concern, or at least some type of recognition of the situation, was expected and almost always welcomed. Tirin dropped the used towel in the wicker basket and exited. Lucien clenched his jaw, the silence gnawing at him as the door clicked shut.

"You ain't even gonna fuckin' say nothin'?!" Lucien erupted.

It didn't take an alpha to hear that, and the door opened as Tirin re-entered the bathroom. He leaned up against the door and this time, his eyes found Lucien's and stayed with him.

"I thought my silence might relieve you of the burden of lying," Tirin said.

Lucien found it very difficult to look at Tirin in this moment. He was so much more than a friend or a mentor to him. Alphas only have love for a few, but never was there a day in Lucien's life that he didn't know that he was one of them. He always told Tirin every-thing; there were secrets Tirin held that neither Julien nor Rayna knew. They were between the two of them, and they would stay that way until Lucien felt otherwise. It broke Lucien's heart that he never told Tirin because, even though the proud alpha would never say it, Lucien saw in his eyes that his hardened heart was cracked because he thought that Lucien didn't trust him enough. Lucien had emotions surging from places he previously didn't know existed and he burst into tears.

"What was I s'posed to do?!" Lucien cried. "She'd have died if I ain't help her!"

Tirin said nothing, gave him nothing. He just stood there and listened.

"She's my sister! What was I s'posed to do?!"

"Protect her," Tirin said, "and perhaps if you had asked for some help in doing that, you wouldn't look like this."

As much as Lucien wanted and needed to tell Tirin everything, he made a promise to his mother years ago that he would not break.

"...I ain't think I'd be doin' it fo' this long. I'd thought she'd be strong enough to do it herself by now."

"How could she learn to fight for herself, when you've been fighting for her all these years?"

"Cree told ya', didn't she?"

"Eight years ago, after the fourth of July."

"She tell you why I couldn't tell ya'?"

"Couldn't? No. But she told me why you didn't. And you were wrong. We would not have stopped you. We would have trained you to do it better."

Lucien closed his eyes and nodded because he knew Tirin would have.

"I can't keep doin' this, T," Lucien said as more tears pushed from his face. "I can't... The pain, it's gettin' worse. I ain't strong enough."

"No, but she is," Tirin said.

"She's not!"

"She is! She's a witch and if she's anything like her mother, she has enough strength inside of her for both of you."

"I can see inside her and I know that ain't true."

"Perhaps you're looking in the wrong places. To this day, I have never seen anyone more powerful than your mother, and I have never met anyone more afraid to wield the power that was given to them. She held back and pushed it down for years."

"...Why?"

"She feared the demon inside of her. She thought it would control her and make her a bad person, so she suppressed it. That was her mistake. In order to control it, one needs to embrace it and in doing so, they embrace who they are – what they are."

"You think Dani's got a demon?"

"There is a demon in all of us, Lucien. Whether we do good or bad with it, is up to us. You must get your sister to embrace her demon or you must continue to fight for her until you no longer possess the strength to do so. On that day, if you do not die, she most certainly will."

"How did you get my mom to accept hers?"

If he was capable of smiling in that moment, he would have.

"…With love," he said. "…Are you okay?"

Lucien nodded. Tirin gave the air a few quick sniffs, checking for any unseen injuries or ailments. Satisfied, he turned and walked out.

CHAPTER 50

The Ol' Red, Now Blue

It's a strange thing to grieve a truck, but for Kaitlin and Dani, the ol' red, now blue was more than just a vehicle—he was family. The two held onto each other for support as they gazed upon the ol' truck, snuggled comfortably in its resting spot in the junkyard. Kaitlin had wanted Dani to stay behind and rest, as the previous day's battle with The Talisman had taken a deep toll on the absentee heir to the Gerard fortune. Her head was bandaged and she still showed multiple bruises on her face, but she refused to stay behind. If this truly was the end for their whimsically-wired warrior, nothing would stop her from paying her respects.

For more than sixteen years, that truck had been their trusted friend. He was more than just a means of trustworthy transportation. Faithfully, he crisscrossed them back and forth across the country, sometimes on no more than a moment's notice. When called upon during tense and precarious occasions, no matter the time or weather conditions, he always started. It was so incredibly hard for Kaitlin to call for a tow truck the one and only time he didn't. Countless meals had been shared within him, and during times when money was short, he offered the protection and security of an enclosure as they slept under the moon's light with him. He even faced off against The Talisman—their most formidable enemy—and paid a heavy price for it. They all did.

The Junkyard King exited his office with five hundred dollars in hand. Aside from being the ruler of this kingdom, he fashioned himself as a bit of a tinkerer. Because of the ingenious design, not only of the conversion, but of the ignition and clutch as well, he felt morally obligated to offer a mere modicum of the money he might make if he was able to restore this illustrious instrument back to glory. Kaitlin didn't accept the money. Something about it just didn't seem right. She felt it would have disrespected the memory of her friend.

The Junkyard King was not the least perplexed by her refusal of the offering. He understood better than most. He stopped as he approached his office, wheeled around and called out to them before they exited his emporium. He bid them to wait a moment more as he rushed over and jumped behind the wheel of the ol' red, now blue truck. He turned the ignition backward toward himself. The truck wheezed, coughed, groaned—and then, with great effort, roared to life one final time. The Junkyard King smiled as he exited the vehicle and took his hat off out of respect and nodded.

"I wasn't sure he would talk!" The King called out to them from across the yard, "but I had a feelin' he might wanna say good-bye!"

Kaitlin and Dani cried as they waved goodbye to The ol' red, now blue truck. Their knight in shining armor.

The following evening, Dani sat in the south side window seat of an eastbound train. Outside of a small bandage on her head, there was no trace of the bruising she had suffered two days ago. Remarkably, she had healed,... on the outside, anyway. Kaitlin was asleep in the aisle seat next to Dani, her head making a pillow out of Dani's boney shoulder. She was exhausted. While Dani had slept and healed over the last two days, Kaitlin watched over her, as she always did. Now it was Dani's turn to reciprocate. As much as Kaitlin tried to downplay it, even asleep she looked troubled and worried about traveling back into the state she swore she'd never set foot in again. Dani's eyes were fixed on an old, worn-out newspaper article she kept in a folder with a few other personal things, most of which she was very proud of, like any article featuring Lucien. There were several pictures of him in "puff pieces" about the family or of his solo accomplishments, but none within the last six years. She wondered if she'd even recognize her brother if she saw him on the street, or him - her.

There were also a few pictures of her and Austin and some with her friends from the prom. Those memories were for another day; today she only had eyes for one particular article, the very first one she had collected: "Gerard Heiress & Son Kidnapped." It had a picture of Camille, Lucien, Daniel and Julien. It told a sorted story detailing the events of that infamous night. The story on that page was so different from how she remembered it. How her grandfather was killed trying to protect them, and how the bodies of her mother and the younger twin, Daniel "Dani" Gerard were never found. An older woman with a delightfully serene disposition sat across from Kaitlin, staring at the beautiful, albeit bandaged, child. The woman had a reminiscent smile on her face and a longing glare in her eyes. Perhaps she saw something of her younger self in Dani's solitudinous spirit that kept her from sleeping, as she and Dani were the only ones awake on the train.

"You can't sleep either, huh, baby?" the old woman asked, her voice as soft as the passing desert night.

Dani looked up, startled by the kindness.

"...I don't sleep on trains," Dani replied with a shy smile, then lowered her head back down to her article.

It was just after midnight, and the Gerard estate was quiet. Quiet enough for you to hear the orchestra of sounds coming off of the Mississippi River: the call of the whip-poor-will's, the shrill of the gray treefrog, and the constant conversations of the katydids. The melodic music of the night. Nothing was out of the ordinary or suspicious, other than Lucien, who chose to exit the estate through the darkened veranda in the back instead of going out the front door. Rayna appeared out of the shadows as he stepped off the patio floor.

"Tell your sister I said, 'Hi,'" Rayna said, startling him.

Lucien nearly jumped out of his pants.

"Da' hell?!" Lucien said. "What 'chu you doin' out here?!"

"One might ask you the same."

"I s'pose if I told you I was goin' to Malaffections..." He stopped himself. He knew how ridiculous it was to lie to her. "I gotta try and stop her. The damn fool girl gonna get herself killed."

"I understand," Rayna said.

"Why'd you lie to me, Ray?"

"Because I love you. And I've never figured out how to tell a boy that his father killed his mother," she said. "'By accident' just didn't seem to be a good enough reason at the time. I'm sorry. I won't do it again."

Lucien showed his understanding with a hug that made both her heart and her lips smile. He kissed her on the cheek and turned to walk off.

"Stay away from Jean Laveau, Luc," she said. "Let Cree and the others handle it. "You certainly have no reason to concern yourself with him anymore. And it's not the type of thing the future CEO of Gerard Enterprises needs to involve himself with."

"I ain't afraid of him, Ray."

"You should be," she said, then her eyes drifted away and the smile fell from her face. "He's the most dangerous man I've ever known," she said as if she were saying it to herself.

Lucien's brow furrowed. Something seemed different about her tonight. Before he could explore it any further, she snapped herself out of her self-imposed state of stupor.

"Especially now that he's, apparently, not alone," she said, now in her usual, sarcastic tone. "Do not go near him. Do you understand me?"

Rayna took great joy in spoiling Lucien. She usually let him do just about whatever he wanted. This was not one of those times, and he knew by the tone of her voice and the look on her face, not to challenge her.

"Yes, ma'am," he said.

"And tell Dani to go easy on my vampires, please," she smiled. Lucien nodded and smiled back. Then, with the utmost seriousness in her voice, "And tell her not to come home on Wednesday. There've been a whole lot of people from London gathering around New Awlins this week, and I don't think they came all this way for the jambalaya."

Lucien nodded again, this time with a concerned look on his face. He didn't know that. Rayna also had a concerned look on her face as she watched him walk away, but her concern was for something completely different than his. She revealed the tarot card she had been saving for sixteen years. The one she turned over about Jean Laveau. "The Lovers" card. She stared at it a few moments before she put it back in its hiding spot. Then, instead of going into the house, she moved back into the shadows from which she came.

CHAPTER 51

Jean's body rested on a steel autopsy table. The table was rolled up against and attached to a matching steel sink with a long rubber hose and a spray nozzle attached to one of the faucets. This state-of-the-art table was equipped with built-in ventilation and four hydraulic pedals at its base that raised, lowered, or tilted the table on either of its axes. Adjacent to this stately stand was an equally impressive steel push-cart - matching, of course, with a single hydraulic pedal to raise and lower the cart appropriately.

There were at least thirty different tools, widgets and thingam-abobs, meticulously laid out in a particularly specific order. Outside of Jean's crusted and creepily un-decayed body, the room was pristine, although it was Jean's crusted and creepily un-decayed body that gave the room prestige. Enough to fill every coroner in the state with envy. They all wanted the opportunity to find out what mysteries this phenomenal enigma held. *How was this body left in such a composed state, yet the other was fully decomposed?* These and other similar questions were exactly why the body was brought here, to the university's anthropology department, and not given to one of the many county coroners who had requested it.

There was only one man in the state of Louisiana qualified enough to answer these cryptic questions, a Dr. Vernon D. Tanner, the Dean of the Anthropology Department at the Louisiana State University and the number one forensic taphonomist in the state. He was actually the only one in the state, so that narrowed the field a bit and made the governor's decision quite a bit easier.

He entered the lab dressed to impress with black slacks and a buttoned-down white lab coat over his pink collared shirt and black bowtie. Although technically no one else was there to be impressed, he had set up three remote cameras around the room to record the entire affair. Dr. Tanner was a greedy, conniving, selfish little man in his late fifties and as some might say, a bit of an ass. He could have held an open autopsy in a lecture hall type of setting where everyone could witness this phenomenon simultaneously, but he refused. He wanted to see it all first, reap all the rewards and publishing rights to his findings, and make his colleagues and everyone else pay to see them. A decision he would regret.

Outside, on the LSU campus, Cree and her assault team of Randy and two vampires, Doty and Rufus, moved toward the Medical Laboratories building with a definite purpose in their pace. Cree had scouted the building earlier in the day and formulated a plan, so everyone already knew where they were going and what their specific job was. All that was left was to execute.

"Alright, everybody knows what they're supposed to do. Let's keep the casualties down, and remember: if any of you see a girl who looks to be around twenty years old, five-foot-sevenish with possibly long, brown, curly hair, DO NOT engage her and find me IMMEDIATELY. She's a witch, she's powerful, she's got an attitude and most importantly, she's the big boss's daughter. You touch her, you die. If she doesn't kill you, her daddy definitely will," Cree said.

"What if she's got the dude?" Rufus asked. "What're we 'posed to do, let her have him?"

"No. We don't bring Laveau back, we're all dead," said Cree.

"Then what do we do?" asked Doty.

Cree stopped at the front of the building and turned to them. She was a little perturbed over the questions and even more so over the fact that she didn't really have an answer.

"Look, your boss and my boss picked us for this job for a reason. Because we get shit done. So enough with the fucking questions. GET IT DONE. Go!" Cree ordered.

Randy zipped away and the two vampires disappeared, as vampires do, leaving Cree alone in front of the building. She turned and marched in through the front door.

Inside, Dr. Tanner seemed to be enjoying himself way too much. He pushed a button on his remote control and "Carmina Burana" started to play over the loudspeakers. He adjusted the volume so the song could be heard in the background without overshadowing his voice on the audio recordings of video cameras. Next, he tapped the remote and adjusted the lights in the room to the perfect temperature for the three cameras to pick up everything. He lowered the magnifying goggles over his black plastic-framed glasses and prepared himself for what he considered to be the crown jewel of all autopsies.

"Good evening. I'm Dr. Vernon D. Tanner and I'm 'bout to walk y'all through, step-by-step, as we uncover the secrets this young man, right here has been keepin' from us for all these years," Tanner said, directly into the camera. "Let the record show that it is the twenty-ninth day of July, two thousand seventeen. The time on the clock says it's one-thirty a.m. We startin' late 'cuz I taught class all day today, then I took a good long nap so I could be fresh for this one here." He smiled as he picked up a scalpel and went to work. "There seems to be some type a,... vial encrusted around this boy's neck. Let's see if we can get this thing off."

Tanner took the scalpel and tried to cut away at the caked-on mud and debris around Jean's neck to remove the vial. Because of the deterioration and the amount of dirt that had accumulated over the years, it was difficult to discern the difference between debris and Jean's actual flesh. He gave up on the scalpel and instead reached for some small surgical forceps. By accident, he made a small incision—and to his horror, Jean's neck began to bleed.

"Oh, shi--!... That's... That's impossible," he stated in disbelief, momentarily forgetting he was recording himself.

"Funny, I said the exact same thing," Cree said, startling Tanner.

Cree had entered the room without making a sound and was leaning up against the wall, watching him. Caught off-guard, Dr. Tanner accidentally squeezed the delicate vial and it broke. All of the mysterious liquid it contained was quickly absorbed into Jean, through the incision on his neck. Hagatha had been quiet for the last few days. Badgering Jean for sixteen straight years would take a toll on anyone, so she took a few days off to rest and prepare herself for a moment just like this.

"AHH-HA-HA-HA-HA-HA-A-A!!! She cackled in Jean's head. *"Wake up, my lover, my love, my key."* Then, her voice changed to something deeper and more ferocious than before. *"Wake up, I command you. UNLOCK ME!"*

"Shit!" Tanner exploded. "Look what you made me do!"

"Sorry, Doc," Cree said, "but I think your work here is done."

"How the hell'd you get in here?! Where them God damn guards at?!"

"They've been relieved. So have you. Again, sorry."

Cree zipped across the room, snapped his neck, and the good Dr. Tanner collapsed on the floor.

"The path is clear," Rufus stated as he entered the room. "And I found a car in the back. Green Jeep Cherokee," he said, showing the keys. "One of the guards'. We're good to go."

"Where's Randy?" Cree asked.

Randy entered the room as Cree destroyed the second of the three cameras in the room.

"The building's swept. We're clear," Randy stated.

"Beautiful. Roof, cover Doty at the front. We'll bag this boy and be outta here in five."

Cree looked up and Rufus was gone. He may have even disappeared before she had finished. Cree shook her head in disgust as she disabled the last camera.

"Fuckin' vampires," she whispered to herself.

Randy made his way to the table and cast his eyes on the infamous Jean Laveau.

"So this the guy I have to thank for me being a beta?" Randy said with just a tad more sarcasm than Cree cared for.

"You're a beta because your boss was an asshole. You'd do well to remember that," she said as she stared him down.

Randy reeled his attitude back and nodded to Cree out of respect for the order. It didn't matter if he could kick her ass and honestly, he wasn't sure if he could. She was number one and he was number two, and they had a mission to complete.

"Let's find something to put this son of a bitch in and get out of here," Cree said.

She turned away before she noticed Jean's left index finger twitch.

Up front, Doty had locked the front door and she and Rufus were sitting behind a counter, talking it up and laughing. What she didn't do was secure the elevators. With her hair pulled back in a tight ponytail and donning a baseball cap with a simple sweatshirt and jeans, Doty didn't immediately recognize the Gerard heiress as even being a girl until it was too late.

"Hey, buddy, uh-uh, turn around. We're closed," Doty said.

"How can you be closed? I thought college buildings were supposed to stay open all night?" Dani asked, still moving forward.

"Dude, if you don't turn the fuck arou,-- OH, SHIT!" Rufus exclaimed, "it's her!"

Rufus and Doty instinctively showed their teeth. They weren't trying to be threatening, it was merely reflexive – it's what vampires do. Unfortunately, it scares the shit out of people. It makes people think that they mean to harm them in some unpleasant way. It had that very same effect on Dani, which was a problem because she's more dangerous than they are. She felt threatened, so she jumped into full mactrouge. This, of course, set off an alarm in Lucien's head.

"SHIT!!" Lucien yelled. "Why's this girl always fightin'?!"

He was stuck at a light, two blocks away from campus. He cleared his mind and concentrated on putting calming thoughts into Dani's head.

"Calm down. They're not here for you. Don't fight. Be calm,"

Over and over he repeated those thoughts, hoping it might work. There was no way he could pop into mactrouge, not now; there were way too many people around and that was one rule he could not break. Never show what you are in public unless your life is in mortal danger. He just hoped that his sister's was not. Dani did hear his thoughts, but she still did not know they were coming from Lucien. It was just her inner voice talking to her again. Her hair fell still, but the glow in her eyes warned she hadn't fully let go.

CHAPTER 52

 ome home."

"My father send you here?" Dani asked as she continued to move forward, but with caution.

"Yes," Doty said as she cautiously moved backward. "We're just here for Laveau. We've got no quarrel with you."

"If your plans involve taking him, then I've got a quarrel with you."

And that was where things got out of hand.

Back in the lab, Randy had just found a heavy-duty bodybag to put Jean in.

"I heard he killed over a hundred that night," Randy said.

"I don't know how many there were. But I do know that three of them were my brothers,--"

Jean's eyes snapped open. In a blur, he lunged from the table and tore into Cree. She had no chance; he was like a wild animal as he slashed and ripped at her. Randy charged over to help and Jean spun into a shadow and instantly came out of one behind Randy. Jean put him in a chokehold and sunk his teeth into Randy's shoulder. Randy roared from the pain as

Cree rose up to fight. Jean opened his mouth and unleashed a flood of swamp water with impossible force. Cree was pinned against the wall and could neither move nor breathe. She was literally being drowned by the volume of water she was consuming and she would have drowned if Rufus hadn't come limping in. He looked like he had just come out on the bad side of a good fight and things were about to get worse for him.

"She's here! The girl, she's,-- OH SHIT!"

Jean stopped the water flow he was sending at Cree and she collapsed. In one motion, he twisted Randy's head completely around and off. Then he went for Rufus.

"More blood!" Hagatha cried. *"I need more blood!"*

Jean grabbed Rufus, threw him into the far wall and was on him again before Rufus could recover. Jean sunk his teeth into him and began to drain his body of blood. This was what Hagatha wanted, what she needed. She was using Jean to get it and he seemingly could do nothing to stop her. He sucked every ounce of blood from Rufus's body until Rufus finally exploded into dust. The blood began to re-animate the damaged and partially-decomposed tissue as it coursed through his body, but Hagatha needed more for her purpose. Much more. So he went back to work on Randy.

Meanwhile, Dani was working her way down the hall with Doty. Dani dragged Doty by her hair and slammed her face through every single glass door they passed on their way to the lab.

"You thought I was a boy?! REALLY?!" Dani yelled. She was still a little touchy about that.

Dani launched Doty through the swinging doors into the lab and Jean welcomely received her. He bit into Doty as Dani entered the room. Dani saw what looked to be a monster and jumped into full mactrouge. She formed an energy ball and launched it at Jean. Jean's eyes flashed, but this time, only one of his eyes was cerulean. The other pulsated a deep, dark red hue. He deflected the blast and charged Dani and grabbed her. She reversed his hold and slammed him, face first, into the wall. Jean melted into the shadowy wall and disappeared. A split second later, he came straight back out and grabbed her by the neck. Dani recognized the shadow move and she knew only one person who could do it. She knew that somehow, this hideous creature was Jean.

"No! Not this one. She's one of my sisters. Release her!" Hagatha ordered.

"Jean, it's me. It's Dani!" Dani gasped.

Jean heard Hagatha in his head and Dani's plea at the same time. He also seemed shocked to hear his own name. He loosened the grip on her neck but did not release her.

"Da-ni?..." he whispered. "Dan-iel, perhaps?..."

"Danielle," she said.

The glow faded from Jean's eyes.

"Ahhhh. Dan-ielle. P-P-Pret-ty."

"He remembered," Dani smiled.

This was the exact same sequence they used when they first met, all those years ago. Jean released her. For a brief moment, they connected and Dani's smile widened.

"...You... made it," Jean said.

It seemed as if he tried to form a smile on his face, but like so many of these moments, that one was fleeting.

"Dani?" Cree said.

Cree had regained consciousness and overheard Jean say Dani's name. As she tried to stumble to her feet, Jean's eyes flashed again and he charged past Dani and slammed Cree into the wall.

"No, don't!" Dani screamed. "Jean, don't! Don't kill her!"

Jean held Cree against that wall with his hand clasped around her throat. He struggled to oblige. He heard Dani's request, but he was also hearing the screaming orders of another.

"Kill this one! We need her blood! More blood! MORE!! I command you, KI-I-LL HER-R-R-R!!"

Dani could not see Jean as he struggled to combat the pain. Cree saw the war waged in his gaze, one eye flaring red, the other trembling blue.

"Jean, let her go, please," Dani asked.

Jean closed his eyes.

"Te-- Tell, h-h-him, I am... coming."

"T-Tell them... all-l-l. GO!"

Jean fought off Hagatha's demands and released Cree, but the price was pain. He staggered away from her. Cree didn't know what to think. She didn't understand why Jean let her go. Part of her was thankful; she was severely injured and in no condition to fight, but another part could only remember how he killed her three brothers. She wanted nothing more than to kill him right now, or die trying. Dani could see her struggle, and just like she had stopped Jean a moment ago, she stopped Cree from committing suicide.

"Cree," Dani said. Cree turned and saw Dani shake her head no. "Go home. Please."

As painful as it was for her, Cree nodded and staggered to the door, then stopped.

"Come with me," Cree said. "We'd all die before letting anyone hurt you. Please. Come home."

For sixteen years, she'd waited for someone to say that to her. Seeing Cree was like a loving embrace; her heart filled with all the memories of her checkered childhood. As hard as that time was, it was ice cream and cake compared to the last sixteen years. She badly wished to go with her, but when she looked at Jean, huddled in the corner in obvious pain, it reminded her of another.

"What about Kate?" Dani asked.

She already knew the answer, but she had to ask. Cree lowered her eyes and shook her head. Dani sighed. Some people believe you become numb to pain after your heart has been broken enough times. They're wrong.

"I can't," Dani said with longing and pain. "Be safe. Go."

Cree wanted to cry and she probably would later, in private. She looked back at Jean with hatred in her eyes and then left. Dani walked over to Jean, being very careful not to agitate or upset him. She had shared so many nightmares with him over the years; saw his torture, felt his pain, but she never completely understood it and until this moment, she never knew how much of it was true.

"What happened to you?" She asked.

It pained him to talk to her. He needed every ounce of his strength to fight off the wanton wishes and dreadful desires of the beast in his head.

"Why?!... Why did you come here?!

"I came for you. Just like you came for me."

"No, child! You cannot... Uhnnh, aaaahhh. Just go... Go! L-Leave this place! PLEASE. Leave me," Jean cried.

He saw his reflection on a metal cabinet he leaned up against and was horrified by it. Hagatha laughed heartily. She so enjoyed his pain.

"Okay-okay. It's okay. Kaitlin will know what to,--"

"Kaitlin, Yes-s-s-s! Take us to Kaitl-i-i-in!"

"NO-O-O-O!" Jean screamed.

Dani didn't know he was talking to Hagatha and not her. He closed his eyes and fell backward into the shadow he was leaning against.

"Jean, no, wait! Don't go!" Dani screamed. "Jean?! Jean, Come back! Please, don't leave me! Don't leave me alone again... Please..."

Doty staggered to her feet behind Dani. Jean's eyes opened and he zipped out of the shadow, past Dani, knocking her down. He grabbed Doty and finished what he had started before. Dani could barely watch the savagery he displayed. He ripped through her until there was nothing left. Then he turned to Dani with only his right eye open, the red one. The left one, for some reason, was tightly closed. He glared at her with that one red eye as the blood dripped from his mouth and in that moment, for the first time, she understood that he had brought the heinous presence, in their shared nightmares, with him. Dani glared back at the single red eye and saw what true evil looks like. True Evil took umbrage to her impertinent glare and spoke to her through Jean.

"Leave, now, little sister. While I still allow it."

"Sister?" Dani thought. *"Interesting choice of words,"*

Dani gave in to the wishes of this evil that held her friend – for now - and she exited the room.

CHAPTER 53

"*You look like you've seen a monster.*"

Dani ran out of the building and raced across campus. She needed to get to Kaitlin. Perhaps even bring her back to help. Distracted, she rounded a corner and ran into a group of four, nearly tackling one of them. Fortunately, he was strong enough to catch her. Perhaps, a bit *too* strong.

"Whoa! Easy, princess," the guy said.

He was wearing a letterman's jacket, which was appropriate for someone his size. He was built like a linebacker.

"Sorry,--" Dani tried to apologize but was interrupted.

"You all right?" he asked. "You look like you've seen a monster."

Then an all-too-familiar voice answered for her.

"Oh, I'd say she's seen many, Rex," Malcolm said as he emerged from the bushes with Bryson by his side. "Apologies that I couldn't make the last outing, Luv, but I wouldn't have missed this one for the world."

All at once, random memories of Austin's death popped into

Dani's head like pictures from a slideshow. Each one brought its own specific pain. That pain turned to anger, then to rage. Nothing else mattered to her now. All she saw was Malcolm. It was a youthful mistake, as there were still four other bodies present.

"You're dead,--" Dani almost said as her eyes flared red.

Right then, Rex, the big linebacker guy, sucker-punched her and knocked the red right out of her. He sent her flying into the arms of one of the other unwisely ignored combatants.

On the other side of the campus, Lucien had pulled into a parking garage and was looking for a space when Dani got hit. He felt that punch almost as much as she did, and he nearly crashed.

"What the fuck?! Shit!"

He sped up to the roof where there was only a smattering of cars. He pulled into the far corner and readied himself.

"Mactrouge, mactrouge," he frantically whispered. He thought about getting out of the car, but he didn't know exactly where to find her and he could feel that she needed him now. He had to stay present. "Come on, do it!" he yelled.

He was right. She did need him. Badly.

"Tipper managed to deliver your message," Malcolm said. "Now I believe she has one for you."

Dani landed in the arms of the vampire she'd once spared—the same one who watched Austin die. Dani mangled her pretty good that night, but she had long since healed and this was personal for her. She turned Dani around and knee'd her in the face, then grabbed her by her hair to stop her from falling and delivered two hard punches to her face that broke Dani's nose.

"Twenty-two days of pain. That's what I suffered through," Tipper explained to Dani, "and I'm gonna make you feel every last bit of it before I suck what blood is left out of your battered body."

Tipper let go of Dani's hair and delivered a front kick to her face. Dani hit the ground like a load of bricks. She was barely conscious and was bleeding heavily from her nose and mouth. She never really had a chance as the four combatants circled and stood over her.

"Oh, Danielle," Malcolm sighed. "You called me all the way here for this? Have to say I expected more."

"I want to finish her! You owe me that!" Tipper yelled.

Malcolm took a slight exception to her tone.

"I owe you?" Malcolm frowned. "Careful, my dear. After what she did to you last time, you're lucky I didn't kill you."

"Sorry," Tipper said in a soft, apologetic tone.

"But you seem to have taken all the fight out of her, anyway. Suppose you might as well finish it. So disappointing."

Tipper stooped down to Dani and smiled as her fangs grew.

Back at the car, Lucien tried to reach his sister.

"Don't quit. Get up, Dani." he thought.

"I can't," she thought.

Lucien pushed out a concerned sigh, for both of them, then took in a very deep breath to prepare himself for the pain he was about to receive – maybe for the last time.

"It's okay. Just open your eyes," Lucien thought.

Dani complied with her 'intuition' and saw Tipper looming deathly close to her. Lucien saw her, too. He burst into full mactrouge and took the reins from his little sister one last time. Tipper grabbed Dani by the hair and pulled her up into a seated position as she moved in to take a bite. Tipper's eyes enlarged when she saw Dani's hair waving around her hand. She panicked and rushed to sink her teeth into Dani's neck, but Dani grabbed Tipper's jaw and pushed her face back far enough so that Tipper could now see that Dani's eyes were red and that she was very, very angry. This surprised Malcolm almost as much as it did Tipper and his brow furrowed.

"Curious," Malcolm said to Bryson.

Bryson did not agree. He growled and barked twice at his two betas and they went into action. Dani punched Tipper in her nose and broke it, then launched her into one of the charging betas, toppling him as she thrust her hand toward the other one, repelling him into a tree. The big vampire, Rex, was right behind her and tried to connect his big boot to her head. She caught his foot and rolled with it in her grasp. He cried out as his knee popped out and dislocated.

"Oh, Rex," Malcolm said disdainfully as Rex writhed on the ground in pain. "Pathetic."

Dani jumped up and grounded herself as the two betas regrouped and began to circle around her.

"She still can't get off the ground," Malcolm whispered to himself. This seemed to puzzle him for some reason.

Dani scooped the air with cupped hands and two balls of fire burst into her palms.

"Ire," she called out and the balls of fire launched themselves at the betas. "INCOENDIUM!"

The balls burst onto the betas and engulfed them. She raised her hands upward and the flames swirled and sweltered over them. Bryson let out a horrid roar as he fell to his knees, feeling the exact pain that his betas were suffering through. Dani clenched her fists and the betas exploded. Malcolm's brow furrowed more.

"No, this isn't right. She shouldn't be able to do that," he whispered.

Lucien fell out of mactrouge and slumped over the steering wheel as a stream of blood fell from his nose. His head felt like it had been split open and his heart was beating so hard that he feared it might explode. He pushed open the door, fell out of the car and vomited. He rolled onto his back and took in a few heavy breaths as he tried to maintain consciousness. His heart began to slow down to a normal pace as he continued to take in slow, steady breaths. The splitting headache remained, but he could live with that. Of even more importance – he would live. Lucien had not seen Bryson and didn't know he was there. Even if he did, there was no way he could take control of his sister again. He needed to rest for a moment, to try and regain his strength. He knew Dani could handle the female vampire on her own, but there was one thing he needed to take care of himself.

"Malcolm," he whispered.

Bryson rose to his feet and prepared to take Dani down until Malcolm stopped him.

"Not yet," Malcolm said.

Dani's hair fell to her shoulders, but her eyes remained red as she popped out of full mactrouge and moved toward Tipper. Tipper staggered to her feet. Without her three cohorts to back her up, she seemed much less willing to square off with Dani. She slowly backed away and looked to Malcolm for support. He had none to offer her.

"You asked to be here, my dear," he said with very little empathy.

"Twenty-two days of pain, right?" Dani asked her. "You were going to show me what that felt like. Okay. Show me."

Whatever ambivalence Tipper may have had was replaced by her hatred of Dani. She didn't need Malcolm's help. She was a highly trained Council vampire and she was not to be intimidated by some young witch who didn't even have full control of her powers. She painfully reset her broken nose, wiped away the blood and moved in to engage.

"After she's discarded Tipper,… kill her," Malcolm whispered to Bryson.

Tipper was an elite fighter, but on her own, against someone with the fighting skills of Dani, she couldn't be more outclassed. Dani dodged and blocked each one of Tipper's strikes and made her pay a significant price for throwing it. Rex received an unexpected kick in the face while he tried to crawl out of the way as Dani battered Tipper around the clearing until she could barely stand. Only her hatred kept her on her feet. Dani kicked Rex again out of petty spite and because he was close enough to be kicked. Tipper threw a weak right and Dani caught her fist, twisted it, then brought her elbow down on Tipper's arm, breaking it. Tipper screamed. Dani then stomped Tipper in the side of her knee, breaking her leg. Tipper slouched to the ground. Dani picked her up by the throat and pulled her in close.

"This is for Austin, you bitch." Dani said.

She drove the screaming Tipper into a low branch, impaling her clean through the chest. Tipper burst into dust. Dani's hair came alive as she turned to Malcolm, only to find Bryson standing in front of her. The big alpha backhanded Dani and sent her flying. She landed on her side and rolled three times before she stopped. Only The Talisman had hit her harder. If she hadn't been protected by the full mactrouge, it may very well have killed her. Lucien reacted like he had received the blow himself. He collapsed next to a small pond on the campus. He grabbed his head and rolled onto his back. He was disoriented and in great pain, but he forced himself to mactrouge. He didn't have the strength to take over for her but, at the very least, he could give her more power.

"Get up. GET UP!" he thought. *"Protect yourself!"*

Disoriented and dazed, Dani released a couple of wild energy blasts, almost killing Rex, who was still crawling around looking for a safe place, but Bryson was long gone from that spot. She struggled to her feet, still very much in a stupor. She spun around in a circle looking for him, but all she saw were trees and shrubbery.

"I know you so very badly wanted me, my dear," Malcolm said.

Dani fired off an energy blast in the direction of his voice, which seemed to move around the clearing on its own. Malcolm was toying and taunting her for his own amusement.

"But in order to do that, you have to go through him," Malcolm said.

Dani fired off another energy blast in what she thought was his direction.

"You've displayed some curiously interesting techniques this evening, but in all these years, you have yet to learn how to get off the ground. It really is your greatest advantage, and without it, I'm afraid you have no chance of defeating him."

Bryson charged in from her left and attacked her. All Dani could do was give ground. He was so much faster than anyone she'd ever engaged. She couldn't even get off an energy blast. Unaware of her surroundings, she backed into a tree. Bryson swung at her, and she was just able to duck under his talons as they scratched four inch-deep lines across the tree. She somersaulted away from him and returned to her feet as another blow came her way. She threw both of her forearms up to block the powerful swing, but the force was so great it bruised her arms. She stumbled a few steps before she tripped over Rex and lost her balance. That one defenseless moment was all Bryson needed to thrust the palm of his hand into her chest. It knocked the wind out of her and bruised a few ribs as well. She flew backward into a tree. The red drained out of her eyes and her hair fell flat as she hit the ground and spit up some blood. Lucien also fell out of mactrouge and spit up blood.

With his left eye still closed, Jean's right eye glimmered red as he finished sucking the last of the blood out of the bodies in the room. Then his body jerked and he grunted in pain as he buckled over and screamed. He writhed and convulsed on the floor until his body flexed to a point where it seemed it might break. He swallowed several deep breaths and when his eyes opened, one was again burning cerulean blue. He scrambled to his feet and took off down the hall. He burst through the doors of the building, leaped off the top step and turned into the black raven once again, and took flight high above the campus. The raven spotted Dani in the clearing below, pointed his nose, and dove hard and fast.

Malcolm was more than a bit disappointed in his antagonistic apprentice.

"It was a valiant effort, I suppose. Certainly not up to your mother's standards, but if nothing else, you are the bravest girl I have ever seen. I only wish I could have seen you at your best," Malcolm said, then to Bryson, "This experiment is over. Finish it, please."

Bryson looked down at Dani.

"For all the betas you killed," he said to her.

Just as he was about to strike, the raven dove, beak first, deep into Bryson's back, then transformed into Jean, who stood up and stretched out inside of him, causing Bryson to explode. Malcolm was astonished.

"…That was unexpected," he whispered.

Both Jean and Dani were soaked in Bryson's blood. Dani could not believe her eyes as she watched Jean absorb all the excess blood through his pores.

"*A-a-a-a-ah-h-h-h,*" Hagatha gasped euphorically.

Jean extended his right arm. Magically, a branch broke off a nearby tree and flew into his hand. He caught it and threw it down through Rex, finally ending his escapade around the clearing, as he exploded into dust. Jean looked to where Malcolm was, but he had already made an expeditious exit. He then placed his focus on Dani.

"You are not yet strong enough to be here."

He looked down at her, favoring his blue, left eye, but he couldn't hide the evil that was still present in the vibrant, red, right one.

"Take Kaitlin and go. I am… not strong enough to protect you."

"…From what?"

Jean turned his head, favoring the right.

"Meeeee," Jean said as Hagatha cackled in his head.

He turned away from Dani and stepped into a shadow.

"Jean, no, wait,--"

He spun back to her, revealing only his right eye and the evil that came with it.

"LEAVE US!!" Jean – or something, boomed.

The ground quaked from the energy he expelled. He backed into the shadow, closed his eyes and vanished.

Lucien dipped his hand in the pond and tossed some water on his face to rinse away the excess blood. He took in some deep, controlled breaths, pushed himself up with a distressed look on his face. He stumbled off, not knowing exactly where he was going. He only knew that he needed to find his sister. He couldn't feel her for the first time since they were little. The headache he was suffering through didn't allow him to feel anything. He could only hope and pray that she was still alive. As his anxiety increased, so did his speed as he raced down a campus walkway until he accidentally collided into Malcolm, who had just burst through some large shrubbery. He seemed to be more concerned about what may be behind him than what was in front of him.

"Pardon me," Malcolm said.

"S'cuse me," Lucien said simultaneously.

Lucien took a few more steps before he stopped with a curious look on his face. He turned and stared at the person moving away from him for a few seconds before he called out to him.

"…Malcolm?"

Malcolm stopped at the edge of the pond and turned back to

Lucien. He looked at him with an expression on his face very similar to the one he was receiving.

"...Sorry, have we met?" Malcolm asked.

"Yeah. Long time ago," Lucien nodded. "You called it a 'Teaching Moment'," he indicated with air quotes. "Remember? Somethin' 'bout consequences and whatnot."

Malcolm thought about that a good moment, until the memory registered on his face. "...Ahhhh. The brother," Malcolm sighed.

"Yep." Lucien nodded. "My sister still alive?"

"Regrettably."

Lucien exhaled his relief.

"Good."

"Eh... That's a matter of opinion, actually."

"Well, like assholes, we all got 'em," Lucien said. Malcolm, agreeably, nodded. "Now, 'bout d'em consequences and whatnot..."

Malcolm held a coyish smile on his face for a few seconds before his eyes flashed red and he popped into full mactrouge and fired a series of energy blasts in Lucien's direction. Lucien dove out of the way and rolled to his feet in full mactrouge. He rolled up and fired off several quick blasts out of each hand that countered Malcolm's offensive. A blast from his right hand exploded on the ground in front of Malcolm and left him off-balance. Lucien threw another with his left hand that struck a heavy branch above the off-balanced Council member, who dove into the pond to avoid it.

"Glacies!" Lucien yelled as he thrust his right hand toward the pond.

The pond crinkled and cracked as it froze over, trapping Malcolm within it. Not even a second passed before the pond exploded upward and sent shards of crystallized ice in Lucien's direction. With a quick wave of his hand, he unfroze the ice, and instead of shards, water harmlessly passed through him. Lucien ran over to the now-empty pond, and Malcolm was gone.

CHAPTER 54

Kaitlin was a wreck. Even though the motel was less than a mile away from campus, she hated letting Dani go there alone, but it was agreed that it was way too dangerous for her to assist. They both knew Julien would send people for Jean and if Tirin was one of them, Dani was not yet strong enough to stop him. So she waited with as much patience as an impatient person could. A soft knock on the door startled her. Kaitlin grabbed her forty-five caliber handgun and moved to the door with caution.

"It's me," Dani said from the other side of the door.

Kaitlin exhaled all the pent-up anxiety she had been harboring, slid the chain off the door and opened it. Finding Dani standing there, covered in mostly dried blood, brought it all back.

"OH MY GOD!"

"It's okay," Dani exhaled, then took in a deep breath and swallowed. "This time, most of it's not my blood,--" she finished before she passed out in Kaitlin's arms.

Twenty minutes later, Dani had reset her broken nose – as she had done many times in the past - and was sprawled out in the tub with an ice pack on her face. Kaitlin sat next to her and dabbed and cleaned her other wounds, as she had done many times in the past.

"You know what your mom's best fighting trick was?" Kaitlin said.

"What?" Dani murmured from underneath the ice pack.

"Not getting hit," Kaitlin said and she was not joking, or trying to make light of this. "Seriously, Danielle, this is fucking ridiculous."

Dani removed the ice pack and revealed two black eyes to go along with everything else.

"I know," she groaned, "I gotta do better. I got to get off the ground, I just don't know h-- OUCH!" Dani screamed and looked at Kaitlin with the saddest, 'How could you do that to me' eyes.

"Ouhh. Sorry... That one's gonna leave a mark."

"...It'd have been worse if he hadn't come."

"Are you sure it's him?"

"Yeah, it's him, but..."

"What?" Kaitlin asked.

"...It's like there's something inside of him, controlling him. It's almost like,--"

"There's a witch inside 'em?" a voice finished for her.

Kaitlin jumped as Dani stood up in the tub and flashed into full mactrouge to find Lucien, soaking wet, standing in the doorway. He was nowhere near as beat up as she was, but it was obvious he hadn't had the best of nights either. Embarrassed by his sister's naked body, he scrunched up his face and turned his head away.

"Awh, Jesus Christ, Dani!" Lucien complained as he used his hand to shield his peripheral.

Dani dropped out of mactrouge. She hadn't seen him in sixteen years, but she knew it was him. She could feel it. Kaitlin, however, could not and she lunged for her gun.

"Ms. Morrison, please don't grab that,--" Lucien tried to say as Kaitlin grabbed her gun and aimed it at him.

"No, it's Lucien!" Dani yelled as she pushed the gun down. "...It's okay."

"You getting the shit kicked out of you is NOT okay!" Kaitlin fired back.

"What, you think I had somethin' to do with d'at?" Lucien asked, still holding his hand to block the view of his still standing sister.

"Your daddy's people nearly beat her to death, then twenty minutes later you just happen to be in the neighborhood?" Kaitlin said.

"Dani, you know those weren't OUR," he directed toward Kaitlin, "Daddy's people. They belonged to a dude named Malcolm Terrence, and,--"

"You know him?" Dani asked with a surprised look on her face.

Lucien tried to answer but was still irreversibly uncomfortable with the naked body in front of him. He kept his hand against the side of his face, allowing him to see Kaitlin only.

"Dani, could you just,-- sit down, or wrap a fuckin' towel, or somethin'. Jesus!"

"Ooou. Sorry," Dani said as she popped back down into the tub and covered herself. "You don't have to be so mean about it."

"I wasn't being mean about it, I just asked you to cover the fuck up."

"Well, maybe if you hadn't just busted in our room, I could've put on,--"

"I ain't bust in, I had to be careful. Wasn't exactly sure which one of these rooms was yours."

"You weren't sure, so you broke in?"

"I ain't break ANYTHIN'--"

"That makes no sense?!"

"You standin' up naked in front of people makes no,--"

"Alright, enough!" Kaitlin yelled.

Lucien peeked around his hand. Dani had submerged herself into the water and covered herself up pretty good, but Lucien grabbed a towel and tossed it at her anyway.

"I mean, we dysfunctional and all, but damn, girl."

Dani caught the towel and threw it back at him, matching his same energy.

"Looks like you need it more than I do. I'm supposed to be wet," Dani said as Lucien made a pained facial expression over her poor choice of words. "What happened to you, anyway?"

Lucien hung the towel on the door and began to examine himself in the mirror over the sink, still avoiding looking directly at Dani.

"Same thing that happened to you. Malcolm," he said as he turned on the water to wash the blood from his nose.

"How do you know him?" Dani asked.

"You ain't the only one he gave a lesson to," Lucien said, then without even looking at her, "How long you gonna point that gun at me, Ms. Morrison?"

"Katie, it's,--" Dani tried to say.

"Until you tell me how you knew we were here?" Kaitlin replied.

"What? You never told her?" Lucien asked Dani as he continued to wash his face.

"Told her what?" Dani asked.

Lucien's soapy face matched the bewildered look he was receiving from his sister.

"Are you fuckin' kiddin' me?" Dani did not respond. "...Oh, my God. You really don't know, do you?" he said as he realized the truth.

"I'm gonna count to three," Kaitlin said as she cocked the gun.

"Katie, sto-o-op," Dani whined.

"I always know where y'all at," he said as he reached for the towel to dry his face. "Well, not always, but most of the,--"

"Oh my God, you can feel me," Dani said as she realized the truth.

Lucien shook his head with a distasteful look on his face. He was still a bit uncomfortable with his sister's vernacular.

"Definitely woulda worded d'at in a different way." He muttered as he began to dry himself off.

Dani welled up with emotion.

"So they've been using you to track us all these years?" Kaitlin said.

"No! That ain't the way it works. If it did, I'd a brought you home a long time ago."

"So they can kill her in New Orleans? What's the difference?"

"You ain't listenin', Ms. Morrison. Only people been tryin' to kill her is The Council."

"And The Talisman," Dani added. Lucien gave her a 'whatever' nod.

"Pop been tryin' to find her so that he can bring her home."

Dani was truly touched by this new information, but at the same time, there was much she didn't understand.

"If that's true, then why didn't you?" Dani asked with an overflow of sadness that escaped through her lips. "If he really wanted to find me, why didn't you just tell him? Why'd you make us suffer through everything we've been through?"

Remorse clouded Lucien's face as he seemed to wonder why himself.

"Well,... 'sides the fact that they woulda killed you, Ms. Morrison,... Momma told me not to," he said softly.

"What?... When?-- Why?!" Dani said.

"...Night she died,--"

"Was killed," Dani interrupted.

Lucien paused and glared at her before he chose to continue.

"...She came to me and... She gave me the power to protect you 'til you was old enough and strong enough to protect ya'self," Lucien explained. "Then she made me promise I wouldn't tell nobody."

"Why?" Dani asked.

"She thought someone in the house wanted you dead. For the longest I thought she was wrong 'bout d'at, but,... someone set The Talisman on you. Probably grandpa." He nodded. "But, anyway, I don't always know where you are. I can only see what you see when you mactrouge and I can only hear your thoughts when there's enough emotion behind them. Sometimes it's obvious. Sometimes it's not. Anyways, I'm sorry."

Kaitlin lowered the gun.

"How long have you been helping her like this?" Kaitlin asked.

"Since the train. D'at one was mostly Momma, but I still felt it. She somehow connected us so I could feel your pain and whenever you pop into mactrouge, I'm supposed to,... give you a little boost. When we was little, it was automatic; it would just kick in. Didn't really have a choice in the matter, but once I got older, I learned how to control it to the point where I didn't have to do it if I ain't want to, but..." he said as he tried to bridle his emotions, "well,... you are my lil' brother."

When they were little, Dani always looked up to Lucien. Even at the age of three, he was strong and confident and always sure about whatever it was that he was doing. She loved him so much, but she never thought that her feelings were truly reciprocated, until now.

"Turn around," she said.

Lucien sighed and turned away as Dani climbed out of the tub and slipped into her robe. She had almost forgotten how much she missed him and in this moment, much to his discord, wanted nothing more than a hug from her big brother.

"Ah, Jesus, Dani!" Lucien cried out as he threw his hands in the air, refusing to touch her.

"Oh, don't be a baby, you're already wet," Dani said.

They both stood there for a few seconds and really took each other in for what was truly the first time in their lives. Right then, they both realized that the one thing they had been missing - was each other. Dani threw her arms around him. Lucien hugged her back. Kaitlin couldn't help but smile.

"I love you so much," Dani said.

"I love you too, Little Brother," Lucien joked.

"Don't call me that," Dani whined.

Lucien's face wrinkled up as he looked at her.

"Jeeze, look at your face," he said. "All them scars,"

"I know. Kate already told me I look horrible."

"Those were not my words." Kaitlin objected.

"Why don't you just fix it?"

"I don't have the power to do that," a disheartened Dani replied.

"Yeah, you do. See, this is what I'm talkin' 'bout. You got all these powers inside you right now, you just don't know how to access 'em. Probably 'cuz you got too much human in you, cloudin' things up - No disrespect, Ms. Morrison," Lucien said. Kaitlin shook her head and rolled her eyes as he continued. "But I think it's confusin' you and causin' you to hold back. You're a witch, Dani, and you gotta let that out. If you don't it's gonna get us both killed, 'cuz,..." he paused, not wishing to say the next words. "I can't keep fightin' fo' you like I did tonight."

"So, you're like, what? Inside of me when you do it?"

Lucien grimaced again from her poor choice of words.

"Why do you-- Just... Don't say it like that."

Dani matched the grimace she was receiving from Lucien and returned it.

"Eeww! Pervo!" Dani said, then punched him in the arm. "Why would you take it that way?"

"Ooww! The hell you hit me fo'?" Lucien yelled.

"Alright, you two," Kaitlin said, already exhausted by them.

"She hits harder than she thinks she does."

"No, I know exactly how hard I hit," Dani replied.

Lucien glared at her as Dani let the tiniest grin escape her face.

"Just-- Close yo' eyes," Lucien said.

Dani complied, and Lucien's eyes sparkled red. He placed his hands over her face and removed all her scars and fixed her broken nose - properly. She pushed him out of the way and looked into the mirror.

"Oh my gosh… I'm pretty." She whispered, surprised by the image in front of her.

"You were always pretty, sweetheart," Kaitlin smiled. "Even with the scars."

"You look like Mom," Lucien said. Dani beamed from his assessment.

"You look like her, too," Kaitlin said to Lucien. He didn't respond. He just looked at her as he tried to hold back a smile. He didn't mind that assessment one bit.

"Now you need to take that pretty lil' face and disappear for a lil' while longer," Lucien said.

"No. I'm coming home on Wednesday."

"Why?" Lucien asked.

"What do you mean, 'Why?' You know why," Dani said.

"If it's anything other than to celebrate our birthday, then you haven't been paying attention."

"He killed Momma."

"Even if that was true, which it's not, entirely, what 'chu think you gonna do 'bout it? You can't fight."

"I can fight. I've been fighting my whole life," she said matter-of-factly.

"Fine, you can fight," he replied in the same way. "But until you learn how to use your powers, you ain't gon' beat nobody, and don't gimme that prophecy bullshit, 'cuz I don't even know if d'at applies to you."

"How could it not? It's about me!"

"You was raised by her," he said, pointing to Kaitlin, "and you got a lot of her in you!"

"You know, I don't know whether to take these as compliments or not," Kaitlin said.

"I know, first it's a bad thing. Now, apparently, it's good. How convenient," Dani added.

"Listen to me," Lucien said. "A lotta folks believe that her influence gives you a choice that no other malafec has. You ain't tied to nothin'. You can fight the prophecy - if you want to."

"And do what? Continue to run for the rest of my life?" Dani asked. "Lucien, I'm tired! I want to come home!"

"And I want you to! Just give me a few months, okay?"

"No!"

"Would you just listen for a second! Pop's gonna be elected Governor in a few weeks. While he's up in d'at big house, Gerard Industries and all the other operations gon' be run by me. Once I'm in charge, I'll deal with Malcolm and The Council and whoever else I need to, to bring you home - SAFELY. And I might even be able to bring you home too, Ms. Morrison."

"How?" Dani and Kaitlin said in unison.

"Laveau's the one they really want,--"

"No way!" Dani said.

"Absolutely not!" Kaitlin said in harmony.

"It's the only way! And I ain't even sure they'll go for d'at!" he exclaimed. "Rayna don't care. Truth be told, she actually likes you; always did. Like me, she's advocated for yo' return from the beginnin', it's just Tirin and Pop," he said as he shook his head. "They ain't havin' it."

"Maybe you should consider just,--" Kaitlin tried to say, but Dani wouldn't even let her finish the sentence.

"NO!" Dani said with an indignant expression on her face. "I'm not leaving you."

"You gotta gimme some time, Dani. I'm tryin' to make stuff right, but you gotta do your part too. Malcolm's got everyone from the east side of London walkin' around New Awlins waitin' fo' ya'. Don't be stupid. Get as far away from here as ya' can. A lot of us know d'at witches ain't these psychotic killers The Council done made y'all out to be. So don't act like one. I'll come get cha' when the time is right."

"I won't let them hurt Jean," Dani said.

"YOU won't let,--" Lucien took a breath. He was becoming angry, and he didn't want to. "You know how many people that motha-fucka killed? Do you?! People who cared 'bout you, and you too, for that matter, Ms. Morrison… Hundreds! He slaughtered 'em,--"

"He was trying to protect your mother and Dani,--" Kaitlin tried to say.

"FROM WHAT?!" Lucien shouted.

This reunion had taken an unpleasant turn and wasn't going the way either one of the twins wanted it to, so before it got worse, one of them decided to end it.

"I love ya', Brah',-- I do, but don't come home. Not now, 'cuz I ain't gonna help you with this. I ain't fightin' for you no more." He punctuated. Then, almost as an apology, "I can't."

He looked at Ms. Morrison, then again at his sister, then turned and walked out.

CHAPTER 55

"*Just because your name's on the building, don't make it yours.*"

Rayna was perched atop her favorite desk corner in what seemed to be an intense conversation with Tirin when Julien stormed into his office with Serena and Lucien in tow. He made a B-line straight to Rayna with some intensity of his own.

"I asked you to send the best you had," Julien said.

"I did!" Rayna said. "Who knew that he'd pick last night to wake up on the wrong side of the bed."

"See? That's why I wanted you to go!" Julien yelled.

"And do what? Die with the others?" Lucien asked. "Why you so quick to throw her in harm's way all da' time?"

"We're malafecs, son. We're in harm's way every day. Maybe if she'd've been there like I asked her to, she could have figured something out, or worst-case scenario, aborted the mission and saved lives! But you didn't think about that, did you?"

Lucien didn't answer, because he hadn't thought about that.

"How's Cree?" Julien asked Tirin.

"Alive," Tirin grunted.

"What put her in Mr. Laveau's good graces?"

"She was the messenger," Rayna said. "Apparently we no longer need to pursue Mr. Jean Laveau, as he intends on making it his life's mission to pursue us, the three of us, to be specific."

"…Good. That makes it simple," Julien said.

"No. Not good, Julien," Serena interjected. "This is absolutely the worst time for something like this! We're less than two weeks away from winning this thing!"

"Naw, Laveau likes to keep things quiet. He'll want to be discreet, which suits me just fine," Julien responded. "Let him come."

"It's different this time, Julien. He's got You-Know-Who with him," Rayna said. "Being possessed by the most powerful witch in history can't be a good thing. Just not sure whether that means for us, or for him."

Julien didn't respond.

"Cree also made contact with Dani," Tirin said.

"What happened?" Julien asked as his tone changed to one of concern.

"She was the reason why Laveau let Cree go." Tirin said.

"Good…" Julien said before getting lost in his own thoughts. "She didn't hurt anybody, did she?"

"No, Laveau took care of that," Rayna added.

"Cree also asked her to come home with her and it seemed as if she wanted to, but…" Tirin hesitated, which was unusual for him.

He would pause and take his time when choosing his words, but he never hesitated – until now. Julien noticed the difference as well.

"What?…" Julien asked.

Tirin would not respond, so Rayna did.

"She wouldn't come without Kaitlin. Which means, if you two can get over yourselves and leave that poor woman alone, you can get your daughter back."

"It's not that simple!" Tirin roared.

"YES, IT IS!" Rayna shot back, more fiercely than usual.

Tirin didn't back down, but he didn't challenge her, either.

"Pop," Lucien interrupted, "Kaitlin's been there for her for sixteen years. I helped her fight, but she kept her alive. That's gotta mean somethin'." Then he looked at Tirin. "I know you love her just as much as you love me. Why can't Laveau be enough?" Tirin didn't respond. "Kaitlin ain't kill nobody, Pop. Yeah, she brought him here, but that's 'cuz Momma asked her to. Ain't none of this her fault."

Julien sat at his desk and simmered for a moment. He knew Lucien was right; it's just that, when you hate something for so long, it becomes a part of you and with each passing day, becomes increasingly more difficult to let go. Finally, he looked up from his desk and his eyes fell upon Tirin and everyone else followed. Tirin was angered by the unwanted attention that was dumped on him. Julien didn't ask with words, but the look that he gave Tirin was enough to offend him. He turned and sped to the door, then stopped. He stood there for a few seconds before he spoke.

"No one kills Laveau, but me-e-e-e-e," he growled as if it pained him to say it, then he turned back to face them for confirmation. Rayna nodded. Julien closed his eyes and clenched his fists. It looked like he shook his head for a brief moment before he nodded. It was enough. Tirin jetted out of the room.

"Thanks, Pop," Lucien said.

"Now we just have to figure out how to do that," Rayna said.

"Well, can we do that later?" Serena asked. "We really need to put some time into the Evans project before this afternoon's meeting."

"Wait, what?" Lucien said, confused. "You're not still considerin' that, are you?"

"Why wouldn't we be?" Julien said as if he was irritated just by the question.

"Pop, that acquisition is a mistake. One that we may never recover from."

"Is that a fact?"

"Lucien, we've been working on this for almost a year now," Serena said. "It's the right thing to do, and the timing couldn't be better."

"Y'all didn't even read my proposal, did y'all?" Disappointed by their silence, Lucien shook his head. "Pop, Gerard Enterprises may not survive the stress that acquisition will put on this company."

"Just how in the hell you figure that?" Julien said.

"Look at the numbers."

"I'm the one who ran the numbers."

"Well, maybe you missed somethin' because,--"

"Maybe I missed something?" Julien laughed. "This coming from our resident high school dropout."

"How long you gonna hold that diploma over me?"

"Probably 'til you get one."

"Outside of bein' a requirement for college and gettin' an entry-level job, what do I need one fo'?"

"I think you just answered your own question, son."

"I ain't goin' to college, Pop, and I work here."

"You work here 'cuz ain't no company in their right mind gonna hire a high school dropout!"

Frustrated, Lucien looked to Rayna, who wanted nothing more than to save this boy right now. Julien stopped it before she had a chance.

"No!" Julien yelled at Rayna before finishing with Luc. "Don't look for her to finish your fights in here."

That hit a nerve.

"I'm fluent in seven languages, one more than you, and I surpassed every teacher in d'at school you sent me to, when I was fifteen. There wasn't nothin' more for me to learn there."

Maybe math, 'cuz last time I checked, English, French, Italian, Spanish, Japanese and Chinese equals six, not seven."

"Chinese got two languages, Pop. Mandarin and Cantonese."

"See, this is the kind of stupid shit I'm talkin' 'bout. Why the hell would you waste good thought learning Cantonese?!"

"'Cuz that's what they speak in Hong Kong — the second richest city in the world," Lucien said.

There was no turning back now. Even if there was, Lucien didn't want to. He had been waiting for this moment and now was as good a time as any.

"That's why I learned it," Lucien continued. "We been the number two supplier and manufacturer for sulfur in the southeast region for the last twenty years,--"

"That's why we're buying Evans Industries! And then next year we gon' begin a company-wide expansion that will eventually push us into that number one spot. That's how real business is done, son."

"There's only so many consumers for our products, Pop. Unless you can somehow persuade the ones buyin' from the number one company in the region to switch over to us, nothin' changes, other than the fact that you just spent more than three-quarters of our assets to become bigger. Bigger, don't always make it better. I'm talkin' 'bout takin' Gerard Enterprises global."

Julien winced and turned his head away as Lucien continued.

"There are so many business opportunities for us outside of this country, Pop. You talk about increasin' our yearly wealth by tens of millions by manufacturin' the same crap we've been doing since this company started: fireworks, fertilizers and fungicides."

"An eighth of the country depends on us for that 'crap', as you call it."

"What if an eighth of the world depended on us for somethin'? Then instead of tens of millions, we'd be talkin' 'bout billions. And we'll be usin' the exact same processes we already have in place to make sulfuric acid and vulcanizin' rubber, 'cuz that's all we really do. D'at ain't gonna never change. All we need to do is just tweak our manufacturin'. We convert one of our fertilizer plants – just one! And instead of pushin' out fertilizer, we push out cell phone batteries and cases."

"CELL PHONES?!" Julien said with a mix of anger and impatience.

"Everybody in the world don't use ours, or anybody's fertilizer, Pop, but just about everybody in the world uses a cell phone."

"They got people all over the world doing that! Why the hell you think they would use ours?!"

Lucien quickly moved to his father's desk and grabbed two unopened proposals off the stack.

"Because ours'll be better. The last three months I've been in contact with this group down in Australia. They got a theory 'bout a lithium-sulfur battery that's gon' change the world. All they need is money, which we got plenty of. We saddle up with them and we'll be at the forefront of this industry."

"A theory? Everybody's got fucking theories, Lucien!"

"It's not a theory, it works! You can go a week without chargin' your cell phone with these things. The bigger model is strong enough to power an electric car for more than a thousand miles. I did some projections; by twenty-twenty, two percent of this country will be usin' electric vehicles. By twenty-twenty-five; twenty percent of the world. Pop, we could be doin' what Grandpa always wanted us to do. Lead the industry."

"That's funny you mentioned him. He didn't finish high school either, so I'm sure he'd wager the future of this company on the projections of another dropout. I won't."

"I'd like to see that college-educated mind you so proud of, tell me my numbers are wrong."

"Watch yourself," Julien warned.

"Instead of buying Evans, we should be biddin' on that land south of the reservoir."

"For what?! That land is worthless."

Lucien waved the second proposal he picked up from the desk.

"Another one of my unopened proposals y'all 'forgot' to look at," Lucien said with a bit too much cynicism and sarcasm for Julien's taste. "We can cultivate that land with the fertilizer we manufacture and within a year we could have one of the biggest cannabis farms in the country."

"Are you out of your fucking mind?! Why are you wasting my time?--"

"Is ten million dollars a month a waste of your time?" Lucien asked. Julien listened. "Progressive states like Colorado and Wash-ington passed laws in twenty-twelve legalizing it. Other states, like California, Maine and Oregon jumped on the bandwagon soon after. All it takes is for the Governor to--" then with as much sarcasm as he could muster, "--draw up this thing called a bill, put it to vote and when it passes, it becomes a LAW. And look who's runnin' for Governor of the fine state of Louisiana."

Julien was so frustrated in this moment that he couldn't see that Lucien was right. Lucien was so angry in this moment that he no longer cared.

"Maybe ya' wouldn't a' liked the ideas, but you could have at least given them a fuckin' curtesy read. But why would ya' do d'at, I'm only your fuckin' son."

"Maybe you hadn't noticed, but there's a lot going on 'round here. You wanna get into this with me – fine, we will, but this ain't the time. Once I'm in office, Serena'll be running the everyday operations here and,--"

"WHAT?!" Lucien shouted.

"What about Luc?!" Rayna jumped in. She had stayed out of it for as long as she could. "No disrespect, Serena. You know I adore you, but this is a family business. Julien, he's your son!"

"Who doesn't have a high school diploma, let alone a college degree!"

"You gave away my company?--"

"*Your* company?"

"--My birthright, to her?!" Lucien started.

"You watch your mouth, boy. Just because your name's on the building, don't make it yours."

"Luc," Serena interrupted, "I'm just filling in a while until you become a little more,--"

Lucien pointed his index finger in Serena's general direction, silencing her, as he stared his father down. He wasn't interested in hearing anything she had to say. He dropped the proposals on the desk and left the room. Rayna was furious.

"...You started working here when you were twenty," Rayna said with a bitterness that Julien didn't appreciate.

"I wasn't working here, I ran the God damn place, and I don't need you to remind me of my own history!" Julien yelled.

"I looked at those proposals," Rayna continued. "Both of them were absolutely brilliant."

"You would think so," Julien said.

"So would you, if you gave your own heir the courtesy of looking at them!" Rayna yelled as she stormed toward the door. "And by the way, HIS numbers - flawless!" She said as she exited the room.

CHAPTER 56

"Nobody has seen me since I was a four-year-old boy!"

It started as just another normal night in New Orleans, but by the time this abnormally nightmarish night would end, what once was, would no longer be. A lone vampire strolled down a stark street as a balmy breeze carried a cackle through the air. He looked back and noticed nothing but the barren boulevard behind him. He smiled as he turned to continue his trek. He knew he wasn't alone and he couldn't have been happier about it as he darted down a dark, desolate, abandoned alleyway. He stepped in the shadows and waited for his would-be assailant with a sinister smile. A pair of eyes opened on the darkened wall, over his shoulder. Jean oozed out of the shadow and unfurled himself from the wall. Before this, so called predator could react, he found himself to be prey as Jean ripped into him and silently sucked all the blood from his body.

"*AH-HA-HA-HA-HA-HA-A-A-A. Yes-s-s-s! More! Feed me more-e-e! Ha-ha-ha-ha-ha!*" Hagatha commanded.

❄

A badly beaten man crashed into the fruitful foliage that surrounded the bayou and ran rampant into the unknown abyss. His screams and cries for help went unanswered, as the only beings within earshot of his pleas were not there to lend him a hand. A half a mile away, Tirin's number four beta, Tracey, bartered with his number five beta, Bobby, over who would be first to reach the flustered fellow and end his life.

"Five hundred bucks if you get to him first," Tracey offered.

"Fuck that. I don't want your fuckin' money, I want your title," Bobby said. "If I get 'em, you tell Tirin that I beat you and I move from five to four."

Tracey didn't much like that bet. The number five beta got the grunt work and the shittiest jobs, which is precisely why Bobby no longer wanted that title. Normally this wouldn't be up for debate, as rank was determined by seniority, but since the four deputies came up through the ranks at the exact same time, it was debatable.

"Come on, man, he's gettin' too far. What d'ya say?" Bobby asked.

"Fine, but if I get him, I want the five hundred," Tracey answered.

"Deal. GO!" Bobby yelled as he took off, giving himself a not agreed upon, head start.

Tracey lodged no objection, and the hunt was on. Each on a separate path, the two of them surgically sifted their way through the bayou and within a minute's time, both had stalked the mirthless man to the edge of the deep water, leaving nowhere for him to go. Over his right shoulder, a growl was heard; to his left, the sound of a branch being snapped.

"Somebody help me! Ple-e-ease!" the man cried out.

Out of the darkness came two pairs of eyes. As one charged toward the defenseless man, Jean leaped out of the swamp over the man's head and tackled Bobby the Beta. Jean bit a large chunk out of Bobby's throat as they hit the ground. Tracey zipped over to attack and Jean opened his bloody mouth and spewed a powerful stream of swamp water at him. The force knocked Tracey down. With Bobby pinned, Jean continued aiming the hose-like blast into Tracey's mouth, choking him. He momentarily stopped and turned to the petrified man.

"RUN AWAY!" Jean screamed.

"NO-O-O-O-O, don't let him go! I want him, too! I need him!" Hagatha screamed.

"RU-U-UN!" Jean yelled.

The man was not about to argue with him and took off as Jean went to the gross work of sucking blood for his master.

Several miles away in the city, Tirin sat in a hunched position on a building, two stories up. His eyes were closed but his nostrils were working overtime, flaring and twitching at an astonishing pace. Then his eyes sprang open. He felt a sharp pain and his body jerked from it, causing the agile alpha to lose his balance. He fell from his perched position and tumbled toward the ground below. His body crashed through an awning and obliterated a table of an outside café. A crowd formed around him as he struggled to rise before being cursed with another sharp pain. His body convulsed for a second until it ended. He roared and transformed into full alpha as the frightened crowd fled in all directions.

Kaitlin and Dani found a first-floor room in a well-hidden motel thirty minutes outside of town. Just on the edge of a swamp, it nuzzled nicely in between a thick section of trees and shrubbery, shrouded from the street and well off the beaten path. Dani wanted to keep Kaitlin as far away from the city as she could. She would have preferred Texas, but Kaitlin poo-pooed that suggestion before Dani could get it out of her mouth. The waxing moon shined like a beacon in the night sky as Jean slipped out of the shadow of a tree and crept dangerously close to the window of their room. He tried to stay away; he wanted to, but Hagatha did not. She had not forgotten about Hazel and was determined to make Jean pay for the life he had taken. Kaitlin's life was the price and there was no negotiating it. The battle between the two of them for control of his body was intensifying and he was losing. The red eye peeked into the window. The blue one could not resist a gander as well. They saw Kaitlin, alone, on the bed with four freshly-sharpened stakes and a box of silver bullets at her side. She was giving her gun a thorough cleaning as she conversed with Dani, who was in the shower. Jean could not discern the details of their conversation, as he was embroiled in a particularly loud one of his own.

"*Oh-h-h-h, look at how pretty she is-s-s-s. Even more so than in your dreams-s-s,*" Hagatha hissed. "*She looks delicious!*"

"*I... will not allow you t-to, touch,... h-her,*" Jean thought.

"*Closer-r-r-r. Move closer to her. Let us take a peek.*"

"*NO!*" Jean thought.

"*YES!*" Hagatha screamed as Jean grabbed his ears. "*I just want to take in her scent. Just a smell is all. DO IT!*"

"I'm gonna have to pick up some more bullets in the morning!" Kaitlin said loud enough for Dani to hear.

"No, Kate, I'll do it!" Dani yelled back. I don't want you going anywhere near the city!"

"I don't know that either one of us should, besides, you're the one they're actually looking for, not me!"

"Nobody here has seen me since I was a four-year-old boy," Dani said, her half-smile hiding the fear behind the joke.

Jean's torso melted into the room through the shadow on the wall behind Kaitlin and extended his arm and reached out for her.

"You look just like your mom! They may pick up on that!"

"*Take her-r-r-r! Take her now!*" Hagatha commanded.

Dani walked in the room with a towel on her head as she dried her hair. Jean ducked back into the shadow and out of the room.

"We just have to be super careful," Dani said. "We'll find Jean and get as far away from here as we can."

Outside their window, Jean huddled in a ball, unable to look at Kaitlin as Hagatha's thoughts crashed through his mind. He rocked himself as he clenched his hair in his fists and tried to drown out her angry screams so that he might at least hear Kaitlin's voice.

"You really think we'll find him here?" Kaitlin asked.

"Unfortunately. I know he's close. I can feel him. He's suffering, but he's fighting it..." Dani said. "Just,... you have to prepare yourself."

"For what?"

"He… may not look the way you remember."

"AH-HA-HA-HA, HA-HA-HA-A-A!" Hagatha cackled.

Jean ran and jumped into a shadow and disappeared.

Later that night, in a highly honored haberdashery, Jean discarded his dreary, dirt-encrusted duds for something more pertinent to his purpose. He bedecked himself in a pair of shiny black boots, a tailored black shirt with matching slacks, and a flowing, black coat to hold all of his special trinkets. On his head, he placed a broadly-brimmed black bonnet that hid the inconsonance in his eyes and most of his face. Now he was ready. Hagatha chuckled her approval, and he spun into a shadow and disappeared.

CHAPTER 57

"Talk like that might make a girl think she was in danger."

Dressed in one of the most seductive and revealing of her ensembles, Rayna strolled the streets of New Orleans that most would not walk during the day. She was looking for something, or rather, someone – special. Although, her tastes on this night were more specific than most. In the dirtiest of alleys, pinned up against the dirtiest of walls, she had a distinctively dirty young man, who was definitely down with some particularly naughty intentions. If only he knew what she had in mind for him. With an uncensored passion they kissed as he maneuvered his hands down her body and she maneuvered her mouth down his neck. His jugular pulsed as her teeth protruded and just as she was about to give this distinctively dirty little boy of a man everything he was definitely down for, the song "I Just Died In Your Arms Tonight" began to play. She smiled as it echoed through the alleyway, but just like the distinctively dirty young man she had been toying with, she had no idea that she was the one who'd been caught. Over her right shoulder, twenty yards away, Jean stood with a small music player in his hand. Completely silhouetted, his coat rippled in the breeze.

"Still playing with boys?" Jean asked.

Rayna laughed then gazed into the eyes of the distinctively dirty young man.

"I like boys. They taste so-o-o-o-o go-o-o-o-d," she said.

"Why not try a man?" Jean asked, his voice low and deliberate.

Distinctively Dirty felt a bit disrespected by that last question.

"Who the fuck is this guy?" Distinctively Dirty asked, and even though he was still definitely down, no one was really paying him any mind anymore.

"Any volunteers?" Rayna asked.

Jean stamped one step forward. Her back still to him, she couldn't see, but she heard the step and it made her laugh even more. Distinctively Dirty found no amusement in this little game of theirs and he had every intention of stopping it as he moved away from Rayna and stepped toward Jean.

"Hey, Jack," Distinctively Dirty said. "You better step the fuck ba,-
-"

Jean raised his head so that Mr. Dirty could see his glowing eyes underneath the brim of his hat, and that was really all he needed to see. Seems he was only somewhat dirty, and he was nowhere near as down as he made himself out to be. He took off out of the alley without even looking back at Rayna.

"Whatever happened to chivalry?" she said, amused in this somewhat serious moment as she turned to face Jean. "Thanks! I'll be fine!" she added, over her shoulder, but Distinctively Dirty was long gone.

"That may not be true," Jean said.

Jean's sober words caused a somberness to fall upon her face.

"I know what you're here for," she said as she produced the "Lovers" tarot card she'd been holding onto for sixteen years and showed it to him. I've always known this day would come, but if you think I'm gonna just give it to you because you've got a sexy hat and coat, you will be painfully mistaken."

"Then, perhaps, I shall just have to take it."

"Why, Mr. Laveau, talk like that might make a girl think she was in danger."

"Imminent," Jean said, stepping further into the light, letting the breeze ripple his coat.

"Should I scream?"

"You will."

Rayna laughed for a third time and all three were pure and genuine.

"Mmmmmm... I always liked you," she said, as the smile fell from her face and her eyes filled with rage.

Had they not fought before, he would have been completely taken by surprise with the speed and power she possessed, but this time, he was ready. Rayna attacked him with a barrage of kicks and punches that gave Jean no choice but to give ground and move backward. This time he avoided her skillful assault, but found himself backed up against the alley wall. She threw a right cross and Jean moved to his right as her fist smashed into the brick wall. Jean spun around her and pushed her body into the wall, then pressed his body against hers in a most sensual way. It turned Rayna on and angered her at the same time.

Tirin again found himself 'fishing' on the roof of a building, this time four stories up and well away from the ledge. He caught a whiff of something familiar on the wind, and took off without hesitation.

Back in the alley, Rayna threw an elbow. Jean ducked under it and came up between her arms and pinned her to the wall, pressing up against her front. He kissed her. She liked it, but still grabbed and twisted his arm and slammed him face-first into the wall. Jean melted into the shadow and instantly came back out, face-first. The move was unexpected and caught Rayna off-balance. He grabbed her and pushed her body to the other side of the alley and slammed her against that wall, purposely ripping her dress. She used her strength and reversed him around. He reversed right back and slammed her again. He pinned her against the wall and kissed her with a passion that was reserved for another. She threw her legs around his waist and squeezed. Jean screamed and released her arms. With her arms free, Rayna punched Jean in the face twice, then wrapped her arms around the back of his neck, pulled his head into her chest and held him there as she tried to suffocate him.

Jean's knees buckled as Rayna increased the pressure of her squeeze and laughed, feeding off of his pain. Jean tilted his body back then slammed her into the wall again, forcing her to release his head and giving him a quick breath. She grabbed him and kissed him with a passion equal to the one she received, then flexed her legs around his waist and squeezed tighter. He gasped in pain and ripped her dress more as she grabbed his head and resumed the suffocation-hold against her breasts. She squeezed as hard as she could, hoping she might snap him in two. With all the strength he could muster, Jean stumbled back a few steps, then launched himself toward the wall and planted Rayna in it. A few bricks dislodged and crumbled, and she released him. Jean fell to his knees. Rayna reeled from the impact, breathless and conflicted by the thrill of it. Jean rolled into a shadow and disappeared. Rayna laughed in victory, thinking Jean had fled, and turned straight into him as she attempted to exit the alley. Jean grabbed her by the throat with his right hand and viciously slammed her into the wall as the red eye became dominant and the cerulean one began to fade. Defiant to the end, Rayna stared into that red eye and did not flinch when she saw what true evil looked like. He released a low, evil breath of a growl as he stared back at her.

"Priest, my ass. Go on, you fucking monster. Do it... DO IT!" she yelled.

Jean moved in close to her face and like a soft breeze, ran his lips over it. She was incensed by him as her breathing increased. He spun her around, put her in a full nelson and held her against the wall. She stopped struggling, unable to break free of his hold. Jean held her there, immobile and vulnerable to the only thing in her life she'd ever feared. It was both her curse and her greatest power. Many times she had thought losing it might be a relief; a burden she no longer had to carry. Losing this battle now would free her from that, but in her own perverted, sick way, she always figured the man she'd lose it to would be Julien. Although he angered her as much as she angered him, he was the only man she ever truly loved. A tear escaped her eye as her unrelenting defiance slipped away.

"What are you waiting for?!" she cried, "JUST DO IT!!!"

Jean couldn't hear her screams, as he was lost in his own battle; the never-ending war with Hagatha being fought in his head.

"*Why do you fight me?! It is she that put you here! She is the one to be punished! Finish her!*" Hagatha ordered.

"*No. Not like this. Not this way,*" Jean thought.

"*It is the only way you can defeat her! Finish it!*"

"*NO!*"

"*Finish her, or I will show you pain beyond your,--*"

"*ENOUGH-H-H-H!*" *Enough. For sixteen years, I have listened to your threats. Endured your torture. Been a prisoner to the pain you have inflicted upon me. No more. You cannot hurt me beyond what you already have. Your threats no longer carry weight. I have endured and will find a way to continue to do so. I cannot yet rid you of my body, but neither can you free yourself of it. So instead of this body being MY prison, it shall become yours, as well.*"

"*You are not strong enough to hold me!*"

"*Perhaps, but I have proven you are not strong enough to hold me, either. You will no longer hold sovereign over me, witch.*"

"*NO-O-O-O-o-o-o-o-...*"

Jean released Rayna and backed away. Confused, Rayna swiveled around, ready to continue.

"What are you doing? Why have you released me?"

"It is done. There is nothing more between you and I," Jean said as he turned away from her.

"Don't turn away from me! This isn't finished! You haven't taken anything!" she cried, her voice breaking.

"Your card was wrong. *YOU* were wrong."

Rayna looked down at the card as her eyes flitted back and forth.

"No..." she said as her eyes flitted. "No. I can't be wro-- You were supposed to,-- But,... you have to!"

Jean stepped into a shadow and disappeared.

"No! Come back here!" she screamed. "Do it! DO IT NOW!! YOU HAVE TO! YOU HA-A-AVE TO-O-O!"

Rayna collapsed to the ground in tears as the song, on repeat, continued to echo through the alley. Tirin, still following the scent, sped down the street and stopped at the top of the alley. The faint song, wafted through the air, in the distance. He sniffed and proceeded with extreme caution before he picked up speed. Rayna was curled up against the wall crying, her eyes still flitting through her tears as she stared at the card. A wistful sigh escaped Tirin's lips, then he knelt down beside her.

"...He didn't do it... But,... he has to,... right? He has to!" she cried. Tirin reached out to her and she pushed him away. "No, leave me alone! He'll come back! He has to come back!"

She pounded Tirin's chest with her fist and he withstood it until she could pound no more. Her scream filled the alley as he embraced her and held her tight, something he had learned a long time ago from Camille. Jean rose up from a shadow on the ground behind them. Tirin caught his scent, rose and turned to face him.

"This ends between us, now," Tirin said.

"Day and night; night and day, for sixteen years I lay there. Dreaming of all the different ways I would kill you."

"Ye-e-es-s-s. Kill him! Let us drink his blood; feel his pain."

"Show me those dreams, Priest," Tirin said.

"...No. Death is not to be your punishment, Lycan."

"What?!" Hagatha said.

"You get to live," Jean said, "knowing everything you ever cared about was destroyed by me."

Hagatha laughed as Jean turned his back to Tirin.

"No! Fight me! FIGHT ME! FIGHT ME-E-E-E-E!"

Tirin charged as Jean sunk into a shadow and disappeared. Tirin's roar echoed through the alley. Then, silently, he lifted Rayna into his arms and carried her into the dark, as the song played on.

CHAPTER 58

"*A black cat and a broom*"

It was well after the bewitching hour as this nightmarish night continued. Kaitlin was fast asleep when Dani dressed herself and snuck out of their room. She didn't know what the 'morrow would bring, but she knew she could not leave without seeing her mother. For the longest time, she knelt in front of the ornamental monument that marked her mother's grave, hoping to hear her voice on the wind, or… something. She didn't know why she was there or why she was even kneeling. Malafecs don't pray and visiting dead loved ones in cemeteries wasn't something that was done. She knew both the grave and monument were just for show. She didn't know where her mother's remains were, but she knew they weren't here. She didn't care. Something inside of her just wanted to be there. The human side, perhaps. She had learned from her years with Kaitlin that humans need places like this. Standing, sitting - kneeling beside a grave site seemed to tether humans to the people they'd lost, as if the physical world could hold the echoes of a relationship that no longer had form. Cemeteries were the place where the dead lived and even though she knew the physical address in this particular graveyard was untrue, the monument with Camille's name inscribed on it, gave Dani a comforting delusion, of a nonexistent presence, and all the memories that came with it. For Dani, on this night, that was enough.

"Hey, Momma," she said to the monument as if she expected it to return her greeting in kind. "I'm home... Sixteen years, eleven months, thirty days and..." She paused momentarily as she searched for the answer. "I don't know how many hours." She muttered, ashamed and more than moderately miffed by her inability to process the equation. "...Katie tried, but I was just never good at math like you... I tried, I just... wasn't... I'm sorry." Dani whispered the unnecessary apology to the memory of the woman that, to this day, she wanted nothing more than to please and, still – wrongfully so – felt that she never did.

She sat back on her heels and impatiently waited; hoping for a sign to magically manifest itself to her in that moment, be it an unintelligible whisper on the wind, or an infinitesimally tiny flash in the warm night's sky. Anything to fill the, not so minuscule, hole in her heart. After a few painfully uncomfortable moments, she accepted the fact that that hole would not be filled on this night – or any other. She felt foolish for being in this cemetery, on this night, kneeling in the dirt, talking to a piece of granite with her mother's name on it.

"How ironic. A witch in a cemetery. All I need is a black cat and a broom." She whispered to herself, hoping that the self-mockery might ease her suffering. It did not. The sarcastic sentiments merely served as a key that unlocked a sixteen-year-old gate full of unprocessed emotions that needed to be released. "I miss you so much," she gushed, trying her best not to cry and failing miserably. "I HATED you for what you did to me! It felt like you were punishing me for being a girl and I didn't understand why! Not really. You were always yelling at me to, 'be a big boy' or go off and do some fucking rhymes! Momma... I'd give anything to hear you yell at me now! I didn't understand what you were doing, but I do now and... and..."

She closed her eyes and inhaled sixteen years of heartache, and misery, and shame. She had held onto it for far too long and it needed to be expelled. So, she did. "I'M SORRY I WAS SUCH A BRAAAAT!" She wailed. "And I'm sorry that I'm not as smart as you, and that I don't fight like you," she sniffled and snorted. "Katie says I get hit way too much. I try not to, but I don't know how to do the things you did, and I wish you were here to teach me!... I don't know that I can fulfill my destiny without you!" She took a long, labored breath as most of the angst had been released, then used her sleeve as a tissue to wipe away the mucus that had been expelled from multiple places on her face. A melancholy calmness was all that was left. "And I know what Luc said about dad," she sniffled. "That it was an accident and," she closed her eyes and painfully shook her head. "How do you accidentally kill the person you love?" She whispered with a bitterness that came from deep within. "I don't know that I can forgive him for taking you away from me. But what difference does it make? I'm not even sure I can fight anymore." Then, almost to herself, "I don't know where I end and Lucien begins. I feel like such a puppet. I just wish you were here to tell me what to do."

"You can start off by listenin' to your older and much wiser brother."

Dani jumped up and whipped around to find Lucien standing behind her.

"...That's not funny," she said as she wiped away her tears.

"It wasn't meant to be," he said in a very portentous tone.

"What are you doing here?" Dani asked.

"I could ask you the same," Lucien said. "I thought I made it clear how dangerous and stupid it was fo' you to come here."

"Don't call me stupid, Luc."

"I ain't callin' ya' stupid, Dani. I'm callin' what you did, stupid."

"It's the same thing and I don't like it."

"You wanna take it that way, fine. You do stupid things, people gon' call 'em out, and I think puttin' yours and Kaitlin's lives in danger is stupid."

Dani wasn't really a big fan of her brother at this particular moment and she was inclined to let him know.

"Yeah, well, I don't really care what you think."

"Oh-h-h-h. Sounds like you wanna be the older brother na'."

"Just 'cuz you're,-- what? One, two minutes older than me, you think that makes you my boss?"

"I think sixteen years ago ya' momma made me your boss and I been regrettin' it ever since."

"Fuck you, asshole!"

"Ahhhhh. Now you mad," he said, mocking her. Then his tone changed to something bitter and hateful. "Look at you! On your fuckin' knees, in a cemetery, praying like a human!"

"Shut up!"

"Or what?! What chu' gon' do, lil' human girl? Cry some more? Or you wanna pray some more first?"

"How 'bout I kick your fucking ass!"

"How 'bout you come try."

Dani popped into full mactrouge, and Lucien followed suit. The only difference was that he raised up off the ground and floated. Dani attacked her brother with a speed and ferocity she didn't know she possessed and as skilled a fighter as she was, she never laid a finger on him. He was just way too fast for her. He never even tried to hit her. He just danced her around in a circle, tired her out, and made her look foolish in the process. Out of breath and having expelled all of her pent-up energy, she stopped trying and fell out of mactrouge. She was done. Lucien, however, was just getting started.

"That's it?! That's all you got?! Fuckin' pathetic." he said as he hovered before her. "I can't believe you're my sister."

"Stop it!" She yelled.

"Naw, you wanted to fuckin' fight, so now we gon' fight." he said and then pushed her. "Fight!"

"I can't! You were right; I don't know how, now leave me alone!" She cried as he pushed her again. "STOP IT!"

Dani turned and tried to run away, but he wouldn't let her. He zipped around in front of her and blocked her path.

"Just leave me alone!"

"Make me." he said as he charged his hands and pushed her again. His push now came with an uncomfortable shock.

"O-O-W-W, Lucien, STOP IT!" She screamed, but there was no one to hear her cries.

"Fuckin' baby. You didn't cry this much when we were kids playing blocks," he said as he shocked her again. Dani screamed and fell to her knees in tears. "GET UP! The time for prayin' is over. Did you pray sixteen years ago when my momma died? The day you stole her from me?"

"I DIDN'T KILL HER!"

"SHE HELD A SPELL FOR FOUR YEARS BECAUSE OF YOU!" Lucien screamed. He also had some pent-up emotions to release, and now seemed to be the time to do it. "She gave up her lifeforce so YOU could live. And now you wanna give up the life you stole from her over some stupid prophecy? I was angry when I found out what Dad did to Mom, but in truth, he didn't put her in that grave, YOU DID!"

"NO-O-A-A-A-AAAAA!!" Dani screamed, her voice deeper and more guttural than before.

She burst into full mactrouge, but there was now an evil presence in her eyes. This time, she floated off the ground. She charged at Lucien with more quickness than he could avoid. She got her hands on him and bull-rushed him across the cemetery and slammed him into the wall, pinning him there. If he hadn't been in full mactrouge, an impact like that would have definitely called for a trip to the emergency room. Even still, it left him a little dizzy.

"Now, d'ats my little sister," Lucien smiled.

Many times over the past day, these two had mirrored each other in both thoughts and expressions. Not this time. Dani was anything but smiling.

"I could kill you-u-u," she whispered in a cold, hollow tone that would rival Hagatha's.

"Ehh, maybe,... but I bet chu' won't," Lucien said with a bit of misplaced swagger in his voice.

He fell out of mactrouge, but held onto his smile and her gaze, and he showed her no fear. Dani's hair settled as the red faded from her eyes and both of them slid down the wall and planted their feet firmly on the ground. Dani was embarrassed by what just happened and uncomfortable with the thoughts and feelings that were racing through her body now.

"I knew there was a witch in you, but damn, girl, you had her buried deep!" Lucien laughed until he saw the look on her face. "No, no, no! Don't you push it down-- Dani? NO. Dani, Look at me. LOOK

AT ME! What you feel right now is the demon – your demon. Embrace it," he said. Dani shook her head as she tried to bridle her emotions. "Yes, Dani, look at me. Stay with me," Lucien said, locking eyes with hers. "It's okay, sweetie, it's okay. I'm okay. You ain't do nothin' to me. Okay? Now breathe. Come on, deep breath," he said as he took in breaths with her.

"I almost killed you," Dani whispered as the tears streamed down her face.

"No, you didn't."

"I wanted to!"

"BUT YOU DIDN'T… That's what's important, that's everythin' right d'ere. Shit, I think about doing bad stuff all the time – everybody does. I don't 'cuz I ain't bad and neither are you." Lucien explained. "The demon is the source of our power. It is neither good nor bad, it only personifies who you are. You're a witch, Danielle Gerard. Don't fight it or push it down, 'cuz ain't nothin' wrong wit' it, other than the misconceptions that others may try to put on you. Come on, na', big inhale." Lucien took in a big breath and held it before exhaling it out. Dani did the same. "Yes. Breathe all that in. Go-o-od. Good… How you feel?" Dani nodded as she wiped her tears away. "You alright?"

Again Dani nodded, then she reached out and embraced her brother and he held her tight. Their connection was so much more than the telepathic link that bound them. Together they were one and they both could feel that they were never meant to be apart. Lucien beamed with pride as he glared at his sister with a playfully suspicious eye.

"I think you still got some more demon buried down in there." Dani's shoulders slumped in unison with her solemn sigh, "but, I guess we can deal wit' d'at another day. Come on," he said as he slid his arm around her neck. "I'll buy you a drink."

"Oou. Can you get me a margarita?"

"Da' hell you know 'bout margaritas?"

Dani rested her head on his shoulder as they walked toward the gate.

"I know that sometimes they come with a Cadillac," Dani quipped.

Lucien burst into laughter.

CHAPTER 59

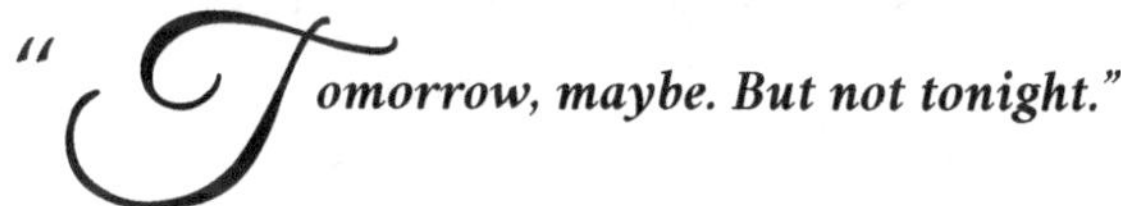

Dani started to climb up the stone wall of the cemetery.

"What're you doin'?" he said as if she'd done something wrong. "Get down."

She jumped off the wall, confused as to what she had done. Lucien's eyes flared red.

"Apertum," he said as he flicked his fingers.

The gate unlocked quicker than his eyes could fade back to normal.

"Is that how you broke into our motel room the other night?"

"I ain't break into your room, I--"

The gate slammed closed and re-locked itself before they could walk through.

"What is this, a test? Seriously?" Dani asked. "I kept up on my latin, Lucien," she said, almost insulted, then waved her hand. "Apertum." Nothing happened. "Why didn't it work?"

The answer to the question might have something to do with the two Dobermans that sat quietly on the ground about thirty feet behind them.

"Shiiit," Lucien said.

Dani turned to see the Dobermans as they dissipated and rematerialized into The Talisman. Lucien popped into full mactrouge and readied himself.

"Dani, run! I'll hold him off as long as I,--"

"No."

"DANI!--"

"I'm not running from him anymore," she said as she walked toward him.

The Talisman nodded his head to her and smiled.

"Sixteen years, been chasin' you. How fittin' to find ya' here. You dun' had a good run. Better dan' most. Ha! Better dan' any! It no longer 'bout da' pay - you well overdue. Got a reputation to uphold, so tonight, girl, one way or anotha', ya' comin' wit' meeeeee."

He extended his hand to her as Lucien charged up and formed an energy blast in his hands.

"Tell ya' new friend, any get in way of Talisman, fall,--"

"--Prey to Talisman, yeah, he knows. He's not my friend; he's my brother, and he's heard it before."

"What, we ain't friends now?" Lucien asked.

"Shut up, Lucien, you know what I mean," Dani said.

It's unclear whether her new found fortitude was because Lucien was with her, or the fact that now she had the ability to get off the ground. Whatever the reason, there was something dangerously different about Dani.

"Don't make 'dis difficult, child. Take my 'and and come wit' me peacefully."

"No. It's definitely going to be difficult," Dani said. "I've been afraid of you my whole life. I'm not afraid tonight. Look, no pee," she said, indicating her pants.

"Jesus, Dani," Lucien grimaced.

"My time's not up yet, old man. Tomorrow, maybe. But not tonight."

The Talisman looked at his watch and snapped it closed.

"Tink I got sometin' to say 'bout d'at."

"I think I do too," Dani said as she exploded into full mactrouge and lifted herself about a foot off the ground.

Lucien let out a sigh of relief that he didn't have to prod her into it again.

"You can form an energy blast on yo' own, can't chu'?"

Dani turned and frowned at him, then answered by pulling a giant energy blast from her Qi and forming it in her hands.

"No, d'ats too much!" Lucien shouted. "You're too close for one that size!--"

Dani ignored him and released it. The explosion sent both her and The Talisman flying in opposite directions. Lucien zipped to his left, away from his sister, to create a stronger line of attack.

"Get up!" he yelled to Dani.

Surprised and a bit shaken by the blast, Dani was no worse for wear as she hopped up and readied herself.

"Move to your right and we'll attack him like betas do!" Lucien yelled as Dani drew energy balls from each hand and charged forward, disregarding Lucien's command. "NO! You gotta circle around him!" Lucien yelled.

Dani flew straight toward The Talisman and pelted him, one by one, with her energy balls. Angered, Lucien split his in two and began to do the same. The Talisman was not used to this type of attack. The multiple blasts rocked and knocked him backward. The last one dislodged the glasses from his face. Dani dove into him and sunk the nails of her right hand into his torso and The Talisman screamed.

"Damn, girl," Lucien muttered, both impressed and a little concerned.

She looked into The Talisman's uncovered eyes and saw what no one was supposed to see: his own personal hell. As punishment, he gave her a taste of it. Tiny Fat Lady Demons flew out of his eye sockets and began to viciously bite and peck at her. She fought through the irritating pain and drove the nails from her left hand into his torso and let the energy from her Qi grow. The Talisman yanked her hands from his torso as the swirling energy surged between them. Lucien shielded his eyes.

"PRA-E-MI-UM!!" Dani yelled.

BOOM! The explosion sent Dani hurling backward. She had fallen out of mactrouge and was unconscious and unprotected. Lucien zipped over and caught her before she smacked into the cemetery wall. The Talisman struggled to his feet and found his spectacles as the tiny demons scurried back into his eyes. He placed his glasses back on his face, then extended his right arm toward his staff and it flew into his hand. He extended his left hand to Lucien and Dani.

"Dani, wake up! WAKE UP!" Lucien yelled.

The Talisman took aim and shot a lethal blast toward Dani and Lucien. With a wave of his hand, Lucien lifted up the pavement in front of them and it shielded them from the blast. The pavement exploded and The Talisman accelerated through the debris and grabbed Lucien by his neck. He breathed a yellow mist in his face that temporarily blinded Lucien, who fell out of mactrouge as his eyes glazed over.

"Enough games! No more foolin' 'round!" he said as he slammed Lucien into the wall and held him there. He tapped his cane on the ground and it sprayed a black tar-like substance over Lucien that glued him to the wall. "Now, it time fo' you to die, boy, and you," he said to Dani as he picked her up by her neck, "it finally time fo' you to come wit' meeee."

"I may have something to say about that," came a voice from over The Talisman's shoulder.

The Talisman turned and saw Jean standing under a streetlight. His body was silhouetted as the light from the lamp rained down over him.

"'Dis no concern of yours, Laveau. Go 'bout yo' business elsewhere's."

"Tonight, my business lies here."

"'Din' pick out a plot and mark ya' grave."

Jean tilted his head up. His blue eye crackled and his red eye fizzed. The Talisman pinned Dani to the wall next to Lucien as she struggled to regain consciousness, then sprayed the black tar-like substance all over her.

"Stay-y-y-y," he laughed as he turned to face Jean in the road down the middle of the cemetery.

They stood about twenty yards apart, "Old West Style," ready to battle.

"Listen close, young 'ens," he said to Dani and Lucien.

"Can ya' hear it?" He whispered.

"Ooooo. This should be funnnn," Hagatha said.

Jean's hands began to glow and the wind picked up. The Talisman made the first move. He bounced his staff off the ground and it launched toward Jean. The twin snake heads came alive and grew ten times their normal size. As they lunged to strike him, branches from a huge tree reached over Jean and snatched the snakes out of the air and ripped them in two. That did not sit well with The Talisman, at all. He pointed his index finger at the tree and darts of fire jetted out and set the tree ablaze. Jean pulled a ball of energy from his Qi, wrapped it around his left fist and punched the ground, sending a rippling wave across the pavement toward The Talisman. Jean trailed the wave as it hit The Talisman, pushing him off-balance. Jean threw a well-timed energy blast, then followed it by punching him with his charged fist, knocking The Talisman through the cemetery wall. In an instant, The Talisman exploded out of the rubble into Jean. He grabbed Jean and slammed him into the wall, yanked him out, and repeated it. He then snatched Jean's limp body close to him as the energy force that surrounded Jean began to fade.

"Can you hear it now, girl?!" The Talisman asked Dani. "Can you hear da' death comin'?!"

Both Dani and Lucien's eyes were still glazed over. They could neither see nor do anything to help.

"Jean, no!!" Dani cried.

"Hell's callin', Laveau."

Jean tilted his head up and locked eyes with The Talisman.

"Maybe," Jean said as his eyes traveled down to The Talisman's breast pocket. The Talisman looked and saw that Jean's right hand was firmly attached to his coin pocket. The smile fell from The Talisman's face, and for the first time since his legendary craps game, he had the look of fear.

"But not for me," Jean finished.

Jean ripped off The Talisman's breast pocket and the coins spilled onto the ground. As the coins scattered, the curses and contracts of a hundred lives dissolved into the night.

"NOOOOOOOO!!!!"

He tossed Jean and got down on his hands and knees. He scrambled around like a madman as he tried to recover the bounty of coins rolling and bouncing on the ground. Jean somersaulted and landed on his feet with his eyes charged. He waved his hands and created a funnel cloud that swept up the coins and took them away. The Talisman looked up at Jean as he clenched his fists.

"You may have saved herrr," he said with a malice in his voice that had not presented itself before, "but ya' still gonna have to deal wit' meeee."

Jean raised his left hand. In his grip gleamed The Talisman's pocket watch, the final link to his power.

"Not tonight," Jean said.

Jean threw the watch to the ground and it exploded. Lightning crackled across the sky as The Talisman began to seep into the ground below him. He didn't fight it. He just stood there with his eyes affixed on Jean. He smiled and tipped his hat to him.

"I'll be comin' fo' you, Laveau."

Jean nodded his respect and like that, The Talisman was gone.

CHAPTER 60

Dani and Lucien's eyes went back to normal and the tar dissipated as they slid off the wall. Jean, having been injured during the confrontation, fell to a knee. Dani ran over to help him. Lucien didn't know what to do. The man did just save his life, but for him, it was complicated.

"You okay?!" Dani asked as she helped him to his feet. "How'd you do it?! How'd you kill him?"

"You cannot kill what was already dead," Jean said with a terseness she did not deserve. "He will burden you no more. You are free. Now le-e-eave," he said through clenched teeth. "You are not supposed to be here."

"Well, we agree on one thing," Lucien chimed.

Jean looked at Lucien with a meticulous eye and Lucien didn't care for it.

"What's up?" Lucien asked as he walked up to them. "Somethin' on my face, or somethin'?"

"Luc, knock it off," Dani said as she inserted herself between them.

"Naw, he the one starin', and I want to know what he's lookin' at."

"This one is his son," Hagatha whispered.

"You're the son," Jean said.

"That's right. You got a problem with d'at?"

"LUCIEN," Dani warned.

"I ain't afraid of him," Lucien said.

"You don't have to be afraid, to die," Jean responded.

"Okay, seriously, you two," a frustrated Dani replied.

"Kill him as a statement. Let the father-- No, wait!... He carries the essence of one of my sisters-s-s-s. Interesting..."

"You carry your mother's light within you?" Jean whispered incredulously. He didn't even realize he said it out loud.

"Let this one li-i-ive."

"Yeah, I do. And what part did you play in puttin' out d'at light?" Lucien asked.

"LUCIEN," Dani gasped.

"Ask her yourself. Or do you not yet have the power to do so?"

"What the hell's d'at mean?" Lucien asked.

"Mmm. Perhaps you should not be here, either. Take your sister and leave, while you still can."

"I'm not going anywhere! And both of you, stop talking about me like I'm not even here!"

"You should not be here! You were supposed to leave! To save yourself! To protect Kaitlin!" Jean said in an admonishing tone.

"I am!" Dani yelled.

"YOU CANNOT EVEN PROTECT YOURSELF!" That hurt Dani's feelings and it hurt him to say it that way. "...Not yet, little one. It is not yet your time! There are dangers here that your innocence will not allow you to see."

"Is that from you, or whatever it is that's inside of you?" Dani asked.

"It's The Old One," Lucien said.

"WHAT?!"

"Your buddy's got the baddest bitch of all time swimming around inside 'em."

"Careful, son of my sister. Be careful," Hagatha warned.

"If you have love for your sister, please,... take her and leave," Jean said to Lucien. "Her innocence will be her undoing, and perhaps yours, as well."

"And what about yours?" an all-too-familiar voice said from over Jean's shoulder.

It hit him in the head like a two-by-four. All his dreams and fears and nightmares rolled into one beautiful package. Dani and Lucien gasped. Their presence in this moment was still up for debate, but the one thing they all agreed upon was that Kaitlin should DEFINITELY not be there. Although, there was one who was so very glad she was.

"O-o-o-oo, yes-s-s. I know that voice. Turn around; turn around," Hagatha sang playfully. *"Let our eyes fall upon her once more."*

"No," Jean gasped in a response meant for Hagatha, but Dani heard the pain that went with it.

"Katie, what are you doing?! You know it's not safe for you out here," Dani said.

"From the looks of things, it doesn't seem like it's very safe for you either, Danielle!" Kaitlin said in the sternest of voices that made Dani back off as she approached.

Kaitlin walked right up to Jean and waited for him to turn. Dani pushed Lucien aside. Kaitlin waited, but Jean would neither speak nor turn, so Hagatha did.

"Turn around; turn around," Hagatha sang. *"Let us take just a peek."*

Jean had managed to achieve a stalemate with Hagatha. Under the circumstances, it was probably the best he would ever get, but when it came to matters involving Kaitlin, Hagatha would never relent.

"When Dani told me you were alive, I didn't believe it at first. I didn't want to. Didn't want to get my hopes up…"

"What will surprise her more? Your face, or our teeth as they puncture her skin?"

"It's been two days… Why haven't you come to see me?"

"Yes, Jean, tell her. Tell her the truth."

"No," Jean feebly answered Hagatha, although Kaitlin thought his response was meant for her.

"Why not?" Kaitlin asked.

"Tell her it's because of me-e-e-e."

"It… It is not safe."

"--Because I won't stop until I have her."

"I've never felt safer than when I was with you." Kaitlin said.

"You are… n-not supposed to be here."

Kaitlin tried to move in front of him, but Jean kept turning, afraid to let her see his eyes as Hagatha kept talking to him.

"Whether it be today, tomorrow, or whenever. In your weakest moments, I will be steadfast"

"Why won't you look at me?"

"BECAUSE HE'S A MONSTER!"

"NO!"

"When you're sick or injured or even fast asleep, I will roll over on top of her and slaughter her!"

"Jean, we care about you, both of us." Kaitlin said.

"No!" Jean sobbed. "She is not strong enough to be here and, and you… you should not have let her come!"

"I will invade her dreams and devour her from the inside out!"

"She came because she cares about you and wanted to help. Let us help you."

"Her last breaths will be used for screams and the last thing she'll see on this earth will be your horrid face!"

"STOP IT!!" Jean yelled at Hagatha, but Kaitlin heard it as well. "The man you loved is gone!" he cried, bracing for her to recoil."This; this is all that remains! A rotted shell filled with nothing but evil!"

"AH-HA-HA-HA, HA-HA-HA-A-A!"

Kaitlin didn't flinch. She smiled and touched his face.

"You once told me that evil was a combination of selfishness, igno-rance and hate… Let the hate go and come back to me. Please. Don't let your thirst for revenge break us apart again." Kaitlin said. "Leave this place with me,… with us, tonight."

"SAY YES! SAY IT! Say it so I can wash my hair in her blood! Say it, and I will pour her remains in a tall glass and drink them! SAY YES, and I will make her cry out loud until,--"

Jean quivered as he fought the hidden battle inside, longing for what once was. He closed his eyes as the voice in his head escalated and a single tear pried its way through. Then another, and another.

"....I.... c-can't," he cried as he buckled over. Kaitlin tried to help him but he scuffled back away from her. "I CAN'T! ...NO-O-O-O AH-H-H-H!"

He spun into a shadow and vanished. Kaitlin broke down and both Dani and Lucien moved to comfort her.

CHAPTER 61

 *ne day, a ten-year-old warlock boy brought home a full-grown woman and she never left…*

The next day, Rayna sat in a chair in Julien's office. Not on her posh pillows on the floor in her corner, not perched on the corner of his desk. A chair. Although she showed no emotion on her face, anyone who cared to look could see there was something missing. Tirin gazed out the window as he always did, but this time he wasn't really looking at anything. Julien entered in a whirlwind with Serena on his tail.

"What do you mean, close?" Julien asked.

"Your lead's been cut to less than three percent in the past two days," said Serena.

"How's that possible?"

"He's questioning your past, Julien. We all knew it was just a matter of time before he played these cards. How your father acquired his businesses, you never serving in the military, what happened to your wife and daught-son. The list goes on."

"What can we do 'bout it?"

"Nothing," she said in an incredulous voice. "You'll lose if you engage him. Our best move is to deflect and refocus the narrative."

"You don't become governor of Louisiana by 'refocusing narratives! Ray, get the cards and tell me how we can shut Mr. Stevenson's mouth." Rayna did not answer. "Ray!"

"I-I... I cannot."

"What are you talkin' 'bout? Why?"

"...The cards... They no longer speak to me."

"What are you,--"

Julien turned and looked at her. His mouth was open as he gazed and it seemed as if he kept trying to shut it, but it wouldn't stay closed. He looked at Tirin, who would not face him. Serena fidgeted as she tried to crawl out of her own skin. Rayna just sat there with her eyes fixed on the floor. Julien walked over to her and snatched her out of the chair.

He wanted to be mad at her, but he couldn't. He seemed more hurt than anything.

"...Why?"

"I'm sorry!" she cried.

He let her go and fell back against his desk.

"Rayna-- ....Who?"

"Last night, while I was in the Bowery, Laveau found me, and,--"

Hearing Jean's name pushed him over the edge and in a fit of rage, he overturned the desk.

"HOW COULD YOU LET HIM,--?!"

"I DIDN'T!... He didn't-- We didn't..." She started to cry and could not speak. Then she took a breath and exhaled everything. "But he was supposed to... Sixteen years ago I pulled the card and he was supposed to, because the cards are never-- I'm never!... I waited - all these years... I'M NEVER WRONG!!... We fought and I hurt him, Julien, I did, but,... He had me and then,-- he didn't. He just didn't. He was supposed to! He had to! But he didn't! My cards said he would! They told me he would, but he didn't!... He didn't! He just... left me there..."

She latched onto Julien, who was lost in his own bewilderment. He didn't understand. If he did, perhaps he could have talked her out of the self-abased state she had put herself into because there was nothing really wrong with her, other than the fact that she was wrong, but that one wrong was more than she could take. It seemed like she cried forever before Julien, with a delicate touch, pulled her off.

"...Tirin,... take her home, please," Julien whispered.

It was not his intention to pass her to Tirin like something that no longer had much value, but his silence made her feel that way. Their relationship had always been a complex mystery to everyone but them. She was his bodyguard when he needed protection, his mother when he needed care. She was his sister at home, his girlfriend in public and his advisor in business affairs. She had always been whatever he needed her to be and he loved her for that. I don't think he realized how much until today.

"JD, please don't be mad at me,--"

"I'm not mad. I'm not mad. You just,--"

"I can still help with,--"

"Just... Just gon' home, Ray."

Julien moved to the window and turned his back to her. Serena stared at the floor, afraid to look at her. Tirin walked over and took her hand and brushed the hair out of her face. She cracked an appreciative smile and walked to the door. She stopped to look back at Julien, but he never turned around. She needed him to tell her that it would be okay; that everything was alright, and he wanted to tell her that and so much more. He just didn't know how. When she walked out of the office, she felt like everyone in the campaign pit's eyes were on her. Proud to the end, she held her head high as she walked to the elevator. The door opened and Lucien popped out.

"Hey! I need to talk to ya'," he said with an abnormal amount of enthusiasm and excitement. "You ain't never gonna guess what-- What's wrong? Where ya' goin'?"

She smiled and caressed his face.

"Home... It seems my services are no longer needed here."

"What the hell you talkin' 'bout?" he said, thinking it to be a joke until he looked at Tirin and realized it wasn't. "What happened?" he asked with the concern a son would have for their mother.

Lucien's brow furrowed, as Tirin would not respond, and he

finally noticed the dilation in Rayna's eyes and the dazed expression on her face.

"Happy Birthday, my beautiful boy," she said.

"Happiest of days, Lucien," Tirin said with a profound insight known only to him.

"Thank you," he said softly.

"Ah, come're. Give me a squeeze," Rayna said as she pulled him in and wrapped her arms around his neck. She released him and gazed into his eyes with pride. "If I ever had a son... I would have wanted him to be - just - like - you," she said as she touched his nose with her index finger on every word.

She kissed him on the forehead and entered the elevator with Tirin at her side. Lucien turned and watched her in complete bewilderment as the doors closed.

Julien stood in the office, fixed and sober as Serena lectured him about things that no longer seemed important to him. Lucien's entrance brought him back from the dark, faraway place he had gone to, but it seemed as if he and his son may venture into another.

"Happy Birthday, Lucien," Julien said in solemn, somber tone, no mirth or merriment in his voice. "If you have a moment, I'd like to talk to you about your proposals,--"

"What'd you do?"

"...Excuse me?"

"I just saw Ray..."

Julien didn't respond as his head dropped. He couldn't talk about this, right now, he was still processing and wasn't ready. Serena walked over to the door and closed it.

"What da' hell'd you do!" Lucien asked again, giving him little choice.

"I'd bring that down a notch, if I were you."

"I think you don' made it clear that you ain't me so I'm gon' ask you again,--"

"LUCIEN!... Son,... Please. This ain't the day."

"Why not, Pop? The fuck you gon' do to me you ain't already don'? You don' spent most of my life ignorin' me tryin' to find ya' daughter, my brother. You gave away my birthright to this bitch here, and oh yeah, you killed my momma, too."

Julien slapped Lucien as a red glimmer traversed across his eyes and vanished. Lucien took the blow and held his ground.

"Uhhh,... Why don't I give you two a minute," Serena said, then wasted no time in getting out of that room.

"For sixteen years, she's been like a mother to,--"

"SHE'S NOT YOUR MOTHER!! Julien screamed, then calmed himself and looked away. "...She's not your mother," he whispered to himself.

Lucien stared at his father with disgust.

"...She's the only parent I ever had."

That was probably the worst thing Lucien could have ever said to him. Julien let his words spill over him and held onto them because a big part of him believed it to be true.

"...I'm sorry, kid," Julien said as he dropped his head and fixed his eyes on the floor. Julien loved both of his children more than anything on this earth, unfortunately, most of the time his focus seemed to be on the one that wasn't there.

"You should try saying that to Ray sometimes," Lucien replied. "But she probably wouldn't believe it either."

Lucien turned and walked out. Outside, he leaned up against the closed door and wished he could take back everything he just said. He didn't mean it. That's why he stopped, and he probably would have gone back inside and made up with his father had Serena not parked herself outside the door and waited for him.

"Lucien," Serena said in her usual timid and apologetic way.

Lucien looked up and saw her, then pushed down all the remorse he was feeling and stormed past her as she struggled to keep up with him.

"...Lucien, I-I just wanted you to know that I've learned so much working under, I-I mean, with your father all these years. I'm so very certain if we work together that,--"

"Save that crap for the cameras, Serena," Lucien said, then he stopped and turned to her. "Just 'cuz I ain't go to college like him, don't think I'm stupid. I know you." He then looked her straight in the eye and whispered, "And I know what chu' really want."

"Okay," Serena answered, and that was the last word that was ever spoken from 'That Serena.' This, 'New Serena' glared right back at Lucien and whispered, "Then you must know how stupid it would be to underestimate me - just because I'm human," New Serena said in apparently her now usual, untimid and unapologetic way. Lucien smirked and continued on his way. "It'd probably be the last mistake you ever made." She announced.

Lucien kept walking as the smirk turned into a smile.

"And there she is," Lucien said as he rounded the corner.

Tirin paced the roof of the campaign headquarters like he was trying to grind himself into it. He wanted to rip a limb off of someone, but there was no one available at the moment. Rayna sat on the ledge with her bare feet dangling over the side. She tossed her cards, one by one, and watched them float down to the street below. Tirin moved to the ledge and sat next to her with his back to the street. For the longest time, they sat there in silence until he finally found the words to speak.

"I'll find him and kill him. I'll bring his heart to you in a jar to add to your collection."

"You can't. He's too powerful," Rayna said.

"He's just a man!" Tirin roared. "No one man can defeat us!"

"...Sweetie, he already has," Rayna said as she tossed the last card. "You know I love you, right?" Tirin responded with a single nod, and she kissed him on the cheek. "Take care. After tonight, you may be all that's left of us," Tirin found her eyes, and she smiled. "Bye."

She pushed herself off the ledge. Tirin reacted the only way he could; he dove after her. He tried to grab her, but she fought him off with all the strength she had, and that was considerable. She was, after all, half-vampire, which proved to be the deciding factor in the end. She kicked him out of range and opened herself up for impact. Tirin transformed just before impact. It was a long way down, and he didn't know if even that would save him, but he didn't care. Rayna obliterated the parked car she landed on. Tirin landed feet-first on another car and crushed it. He howled in agony but from two very different pains. Despite the onlookers, who had begun to form a crowd, he tried to drag his bruised and bloody body toward Rayna, but it was too late. The only thing he could do now was cry. He let out a heart-breaking roar that filled the city, then he limped away as best he could. Sirens blared in the distance as Lucien, along with a few others, came rushing out of the building to see what the commotion was about. Then he saw Rayna.

"AH, NO! NO-O-O-O!!" he screamed as he ran to her. "SOME-BODY PLEASE! PLEASE!... Hurry! Call an ambula,--"

He touched her face, and her head rolled away from the rest of her body. He screamed as her form began to deteriorate at an expediential rate. Her desiccated remains quickly became delicate and brittle in his hands. With the utmost care he tried to collect and cradle her, but still she cracked, splintered and disintegrated into dust... Then a soft, summer breeze rose up, sifted through Lucien's hair and gently blew away any sign she ever existed.

Later that day, the pit area was empty, the volunteers were gone, and the campaign was over. Julien sat alone in his darkened office and cried.

There were many stories and rumors about how Julien Dumont Gerard and The Priestess Rayna Loralei Rachel met, and of what their relationship truly was. But no one, other than the two of them, knew anything more, than that one day, a ten-year-old warlock boy brought home a full-grown woman - and she never left,... until today.

CHAPTER 62

"*W*elcome home*"*

Kaitlin zipped up a backpack full of stakes and various other devices for killing things that are not easily killed, then picked up her gun and checked to make sure it was fully loaded as Dani walked out of the bathroom.

"We could still bail and get Birthday Pizookies at BJ's," Kaitlin said, not meeting her eyes.

Dani's eyes glinted red as she walked up behind Kaitlin and touched the back of her head. Kaitlin collapsed into Dani's arms. Dani picked her up and, with love, laid her down on the bed. She then stroked Kaitlin's hair away from her eyes and mouth.

"Maybe next year, Mom." Dani smiled. "I love you."

Dani kissed her on the forehead and exited the motel room. Thirty minutes later, Dani got out of a taxi at the front gate of the Gerard estate. After sixteen long years, she was home. She stood there and took in the place as the taxi drove off. It looked different than what she had remembered; smaller, scarier. She moved to climb over the gate and stopped herself when she remembered the cemetery lesson.

She smiled, and her eyes flash red. The word slipped off her tongue with more ease than she expected.

"Apertum,"

The gate opened as the red in her eyes faded. She took a breath, then walked down the quarter-of-a-mile path to the main house. At any second, she expected a throng of vampires to descend and try to impede her approach, but there was not a single soul or soulless creature to be found.

"Strange," she thought.

Even if no one was home, under no certain terms would Rayna ever leave the place unguarded. It gave her pause, but it did not stop her advancement down the dreadfully dark, luridly lit lane. With the front door in view, things got stranger. Not only were there no vampires at the door, but it was wide open. It almost looked as if the place had been abandoned until a single light lit up inside. An invitation that she was not the least afraid to accept. After all, this was her home, too. She climbed the steps and walked inside as if she were coming home from the movies.

"Dad! Daddy! I'm home!" she called out with a playfulness unsuitable for this ominous occasion. "It's me, Danielle... Your son."

The door slammed shut behind her. Dani turned, and no one was there. The playful exterior she had when she walked through the door vanished, and her eyes ignited as her hair took to flight.

"So, you find this amusing," Tirin said as his voice echoed through the house. Dani whipped around but could not see him. "To return here after all these years, on this day. With blood in your eyes..."

The echo made it seem as if he was everywhere. Either that, or he was just moving around her that fast.

"Very well," he continued. "Who is it you wish to kill first? Which one of the men who looked after you when you were young? Abel?... Guillermo?... Jimmy Lee?... Or perhaps,... me-e-e-e-e."

Dani turned as Tirin stepped out of the shadowy hallway into the light. He was healing, but the bruises and cuts on his body were still evident. As he moved toward her, she noticed a slight limp as he favored his left leg. As a little girl, she always thought Tirin to be the scariest man in the world. He was always so cold and hard. She never understood why her mom loved him so. Standing before her now, he didn't look scary, hard, or cold. He looked tired, vulnerable, and, most of all, he looked sad. Dani's eyes returned to normal and her hair fell back to her shoulders. A tear streamed down her face as the reality of the situation set in. She felt foolish and was embarrassed by the thoughts she had brought into the house with her. Tirin moved over to her, and she let her head rest on his chest. He tried to remain stoic as she cried in his arms.

"It's never easy, killing," he said. "Especially someone you love."

"I don't want to fight you," Dani said.

"You don't have to. Our fights are not with each other."

He stepped back and looked at her. He beamed with pride at the beautiful young woman she had become.

"...You look just like her."

"Thanks. Lucien says so, too."

"Mmm. Yes. Her spirit roams within you," he said. "but you've always had your fathers eyes."

Dani didn't know how to process what was supposed to be a compliment. She became self-conscious in the moment as her eyes diverted away from his, and her focus became fixed on the floor.

"I loved your mother. She was,… perhaps, closer to me than anyone… Even Dane."

That brought her eyes back to him.

"She felt the same way about you. You and Kate were the only friends she had."

Tirin could not hold his tears back any longer. He closed his eyes, then opened them and let them flow free.

"I'm not here to stop you," he said. "We all must follow our paths. I just thought you might appreciate that lesson." Dani nodded her thanks to him as he continued. "I have but one last thing to offer you before we say goodbye," Dani looked up at him and held his eyes in the way that her mother used to. "No matter what you think or may have been told, I promise you that no one on this planet loved your mother more than he did. What happened sixteen years ago was tragic, and he's lived with it every second of his life since. Remember that, as well."

Tirin embraced her again, then left a loving kiss on her forehead.

"Welcome home, Danielle... and Happy Birthday," he said, then turned to leave.

"T," Dani called, stopping him at the door. "Where will you go?"

With his back to her, Tirin looked to the sky as if the answer to her question was written up there, in the stars. Then, like so many times before, he chose his words carefully.

"To hell, for the things I've done and... will do... Especially tonight."

It seemed like he wanted to turn back and set his eyes upon her one last time, but he didn't. He pushed off the door frame, and, in a flash, he was gone.

CHAPTER 63

"*All I ever wanted...*"

The old Dallas Club had been virtually untouched for sixteen years. The roof had fallen in, but four walls remained, for the most part, intact. There was a small memorial stone for Camille encased in the ground, where the dance floor used to be. Julien sat on the chair in the shoeshine stand, the same spot he sat in sixteen years ago, waiting. He was silhouetted, but the bitter rage in his eyes could still be seen. He was waiting for a fight. A large cloud moved away, unblocking the light from the waxing, three-quarters-full moon, and the place became illuminated. As one last shadow dissipated, Jean appeared in its place. Julien didn't move. He just sat there and looked at him for a while before he spoke.

"You may not know this but,... there's a little-known law in the South that prohibits the knocking down or demolishing of any building over a hundred years old, as long as it has at least three walls intact. It was put in the books to stop these bozos from erecting a strip mall over a,... possibly historic site," Julien said as he stepped down from the chair and walked into the light.

A little more than a block away, Lucien headed toward the building with Opal, Alvin, and Mace, along with ten other vampires. He stopped at the corner and scanned the area with a suspicious eye.

"Alright, y'all remember what I told ya'," Luc said. "Be stealthy and stay hidden. Hopefully I won't need ya'. Go on. Disappear."

They all took off in different directions and did what creatures like them do best; they disappeared. Lucien rounded the corner and was careful to stay in the shadows as he made his way toward the old club. He snuck up to the building and hid behind some rubble. With no emotion, he watched and listened from a large hole in the wall.

"This particular building was first put up in eighteen twenty-three," Julien continued. "They say, yo' momma, Madame Marie Laveau, at the age of twenty-nine, used to read fortunes, right about where you're standing. Funny. Nowadays, you can't go twenty feet down Bourbon Street without seeing a poster or some hint of her existence somewhere. Some people even think she's still alive… What 'chu think 'bout d'at?" he asked. Jean didn't respond. "We bought the place in nineteen ninety-four. It had previously been a Christian Science bookstore. Hmph," he chuckled. "We did some, EXTENSIVE renovations, if you know what I mean, and in ninety-five, opened up 'Club Dallas' …My wife was murdered in this very spot, right here, in ninety-nine." Then there was the slightest change in his tone. "But you already knew that, didn't you?"

"I did not kill Camille, Julien, you,--"

"LIAR!... Maybe you didn't pull the trigger, but make no mistake, she died,--"

"Because you were not strong enough to protect her." Jean interjected.

That hurt. The truth always does.

"…I don't remember you faring all that well in that department either, Mister. But, knowing your history, maybe you didn't really want to." Touché. "You should have died that night sixteen years ago, not her – YOU."

"…I did."

"Yeah, well… Prepare to do it again."

Julien rose just off the ground as his body charged up and Jean's eyes and fists began to glow as he readied himself. Then, just before they could strike, the ground between them cracked with a thunderclap of red light. They both turned to find Dani where the door used to be, framed by debris and silence. Lucien sighed and shook his head in disbelief.

"Camille?..." Julien gasped to himself.

Julien powered down as his body lowered and his feet reconnected with the floor. He took a step in her direction and she put up her hand and stopped him. She paused for a second, exhaled, then walked over to Jean without looking at her father. She looked into both of Jean's eyes before she narrowed her focus on the cerulean one.

"I know you're hurting, and angry, and I know who's in there with you now, but the only way you do this, is if you kill me first. And I know you won't do that," she said, then turned her focus to the red eye. "And I know he won't let you do it, either."

"He cannot stop me, you ungrateful child! I spared your worthless,--"

"You cannot win this, little one. It is not your time yet."

"...Well then I wouldn't go too far," she smiled.

Jean looked at Julien, then backed into a shadow and disappeared. Dani took another deep breath before she turned to face her father.

"...Hey, Daddy." She said, full of remorse and uncertainty.

"Hey, Dani,--"

"Danielle."

"...Danielle... You look just like,--"

"I know. Everybody says so."

Julien nodded his agreement. Neither knew what to say, so they just stood there for an awkward moment, soaking in sixteen years of regret. Then Julien opened his arms to her. He didn't know what else to do, and that was really the last thing she expected from him.

"...I can't," she said as she closed her eyes and shook her head, the words barely escaping her mouth.

When she said it, she didn't know how much pain those words would cause her when they left her lips. If she did, she probably wouldn't have said them. Even now, she wished she could take it back, but it was too late. That train had already left the station.

"Yes, you can," Julien said.

"No, I ca,--"

"Yeah, you can. You can if you want to, 'cuz I'm right here," Julien said. All Dani could do was shake her head as the tears began to fall. "It doesn't have to be this way between us."

"Doesn't it? You killed momma sixteen years ago and you've been trying to kill Kate ever since!" Dani said, then after a long pause, "Why, daddy?!... WHY?!"

Lucien got emotional from his sister's question. A part of him wanted to know the answer, too. Right then he wanted to stop this, but he refused to interfere.

"...All I ever wanted was to live with my family, in peace, to be happy," Julien responded.

"...I don't think that life was meant for either of us."

"...I guess not... I'm so sorry, Peanut."

She nodded. Her forgiveness came with tears. But when her hair rose and her fists glowed red, it wasn't anger, it was readiness.

CHAPTER 64

Kaitlin woke with a start—groggy, disoriented. Then came the fear. The kind that lingers, even after the nightmares end. She knew Dani could defend herself, as she had proven time and time again, but this was different in so many ways. This was family. She jumped up and ran for the door and stopped just short of it. She nearly forgot she had to defend herself as well. She dashed back to the bed and grabbed the backpack full of stakes and various other assorted weaponry and, of course, the gun. She knew she'd need that where she was going. The only thing she didn't know was that Tirin would be standing right outside of her door when she opened it.

She gasped and exhaled nearly all the air out of her body. It seemed like an eternity before she remembered to inhale some back in. The two of them just stood there with their eyes locked on each other. Both seemed equally surprised and neither looked away. Kaitlin, of all people, knew she wasn't supposed to hold an alpha's gaze, but she couldn't bring herself to look anywhere else. She had almost forgotten the gun in her hand, loaded with five brand-new silver bullets, until Tirin's eyes reminded her. They jetted down to her gun-toting hand for a quick second before they crept back up to her eyes. Then she remembered and, in that moment, became more frightened than she's ever been. She jerked her hand up to shoot. Tirin didn't offer the tiniest feint. He reached out and slapped her hand as she fired, sending the shot slightly off-mark, just missing him. He grabbed her by the throat, took the gun away from her, then stepped into the room and closed the door behind him. She didn't cry out and there was no sound of a struggle. Not even the cricket's song invaded the silence. There was nothing, until her body came crashing through the window and landed on the hard ground of the paved parking lot.

She rolled twice before she stopped. Her face and arms were cut up from the glass, but her eyes remained open as Tirin walked out of the room holding the gun and the box of silver bullets. Kaitlin never screamed. Room lights started to flip on and people in the motel began to come out to see what the commotion was about. Tirin walked over to Kaitlin and stooped down next to her as the disconcerted whispers of shock and fear grew in the background, but none of that mattered to him, not now. He didn't even look at Kaitlin as he emptied the gun and checked the bullets.

"Silver… Good," he said as he looked at her for the first time since she came through the window.

She was conscious, barely, but the only movement came from the blood that dripped from her wounds. Tirin sniffed down her body, stopping at her shoulder. Something in the scent told him it was out of place.

He put the gun down, grabbed her by her hair and yanked her to a seated position. He then knocked her shoulder back into place. Now she screamed. Her cry terrorized the motel's guests; some ran back into their rooms and others yelled at their children and spouses to get back inside. A few people positioned themselves to get a better look at the goings-on, but none dared approach as Tirin resumed his inspection of the gun and bullets, which smoldered in his hand.

"Wh-Where's Dani?" Kaitlin asked through her tears. "What'd you,--"

"She's the last person you should be worried about now," Tirin said as he loaded the gun. "This isn't about her."

"Tirin, please, don't,--"

"We treated you like family and you betrayed us when you brought that man into our lives."

"I was trying to help my friend!" Kaitlin cried.

"You might as well have killed Dane yourself."

It seems like there's always one guy in these situations – a hero with good intentions, but they never really have any idea what it is they're getting themselves into. It's sad, because in this particular situation, the hero that came out of his room and started to walk toward them wanted nothing more than to help Kaitlin in the most genuine way.

"Hey! HEY!" The hero called out. "Back up off the lady, man!"

He was a decent-sized dude with good height and weight on him, and he had the support of the onlookers, but Tirin didn't hear him. His focus was solely on Kaitlin.

"You and I gonna play a little game, now. Here's how it goes: I'm gonna give you this gun, freshly loaded, with five silver bullets in it. If you can kill me before I count to ten - you win. If you don't,..." he said as the hero arrived, "then you're gonna wish to God you never played this game with me."

"HEY! Get the fu,--"

In one fluid motion, Tirin rose up, turned, ripped the hero's throat out and stooped back down next to her as he collapsed to the ground. Kaitlin screamed as Tirin flicked away the remainder of the Hero's throat, and the onlookers climbed over each other to get to their rooms. Tirin slapped Kaitlin and grabbed her by the face.

"PAY ATTENTION TO ME!" he yelled at her. "THIS IS SERIOUS! LOOK AT ME! These fools can't help you! I'm gonna kill a couple more of them just to up the ante for you!... The only person that can help you now, is you. Good luck, Katie. I really mean that."

He tossed the loaded gun just above her head. She looked up to catch it and just like that, he was gone. A roar was heard as Tirin sped past an open door and ripped through a guy peeking out, causing blood to spray on his door and wall. Hysteria had broken out in the motel parking lot as guests screamed and ran for their rooms and cars. Kaitlin struggled to her feet as Tirin began the countdown.

"ONE!... TWO!" he screamed as he zoomed behind her.

Kaitlin turned and fired, nowhere close to where he was.

"THREE!..."

Tirin jumped through a window into a room and ravaged the couple inside. Kaitlin limped over as fast as she could and fired off a round. Another miss. The lights in the room went out.

"FOUR!"

The couple inside was still screaming. They begged for help as Kaitlin moved to the window.

"FIVE!" Tirin growled as he exploded through the door, startling Kaitlin.

She fired again and missed.

"SIX!... SEVEN!"

Tirin sped behind Kaitlin and raked her back with his claws. She fired in the air as she screamed, wasting another precious bullet. Blood began to seep through her shirt as she fell to her knees.

"EIGHT!... Get up!" he bellowed. "GE-E-ET U-U-UP! NINE!"

She stumbled to her feet, sobbing and shaking so much that she could barely hold onto the gun as Tirin turned and ran straight at her.

"Come on! Do it! COME O-O-O-O-N!"

Kaitlin's father taught her how to shoot when she was thirteen years old. She was a really good shot too, but she had never been faced with a situation like this, where her entire existence rested on a single shot. The time for thought was gone. She took a breath, squeezed the trigger and it was done. Her father taught her well. Her aim was true as that bullet traveled right toward Tirin's head, but her father never taught her how to shoot an alpha. Tirin feinted ever-so-slightly to the right and the bullet zipped past him. He caught her in his arms, slammed her into the motel wall and pinned her there. His chest heaved as he sucked in air to replenish the supply he had expelled.

"...Ten..." he whispered. Then he growled, "you lose-e-e."

Her scream echoed through the lot—sharp, helpless. Then came silence, heavy and absolute.

CHAPTER 65

Lucien watched as Dani rose up about a foot off the ground. She waited for her father to do the same, but he wouldn't. He just stood there, defenseless, leaving himself open for whatever was to come his way.

"What are you waiting for?!" Dani yelled at him. "Get into mactrouge! Defend yourself!"

Julien placed his hands in his pockets and lowered his head.

"I mean it, Daddy!... DO IT!" Dani screamed as she formed an energy blast in her hand and held it.

Julien still would not comply. In an effort to make him, she launched the blast in his direction. He didn't move as it exploded on the ground to the left of him. Lucien clenched his teeth as he watched. He didn't know what emotions were pulsing through his body at the moment, but it was uncomfortable for him. He was angry with his father beyond measure, but not to the point where he wanted him dead. Seeing him in this vulnerable state made him wish that their last conversation had been a different one. As for his sister, as Jean had emphasized so many times, she was not supposed to be here. Did he spend his life protecting her so that she could die trying to fulfill some foolish prophecy? He was just as angry with her as he was with his father and despite all of his efforts to stop this, it was happening now and he didn't know what to think or do. He only knew that he would not interfere, or help, either one of them.

"If you don't fight, I'll kill you!" Dani screamed.

"If that's what you came here to do, Peanut, then I,--"

"Stop calling me that!" Dani choked out. "You don't get to call me that anymore!"

"I'm sorry," Julien said.

"FOR WHAT?!" Dani screamed. "What are you sorry for?! Which one of the hundreds of things that you've done?!"

"...All of 'em," Julien said.

"NO! It's too late! It's too late for that now! Fight me! FIGHT!"

She drew another energy blast from her Qi and launched it at him. It exploded right in front of him. He covered up momentarily to block the shrapnel and debris, then put his hands back into his pockets and resumed his stance. Dani then drew an energy ball from each hand. Neither was close to hitting him.

"NO! YOU'RE GOING TO FIGHT ME YOU SON OF A BITCH!... You have to fight me!" Dani screamed as tears fell from her eyes. It was making it difficult for her to hold mactrouge. "You have to!... You took everything from me! I won't let you take this!"

She zipped across the room toward her father. Julien lowered his head and waited for her to strike, but he did not move. Just then, Jean rose up out of a shadow, blocking her path.

"What are you doing?! Move!" Dani yelled. Jean would not. "I won't let you take this from me either, now move! MOVE!" Dani screamed, but Jean held his ground. "PLEASE! Just get out of my way!" she said as she finally broke down.

It had become impossible for her to stay in the mactrouge state, as her tears kept washing the red from her eyes. She slumped down to the ground and her hair fell onto her shoulders. Hagatha was oddly silent in this moment. Dani annoyed her, as many younger, less-expe-rienced witches can do, but in the end, Hagatha still saw her as a sister and although she found this one to be extremely obnoxious, she was her sister just the same. Jean watched the young woman in front of him. They always had a unique connection and he never understood why, until tonight.

"Danielle,… do not let this anger ruin your life as it did mine," Jean said as he bent down to her.

"But it's my destiny," Dani cried.

"No. A prophecy does not set one's destiny." Jean said. "A tarot can only hold power if you empower it to do so."

Jean's voice lingered in the silence that followed, a truth neither past nor prophecy could refute. He reached out his hand to her. "Come, little one. It is time to let the hate go. It does us a disservice and we have been slaves to it for far too long. Kaitlin has waited for us both to understand that. Let us not make her wait any longer."

Both Lucien and Julien took note of Jean's powerful words, as well as one other uninvited guest.

"I'm afraid poor Kate will have to wait a tad bit more," Malcolm said. "It was a beautiful speech, though. It really was quite moving."

A Council warlock, in full mactrouge, along with a vampire, entered through the cracks in the wall behind Julien. Another pair appeared outside, behind Lucien. Dani took Jean's hand and as he pulled her up, a third Council warlock with two vampires at his side entered the arena and crept up behind Dani and Jean. As Jean turned to them, he saw the red laser dot from a sniper rifle as it appeared on Dani's forehead.

"I especially liked the part about a card holding power over you, but only if you empower the card to do so. That was really very poetic," Malcolm said. "You are a fascinating fellow, Mr… Laveau, I believe it is? Hmm? Jean Laveau? From Haiti, correct?"

Jean turned back to him, but would not respond. Dani, however, had a lot to say.

"You're such a fucking asshole."

"Don't be base, Danielle," Malcolm replied. "Let's not ruin this wonderful reunion with a tainted tongue. All these years away and this is how you speak in front of daddy? Tch, tch, tch."

Dani took a step toward Malcolm. Jean blocked her progression with his arm, saving her from her temerarious thoughts, as she was unaware of the laser dot on her forehead or the hidden sniper waiting on a rooftop until Jean pointed it out. Dani suppressed her impulsive intentions, but her tongue was still free to speak them.

"I'm going to kill you," she said.

"That would be a neat trick," Malcolm smirked.

"Are you that afraid to fight me that you always have to have others do it for you?"

"Sweet child, have you forgotten who it was that taught you?" Malcolm answered. "Then again, you are twenty-one now. A full-grown menace to society, and it appears you've finally learned how to get yourself off the ground over the last couple of days, or perhaps we have your brother to thank for that. Hmm?"

Dani didn't answer, but her expression told him his surmise of the situation was solid. Dani glanced up at the sky. The moon had been hidden for some time by an assemblage of agonizingly slow-moving clouds, but an advantageous opening was approaching. She glanced at Jean, who tilted his head down. He knew.

"Ah. What a surprise. The inordinately sheltering sibling," Malcolm said as the Council warlock escorted Lucien into the arena. "I'm really quite curious how it is you've been helping your sister all these years. Perhaps you'd be good enough to share that secret with the rest of the class before you die."

"Fuck you, asshole," Lucien said.

"I must say, your children really are quite charming, Mr. Gerard. You should be proud," Malcolm replied, not at all trying to hide the sarcasm in his voice.

"Why don't we just keep this between us," Julien said as he stepped closer. "I'm the one you really want."

"No. I actually want all of you, and that's close enough," Malcolm said, stopping Julien from inching his way closer. The playfulness he always displayed had perished. "If one hair on his head so much as twitches, destroy him," he ordered the Council warlock behind Julien. "You are all guilty of crimes against The Council. The punishment for that is death."

"Dude, you're fuckin' high," Lucien said.

"Your father and this one here," Malcolm said, indicating Jean, "have both KILLED prominent members of The Council. YOU attacked me with malice intent,--"

"YOU WERE TRYIN' TO KILL MY SISTER!"

"--WHO SHOULDN'T EVEN BE ALIVE!" Malcolm yelled with more emotion than he had ever displayed. Even the other Council warlocks took notice. He took a couple of breaths, then returned to his normal disposition.

"A mistake on my part that will immediately be rectified," he said as his eyes glared at Dani. "If only Kaitlin was ambling about, I'd have the entire Scooby gang. A most annoying woman; I'm sure she's not far away. Charles," he said to one of the other warlocks. "Make note and remind me to do a quick sweep of the area after we've dispatched the four of them."

Charles nodded.

"If you think a bullet can stop me from ripping,--"

"Oh, I'm certain this one can," Malcolm said as he pulled a bullet out of his pocket and displayed it between his index finger and thumb. His eyes flashed as he placed it about shoulder height in the air and released it. The bullet sat perfectly still in the air as he continued. "It was designed for situations such as this. It's a hollow-point vampire bullet, filled with the toxin of ten vampires. Neither Kaitlin, your brother, nor this dapperly dressed gentleman can save you from this. One word from me and Danielle, Daniel, Dani Gerard and whatever other names you are known by, will no... longer... exist..."

Malcolm's sentence dragged on because his attention was drawn to Lucien's gang as they casually seeped into the arena and flanked Malcolm's people. Two final vampires appeared in the doorway behind him.

"Naw, don't let 'em interrupt. Please continue," Lucien said.

"Hmph. Interesting. You don't really believe you can win with these hooligans, do you?"

"I don't know whether or not I'll win, but I'm damn sure you gon' lose."

"Tell them to stand down, or your sister di,--" Malcolm started to say as the moon broke free of the clouds and gave Jean a much-needed shadow. He stepped into it and vanished before the Council warlock could react. Malcolm was momentarily mystified by the deceptive disappearance, then his eyes widened when he realized what had happened. "...He's a moo-tone-wah?" Malcolm whispered to himself. "...SHOOT HER!" he yelled.

Dani closed her eyes and exhaled, hoping that Jean had found what he was looking for. A scream was heard over Malcolm's shoulder, off in the distance. Then there was silence. Jean popped back into the arena with a sniper gun in his hand, this time behind the Council warlock and the two vampires that had flanked him and Dani. His eyes flashed and the weapon fell apart. Then he flexed his wrist and a retractable wooden stake slid down his sleeve and fell into his hand. Dani's hair began to lift up off her shoulders and when she opened her eyes, they were blood red.

"You were sayin'," Lucien smiled.

Malcolm only had a split second to make a decision; a choice, really. Jean's ability to moo-tone-wah created a serious problem for him. If he did nothing, Jean would step into the shadow he just popped out of and wreak all kinds of havoc on him and his men. His only other choice was to take away the shadows by flooding the room with either darkness or light. The shock would cause his men to lose their advantage and Julien and Lucien would most likely mactrouge in the confusion. He would still have his vampires, but so would Lucien. Dani was the wild card, and she had her red eyes trained on him.

There was no right or wrong answer in this situation, only a choice, and then he would have to play his hand accordingly. Malcolm's eyes flashed red. He slammed his hands together and intensified the light in the arena, two-fold. He chose light because the brightness would momentarily disorient everyone - including him - and because witches can see perfectly clear in complete darkness. The disorientation lasted only a few seconds, but it was enough. Both Julien and Lucien popped into mactrouge.

"LUC!" Julien yelled, not as a warning but as a signal.

Neither Julien nor Lucien had time to turn and face the warlock behind them, so as soon as the disorientation ended, they both fired shots at each other's warlocks. The Council warlocks blocked the blasts, but they also had to deal with the deadly vampires. Julien and Lucien did, as well. Jean may not have been able to dance through the shadows, but he was well-versed and capable of bringing his particular style of destruction in any situation. Two skilled vampires would be a handful for a normal warlock, but Malcolm was anything but normal. He easily dispatched his two toothy assailants, but once he saw more flocking toward him, with Julien heading his way and Lucien taking aim at him from across the room, he knew the odds were not in his favor. He saw that Dani had turned away from him and was making short work of the warlock covering her, and he took advantage of the opening. The bullet from his pocket was still floating in the air, pointing in Dani's direction. He looked at Julien and flashed a sinister smile.

"DANI-I-I-I!" Julien screamed as Malcolm leaped for the bullet.

Julien couldn't reach Malcolm in time to stop him, so he changed direction and zipped toward his daughter instead. Malcolm touched the bullet with his index finger, magically igniting the tiny explosive charge in the primer, which rocketed the round right at the unwavering witch. Julien dove to tackle Dani. His trajectory placed him in the path of the predestined projectile and the bullet found a home in his back and did not leave. He collapsed into his daughter's arms.

"Daddy?..." Dani gasped.

Dani fell out of mactrouge as she eased her father to the ground.

"NO-O-O-O! NO!" Lucien cried out. "Where is he?! WHERE IS HE?!" Lucien screamed. Jean looked toward the doorway, but Malcolm was gone. "Oh, you son of a bitch! You're dead! You hear me?! YOU'RE DEAD! MACE!!" Lucien screamed as he fell out of mactrouge. Mace zipped over to him. "Find that mother fucker for me, please!"

Mace zipped out of the arena as Lucien rushed over to Dani and knelt at her side.

"Daddy, don't die," Dani cried. "Please, not now... I don't want to lose you again."

Julien gurgled and coughed up some blood. Dani turned to Jean.

"Help him! PLEASE!" Dani pleaded.

Jean shook his head, "There is nothing I can do."

"You saved Momma, you can save him!"

"Your mother's wound was from a single vampire. There is ten times the amount of toxin in that bullet." Again, he shook his head, "I am sorry."

"No… It's not supposed to be this way," Dani cried.

"It's okay, Peanut… It's okay," Julien coughed out. He raised his hand, touched her face, and smiled. "Just like your momma," he said. Then he looked at Lucien. "Those proposals… they were so good… I'm sorry I didn't look at them before… I just,--"

"I don't care about that, Pop." Lucien cried. "I was just trying to make you proud."

"Aww, boy… You always did."

Julien reached inside his collar and pulled off the blood heart necklace clasped around his neck. He always knew how much Lucien loved it and he put it in his boy's hand. Then he looked at Dani and smiled as he grabbed her hand and kissed it.

"My little girl," he smiled. "…Finally got you home… Happy Birthday, Peanut…"

"Thanks, Daddy," Dani said.

Julien took both of their hands and clasped them together.

"I… L-Love… youuuuu…" he whispered, then he smiled and closed his eyes.

Lucien broke down. Mace zipped back into the arena, out of breath. He walked over and touched Lucien on his shoulder.

"I'm sorry, Luc. I checked the entire neighborhood twice but,… he's gone."

"AWH-H-H-H-H-H-H!" Lucien screamed.

He was so caught up in his own emotions that he didn't notice his sister had stopped crying, and that she was hyperventilating next to him. Jean did, and it forced his hands and eyes to glow as he took a defensive stance.

"Lucien. Move away from your sister, please."

"What?…" Lucien said as he looked at Dani, just now noticing that her hair was floating with a life of its own. "…Dani?"

Dani took a deep, haggard breath and exhaled out any benevolence that remained in her body. Her fingers began to bleed as, one by one, razor-sharp talons erupted from her fingertips. Her hands became energized and her eyes crackled blood red. Then, for the very first time, her naturally tanned skin seemed to absorb a greenish hue as she rose up and released a long, bloodcurdling scream. Hagatha had been quiet for a while, but no more, as she let out a deep, throaty laugh.

"Heh, heh, heh, heh, heh, heh. That's the girl I've been waiting for," she whispered to Jean.

"STOP." Lucien firmly stated to his gang. "No one. Move."

Dani hovered around her father and lowered herself to face Lucien eye-to-eye. She growled in his face as saliva dripped from her mouth.

"Who's the little one now, Brother?" Dani whispered. Lucien held her eyes but did not respond. "I want that necklace. GIVE IT TO ME," she ordered in a deep, hollow voice.

"Oh-h-h, I like her so much better like this," Hagatha said.

"…No. It's mine," Lucien responded.

"Perhaps you want me to take it from you," she said as she unfolded her bloodied taloned hand in front of his face. "Give it to me, or I'll rip it out of your dead hand."

"…You won't kill me."

Dani smiled as she positioned her index finger terrifyingly close to Lucien's eye. Jean had been fully powered and ready to strike since Dani's hair took flight but when he looked at Lucien, it gave him pause. Jean had sensed Camille's essence at the cemetery last night, but now, looking into Lucien's eyes, he saw her clearly; fully. She exhaled a long breath and blew the recollection of their first encounter through his mind.

"I only wonder why you would risk so much to save her now if you plan on doing the same thing to her as you will try to do to me, once she reaches an age that makes you - uncomfortable."

In his lifetime, Jean Laveau had seen more than most could ever imagine, but seeing Camille rise up from Lucien's body was an astonishing sight even for him. Like a ghost, she floated out of Lucien's body and walked over to Jean with a warm smile on her face. She glanced at his energized hands before her eyes met up with his.

"*It's a primal darkness that clouds our vision.*" Camille clearly stated, but only he could hear her. "*We feel lost; frightened,... alone. And we respond in kind to whatever it is we are given,*" she said as she reached out and clasped his glowing hands and held them in a loving, friendly way. "*<u>Talk</u> to her, Jean. Guide my daughter back from the darkness, into the light.*"

Camille's eyes flashed. Her chest illuminated and a burst of energy surged down her arms, into her and Jean's intertwined hands. It travelled up through Jean's body and found a home in his head. Jean's eyes squeezed shut. He inhaled a mighty breath and held it as Hazel's painful memory flashed through his mind. He gasped as he exhaled and a sorrowful tear burst through his eyes and ran down his face. Camille saw his pain and gasped as she released him. They stared at each, neither knowing what the other would do, but both completely understanding how the other felt. Jean powered down. His hands faded to normal and his eyes moved to Dani.

"Danielle," Jean said in a soft, calming voice. It seemed to irritate her as she whipped her head around and glared at him. "There is love all around you, child... but you must allow yourself to feel it. Grasp onto it and hold it tight, for the love is the light that will guide you from this darkness. It is the light that will guide you back to us."

Dani stared at Jean for a very long, uncomfortable moment, then she carefully withdrew her finger from her brother's face. She closed her eyes and began to quiver as she internally tussled with the demon inside of her. Lucien, however, would not give her the peace of a solitary struggle.

"Don't you dare push it down," Lucien whispered in an angry, antagonistic voice. He knew what his sister was trying to do, and even though it was only seconds ago that his life was on the precipice, he refused to let her. "Embrace it ALL, Dani. All of it! Breathe into it!"

"Lucien,--" Jean warned.

"Lucien. S-Stop, pleas--" Dani said as she tried to contain herself.

"BREATHE IT IN, GOD DAMN IT!" he yelled at her.

Dani opened her blood-red eyes and grabbed him by the neck and squeezed - HARD.

"You're a witch," Lucien gasped. "You gotta,... embrace it... All of it... Stop bein' a-ashamed."

Jean took a step to stop it, but Camille mirrored him to keep herself between him and her children.

"You must allow her to hear it." Camille said. *"She must understand it and believe it to be true."*

"At what risk?" Jean asked. *"Your son? This city?"*

"My son carries my strength. My daughter holds my fire. I trust them both." Camille said. *"I'm asking you too, as well."*

Jean clinched his fists and his body became tense.

"Please," Camille implored.

Jean held Camille's eyes and waited for what was to come next.

"You gotta,... take control of it, Dani,... or you'll,... become everythin',... you're tryin',... so hard,... not to be..."

A tear fell down Dani's face, followed by another and another. She released Lucien and exhaled as if he had been holding her breath for a very long time.

"Thank you, Jean Laveau," Camille smiled, then rose up and swooped back into Lucien's body and disappeared.

It seems as though she was not done with him - yet.

"That's it,... Breathe," Lucien said as he struggled to take in a breath and exhale with her. "Breathe."

The red faded from Dani's eyes. The talons receded back into her fingers, and the wounds they produced healed. Her skin faded back to its normal complexion, and her hair settled and rested on her shoulders.

"Yeah," Lucien nodded. "That's what I'm talkin' 'bout."

Dani lunged forward and embraced him and Lucien hugged her back as Jean exhaled his relief.

"Welcome home, Brah," Lucien said.

"...Don't call me that," Dani exhaled.

"And Happy Birthday."

Dani gave him a somber smile, then looked at her father's body. There would be no birthday celebration tonight. A siren was heard in the distance. The siblings looked at each other with both true affection and remorse, then Lucien rose and pulled Dani to her feet.

"What do we do?" Dani asked.

"We need to get the hell out here," Alvin, the vampire, said.

"And you need to go," Lucien said.

"What? Why?!" Dani asked.

"'Cuz somebody's gotta make everythin' right in this city again, and it can't be you. The Council's still here, and they still want you dead," he said as he looked around at the bodies. "Probably even more so now. They can't allow a full-grown witch to be walkin' 'round talkin' to people."

"Then what I'm I supposed to do?"

"…Run away," Lucien replied as a tear fell off his face.

"I'm sick of running, Lucien," she cried.

"I know, but stayin' here'll make it way too easy for 'em. Gimme some time, Sis. I'll make it right, somehow, then I'm a bring you home. I promise."

Dani nodded as her shoulders slumped and she wearily turned and cast her eyes on her father's body.

"After all I did,… he still saved me," she said, not trying to hold back her tears.

"Pop always tried to do da' right thing. He just got confused when it came to how."

"Luc, we gotta go, man," Alvin said.

Lucien nodded, then turned to Jean. He looked in his good eye.

"Thank you - for everythin'. Take care of 'em, and I'll get 'em back here as soon as I can." Luc said. Jean nodded. Then Lucien glared into Jean's other eye. "On another note, if I find out you had somethin' to do with Rayna's death, there won't be a cave on this planet dark enough for you to hide in."

"Oh, Lucien," Dani said with an unapproving brow scrunched on her face.

This was not the time, and it definitely wasn't the place for this conversation. Dani tugged at Jean's hand and pried him away from her sullen sibling and the two of them ran off. Lucien then turned his acrimony toward his crew as they were all that was left as the sirens closed in.

"Y'all need to go! Quick!"

"What about you?" Mace said.

"Somebody gotta clean this shit up, and it starts now, with me," Lucien barked. "Opal, be ready and wait for my call." Opal nodded. "Alright, y'all go! Gon'! Disappear!" he ordered. Mace was hesitant. Lucien exhaled some of his aggression before he responded, "It's cool, Brutha'. I got this."

Mace released a soft, frustration-filled growl, then he and the vampires did what they do best.

Alone, Lucien dropped to his knees next to his father. He lifted him up and held his lifeless body in his arms. A sorrowful sigh released a tear from his eye along with all the pent-up emotion he had been toting around for what seemed like his entire life. So many things he wanted to say that he no longer could. So many things he needed to hear that he never would. His heart ached from the pain that so often comes with regret. It's a horrible weight for one to bear, and try as we might to release it, it can secure a tenacious grip on a soul. Julien ferried his regret around for sixteen years. Now it was Lucien's turn. His burden, his bloodline, and this broken city, all of it was his and his alone to shoulder.

The red and blue flashing lights frantically flickered off of what was left of the walls as the New Orleans PD poured into the busted building with guns in hand and their sights, surprisingly, set solely on the young heir. Seems the broken city was no longer in need of repair, at least, not by him.

hat smile

In cities with a high malafec population, the steady sounds of sirens and the aggregate abundance of ambulances were a constant. An expectation that, perhaps, should not be so easily expected. Curious how it seemed there was never one to be found when you really needed one. Even more curious, how sometimes, when they were there, it wasn't enough. This held true for most metropolitan centers where there was an insufficient number of police to patrol the highly populated areas. On this night, though, there was no amount of sirens, ambulances, or police that could undo the carnage that was left on display in the parking lot of this motel. The flashing lights from patrol cars forced Jean and Dani to put their fears and concerns on a brief hold as they approached with the utmost caution as to not be detected. Once they realized that the officers in the two patrol cars and the paramedics in the ambulance were just as maimed - or dead - as everyone else, caution was left by the wayside, and fear, once again, became their traveling companion.

They prayed Kaitlin had not listened and that she had done exactly what she was not supposed to do - LEAVE. They hoped she was off somewhere where she certainly should not be, traversing unknown dangers on dodgy, darkened streets, looking for Dani. They ran up to the dark room, ready to burst in if necessary, but instead found the door ajar,… and the window broken.

"KATIE?!" Dani screamed as she pushed through the door.

She tried to turn on the lights, but the lamp had been knocked over, and the bulb was broken. Dani turned to continue the search elsewhere, only to be stopped by Jean, who noticed that the floor was wet. The bathroom door was cracked, and a slow, steady stream of water flowed from it. Red water.

"UHH," Dani gasped as tears gushed from her eyes.

She ran through the door, flipped on the light, and screamed. Then she screamed again,… And again…… And again.

Kaitlin Morrison was a woman who loved life, and she lived every moment of hers to the fullest. She challenged it, flirted with it, and refused to fear it, even when she was afraid. When one has a spirit as great as hers, fear can never rule it. She took on every obstacle head-first and embraced it. She shared her heart with everyone who was fortunate enough to have ever met her. She gave herself fully to everything she did and to everyone she knew, and she did it with a smile. That beautiful smile. It was, perhaps, her greatest weapon and undoubtedly her greatest gift. She wore it like a badge of honor on her face for all to see. She gave it to everyone who crossed her path, whether they knew her or not, and although she was no witch or sorceress, the effect it had on others was magical. She changed everyone she came across for the better. No one knew that more than Jean.

He entered the bathroom and found Kaitlin's naked body lying in the overflowing, blood-filled tub. He was paralyzed. Not even Hagatha's wickedly inappropriate cackle could affect him now; he was numb to the world. All he could hear was Dani's incessant, unceasing screams. His body went limp, and he fell to his knees, then slumped up against the doorframe to stop himself from falling further. Dani shut off the water and soaked herself as she unsuccessfully tried to pull Kaitlin's body out of the tub. Kaitlin's head rolled to the side, and

Dani discovered a deep, nasty lycan bite on her shoulder. She tried to apply pressure to stop the bleeding, but there was no need. The deed was done.

"No, no, no, no, no, no, no. Jean, help me get her out," Dani cried. "Jean, help me. PLEASE!! HELP ME GET HER OUT!!" she screamed, but Jean would not move. "Oh, God - NO! NO-O-O! NO-O-O-AAAAAAAAHHHHHHHhhhhhhaaaaaaaa..."

Dani held Kaitlin in her arms and wailed as Jean sat in silence on the wet, blood-filled floor. Then his body twitched from what seemed to be nothing more than the teeniest tilt of his head followed by a slight, shallow squint. The squint elicited a small, nearly insignificant increase of intelligibility in his vision, but it was enough. What was a blurred slathering of nothing on the shower wall suddenly became clear. It was a message. He could barely breathe as he read the hand-written note – a question, really - on the wall above the tub, scribed in Kaitlin's blood:

'Now, will you fight me?'

Jean's mouth fell open, and he inhaled as much air as he could take. He closed his eyes in an attempt to hold back the onslaught of emotion that was rising, but it didn't work. For sixteen years, he had suffered through Hagatha's unrelenting taunts and torture, but not once during that time had he ever suffered through more pain than he did at that very moment.

"Uhhhnnn," he gasped, arduously.

Again, he inhaled and sucked in as much oxygen as his body would hold. With an unearthly patience he exhaled through his teeth as he reopened his eyes and glared at the question staring back at him on the shower wall. Judging from the purse of his lips and the cerulean blue hue that flickered and fluttered across his left eye, it's a pretty safe assumption that he will.

THE END

ACKNOWLEDGMENTS

Dillon. Dakarai. Shruti. Dianne. Zoe. Stephanie. Marlena. Zion. Melvina. Buddy. Elizabeth. James E. Melvin. Robbie. Lenny. Bob. David. Jon. Bronson. Hannah. Woods. Beth-Anne. Boogie. Leon. Bert. Megan. Stuart. Carmen. Kevin. Mariah. Gladys. Jayme. Cole. Chip. Chloe. Dyrk. Daggs. Jones. Rod. Cheryl. Denaye. Tara. Jeff. Tirion. James. Chinh. Duy. Courtney. Lisa. Tanya. Michelle. Alma. Brad. Stacey. Mark. Tracey. Kate. Tree. J. G. & Breezy. Robert. Joshua.

Thank you. For the inspiration.

You all played a part.

ABOUT THE AUTHOR

D. A. BARNEY was born and raised in Cleveland Heights, Ohio and for as far back as he could remember, there was a voice constantly whispering strange things to him. Beautiful things - amazing things and sometimes, even scary things. He began to write the voice down, and the rest is history. He and The Voice received a BFA in Film from The Ohio State University where they specialized in writing and directing. Since then, their scripts have won eleven awards in competitions and film festivals around the world. This is their first foray into the surrealistic world of book publication. It will not be their last. Stay tuned.

Check out the website for definitions, profiles and other cook stuff at www.thewiccanreport.com

facebook.com/TheBewitchingofCamille
instagram.com/thebewitchingofcamille
tiktok.com/@the_wiccan_chronicles
youtube.com/@TheWiccanChronicles